WANTON and WISE

F E WHARMBY

ISBN-13:978-1515268789
ISBN-10:1515268780

Copyright belongs to the author

British Library Cataloguing in Publication data.

I dedicate this book to my lovely daughter,
Janet, who was promoted to glory at the age of 41.

All profits from the sale of this book will be donated to the Salvation Army.

Chapter 1

Mr and Mrs Waspill, both manacled, clung to the wooden sides of a cart pulled by a mule. They were a sorry sight, she in a ragged shift, only just this side of decent, and he in a pair of ripped trousers, stained green by algae, and black from a filth-covered prison floor. The ugly noise of wooden wheels rumbling over cobblestones, shouting, and people jeering and mocking, echoed between high buildings. The sounds, wafted by the breeze, alerted the men waiting to perform their usual grim task on the scaffold platform which was set up and ready for use in the town square. A reverend, waiting on the platform, read aloud from the scriptures. The skirt of his long black cassock, and his thin grey hair, wafted in the breeze. The crowd waiting in the square fidgeted expectantly. It was seldom that a husband and wife were brought to be hanged together, and people had travelled from great distances to see the show.

The cart lurched to a halt near the scaffold, and the crowd roared insults and spat at the terrified couple. Parish officers pulled Mrs Waspill out of the cart, and up a short flight of wooden steps, then turned to deal with her husband. At the sight of the pair of dangling nooses on the scaffold, they became hysterical. He was dealt a blow that broke his arm. Howling with pain, he limped up the steps and stood next to his wife, holding his broken arm. The couple began to shout and curse each other for being in this sorry state, and a ripple of laughter ran through the crowd. This was unexpected entertainment.

Earlier in the year, Mr Waspill had stolen a cargo of grain from a farmer. Friends of the farmer who were drinking in an alehouse had overheard Mr Waspill boasting of the incident and had immediately reported their information, both to the farmer and to the authorities. In due time the thieves had been apprehended, and brought to the gaol in Nottingham Town. The magistrate had heard their plea and drawn the conclusion that the pair were guilty, and the inevitable sentence had been delivered.

A grim-faced group of men, who worked on canal barges, stood on one side of the square, apart from the crowd, quietly watching the proceedings. If people noticed them, they avoided passing close by. The men were all dressed in dark coats with high lapels and moleskin trousers that widened out from the knee to cover high-laced boots, and each man carried a broad brimmed hat.

Mr Waspill fell quiet when a hood fell into place over his head, but the tearful protests and screams of his wife could still be heard as the noose tightened around her neck. As two pairs of legs kicked air, the noise rising from the crowd could be heard more than two streets away.

As the reverend closed his Bible, the bargees replaced their hats and, speaking quietly to each other, turned for home on their barges. The remainder of the crowd filtered away into the nearby streets, leaving the dangling bodies. Eventually, the bodies were taken down, wrapped in rough calico, and dropped into a paupers' grave on the outskirts of Nottingham Town.

Two days later, Bill Waspill stood over his parents' grave, weeping. He wore moleskin trousers and high-laced boots of the bargee. His spare clothes, tied in a bundle, lay beside his feet. Bill had been the Waspill's only child and had been made to work on the barge from an early age, but he had fond memories of a happy childhood. Although he knew his father sometimes made money irresponsibly, in Bill's opinion his parents were perfect.

'I'll get them who did this to you. Don't you worry, Mam and Pa. I'll not rest until I find the people responsible, and I'll make them pay. They'll shed tears every night for what they've done to you,' he sobbed.

Bill, now twenty-eight, was tall and, thanks to the work he did, muscular. He kept his straight, dark brown hair shoulder length, and had a thick moustache. His brown eyes were small and close together, set into a thin face. He could be charming, and when he wanted, he could speak in a refined manner, but those who knew him kept a careful hand on their purse, and certainly kept out of his way when he was drunk.

He had been working on a new canal in Derbyshire when the news of his parents' difficulties reached him. It was shouted across the water by a passing bargee that his parents were imprisoned and about to be hanged in Nottingham Town. Anxious to comfort his mother and, more importantly, to obtain possession of the barge owned by his father before his death, Bill had paid a carrier for a lift to Nottingham. If he could get his hands on his parents' barge, he would have access to a profitable livelihood as a bargee.

With a last sad look at the grave, Bill returned to the town and found a cheap lodging house. Pleased to see that his room had a lock and key, he didn't bother to unpack and, leaving his belongings in his room, set off towards the River Trent. His first priority was to find anyone working on the riverboats that he might know. He was in luck. An old friend of his late parents had moored his narrow boat on the Grantham Canal, not far from the Trent Bridge.

'The horse has gone long since, stabled in a field near the town, but your pa's old barge is further along the canal. You won't be able to use it, me lad, because it now belongs to the parish. It'd be stealing, and you'd end up getting what your mam and pa got,' the man said, looking at Bill's face.

'What can they do with it? It'll just lie there in the water and rot, and be no good to anyone.' Bill shrugged and kicked a stone into the water making a nearby duck fly away, quacking in alarm.

Giving Bill a speculative glance, the man sent a brown stream of spittle into the water before saying, 'If I was in your shoes, I'd see if I could find the reverend who was at the execution. He seemed to be a kindly soul, and might help you.'

'What was his name?' Bill's head came up. He felt hopeful until the man lit a pipe and shook his head.

'Can't tell you that.'

'Don't matter. There's plenty of other folk who was there, and they'll be pleased to help me,' Bill said with another shrug of his broad shoulders.

He strode away along the towpath. Not many of the boat people would willingly give Bill Waspill information. Bargee families were a very close knit community and frowned on those, like the Waspill family, who brought their honest reputation into disrepute.

Bill trudged back to the town and had a word with a tavern landlord who had premises overlooking the town square. A coin pushed across the table bought the information he sought. His charming manner was a great help on the following afternoon, when he called at the rectory next to the Parish Church.

He had polished his boots and found a clean shirt to wear. His hat, well brushed, sat at an angle that showed off his hazel eyes, and his smile was candid as the door opened to his knock. The housekeeper took him into the garden, where the reverend was deadheading sweet-scented roses.

'Yes, I was there,' he said when Bill, hat in hand, questioned him. The kindly man listened, and nodded slowly as Bill explained how much the return of the barge meant to him. 'Be here at sun-up tomorrow, and I'll accompany you to the courthouse. If you're lucky, we may even be able to speak with the magistrate who passed sentence on your parents.'

'Do you know his name, sir?' Bill crossed his fingers. His mouth turned down when he saw the man shake his head.

The following day the men were up early, and after a long wait in a dreary corridor, they were shown into an office with six high desks, each illuminated by a tallow candle. The reverend informed the clerk seated at the nearest desk who Bill Waspill was, and told the man it would surely be in the best interest of the parish to transfer the ownership of the late Mr Waspill's barge and his horse to Bill. It took most of the day before the necessary documents for the release of the barge and horse, and proof of the new ownership were given to Bill. The name of the magistrate who had dealt with the case, Mr Cooper, was inadvertently mentioned and Bill was quick to notice the indiscretion made by the clerk, but he didn't let the man, who was busy writing with his feather quill pen, see that the name meant anything to him.

During the following weeks, Bill made it his business to find out all he could about Mr Cooper and his family. He found that they lived on the outskirts of Nottingham Town, very near a newly-built canal. He spent days waiting outside the magistrate's house to see Mr Cooper. His vigil paid off, and he was rewarded with a glimpse of the man and his family as they were driven in a carriage through the large iron gates of their home in the direction of the town. 'Yes, you'll all rue the day you passed the death sentence on my mam and pa!' he shouted to the retreating vehicle.

It was almost six months before he finally devised the plan of abducting one of Mr Cooper's daughters. It wouldn't matter which, although the youngest girl, Merrilla, was a beauty.

Bill was waiting one day on a street corner in the old part of Nottingham, when he noticed Jeremy. The boy had a pinched look to his dirty face, and had a small and scrawny body, as though regular meals were unknown to him. By the way the lad glanced into shopping baskets and eyed the pockets of the passing crowd, Bill knew he had found someone who would help him put his plan into action. A tankard of ale and a meat pie later, and Jeremy was his slave.

Bill didn't take the lad fully into his confidence. He decided to try out his plan first. One night, the pair abducted a pretty servant girl from a farm, and successfully sold her to a brothel madam for a good price. They were jubilant. Easy money. They then persuaded a lowly female servant from the town, who was the worse for drink, to join them on the barge. When he had finished using her for his pleasure, Bill waited until it was dark, gagged her and took her to the same brothel. Other girls suffered the same fate; and no one thought to search a boat for a missing girl as it travelled along rivers and canals.

He was ready to put his main plan into action. He would attract Merrilla Cooper's attention and lure her to her fate. The daughter of Mr Cooper, the magistrate would become a common prostitute, like many girls who were unwise enough to leave the protection of their family.

Merrilla Cooper's soft kid boots made almost no sound as she walked to church with her family. When she crossed the wide iron bridge over the canal her attention was drawn to groups of people on the canal banks, where ragged children listened to a hurdy-gurdy man turning a handle at the side of the box, making tinkling music. A monkey, wearing a red jacket and holding a tin cup, was attached to the machine by a chain.

Further away, some men sat on flattened weedy grass, playing a game of cards. Shouts almost drowned out the music when they began quarrelling, and Merrilla saw them get to their feet and begin to fight. One man fell into the water and had to be helped out by his mates. The words 'cheating scum' and other epithets floated to her; she had heard them before in the city, but the meaning of the words was unknown to her.

She moved her gaze to where half a dozen shameless-looking women sprawled. Because of the heat, they had pulled their long skirts up high, showing knees and thighs to anyone looking in their direction. Some of them were drinking from stone bottles. Hot and thirsty, Merrilla licked her lips, and wondered what might be in them.

Lying in the shade of a bush, a man pulled a young woman close to him, exposing her breasts then, disregarding a couple of laughing and taunting urchins, he straddled her, giving those around him a coarse display.

Catching sight of Merrilla's shocked expression, the woman pushed the man away and adjusted her clothing as she shouted to her, 'I'm no whore. I'm as good as you, miss, if not better.'

Her face hot, Merrilla lengthened her stride to catch up with her sister. With lips pursed, and in an unconscious imitation of her mother, she muttered, 'Disgusting.' She remembered she should have been walking two paces behind her sister with her eyes cast down, instead of gazing at sinful vistas, and promised herself not to look the following week. Well, maybe just a peep...

Pressing her prayer book to her waist, she tried to ease the painful dig of her whalebone corsets. Whilst gratified by the way her developing breasts were pushed up and her waist span reduced, she wondered if the discomfort of a constriction on such a warm day was worth it.

Her father, a stout man, wearing his favourite green silk coat over a long embroidered waistcoat, and a tricorn hat trimmed with ostrich fronds, marched at the front holding a Bible close to his heart. The heavy line of his jaw, his straight thick eyebrows, and his firmly closed lips gave him a forbidding expression. Mrs Cooper, a fair, slender woman, walked a couple of paces behind him. Their two daughters, Maude, who had her father's stout build, and sixteen-year old Merrilla, the younger, brought up the rear of the line.

A blossom landed on Merrilla's prayer book. It balanced for a moment before falling to the ground. She wondered briefly from which tree it had fallen, but continued walking, deep in thought about the scene she had witnessed, and forgot about the blossom.

The following Sunday, Merrilla felt a slight sense of disappointment when a shower of rain meant the canal banks were deserted. She thought she saw somebody watching her, partly hidden behind a tree. The family were almost across the canal bridge when two sloe-blossoms, bound together with grass, landed on her prayer book, before blowing away in the wind. Noticing the direction from which they had come, her green eyes frowned a warning at a young man who stood smiling at her, seemingly unaware of the damp morning. He was obviously dressed in his best clothes, but the style showed him to be socially at a disadvantage. With a contemptuous toss of her head, she muttered, 'Oaf,' and continued following her sister towards the church without losing step.

The parson droned and some of the congregation were dozing when her thoughts turned to the stranger on the bridge. *Curious, he looked common, yet... Yes, he is rather handsome in a dark way.* Remembering how his eyes sparkled when he bowed to her, her heart began thumping. Her spontaneous smile instantly vanished, and she lowered her eyes as her mother, leaning forward in the family pew, gave her a disapproving glance. She touched the ribbons tying her bonnet and sat up a little straighter, remembering the young woman she had seen the previous Sunday. She wondered what the word 'whore' meant.

Sundays came and went. Merrilla dreaded her sister or parents noticing him but she half hoped he would be there, leaning with both elbows on the green-painted wrought-iron bridge. Each time they approached the canal bridge and she eyed the front of his trousers, she felt a strange sensation in her stomach, and clenched her buttocks as she walked. Sometimes he would be in the company of a scruffy lad who appeared to be about the same age as her. Waiting until her parents and Maude had passed, the young man would toss a bouquet of flowers and grasses. Each time the bouquet, with its wonderful assortment of colourful wildflower blossoms, grew larger. Smiling, he'd lift his hat, and bow without taking his eyes away from her. Each week the flowers fell to the ground.

The last posy to land on her book was of violets. Extremely fond of these sweet-smelling flowers, she held onto them without glancing in the young man's direction.

'Bill, she held them. You has done it at last.' The shabby boy gave a little jig with excitement as he watched Merrilla walking away.

A queer little smile flittered across Bill Waspill's face and he playfully punched the boy lightly on the shoulder. 'Yes, Jeremy. One step at a time, though. The next trick is to get her to speak to me—handsome bargee Bill. Yours truly.'

Bill grinned widely, showing a full set of teeth under a lavish moustache. As usual, he wore his best coat with high, wide lapels. His trousers of fawn mock moleskin, belling out from below the knee, partly hid his high-laced boots, bright with black polish.

His hat tilted at a jaunty angle, he twirled his cane in time to his cheerful whistling. Following his young friend onto the canal towing path, he placed his arm over the boy's shoulders giving a low chuckle as they approached a long red and green barge in desperate need of a coat of paint. 'Best you get the boat cleaned and polished ready for our honoured guest, Jeremy,' he said.

The boy nodded and, walked towards the cabin door. 'Do you think you'll get her to come here? I bet she's never met a bargee before, or even put her foot on a barge. She's bound to turn her nose up. I dare bet my best cap she'll think it's shabby.'

In a flash, Bill's mood changed. His eyes narrowed as he snarled, 'She'll think it's a bleeding palace by the time I've finished with her and her high and mighty family!'

'All right, all right, keep yer bloody 'air on. I only said.' The boy hastily backed away from his mate's sudden flare-up.

Merrilla, alone in her bedchamber, stroked her cheeks with the violets, caressing the delicate soft petals and enjoying their sweetness. Knowing her parents would have asked from where the flowers had come, she was, for once, pleased that she had walked in line behind her family, and had concealed the violets in her reticule until she had reached the privacy of her room.

Why on earth would a man throw flowers at me? It's not as though we've been introduced. I could understand if it was Maude, she's older and a beautiful lady. She doesn't have freckles like me, but then she has never had flowers thrown at her. Or maybe she has and has said nothing.

Smiling dreamily, Merrilla put the blooms to her nose and drank in the delicate perfume. Then, with a regretful sigh, she wrapped them in a handkerchief and placed them deep inside a drawer, away from prying eyes. It was only just in time. Her maid tapped on the door and entered the room.

The following hours were spent as most Sundays. After lunch, the family sat listening to Mr Cooper reading passages from the Bible. Merrilla, as usual, watched the hands of the clock creeping round its face, and was severely reprimanded for fidgeting. At six o'clock it was time to change for dinner, but before the sisters rose to leave, her father held up his hand. 'Next week I'll be staying in Nottingham Town. I need to visit my factory, and I'll be attending a meeting with a number of other magistrates. Also,

13

I'll be hearing a lecture on factory reform. This will take several days.'

No reply to this news was expected. As Merrilla opened her mouth to ask when her papa would be returning, a stern glance from him silenced her. She and Maude curtsied to their parents and left the room.

Each Sunday, the family and the indoor servants would gather in the entrance hall for evening prayers prior to retiring. That Sunday, Merrilla had thought her father would never finish but, fortunately, that time, her impatience had not been noticed.

Her maid helped her prepare for bed. Chattering happily, the girl brushed Merrilla's tawny hair until it lay in a cascade of curls over her shoulders. In no mood to listen to the servant's gossip, she wanted to be alone to dream about the young man who threw flowers to her.

As soon as the maid had gone, she climbed out of her high bed and threw a light wrap around her shoulders. Padding across the thick carpet, she took the violets from their hiding place and carried them to the dressing table. Looking glass in hand, she arranged the flowers, one by one, in her hair, and sat dreaming of a tall young man with laughing eyes. She wondered how soft his hair would feel, what it would be like to be kissed on the lips, and whether she'd swoon with delight if he held her close. *He's the man I'll marry one day,* she promised her reflection.

She rose to her feet and danced noiselessly around her bedchamber, giving a sudden giggle. *He's very different from the man with whom Maude has chosen to spend her life. I can't imagine Mr Godsen sending flowers to my sister in such an unusual manner.*

In time, she paid close attention to every small detail of her toilette and would rebuke her maid if the girl didn't curl her hair or iron her ribbons to her liking. Whenever she left home, she'd notice the young man lurking, ready to follow her, often bowing and smiling. Blushing, she'd let her long eyelashes rest on her cheeks, and then glance at the person accompanying her, worrying if they had noticed his antics. Fortunately, they hadn't.

So far, he had not had the opportunity to speak to her, and she wondered who he was, and from where he'd come. Was he in some kind of uniform? No one she knew dressed in that strange fashion.

Merrilla followed her mother into a bookshop to buy her father a present for his birthday. 'Just remember, gentlemen like something learned, my dear,' advised Mrs Cooper before wandering off to speak to an acquaintance.

'Beautiful one, I adore you.' A husky voice made her jump. 'Let me gaze upon your lovely face.' His hot breath stirred her curls as he leaned down to look under her ribbon-trimmed bonnet.

Startled, she blushed and trembled. She hadn't noticed his approach. Her green eyes grew dark with alarm, and she glanced in fear to where her mother stood, deep in conversation.

'You must never speak to me. If my papa ever found out you had spoken to me, he would...would put you in prison. He's a magistrate and owns factories, and is very, very strict,' she whispered in terror. Had anyone noticed? No. She bent her head and bit her lip when he spoke again.

'No matter my precious, I love you. I call you my lady with the sun-kissed curls. Please, will you give me a token I can wear next to my heart? A glove? A button? A handkerchief?'

She shook her head, causing her long ringlets to dance under her straw bonnet. Her mother half turned as though to rejoin her, and she panicked and dropped the book she had been reading. In a split second, he caught it.

'Go away!' she hissed, snatching it from him.

'Only a small token, my lady.' Glancing around, he knelt on one knee, held out both hands, and gazed up at her imploringly. 'You are a flame and I am a moth,' he said.

'How absurd you are, sir.' Shocked by his behaviour but, aware of awakening senses, she turned away. As she moved towards her mother, she allowed a tiny lace-edged handkerchief to flutter to the ground.

With a triumphant chuckle, Bill darted to pick it up. The dropped token meant the end of his chase was near. He gave a jubilant, but silent, 'Yes!'

As he left the shop, he saw Jeremy across the street, lounging against a wall, and walked over to join him. 'A missive, full of love and devotion to my lady, will be the next step, and I know just the person who'll write something romantic for me. I'll give it to her, and she'll fall completely in love with her bargee, Bill.' He grinned as he watched Merrilla's progress along the busy street, always a step behind her mother, and laughed out loud when she lifted her wide skirts in a ladylike way, showing white silken ankles as she stepped into the family carriage. 'Yes, my beauty, 'tis time we got much more friendly.'

He strode along until he came to the basement rooms where the widow, Polly Goodley lived. The woman listened to his tale of burning desire and, grateful for the coins given to her, began to write.

During the next few weeks Merrilla received a daily love letter that she tied with a ribbon and kept hidden under her handkerchief sachet.

As weeks passed, she felt she knew her Bill much better. She fell deeper and deeper under his spell. When reading and poring over the letters, she truly believed every written word. Her secret love grew difficult to hide. Her glowing looks brought sour comments from her sister, but she ignored them. She didn't dare confide in anyone, especially Maude, who would have gone immediately to tell her parents.

She was extremely fond of her grandparents, who had always spoilt their favourite granddaughter. They lived within walking distance of her home, and she usually visited them once a week, with a maid as chaperone. One Sunday in August, she dropped a note as she walked to church. She knew Bill or Jeremy would be following her, and would pick it up. It gave directions on how to find her grandparents' house, how to gain entry to the extensive gardens without being seen, and that she intended to visit them on Friday. After lunch, while her grandmother would be having a nap, she intended to make for the wooded area of the garden and meet him there.

Everything went just as Merrilla had planned. Waiting until she was alone in her grandmother's drawing room and her maid had joined the other servants for tea, she slipped unnoticed into the garden. She hurried along mossy paths past the flowerbeds, until she heard a low voice.

'Merilla, my love, I'm over here.' Her eyes were drawn to Bill Waspill who stepped from behind a bush. "I'm relieved you have no chaperone," he said.

'Oh, Bill, I thought Grandmamma would never have her afternoon nap,' she gasped. 'I must not tarry long or I'll be missed.'

Catching hold of her hand, he drew her closer. 'When I saw you drop your note in the street, I knew you'd use your clever head to arrange a secret meeting. Oh, I do so admire you, my dearest one.' He looked into her eyes and pressed her fingers to his lips.

The crunch of stones on a nearby path made them spring apart. He took a letter out of his pocket and pressed it into her hand. 'Our meetings are too short, but the memory of this day will stay in my heart forever, my dearest one.' He blew a kiss and melted

17

into the shrubbery, out of sight, leaving her with glowing cheeks and a fast beating heart. The letter placed into the pocket of her gown, she hurried along the path towards the sound of her grandfather calling her name.

'Where have you been, girl? What have you been doing among the trees?' he asked, peering short-sightedly past her.

'Looking for you, Grandpapa.' She linked her arm in his and, matching her pace to the old man's tottering steps, they made their way along flower-lined paths, stopping at times to examine a plant or a statue.

As they approached the house, he asked, 'Is your papa at home, Merilla. or is he still away in Nottingham, attending lectures?'

'Mamma received a letter from him yesterday, Grandpapa. She told me he would be home at the end of next week,' she said as she helped him up the stone steps into the house. Glancing back at the garden, she nearly fainted with shock when she saw Bill standing in full view, waving to her. Luckily, the old man was already in the hallway.

Merrilla had no opportunity to read the letter until she had returned home and her maid had prepared her for bed and left the room. With trembling fingers, she held the pages close to the candle, and scanned Bill's declaration of love, until she came to the words. 'Marry me, my beloved. We can sail away in our dreamboat.'

'Oh, yes, Bill,' whispered the infatuated girl. She read and re-read the letter until the candle flickered and went out in a pool of fat.

Her family had retired for the night before the loving words were hidden away with the other letters, but Merrilla lay awake, watching the moon through her window, and dreamily planning an idyllic future in which she sailed on a beautiful boat with Bill Waspill.

Chapter 2

'But why not? Why can't I better meself? I don't want to end up in one room like this, with snotty-nosed brats running around my feet! I want to wear warm boots, have a soft bed, and be clean!' With legs wide apart, and hands on hips, Nancy Turpin spat the words out at her mother. The glow coming from the fire—the only illumination in the room—highlighted her chin, which jutted out with determination.

A loud cackle of laughter came from Mrs Turpin. Seated beside the fireplace, she rocked backwards and forwards in a creaking chair—the only proper chair they had. Her head tilted to one side as she studied her daughter. 'You'll have to change yourself, a lot, if you want to get out of your class.' She stabbed the stem of her clay pipe towards Nancy as she asked, 'What's brought this on? Has you been talking to that Mr Pugh? I've told you before, he's married. Anyway, he's no gentleman, not a proper one, anyway.'

Nancy gave an impatient shake of her head. 'Class? What's class? There's them that's rich, and them that ain't. No.' Her eyes took on a far away look, as she added, 'These last few weeks I've been watching a proper young lady. Her clothes are lovely, and her skin's all pink and white. And as she walked past me, I could smell her. Just like a beautiful flower, she is. Wish I were just like 'er.' She sank down on the earth floor and, rocking a wooden cradle containing a whimpering baby, looked up at her mother. 'I know I must try, Mam, but I can't think of how to go about making meself change. There must be better ways to live than this. One room for each family, rags to wear, and nothing much to eat.'

She didn't realise how fast she was rocking the cradle until her mother placed a hand on her shoulder. 'I've never known anyone do it, but you've always been a bit different to others, our Nancy.

Reckon it's your grandmamma coming out in you. She were different to her sisters, and she married very well.' Mrs Turpin stared into the fire, and reminisced. 'I remembers when I came to live 'ere, my heart full of dreams. When I married your pa we made our home 'ere in the Narrow Marsh district of Nottingham. Fortunate, I was, to have use of a water pump, and share a washhouse with my neighbours—the same neighbours who rallied round in good and bad times, and helped when I gave birth. We was blessed with a child each year. Nine of the babies died, but eight survived, you the eldest.' With a weary expression, she put a hand on her daughter's head, caressing her face with her fingers. 'You'll have to learn to speak proper, our Nancy, same as the gentry. Get nice clothes. And you'll have to wash your hands and face every day, you know.'

Nancy looked up at her, open-mouthed. A sudden puff of smoke blew down the chimney, and they wafted the air with their hands before moving away from the fire. After a bout of coughing, her ma said, 'I think the best thing you can do is go and see Polly Goodley. She was gently reared, a parson's daughter, and brought up in a vicarage, or so I've heard. She writes and reads letters for people. She might be able to help you.'

'Oh, Mam, do you think so? I will better myself, you just see if I don't. If this Polly Goodley don't want to help me, then I'll find someone else who will. Now I'm working more hours at the mill, I can pay someone to show me how to change.'

Their eyes widened with alarm when they heard footsteps outside, and as the iron latch on the rough plank door rattled, Mrs Turpin pulled the chair closer to the table. 'Don't say owt about this to your dad, he'd not understand,' she warned.

Without answering, Nancy busied herself by pouring warm milk into bowls. As her brothers and sisters crowded onto a narrow bench beside the table, Nancy placed a bowl and a crust of bread in front of each child. They sat in silence, dipping the bread into the milk and chewing on the crust.

Mrs Turpin hurried to set a meal of mutton broth in front of her husband. He grunted, and glanced to where she bent over the cooking pot. Ogling his wife's backside, he watched her turn towards him, then bent his head over his plate. Her face was expressionless as she watched her husband eating.

'Childer are fed, Mam. I'm just going down the road a minute. I want to see Mrs Goodley.' Nancy lifted a grey woollen shawl from a nail on the door.

She was about to throw the shawl around her shoulders, when her father growled out, 'Yer what? Polly Goodley? Yer not, yer know!' He seldom looked up from his plate once he had started eating, so that meant he was serious. 'You stop here, girl. Her husband used to lend out money. Him and their daughter were out one dark night collecting debts. They got robbed. He was killed. A cudgel spilled the daughter's brains, and she died a week later. Don't want you ending up like her.'

With an ominous glitter in her eyes, Nancy watched as food spewed out from his mouth, and was spat across the table. Her stomach churned in disgust. Exchanging a knowing look with her mother, she replaced the shawl on the nail. She knew that when he spoke to someone in such a manner it was best to obey, or his brass-studded belt would be used across the person's back.

Mr Turpin was a fortunate man, for he was in full employment at Cooper's factory, in the centre of Nottingham. Working long hours, with meagre wages, he managed to feed his family on plain but nourishing food. A cotton mill, in nearby Pilchergate, employed Nancy for a few hours a day, and she willingly contributed to the family finances. Her brother was also in regular employment. They were rich indeed, compared with some of the other families living nearby.

At bedtime, Nancy managed to whisper to her mother, 'When I leave work tomorrow night, I'll call at Polly Goodley's place.' She jerked her head in her father's direction. 'I should have time to see her and get back home before him.'

They both glanced at him. Hunger satisfied, he lay on a bed of straw and sacking. Nancy pulled a face, and grinned at her mother when he began snoring.

Mrs Cooper pulled on her kid gloves with sharp tugs that threatened to ruin the silk lining. Her voice rose an octave as she said, 'Good heavens, Merrilla, do you need to visit the bookshop again? Surely you don't intend to give all your family new books as birthday gifts?' At Merrilla's pleading look, she blew out her breath and said, 'Oh, very well. I'll take your sister with me to the dressmakers, but don't complain if you have nothing new to wear at your friend's tea party next week. I'll leave you and your maid at the bookshop, and pick you up again on our way home. Don't keep me waiting, girl. Hurry and tell Maude of our change of plan.'

Her foot tapping on the fine red carpet in the entrance hall, she gave an exasperated tut-tut as Merilla lifted her skirts, showing lace-edged petticoats as she ran towards the staircase.

Maude was only too pleased to take Merrilla's place, and joined her and her mother in the entrance hall.

As the carriage came to a halt outside the bookshop, Merrilla and her maid alighted.

'We'll be back here in half an hour. Do not keep me waiting, or I will be most displeased, Merrilla,' her mother said, leaning forward in the carriage. She gave a couple of knocks on the roof with her parasol and sat back in her seat as the driver set the horses in motion.

Merrilla waited until the carriage disappeared around the corner of the busy street before she turned to her maid. 'Mind what I am saying, girl. Keep a sharp lookout for the return of Mrs Cooper and my sister. Call me as soon as the carriage turns into the street. Don't speak to any strangers, and don't wander off.'

Merrilla's eyes roved round the lamp-lit interior of the bookshop, searching for Bill. Her heart sank. He wasn't there. She frowned. Did he not pick up the note she had dropped in the street the day before?

The doorbell jingled, and there he was, holding his hat and smiling at her. She caught her breath with excitement.

At her bright smile, he hurried forward, his eyes darting around the shop in search of any companion. 'My darling. You are all alone? Your Mamma?'

She shook her head and gave a little giggle. 'My maid's outside, watching for Mamma's return.'

He drew her further into a dim, book-lined recess. 'I've been counting the days, my love. It's only been a week since I spoke to you, but it seems like a year.' Lifting her hand to his lips, he gazed into her eyes. 'Tell me, my darling, have you considered? Will you marry me?'

Merrilla blushed. 'I've thought of nothing else since I read your letter.'

He drew her deeper into the recess, and kissed her gloved fingers one by one, causing her knees to grow weak, and her eyes to sparkle even more. 'It'll be best if we elope. Your papa will never let us marry in a church. He'll say we're unsuited, or find some other excuse, but I love you, Merrilla, and I want to spend my whole life loving and caring for you. You haven't told anyone about us, have you?'

'Oh, Mr Waspill. Oh no, of course not. Elope? Yes! Oh. You've taken me by surprise. Elope?' she gushed. 'Do you think that would be best?' She felt dizzy, her heart thudding in the most delightful way.

'When you're my wife, my darling, your papa will have to accept me. By then, of course, he'll see how well I'll have cared for you, and cherished you,' he said, still gazing into her eyes.

'How? I mean, will we be on your boat all the while?' She panted. No one had ever looked at her with such intensity before. His hazel eyes were hypnotic.

The jingling of the bell over the shop door broke the spell. Merrilla moved to the end of the shelves, and glanced guiltily towards the front of the shop, but it wasn't her maid, only another customer.

With an arm around her waist, but not close enough to frighten her, Bill whispered, 'You'll love my boat, my dearest. We'll be so cosy as we glide along the canals and rivers to our new life. I'll show you towns and pretty villages, and teach you the names of wild flowers. Perhaps you'll paint pictures of the birds. When we return to Nottingham, I'll sell the boat and buy a little house with a garden near to your family.'

In excited agreement, she couldn't see any flaw in the idyllic picture he presented.

Narrow boats were constantly passing through her hometown. They all had banded chimneystacks, gleaming paint and polished brass, winking in the sunlight. Decorated water cans sat on the cabin roofs, with contented cats or dogs stretched out nearby. Open-shirted men, steering the boats, cheerfully waved and called to each other. She gave no thought to how the boats were kept so spick and span. It never occurred to her to consider how a girl with her upbringing might cope with the cramped conditions of living on a boat, without a maid or servant to see to her needs.

The movement of a customer on the other side of the bookshelves brought her out of her daydream. 'Bill...Mr Waspill, I must leave... My Mamma...' She reluctantly pulled free from his grasp.

He kept his voice low. 'I'll not be able to see you tomorrow, my dearest. I need to make arrangements for our future. I'll send young Jeremy with a letter.'

She took a book at random from a shelf and walked towards the front of the shop to pay for it. As she opened the shop door he blew her a kiss, and gave a discreet wave.

Nancy Turpin waited and watched outside the bookshop, When Bill Waspill left the shop and walked in her direction, she pulled her shawl over her head and hurried towards him. Her hand hovering above his arm, she said, 'You know that young lady? You know her name, sir?'

Bill took a step back. 'What's it to do with you, doxy? Thinking of robbing her?'

'No, I want to find out where she lives, so I can work in her house. I've heard she's kind to her servants.'

'Forget it. I've seen you before. Got a reputation with the men around here. Street work's the best you can hope for.'

With a sarcastic grin, he hurried away, leaving Nancy with tears darkening her lashes. Stamping her foot with frustration, she shouted, 'I'll show you, mister. I might enjoy a bit of fun with the boys, but neither you nor anyone'll not treat me like dirt. I'll be a lady just like her one day.'

'Taking a deuce of a long time to snare this latest one, Bill,' declared Jeremy. 'Money's getting a bit short, yer know? You spent a lot on getting them letters written. I was talking to Mrs McCreed last night. She said she'd take this latest girl off your hands and use her in the whorehouse. She said not to worry if she ain't broke in. Some men are pleased to do that and will pay extra.' After wiping his nose on his sleeve, he added, 'She pays good money for virgins, Bill.'

The pair sat inside the Winsford, a fine old timbered inn, sited beside the river. Its rough oak tables and benches wobbled on grimy square flagstones, stained dark with spilled ale. Jeremy flinched and stopped scratching his head when Bill banged his tankard down on the table.

'I'll be breaking this one in myself. She's a tasty piece. I've worked hard on getting her moonstruck. After I've done with her, she can either go to the brothel, or we'll keep her on the boat. She'll find out then what hard work is.' Bill was unsure if the boy would agree to his proposition. In the past it had always been fifty-fifty in monetary schemes. 'I'll have the girl, and you can keep whatever she brings with her. Now that's fair, ain't it, Jeremy?' He leant over the table and breathed ale into the boy's face. 'I've me own reasons for keeping her,' he said, in a low voice, seeing no reason to let Jeremy know he had become quite fond of Merrilla, in his rough way. The boy would think he had gone soft, and he had to think of his reputation.

'Yes, I know,' said Jeremy. 'Someone told me that, a year or so back, her papa had your mam and pa hanged. It's said by folk roundabout here that your dad would have got away with thieving if he hadn't got drunk and boasted about it.' At Bill's smouldering expression, he drew back on his bench, ready to jump out of harm's way, but continued, 'She'll never be able to work the boat, Bill. She ain't strong enough. You'll never get to Ripon with her helping you, not all that way. Takes a proper boat-woman, that do. A thin jade like her opening lock gates? Too flash with her dainty hands.'

'She'll not be so flash when I've done with her. Anyway, I can always put her over the side if you're right.'

Bill waved his tankard at the serving girl for a refill. Giving him a saucy grin, she bent low so he could see her breasts. She received a scowl for her trouble. He turned back to Jeremy. 'Look. She's near as dammit to agreeing to come away with me.

A few more days of fond looks, and that'll be it. Now, what I want you to do, on the night she leaves home, is to hire us a travelling coach and swift horses to get us to the boat. I'll let you know in plenty of time what night it'll be. When she's on board, you take the coach back, and join me on the boat later. Plenty of room for you to sleep among the cargo covers.'

He caught the eye of the serving girl again across the smoky room, and lifted Jeremy's tankard, indicating another drink. The girl flounced across with an earthenware pitcher, and, without bending to show her breasts, filled the tankard. Bill pushed a coin across the table, waited a moment until the girl was out of earshot, then turned back to Jeremy, and placed a hand on the boy's arm. 'Best place to hire a coach is from that old inn on the heath. They don't know us there. I've heard how they don't care what their coaches are used for, as long as they get them back in one piece. Anyway, I'm told the man owning them never asks damn fool questions.'

Over the top of his tankard, Jeremy asked, 'You got some coins for this hiring, Bill? The man'll want cash.'

'I'll give you enough money on the night, never fear. You do that, and I'll keep working on Miss Merrilla. The lady. She'll bloody wish she still were by the time I've done.'

His smile caused Jeremy to glance at him with narrowed eyes. 'What about later, Bill? After I've took the coach back? You'll have 'er. Will you still want me to help you on the boat, like before?' the boy asked, shifting on the low bench. The boat was his home, and he was clearly uneasy about his future, not wanting to return to his old life as a petty thief. He enjoyed living there, helping Bill to abduct young farm girls and female servants. After keeping them on the boat for a while, and teaching them the ways of rough lovemaking, Bill always sold them to a brothel. The venture was profitable, but they had never abducted a young lady with a rich family, and constables from London Town might be employed to find the girl.

''Course I want you to stay with me, lad. I can manage to work the boat by myself until we get onto the Cromford Canal, but then I'll need you to help with the locks, and leg the boat through the Gregory Tunnel. There's Meggie, as well. She can be a bothersome horse when the mood takes her.' They sat drinking and making plans in their heads, until Bill added, 'We'll have to be careful, and keep Merrilla in the cabin, out of sight, until we're well into Derbyshire. We can't risk her being seen. There's bound to be a big hue and cry, and probably a reward for her return.' He smoothed and patted his moustache dry with a rag he used as a handkerchief and gave a half laugh. 'The bloody Mr Cooper, the magistrate, will then know how it feels to lose someone close, and he can suffer and grieve, like what us poor folk do.'

'I'll not mind sleeping on the cargo deck. It's no hardship when the weather's good,' Jeremy said, getting to his feet. 'See you later, Bill.'

Bill watched the boy weave between customers seated in the dim room before slipping out through the taproom door. After emptying his tankard, he indicated again to the serving girl to fill it.

Chapter 3

Dusk was making evening shadows when Nancy Turpin peered through a set of iron railings, down to a basement door and window. She seemed to be unnoticed by people nearby, busy with their own business. Her shawl pulled closer, she lifted her stained and patched skirt, and crept down a flight of steps, which, considering the district, were surprisingly clean. The door opened to her timid knock with a suddenness that made her catch her breath.

'Yes?'

The woman holding the door open was petite, the same height as herself, but older, about the same age as her mother.

'If you don't shut your mouth and say something, I'll close the door.'

'I can't.'

The woman's eyebrows rose to a delicate arch.

'If I close me mouth, I can't talk.'

A slight smile curved the woman's lips. Her face was clean and her skin almost unlined. An ecru lace cap, with long strings, perched on top of ringlets, where threads of grey glinted among the brown hair. Her plunging neckline was partly hidden by a white lace-edged fichu, draped over her shoulders.

'You're very pert, miss.'

'You Polly Goodley?'

The woman nodded.

'Me mam told me to come and see yer.'

'Best step inside, girl. I don't do business on the doorstep.' Moving to one side, Polly pulled the door further open and, standing on tiptoe, took a quick peep up and down the street.

Nancy looked around the room with wide-eyed interest. Old, polished wooden furniture smelt of beeswax, a blazing coal fire threw warmth from a black-leaded grate, and a narrow wooden-framed mirror hung over it. Her bare toe made to touch the heavy and brightly-coloured pegged rug, but Polly stood watching, and she withdrew her foot.

It wasn't easy to tell this stranger about her half-formed ideas, her dreams of being dressed in silks and velvet, and of being like the ladies she saw riding in carriages —an idealistic prospect for a young woman who had nothing but a natural beauty, quick wits, and a determination to alter both her looks and her situation. As she finished speaking, she lifted her chin, as though challenging the woman.

Polly had sat at her table, watching and listening in silence as Nancy had stumbled and stuttered out her hopes.

Self-conscious, Nancy's body slackened, and she wrapped her arms around herself. 'Suppose you think me cork-brained, having such thoughts as these?' she said, her cheeks flaming.

'No.' Polly stood and ordered, 'Stand up straight.' She walked around the blushing girl, lifted her arms, and looked in her mouth to examine the state of her teeth. She gave an, 'Mmm,' of satisfaction that no teeth were missing. Then she took hold of a louse-ridden lock of hair and pulled it straight to examine its length. 'Right. What colour should this be?'

'Don't know.'

With a sniff of disgust, Polly moved nearer to the fireplace. 'Lift your skirt. I want to see your legs.'

Nancy showed her knees.

'Are you a virgin, girl?'

Nancy's cheeks burned with embarrassment. Even her mother had never asked that question, although she'd given disproving looks whenever she'd arrived home late, flushed and with sparkling eyes. 'Course I am,' she spat out. Her eyes tightened to cat-like slits with suppressed temper. She loved the company of men, and since about the age of twelve, had thoroughly enjoyed the sensation of their ardent attention. With a great deal of self-control, she had been able to stay pure, satisfying her lovers with her hands and mouth, and allowing them to do the same. She often wanted to give in to their demands, but had once overheard a man boasting about his conquest, and about how the girl would now make a splendid prostitute. Nancy vowed that no one would talk about her in that way. Decent men of her class married only virgins.

Standing with her head tilted to one side, Polly blew through her pursed lips, and with eyes half-closed, studied her.

Blinking fast, so tears wouldn't flow, Nancy bit hard on her bottom lip. *Bloody fool to come here and see this old bitch. She'll not do owt for me,* she thought

Polly broke the silence. 'Yes. You leave home and live here with me. I warn you, though, before I've finished with you, my girl, you'll hate me. I give no guarantees that you'll be anything other than what you are now. Just you always remember; it was you who came to me for help. You give me what you earn at the mill, and I'll keep you and buy your clothes. It'll take a great deal of my time and effort to turn you into something like respectability, but I'm willing to try.'

'Oh.' Nancy's eyes opened wide with a mixture of fear and hope.

'Come, girl. I'm not about to turn you into a pickpocket or a dolly-mop. Who knows? Perhaps one day we may be able to find you work in a big house. Maybe as a parlour maid or even a lady's maid, but you must learn to speak better. It's up to you, mind. You must really want to change.' Polly's tone was curt, and she wagged a finger as she spoke.

Nancy stared, open-mouthed. 'Be a maid to some lady? Maybe work for the young lady Bill Waspill knows? Ooh!'

'First, wash. You must always be clean. Not just on your face, but you know where.' At Nancy's confusion, she added, 'Clean underneath. No ticks or fleas, and no lice in your hair. It'll take me hours to get you clean. I'll not try to gargosel you. It'll be hard work, and you'll have to trust me. First, you'll need clothes without patches and darns.'

With a most unladylike sniff, Nancy rolled her eyes, and then gave her head a vigorous scratch. When Polly slapped her hand, she glared at the woman. 'So tell me, how? Where the 'ell am I going to get new clothes from, lady? And if I do, how the deuce shall I keep them clean, living where I do?' Nancy's voice was bitter. She could already see insurmountable problems, beginning with a lack of money.

'I told you, live here with me. I've a bed you can use.'

'Now tell me how I'm going to feed us both on the bit of money I get from the mill? I work all the hours they'll let me do now, and I run errands for folk. Talking about the mill, how the 'ell am I going to keep clean, with all that oil about?'

Polly pulled a tight face and shrugged her shoulders. 'That, my dear, is your business. I didn't say it would be easy, did I? But I do have something that'll give you a start.'

Nancy's eyes narrowed as Polly walked to the corner of the room and folded a paisley shawl with a long fringe that was draped over a large tin trunk, and lifted the lid of the trunk. A gasp escaped Nancy as the smell of camphor reached her. She gave a cry of delight as Polly lifted various silk and fur items from the trunk, and laid them on a nearby chair. 'There should be... Ah, here we are.' She straightened up and shook the creases from a blue gown of lightweight wool, untrimmed, with a low neckline and tight elbow-length sleeves. After a moment's thought, she held out a pair of black shoes with red heels.

Nancy's mouth rounded into an almost silent, 'Oh!' She held herself as if she were already a lady.

'This gown should fit you without too much trouble. It may need a small tuck here and there. I'm not too sure about the shoes, though. They belonged to my daughter, and when she died

I was reluctant to sell them.' The gown draped over her arm, she added, 'Do you know how to move when wearing petticoats? I don't suppose you've ever worn undergarments, have you?' She frowned when Nancy shook her head. 'And curtsy. Have you been shown how to do a proper curtsy, girl?' Again, lice jumped out as Nancy shook her head and, snatching the gown from Polly, she held it in front of her and twirled around the room. Her violet eyes sparkled with excitement as the gown flowed round her legs.

'Here, give that to me. You'll get it filthy.' Polly pulled the gown from Nancy's hands with some difficulty, and gave her a chilling glare. 'Get off home now, and tell your mother what you're planning. If, and only if, she says you can come and live here, come back. Don't forget what I've said. It'll take months or even years to transform you.'

Nancy's head was full of plans as she hurried home. In the future she wouldn't have time to help people with errands; she'd need every penny she could earn at work. She slid into the room, which was thick with coal-smoke and steam from the cooking pot, expecting to find her father waiting with his belt wrapped around his hand ready to beat her and demand why she was home late. Mrs Turpin gave a wry smile when Nancy glanced anxiously around before hanging her shawl on the doornail.

'You're home first. Did you manage to see Polly Goodley, our Nancy?'

'Yes. She wants to help me. Got some clothes for me to wear. Oh, Mam. Looks like me dreams ain't so daft after all. She's going to train me so I can be a lady's maid, and then I'll be able to work in a big house.' Her face glowed as she took hold of her mother's hands and held them tightly.

'I don't know how we're going to do all this without your dad knowing,' Mrs Turpin said, with a worried frown.

'I shall leave 'ome. Polly Goodley said I could live with her. It'll be the best way, Mam. Dad won't miss my bit of money now our Jack's working at the factory.'

'Oh, I don't know. Should have spoke to him first.' Pulling her hands free, Mrs Turpin sat in the chair, rubbing her chin. 'He gets in such tempers nowadays if things change.'

Nancy wound her arms round her mother and placed her cheek on her face. 'I'm seventeen now, Mam, and I'll have to leave you soon. I'll only be down the road. Childer can always fetch me home if you need me,' she whispered, glancing at her younger sister. The little girl had left the other children playing with some kittens, and was standing nearby.

'What you saying, our Nancy?' the child asked, moving closer to lean on her mother's chair.

'Nowt. Grownup talk. Go and play with the others,' she snapped, giving the child a push.

Mrs Turpin took a deep breath and sat up straight. 'I'll talk to your dad for yer. I'll do it after he's had his dinner. I think you should at least try it. Our little Tommy starts at the Cooper's factory next week, so your dad should not be too upset, and might not miss your money. Anyway, you can always come back 'ome if things don't work out for yer.'

Nancy gave a relieved grin as she rushed across the room to where she kept her few belongings. She had passed the second hurdle.

Later, light from the open doorway lit the steps when she returned to Polly's home. She carried a small bundle, and used it to push the door further open.

'Me mam said I can stay. Me dad ain't home yet,' she gabbled, all in one breath, as her eyes searched for the gown and shoes. She dropped her bundle on the floor, and gave a sigh of relief; the blue gown still lay on top of the trunk. Then she noticed

Polly was wearing a sacking apron, and her sleeves were rolled up.

'Right, my girl, first, I want you to know I'm in charge here. This is my house, and whatever I say, I mean. And whenever I tell you to do something, you'll do it without question. Do you understand?'

Recognising authority, Nancy nodded. For once she didn't answer back.

'I've plenty of hot water. Now, let me have a proper look at you.' Placing her finger under Nancy's chin, Polly studied her face, and stroked her cheek with a gentle finger. 'You've not had the pox, that's one good thing in your favour. Your skin's clear.' She pulled and pushed a capacious hipbath closer to the fire, then filled it half-full with steaming water. A pail of cold water sat nearby. Eyes wide, Nancy bit her lip and backed towards the door.

Polly beckoned her forward. 'Don't stand there gawping. Come and help me.'

When the bath was ready, Nancy undressed and Polly helped her into the water. Squeals rang out when the strong-smelling, soft brown soap lathered Nancy's hair, and ran into her eyes. A film of grey bubbles formed on top of the water. Polly used a scrubbing brush on Nancy's back and neck, ignoring her cries of pain. She did allow Nancy to scour her own legs and arms, but watched with folded arms, making sure no areas were missed.

An hour or so later, Nancy, dressed in a clean nightgown, looked a different person. Her hair, soft and fine, rippled over her shoulders in a flaxen cloud. She put her hand to it in wonder, stroking the silken curls. 'It feels lovely. I'm going to keep it like this always,' she whispered in delight.

As Nancy admired herself in the mirror, Polly's lips twisted with wry amusement. 'Given your neck its first wash in years. Anyway, we've made a start on you. Best you get to your bed now. Good thing it's Sunday tomorrow. We'll have all day to make some undergarments and a bonnet.'

'Them shoes, can I try them on?'

'No. Maybe tomorrow. We'll see.'

The shoes on the top of the trunk tantalized Nancy. As they sewed and altered undergarments, including a bleached linen petticoat with the luxury of a narrow lace trim, she constantly glanced towards the shoes. However, with heavy sighs, she continued setting stitches into the garments—at first, most of them crooked. By late afternoon the sewing finished to Polly's satisfaction, they sat by the fire, relaxing.

Polly couldn't put off giving Nancy the shoes any longer. She went to the trunk and looked at them, shining and unworn. She struggled to hide her tearful emotion as she handed them to Nancy, who tried them on.

'They fit. They do fit, look.' Nancy held out a dainty foot for inspection, delighted to find her foot fitted so easily into the first pair of shoes she had ever put on. Her usual footwear had been a pair of old boots for the winter and, in the summer, bare feet. At Polly's expression, she removed the shoes, and sat with them in her hands, staring at her. 'What's wrong?' Then she remembered what her father had said. 'Oh, did these belong to your daughter?'

'Her father bought them for her. She never saw them. By the time they brought her home, she was past wearing shoes.'

'How long was she ill?'

'The robbers split open her skull. She was covered in blood and didn't know me. I nursed her for just over a week. She died in my arms. In some ways you remind me of her. I'm pleased you've come to stay here. It's given me something to live for and look forward to. Be nice to cook for the two of us.'

Nancy slipped her feet back into the shoes.

'You'll need to learn how to walk in them. It's hard to be graceful in heels,' Polly said, watching her.

Nancy practised walking in them. It seemed easy in the privacy of Polly's room, and she soon became confident enough to swing her hips. Her difficulties would begin outside on the lumpy cobblestones.

Watching Nancy's evident enjoyment, Polly said, 'I'm pleased they fit, and you'll enjoy having them. It's no use for me to live in the past.'

Early Monday morning, Nancy tottered along the street, trying not to catch the heels in the gaps between the cobblestones. The blue gown had needed little alteration and swung in a becoming manner over the starched petticoat. A plain, white linen bonnet covered her hair, framing her heart-shaped face. Polly had insisted she wear a brown woollen shawl with long tassels against the chill of the morning, and an apron of sackcloth, to protect her gown from the grease and dirt in the mill.

'Eh, look at her.'

'Can we talk to you, or do we 'ave ter curtsy first?'

Others joined her young workmates, and they all danced round her, mocking and mimicking her walk.

Chin stuck out, Nancy rolled her lips over her teeth and bit down hard, determined her noisy tormentors wouldn't see how much they were upsetting her. Once inside the mill, the sound of the machines partly drowned the taunts, although she remained the butt of mockery from her smirking friends.

Nancy's main occupation was to supply the army of men and women standing on the machine platform with wooden bobbins. This meant passing close to the moving machinery, and she was careful to keep her skirts from touching the greasy metal railings, although the apron soon became soiled.

About mid-morning, she noticed two male employees speaking to a small girl, who seemed to be grinning and glancing in her direction. The child held a small pot of oil and a brush, for it was her task to crawl under the machines and lubricate the moving parts. Dismissing the thoughts that sprang to mind as fanciful, she ignored the child.

'You'd best go and put on your old rags again,' remarked a woman, a while later as she rolled a tub of raw cotton towards a machine.

Nancy, affronted by the woman, stared at her amused expression, until she saw where the woman pointed. The girl must have squirted ink onto the part of her skirt unprotected by her apron. With a shrill cry, she pulled at her skirts, eyes flashing, and face whitening with temper. Colleagues nearby pointed and hooted with laughter. Nancy glared at them. 'I suppose you all think it's funny? I dare bet none of you lot could afford to buy a gown like this. No, you'd rather spend your money on daffy and gin, then get stale drunk,' she yelled, above the noise of the machinery.

'What's going on here?'

Everyone was suddenly extremely busy.

'Nothing, Mr Pugh.' Bobbing a curtsy at the mill master, she bent her head over her box of bobbins.

Mr Pugh's piggy eyes narrowed and roved over Nancy's trim figure, finishing at the low neckline. He ran a tongue over his thick lips as he stared at the milk-white curvature. 'Name, girl?' he barked.

'Turpin. Nancy Turpin, sir,' She gave the scowling man a nervous smile, before lowering her violet eyes.

'Can you read, Turpin?' Mr Pugh wasn't known for his pleasant manner.

'Yes, sir.' Hands clasped together, she bobbed another curtsy.

'Hmm.'

He strode across the room and spoke to one of the workmen before climbing a rough wooden staircase to his office. Glancing once and then twice at the window, Nancy saw him staring down at her. Her legs shook. It was the first time the mill master had spoken to her. It was more usual for him to stay in his office and send messengers with orders to those working the machines.

She bent her head and resumed work, but her mind dwelt on her misguided lie. *Why on earth did I tell him I could read? I bet a brass farthing he knows I can't. Bloody messed up things before I've even started. Polly'll not let me stay with her if I've no work. She's all on to look after herself.* Nancy's thoughts were interrupted by a shout from one of the workmen, which sent her scurrying to supply him with more bobbins. She found herself kept too busy for the rest of the day to remember her untruthful claim to the mill master.

Darkness was falling when Nancy left the mill. The route home to Polly's lodgings took her through twisting alleyways and dirty narrow streets. Here and there a lamp gave a feeble glow high on a wall. The shouts of street vendors and cursing coachmen rang out all around, but Nancy wasn't afraid; she was used to such places and foul language.

Bill Waspill walked past her and dodged the traffic as though in a hurry, and she wondered briefly if he were still meeting the young lady. She couldn't ask Polly, for the woman never discussed her clients' businesses. Nancy's lips curved in a smile, as she thought, *I don't care, and I'll soon be like a lady, and I'll probably take tea with her one day.*

Her mouth watered when the appetising aroma of a pig fry and thick gravy met her as she opened the door. She threw her shawl towards a chair and, missing its target, it slid to the floor. Disregarding it, she rushed to the table. Raised eyebrows and a stony stare arrested her movements. A hand on a chair back, she stood looking at Polly, mystified. 'What now, for goodness sake? I've only greeted you.'

Polly pointed to the discarded shawl in silence. Nancy bit back a retort as she hurried to pick it up, folded it and placed it on top of the tin trunk, before returning to the table.

'Do you not wash your hands and face before eating?'

With a roll of her eyes and giving a loud sigh, she went to do as bidden. She was halfway across the room when Polly gave a loud shriek, and, pulling her by her skirt, spun her round to face her.

'Your gown! What on earth happened? It's ruined, girl.'

'That's my so called friends' and workmates' idea of fun.' Nancy's expression was grim, and, speaking through clenched teeth, she added, 'I'll get even with that stupid lot at the mill one of these days, just you wait and see.'

'Take it off. I'll soak it, but I don't think I'll be able to remove the mark completely. Oh, it has gone right through to your petticoat. They must be a set of brainless nuddikins. Good thing I made you wear an apron. I suppose that saved your gown a little.' Tut-tutting, Polly examined each garment Nancy handed to her.

Leaving Polly to deal with the greasy stains, she put on her nightdress and bed-cap and, with a shiver, threw her shawl round her shoulders before sitting down at the table. As Polly placed the meal in front of her, she reached over the table and pulled a large chunk of bread from the loaf. She was about to stuff it into her mouth, when the back of a ladle landed on her knuckles. She dropped the bread with a curse.

'You... That hurt. What did you do that for?' she bawled and, putting her tingling fingers into her mouth, sat glaring at Polly.

'Ladies don't lunge across the table like that and stuff their mouths full. You place the piece of bread on your small plate, and break it into bite-sized pieces as you require it. Now, watch

40

me.' Polly pulled a chair next to hers and sat down. 'You sit with a straight back, use your spoon like so, and bring it up to your mouth. Don't lower your head to eat the food like an animal.'

The expression on Nancy's face showed she was unimpressed. 'Take an age to fill yourself that way. You wouldn't get owt if yer did that at our house. Others would get everything. It's first up, best dressed at our place.' She chuckled, remembering a morning a few weeks earlier when her father had been searching for his trousers. It hadn't been until her brother had returned home from work that they had found he'd been wearing them by mistake.

'You're not in your father's house now, you're in mine. And while you're here, you'll eat in a correct manner.' When Polly used that tone of voice, she knew she meant what she said.

After the table had been cleared, and the dishes washed and put away, Nancy told Polly about the day's events at the mill. 'First time Mr Pugh's ever spoke to me. I reckon he didn't know me with being clean and all. He asked me name, then asked if I could read.' Watching the flames from the fire she knew she had to tell Polly, but felt uncomfortable about the lie.

'What did you tell him?' Polly asked. Her arms wet up to her elbows,, she plunged them time after time into warm, sudsy water, frowning and tut-tutting as she rubbed the oil-marked clothes. Nancy glanced at her and then returned her gaze to the fire.

'I...er, I told him yes. Hope he doesn't ask again.'

Clearly hearing the worry in her voice, Polly stopped washing to stare at her, her eyebrows raised in enquiry.

Nancy blushed. 'Well, I did know some letters once. Me mam started teaching me reading and writing, then the other babies came, and I had to start work. Schools ain't for the likes of me.'

'What letters do you know? Can you remember anything?'

41

Nancy's flaming cheeks supplied the answer, and Polly shook her head in exasperation.

'I never gave a thought to your education. Let's see now. I've an old slate somewhere that my daughter used to use, and I have my old Bible. Wait until I've hung these up to dry, and then I'll look for the slate. I'll try to teach you. Who knows? Perhaps one day you'll be able to help me write letters for people.'

The inexpert use of Nancy's thin slate pencil as she drew it across the piece of slate, set their teeth on edge, but neither of them said anything, aware that eventually she would progress to scribing on paper. They worked together with determination, both realising that her future depended on her remembering the basic schooling she had once received. It was nearly midnight when the exhausted pair went to bed, but progress had been made. She was a fast learner.

Each night on her return from the mill, they worked at speech, deportment, etiquette and education. As the months passed, she changed. She no longer lifted her skirts to run. She walked gracefully, with her back straight and her head held high. Her speech improved. It was soft and clear. Bill no longer came to see Polly and Nancy forgot about him and Merrilla. Mr Pugh became interested in her, and when he knew she could read and write, he put her to work in his office. Luckily, she only had to write simple words, and was able to copy those that were more difficult. He also gave her the responsibility of instructing other workers how to distribute customers' orders. The sweet perfume of the soap she used seemed to inflame him, and he found new ways of keeping her by his side. Nancy, using her ingenuity, became a valuable asset to the mill master.

Realising that Nancy needed to mix socially, Polly was pleased when she agreed to accompany her each Sunday to church, correcting her quietly when Nancy made a mistake.

They had lived together for almost five months when, one evening, on returning from the mill, Nancy found her arm grasped, and was spun round to face a threatening figure. Giving a gasp of fear, she put up the other arm as though to ward off a blow. 'Pa! What's you doing here?'

'Don't you Pa me. You ain't a daughter of mine any more,' Mr Turpin growled, putting his face close to hers. She smelt his booze-laden breath.

'Why? What do you mean?' Surprised by his words, she stopped pulling herself free from his clutches.

'You might well ask. ''Ow do you think I feel having you live with that doxy? Laughing stock of the street I am. You were brought up proper, you were, me girl. I had Fred Pullings marked out to wed you. He'll not look at you now you've pulled this stunt.'

The pain Nancy felt as his fingers dug into her arm made her eyes water. 'I ain't done nothing wrong. I'm a decent girl, and don't you call Polly Goodley names. She's kindly towards me,' she yelled, trying to twist away from him, her temper out of control.

'Baa, now she's on her own she's looking for an easy living. I know things about her, I does. Her husband used to be a bloody moneylender. Lent money for folk to have a bet, then when you lost he wanted the money back, and more on top. No wonder he got himself and his daughter murdered.'

Struggling to free herself, Nancy kicked out at her father's legs. Fortunately, she missed, for he would certainly have responded by lashing out with his fists.

'Yer mam's missing the money. She's finding it hard to manage. You're giving that doxy your wages, and your mam needs them.'

She stopped struggling and stepped closer to him. 'So, that's it. You're keeping my mam short. You've three wages going into that house, but you aren't satisfied. Bet you ain't cutting down on your ale, are you? Well, you just think on this, our dad: what I earn's mine, because I'm a woman full-grown. Now I'm seventeen, I've left home, and I'm not coming back.' Like a spitting cat, she stood, ready to fight for her new-found freedom, for the moment, Polly's elocution lessons forgotten.

'You give your mam half your wages or I'll skelp yer myself,' he threatened.

But Nancy was in no mood to be intimidated. 'And I say you'll need all the people in this street to help yer do that,' she yelled.

'Baa!' He gave her arm a sudden push, making her stagger, but she managed not to fall onto the filthy ground. Before turning away he spat a stream of brown liquid towards his daughter's feet, but, knowing her father's habits, she jumped to one side. A frown and a down-turned mouth marred her pretty face as she watched her father stomp away.

Her shawl clutched tightly, she arrived at Polly's, white faced and breathless. It took some time before she could stop trembling and tell Polly why she was so upset.

'Oh, Nancy, we must call at your old home with some money, after we've been to church next Sunday. It's only fitting that you help out your family.'

'I've two brothers working. Me eldest should give Mam more. It's because he's started calling at the tavern for a drink on the way home, and now he's found out what women are for. Its not right that my pa gets all his own way, just because he wants to buy ale for his cronies and paramours.' Nancy sniffed, and dabbed daintily at her eyes with a hemmed piece of rag used as a handkerchief. 'I've heard what he gets up to, when he's out of sight of my mam. He'll have any woman that offers, he will,' she said.

Polly had also heard talk of young Mr Turpin's sexual prowess, all of it uncomplimentary.

'Look, Nancy, if you lose contact with your family you may regret it later in life. It won't hurt to show a little charity. I know—it happened to me. My family disowned me when I married Mr Goodley, and then his family wanted nothing to do with me. They thought I was too lady-like.'

Although interested in this disclosure, Nancy's expression remained stormy, though she brightened at Polly's next words.

'I think you've made such excellent progress. We'll see if your mother can see any alteration in you.'

Nancy nodded, and said with a smile, 'It'll be nice to see my mam. I feel as though I've been left home ages.'

'I've made a surprise for you. This is for you to wear to church. The straw's very golden, and it should look becoming with your colouring.' Polly removed a silk scarf, swathed over a bonnet, trimmed with blue silk roses and a bunch of wide ribbon.

Nancy caught her breath with delight. 'It's beautiful, Polly. Oh, thank you,' she said, bending to kiss the woman's soft cheek, before standing in front of the mirror to try on the bonnet.

Sunday came, and Nancy took particular care of her appearance. The shape of the bonnet complemented her face, and she felt like a queen as she sat with Polly. She hardly listened to the service; most of her attention was on the fashionable clothes the ladies were wearing. When they left the church, they walked side-by-side though the churchyard, their skirts touching, and their bonnets turning towards each other as they spoke.

They halted at the lynch gate.

'Give your mother my regards, Nancy. I'll have a stroll through the churchyard, towards the grave of my husband and daughter and then wait for you here. We can then go home together.'

When Nancy stepped inside her old home, she placed a handkerchief to her nose, and blinked in the pungent, smoky atmosphere. *Surely the stench was not as bad as this when I lived here*, she thought.

'Nice of you to come, our Nancy.' Mrs Turpin rose from her chair. Her eyes roved over Nancy's clothing with something like wonder at her transformation. While her mother scrutinised her appearance, Nancy drew a comparison between this pokey little room and the place she now called home. She lifted her gown and petticoats clear of scurrying beetles, wrinkling her nose in distaste.

'Did Pa tell you he'd spoken to me?' she asked, after their stilted greeting.

'Yes, he said yer looked nice. Like a lady, he said.'

Nancy gave an unladylike snort, which would have earned her a slap from Polly, had she heard her.

'Proud of you, he is. He heard how you've been made a charge hand over the other women in the mill. You've really done well, our Nancy.'

'Mr Pugh. It was him who thought I could do it. He said he has faith in me.' Nancy spoke slowly, remembering to sound her aitches.

'You watch out, me girl. He'll have his 'and up your skirts. It isn't the first time he's tried it on wi' the mill women. They say he's got more than one bastard.'

Nancy touched her bonnet bows and adjusted her shawl, remembering the gentleness with which the mill master had touched her. She looked her mother in the eye and smiled. 'I can handle Mr Pugh. It's easy to mystify that one. Buy me anything, he would. Not that I'd allow him to,' she added at her mother's horrified expression. 'Don't worry about me, Mam. I know how to look after myself. You just look out for this lot here.' They looked at the silent, watchful children. 'You can send one of the boys round to Polly's place each Friday night. It'll save me having to call round here each Sunday.'

As she stepped forward to kiss her mother, she drew back swiftly when the lousy hair and unwashed skin almost made contact with her own. She turned her head away, and made no attempt to touch her mother or the children when she said goodbye. Looking back over her shoulder as she was leaving, she said, 'Can you see a change in me, Mam?'

A look of hurt crossed her mother's face as, bravely hiding her feelings, she smiled, and said, 'I can see a vast change indeed, our Nancy. You're all growed up, you are.'

Nancy and Polly walked along the streets, stopping to gaze into shop windows, and ignoring gentlemen who lifted their hats and bowed, hoping for an introduction. Nancy was quite aware of their attention, and gave a couple of handsome men a discreet wiggle of her fingers behind Polly's back.

'Mam said she could see a vast change in me, Polly.'

'Did she, now? I thought she'd see a difference.'

'I don't know how I could have lived in that sty. It's so neglected, and the floor's overrun with bugs. Oh, I never, ever want to go back there again. I could do with a bath, I feel that itchy.' Her mouth pulled into an ugly grimace, she gave an exaggerated shiver.

'Don't forget who's loved and looked after you since you were born. Never turn away from your mother, Nancy. If you do so, you'll be sorry your whole life long.' Polly gave her a sharp look, but Nancy tossed her head, and shrugged.

When they reached home, she pulled off her kid gloves and threw them carelessly onto the table. Busy removing her bonnet, and wrapping the piece of silk fabric around the golden straw, she looked up and saw Polly frown.

'Don't forget to put those gloves on their stretcher, for you'll not get another pair for a long time. And cover that bonnet properly. You know how badly straw fades.'

Nancy was not upset by the strident voice, still feeling a happy glow with her mother's words ringing in her ears. She gave Polly a dazzling smile. 'A vast change, Mam said. You're making me into a lady at last, dear Polly.' Lifting her skirts with dainty fingers, and twirling around the room, she danced over to place a kiss on the older woman's cheek. 'Do you think I'm ready to work in a gentleman's house yet?' she asked, taking hold of Polly's hand and lifting it to her cheek. 'Who knows? I may even get to marry a gentleman.'

'You've a long way to go, and a lot to learn before that day arrives, my girl,' Polly said. Sadly, she shook her head. 'And the changes must be for the better, my dear. You must not spurn those who love you, or flash your smile at every man who looks your way. Otherwise, at some time, you'll rue the day,' she warned.

But Nancy took no notice as she undressed, and shook out imaginary bugs from her clothes.

Chapter 4

Bill Waspill had hinted, in his letters to Merrilla, that any money she brought with her would be extremely useful. At their last meeting, he had looked into her eyes and spoken softly and appealingly.

'We could buy some new equipment for our boat, Merrilla. It would make us both very much more comfortable. Maybe the bed...?'

Because all of her monthly allowance had been spent, the declaration had worried her, until she remembered that her father kept money in his study. He was still away in Grantham, and not expected home until the following week.

Waiting until her mother and sister were busy with household tasks, she went into her father's study and closed the door. A box of gold coins had always been locked in the top drawer of the bureau, to pay the household expenses. She knew where the key was kept, and it only took a moment to unlock it, remove the box, and open it. An audible gasp escaped her at the large amount of coins.

Voices outside the study door made her freeze but, keeping an eye on the door, she wrapped a pile of sovereigns in her handkerchief and thrust them into her pocket. Then she closed the lid, replaced the box in the drawer, and returned the key to its hiding place. She tiptoed across the room and listened, her ear pressed against the door panel, one hand in her pocket clutching the money, and the other covering her mouth.

At first, all she could hear was the rapid beating of her heart, but then she made out a voice. 'I have not seen Merrilla since breakfast, Mamma.' Maude. She and her mother were in the corridor, just the other side of the door. Merrilla's eyes frantically searched for a hiding place. Slim as she was, there was nothing large enough to conceal her. Then her mother tut-tutted in reply to Maude, and the voices faded as they moved towards the drawing room.

She opened the door and put out her head to peer along the corridor; it was empty. Silent in her house shoes, she hurried across the entrance hall, and scurried up the staircase to her bedchamber, where she closed the door, and leaned against it, thankful she hadn't been seen. Her heart still racing, she glanced round the room, trying to decide upon the safest place to hide the coins. Her jewellery box stood on the dressing table. She grinned in triumph, and was about to plunge the money under the baubles inside, but her grin faded as she scanned the pretty assortment. Not much value there, except a long string of pearls, which had been given to her on her last birthday. She tipped the coins out of her handkerchief and counted them. Fourteen. They needed more. Bill had once hinted in a letter that fifty guineas would make a good start to their marriage. Dare she risk returning to the study? With a giggle, she put the coins in the box. *How silly of me,* she thought. *When I return home as Bill's wife, Papa will be only too happy to give me fifty guineas—and much more, if we need it.*

Her thoughts then turned to what jewellery she would wear on her wedding day. *Oh, I know—Mamma will lend me her ruby necklace. I can wear it, and then let her have it back as soon as we return. No harm will come to it, and Mamma has always said that gems which are frequently worn shine brighter.* No sooner had the thought entered her head than she was tapping on the door of her mother's bedchamber. Hearing no reply, she slipped inside and went to the dressing table. Her mother kept all her best jewellery wrapped in black velvet. She had just put a hand on the handle of the drawer when a knock on the door made her straighten and turn in inquiry. A maid entered, carrying a bowl and an ewer containing fresh water. She placed them on the washstand, and, after curtsying, withdrew. Merrilla searched for the necklace and, finding it with the matching earrings, scooped them into her pocket. The box and the remainder of her mother's jewellery were replaced exactly as she'd found them. She closed the drawer with the knowledge that nothing would be disturbed until her parents attended a function, and by that time she intended to have returned home as Bill's wife, and replaced the ruby necklace and earrings.

Upon returning to her own room, she noticed her own ewer and bowl had also been changed. With a grateful sigh, she poured cold water into the bowl, and splashed her burning cheeks. *I'd never make a successful burglar, my red face would give me away,* she thought. Elated by her success, she danced across the room to place her mother's jewellery with the gold coins. 'Tomorrow. Tomorrow,' she whispered to her reflection in the looking glass. An animated face looked back at her. *I must compose myself. If I appear to be excited it will arouse suspicion and I'll have to face questions from Mamma and Maude.*

As she returned downstairs, she concentrated on walking slowly, with her back straight—dignified, as a young lady old enough to marry should be.

Throughout the remainder of the evening, and the following day, she found it difficult to behave as normal. Her mother planned to spend the morning shopping, and as usual, she wanted to be seen by numerous friends, buying pretty trinkets for her daughters.

'But beautiful girls need to be complemented by lovely things to wear,' Mrs Cooper gushed to an acquaintance who had once remarked on her generosity. Merrilla had felt a flush of embarrassment stain her cheeks. At the time, she had thought that a new saddle for her pony would have been money better spent. Now, when she thought of Bill, and how willing he would be to indulge her slightest whim, serenity filled her.

On arriving home from the shopping trip, she went to her bedchamber, where her maid waited to help her change from her walking gown into a light cotton afternoon gown. She wanted to be alone, but dared not send the girl away until she had done her work. After brushing Merrilla's hair and tying fresh ribbons around her bunches of long ringlets, the maid was dismissed to the servants' hall. She hurried to the door and turned the key in the lock. *At last*, she thought, as she threw back the lid of a large wooden chest, and removed the clothes inside. During the last few days, she had been trying to choose which of her numerous gowns and other pieces of finery to take away with her.

An empty valise and a dressing case were hidden under the bed, ready for use. The dressing case pulled out, she lifted it onto her bed, and began packing the possessions she thought she'd need as Bill's wife. He had already warned her he could only carry a limited amount of luggage on the boat. She packed first one thing, then another, changing her mind time and time again, until the floor of her bedchamber was littered with clothing of every description.

Finally selecting the garments she wanted to take with her, she packed both the dressing case and the valise, before replacing them under the bed. After tidying her room, she packed a bandbox with Bill's letters, the jewellery box with her trinkets, her mother's jewels, and the gold coins

Knowing her maid would immediately notice any brushes and combs missing from her dressing table, she left them there, with the intention of packing them later. There was enough room under her bed for the bandbox. She pushed it out of sight with her foot, and scrutinised the room. Everything seemed as it ought, should anyone give it a casual glance.

When she went downstairs, the drawing room seemed stifling, and she chose a seat near an open window. She tried her best to appear normal by taking up her embroidery and stitching the complex picture, but her thoughts were busy with her elopement plan. Maude had to ask twice if she would accompany her for a walk in the garden before Merrilla smiled her agreement.

'Stay in the shade, girls. The light is strong, even though autumn is almost upon us. We don't want your freckles to show, Merrilla. And do not remove your bonnets, girls.'

They gave her a graceful curtsy before donning light wraps and stepping outside. Merrilla only half listened to Maude's chatter as they strolled along paths bordered with scrubs and flowers. Sometimes they lifted their skirts to avoid pollen staining the light fabric.

At last it was time to leave the garden, and they returned indoors to change into their dinner gowns.

'I will be pleased when I have a dressing room like Mamma. By then, I'll be a married lady of course.' Maude spoke in a way that suggested her time of wedded bliss would be there long before her sister could find a husband.

Merrilla gave her a pitying glance, but fortunately it went unnoticed. *I'll be married long before you, miss, and I'll own my own beautiful boat*, she thought, as she walked along the corridor to her bedchamber.

Mr Cooper did not encourage conversation when his family sat at the dining table. He believed they would speak of trivial subjects, and about things of no interest to him. This habit was observed in his absence. At dinner, Merrilla silently took portions of food offered to her by the butler, and put them on her plate, glad they were small, for her throat was tightened by a mixture of excitement and fear. *This time tomorrow, I'll be having dinner with Bill at our own table*, she thought, and began planning a menu, until the ladies retired to the withdrawing room for coffee.

She did her best to ignore the black hands, which crept with maddening slowness round the dial of the ornate gilt clock on the mantelpiece. For once, she was pleased when Maude seated herself in front of the harpsichord.

'May I turn the pages of music, Maude?' she asked, rising to her feet. As she took a position behind her sister, Maude shot her an incredulous look, usually receiving unkind remarks about her sister's musical accomplishments, but she refrained from making a comment as she sorted through a pile of sheet music.

'Play some of Mr Handel's airs, my dear,' Mrs Cooper called from her seat beside the fire.

Merrilla gave a sigh. She preferred the more lively music of William Boyce, or Dr Berney.

The evening seemed unending to the impatient girl, but at last the time came to place a kiss on her mother's cheek, and to bid her and her sister good night. As she left the room, it occurred to her that this would be the last kiss they would have before she was married. With exciting thoughts running through her mind, she lifted her skirts and hurried to her bedchamber, where her maid was waiting to help her to disrobe, and don her nightgown and wrap. 'Leave my hair. I want to brush it myself tonight,' she said, putting her hand on her hairbrush. She knew she couldn't possibly arrange her hair into ringlets again without help, and she had to look her best, tonight of all nights.

'Yes, miss,' the maid said, gratefully. Merrilla watched in her looking glass as she turned back the covers on the bed, and picked up the discarded gown, stockings and underwear.

'I'll take your gown downstairs to be pressed ready for the morning, miss,' the girl said, giving a smiling curtsy. 'Good night, miss.'

Worried in case she fell asleep and missed her appointment with Bill, Merrilla sat in an upright chair near the open window, gazing outside. *I shall be Mrs Waspill the next time I see this view,* she mused. Her window overlooked the kitchen gardens, and also a yard at the back of the house, which was partially illuminated by lamplight from the kitchen windows. After a while the lamps went out, one by one. She heard faint noises in the house as her family and the servants made ready for bed. At last, all went silent. She caught herself yawning, more than once, and tried passing the time by gathering forgotten items, including her favourite book of poems and a scarf, and tried squeezing them into her bandbox. Worrying that her mother's jewellery might somehow get lost, she decided to wear it.

A clock chimed the hour. Everyone in the house should be asleep, so she padded across the room, removed her best green velvet gown from the closet, and threw it onto the bed. It took her an age to tie the laces of her stays, and her fingers fumbled with the tapes on her petticoats, which tied with strings at the back. She put on an extra petticoat, as her dressing case was too full to place anything else in it.

When she had tried to pack the velvet gown earlier, its bulk had filled the case. The gown had a matching cloak, lined with fur, and, although the evening felt warm, she wanted to take it with her. These garments were more difficult to put on without the help of a maid so, hot, as well as excited, she opened the door of her bedchamber.

With slow movements, a step at a time along the corridor, she passed Maude's, then her parents' rooms. Outside each door, she stopped and listened, but the only sound was that of her mother snoring. After moving to the top of the stairs with her luggage, she descended, knowing which stair creaked, and how to step so the old wood wouldn't betray her.

She had decided, days earlier, that it would be best to leave by the side door, and had checked that the bolts and hinges were well oiled. All that lay between her and her beloved Bill was a short passageway and a door.

The warmth of the day lingered in the night air. This, and the uncertainty of Merrilla's arrival, made Bill Waspill and Jeremy sweat.

'Keep that bloody horse quiet! That harness rattles loud enough to wake the whole damn place,' hissed Bill from his hiding place among the bushes.

'I can't help it. He wants to be off, and I for one don't blame him, neither. You said midnight, and its well past,' came the reply from Jeremy, crouched near to the open iron gates, ready to make a dash if things didn't go as planned.

'Hist. You hear that? It's her. Ah, you little beauty. Come on, Merrilla, come to your Bill, then.'

In the shadow of the porch, her dressing case and bandbox in one hand, and the valise in the other, Merrilla struggled to close the door.

'Come on, Jeremy. Let's go and help the lady. She mustn't wake the household at this stage,' Bill called, stepping into the open, grinning broadly. Jeremy, his eyes scanning the darkened windows above, followed his friend across the lawn. 'Good girl. How I do admire your fortitude and fearlessness, my darling.'

Enchanted by her moonlit adventure, Merrilla gave him a look of adoration as he took the valise from her. He slipped an arm around her waist, and guided her along a flower border to avoid stepping onto the gravel drive. Crunching gravel might alert people sleeping behind dark windows in the rooms above. Jeremy, carrying the dressing case and the bandbox, followed the couple as they hurried across the smooth lawn of the front garden.

'My love! I know you're not used to travelling in hired coaches, but I could think of no other way to whisk you off at the speed we need to travel,' Bill said, in a low voice, as he guided her though the gates and along the road. He handed the valise to

Jeremy, who threw it inside the boot of the coach. It landed with a thud beside the dressing case and bandbox.

Bill helped the willing girl into the coach as Jeremy leapt into the driving seat and took hold of the reins and whip. As the coach moved off, it gave a sudden lurch, giving Bill an excuse to clutch hold of her. Slipping his arm around her, he felt with approval the rich fur and velvet of her clothing and, as he moved closer her flowery perfume and nearness aroused his lustful senses.

Merrilla wouldn't have entered the vehicle so willingly had it been daylight, and had she noticed its peeling paintwork and the cracked leather seats. It was also, fortunately, too dark for Bill to see how she wrinkled her nose in disgust at the musty odour.

'My darling, you'll never know how many times I've dreamed of this moment. Of you and I, roving through life together.' Bill moved a rug from the opposite seat, and draped it over her legs, but kept his hand on her thigh.

A strong smell of horse clung to the rug as she hitched herself further along the seat, shrinking into the corner, a chill of fear running down her spine. She took a panicky dislike to the pressure of Bill's leg as it pressed in such an intimate way against her. *Why is it that I've never noticed how stale his breath smells?* she thought, forgetting they had met in public places, and mostly in the open air, never as close as this. She leaned her head away from him as he edged closer and took hold of her hands.

'Let me take that tender hand and place it to my waiting lips,' he crooned.

She snatched her hands away and placed them on her burning cheeks. 'No, Mr Was pill. Please, no.' Desperately, she thought of some way out of her predicament. She glanced at the window, but the coach was travelling too fast. It would be suicidal to open the door and escape. Her throat tightened with panic. *How on*

earth could I have been so irresponsible to travel to an unknown
destination with a man I do not fully know?

'Mr Waspill I've been so foolish. I cannot travel with you. That is what I came out to tell you. Please, sir, take me back home now.'

'It's Bill, for your pretty lips, my dear.'

'But, sir…Bill…There is something I have forgotten. It is most important that I return home at once.' She squealed with terror when he pulled her roughly towards him. Never in her life had she allowed a man to handle her; indeed, no one had ever needed to. She screamed even louder when he slipped an exploratory hand down her neckline and squeezed her firm, young breast. The scream was silenced as his lips clamped onto her mouth, and he tried to open it with his tongue. Her eyes widened in horror. She tried to bite him, and her fingernails raked what flesh she could reach.

Jeremy heard the drumming of Merrilla's heels, and whipped the elderly horses hard so they made a greater effort to gallop. On reaching the deserted canal towing path, he manoeuvred the clumsy vehicle to a halt near to the long horse-drawn barge that lay motionless in the dark water.

After jumping down from the coach, he tied the horses securely to a nearby bush. His hands stilled and he caught his breath at a whinny and stamping of a hoof. With a nervous chuckle, he realised that the sounds had come from Meggie, the barge horse. She was tethered nearby, and already harnessed, ready to pull the barge on its momentous journey.

'Damn hellcat! Had to knock her senseless. Hurry up, take her legs. We must get her inside quick, before anyone comes by,' Bill growled, as he tried to lift Merrilla out of the coach.

'No one comes past here at night. Too frit of being a goner.' With a grunt, Jeremy took hold of the girl's ankles, grinning as his fingers touched the fine stockings.

They were both panting as they carried the girl's inert body inside the cabin and dropped her onto the dirty floor. Jeremy hurried to light the large three-cornered lantern that hung at an angle on the cabin wall. He gave a long, low whistle after turning to see Bill's blooded cheeks.

'Struth, Bill, she's done a grand job on your face. You'll bear those scars for a week or two, I'll be bound.' The cheeky grin faded when Bill gave him a malevolent stare.

'Dub yer mummer. She'll not better me, my lad. My belt will soon sort her out. You get to the coach and bring her things down here. Then we'll find out what she managed to bring us.' Bill's voice was gruff with disappointment. He gave Merrilla a none-too-gentle nudge with the toe of his boot. She gave a soft moan, but didn't open her eyes.

Out of breath, Jeremy clattered down the five steps of the cabin, dropped Merrilla's luggage on the floor, and then, knowing from experience what could happen, turned back and locked the door. Standing beside Bill, he looked down at her. 'Them bags ain't half a weight. Bet there's some good stuff in there,' he said, jerking his head towards the luggage. Stepping closer to the unconscious girl, he stared at her face.

'If I was you, Bill, I'd smother her whilst you've still got the chance. She'll be nowt but trouble, this one. Stands out a mile, it do. Mrs McGreed won't thank you for bringing this baggage to work with her girls.'

Bill turned to face him. 'Told you to stow it. She's for me, this one. You can have her clothes. They're quality things, and you'll get a good price, but I'm keeping the girl here with me.'

He gave Merrilla another bruising nudge with his boot, and watched as she moaned and opened her eyes.

At first, she had no idea what had happened to her. Then, as she raised herself up, her eyes widened. She looked around, and her terrified gaze fastened on the door. She gave a long, shuddering moan as Bill spoke.

'Don't even think it, my dolly. I locked it, in case you harboured thoughts of fleeing. Listen to me, and listen well, my girl. You're here, and here I mean to keep you.' He ignored the violently shaking head and wild eyes. 'Now, let's get down to business. Take off your clothes—all of them.'

She gulped, and stammered, 'My...my clothes? Why? No. You can't have my clothes.'

'Come on, hurry up. We don't have all night. Jeremy 'ere wants to be on his way.'

'No. I can't.' Her cheeks went paper-white with terror.

'I said take them off. You'll not be the first girl we've undressed.' The menace in his voice was unmistakable.

'Yer'll take them off, or we'll do it for yer,' Jeremy sang, in a childish chant, far more frightening than Bill's threats.

She was still sprawled on the floor. As she moved to a sitting position, she unfastened the clasp of her cloak. It fell from her shoulders onto the ground in soft folds. Giving a low whistle, Bill bent nearer at the sight of the sparkling gold and ruby earrings and the necklet around her throat. He moved closer and she cringed away.

'Cor, guv, you said I could have everything, and you'd have the girl.' Jeremy's eyes rounded with greed.

Ignoring the boy, Bill pointed to the jewellery. 'Let's have them first, girl.'

'No, not these. They belong to my mother. I brought them to wear on my wedding day.' Tears of fear and anger wetted her ashen cheeks as, lifting her long skirts with trembling hands, she tried to move away from the hulking figure. Stumbling, she fell to her knees.

'Do you take them off, or do we do it for you?' Bill's glittering eyes made him very intimidating.

She struggled to her feet, unfastened the necklet and, following the instruction of his pointing finger, removed the earrings, as well as a ring with blue stones, and threw them at him. They were followed, one by one, by her garments, until she stood, dressed in only her shift, in a state of uncontrollable shock, her arms folded across her body, shivering and mesmerised.

She flinched as Bill barked out, 'That an' all.'

Jeremy gave an evil chuckle when her eyes widened in disbelief. Only her nurse and maid had seen her fully disrobed. Dazed, she lifted the hem, drew the shift over her head and tossed it down, trying to hide her body with her hands.

'Here. Cover yourself with this, then get yourself over to that bench,' Bill ordered. He threw her a tattered garment, and pointed at a bare wooden bench fastened to the wall of the cabin.

The garment had once been a dress. Merrilla put it over her head, and tried pulling it down to cover her legs, but at sometime the hem had been ripped off, and it only reached her knees. With fingers covering her mouth, she watched, traumatised, as Jeremy tied the corners of her cloak together to make a neat bundle. He forgot about her soft kid boots that had skidded into a corner. His head bent over the clothes, he didn't notice Bill scoop up the fallen jewellery and put it in his jacket pocket. Throwing the bundle of clothes towards the cabin door, he turned to face Bill. 'You said I was ter have all the things, and you were to have her?' he said, looking slyly out of the corner of his eye.

'Right, and I'll keep my word, but we split the gems, same as usual.' Bill's eyes narrowed. 'You be satisfied with what you have, boy, and make damn sure you get rid of that lot well away from here. Now, you know the route we'll be taking. Grantham

Canal, across the River Trent, and onto the Nottingham Canal, then on towards Cromford. I'll wait there a day for you, and if you don't turn up, I'll make my way along the Erewash, and onwards.'

He turned away in dismissal, but the boy caught hold of his arm. 'Eh. Let's see what's in the bandbox first, shall we?'

Taking a clasp knife from his pocket, Bill opened a blade. They bent over the bandbox as he forced the lock open. Merrilla could have told them the key was in the pocket of the cloak, but she dared not speak. As the lid opened, she sprang forward with a shrill cry, causing Jeremy to turn round in surprise. In a flowing movement, Bill slid the jewellery box under his jacket and held it in place with his arm. Closing the lid of the bandbox, he pushed it along the floor with his foot in Jeremy's direction. Then, turning to Merrilla, he hit her in the face with the back of his closed fist, knocking her to the floor. 'Get out, boy. Take the things and get out,' he snarled, standing over the cowering girl, fist lifted, ready to strike again.

Jeremy unlocked the cabin door, took hold of the bundle and threw it outside. The rest of her luggage followed. As he jumped onto the towpath the bolt on the door shot home, followed by Bill's muffled voice. 'Now, my beauty, we're alone at last. Time we got to know each other properly. Later I'll tell you all about your loving papa, and what he's done to me family.'

Merrilla watched with big eyes as he removed the jewellery box from under his jacket and placed it in one of the decorated cupboards. She returned to the bench and sat with both hands on her cheeks, cowering, as Bill moved towards her. He removed his jacket, laid it on his bed, and unbuckled his trouser belt. She whimpered, sensing he meant her harm. He grabbed a bunch of shining ringlets and pulled her head down. At the same time, the leather belt landed on her back. In her sheltered life, she had always been surrounded with kindness. When naughty, her punishment was to be sent to her room, supperless. Nothing had prepared her for such dreadful treatment.

'No. Bill. No, please nooo....' Her words were cut off by a high scream.

'But you have hurt me, dear one. Now you must be punished. Remember, you scratched me, and I only wanted a little kiss.'

Two bloodied weals striped her soft body as his arm rose and fell. 'You'll never think to scratch me again, my girl,' he muttered. By the time he had replaced his belt, she lay unconscious on the floor.

When Merrilla regained her senses, she was alone. Giving a moan and a whimper, she lifted herself into a sitting position, and sat a moment, looking around the cabin. All the furniture was fixed to the wall, and the floor was composed of dirty, bare, wooden planks. Her body stiff and sore, she struggled upright and, holding on to the furniture and wall, moved with difficulty to the only window in the cabin. A tearful cry escaped her when she realised the early morning daylight was almost obscured by bales of hay to feed the horse. By pulling herself up on tiptoe, she could just see the sky, and the tops of trees. There was no clue as to their whereabouts. A gasp and another moan escaped her swollen lips when the door opened and Bill came into the cabin. He had removed his best clothes and wore his working garments—an old shirt with rolled up sleeves, and a pair of stained moleskin trousers.

'So, my lady, you're on your feet. That's good. Now we can finish your education.'

With a cupboard for support, she watched his hands as he unbuckled his belt and trousers. She bit on her knuckles as he undressed and moved towards her. It was the first time she had seen a man's bare body. The awesome sight of flesh and black hair, his hard throbbing arousal, repulsed her.

'I've waited a long time to bed you, my little virgin, and I'm all ready for you, look.' He leered, and gave a low chuckle at her horrified expression. 'No need to worry, my little flower, you're not the first I've broken in. It'll not hurt if you don't struggle.' His expression was savage when he lurched forward and caught her by the hair and hauled her towards him.

She kicked out and managed to run to the other side of the cabin. 'No.' she screamed.

'What did you say? No? It's Bill, my dear. You don't say no to your Bill, do you?' He lifted his fist.

With both hands shielding her face, she whimpered and slithered across the floor as he strode towards her. Another scream escaped her when he tore the dress from her sore body.

'Silly bitch. Nowt ter fear. But I'll make you heed me, dolly. Your life is going to be different from now on, and you'll be begging for my loving by the time we reach Yorkshire,' he swore as she swooned again.

Chapter 5

'Well, boy?' Bill shouted across the room of the tavern. Earlier that afternoon, he'd locked Merilla in the cabin (giving her a warning not to scream or bang on the door), moored the boat, and tethered Meggie the horse. Since then, he'd sat in the dismal room, drinking the landlord's homemade brew, but sober enough to recognise his partner, Jeremy, ducking his head under the door lintel. The boy coughed and rubbed his eyes with a grimy finger as smoke from the wood fire in the hearth added to the haze that rose from clay pipes. A couple of old men, sitting well away from Bill's shabby figure, were enjoying their pipes and ale, and a gossip.

'I've been looking for you. You come further than I thought. Took the coach back. The man asked no questions about what it'd been used for.' Seating himself next to Bill, Jeremy pushed a coin across the table as a tankard of ale was placed in front of him.

'The things. Did you get rid of all her things?' Bill asked. 'I don't want any comeback from someone recognising any of her stuff.'

''Course I did. A man I know'd from way back owed me a favour. He lives in Nottingham, Eastwood way. Gave me a good price, and I bought a gown and shawl for her, like you wanted.' Jeremy caught the landlord's attention and gestured to the table. 'You eaten, Bill?' When Bill shook his head, he called for two hot meat pies, both with buttered turnip. 'They've posted notices up all over Nottingham. Someone told me they're about Mr Cooper's missing daughter. Merrilla's papa is offering a big reward for her safe return.' Jeremy eyed Bill. The amount was substantial, and they would both be very rich, by their standards, if they shared the reward. The only flaw was that Merrilla would tell the authorities what had happened to her.

'Don't bother about rewards. The girl's worth more to me if she stays and works. She won't be seen by anyone who might know her, not as far away as this. It makes me feel great to think her pa now understands what it's like to lose someone dear to him,' said Bill. After bolting down the food, and cleaning the plate by rubbing his fingers through the gravy and sucking them, he appeared more sociable.

He placed an arm over the boy's shoulders and whistled a tune as they walked along the towing path to the boat. 'You can sleep in the front, under the canvas.' He gave a humourless leer. 'You'll not hear screaming if you stay away from the cabin walls. Where've you put the things you brought for 'er?'

Jeremy jumped onto the deck of the barge. It took only a moment to stow his things. He left the second-hand grey gown, and a woollen shawl Bill had ordered, rolled up on top of a bale of straw. Returning to the towpath, he put the harness on Meggie and hitched her to the boat as Bill disappeared into the cabin.

The only light filtering into the cabin came from a small bull's eye in the roof and the dirty square window, but it was enough to show Merrilla sitting huddled on the bare bench that served as her bed. She looked towards the door with terror-filled eyes. Her tear-streaked face was unwashed, and the ribbons, which once had tied her shining ringlets into bunches, had long disappeared.

'There you are, my dear one. Our friend, Jeremy, has returned to us. I said he would.' He could hurt her further with a lie, so he lurched across the cabin and towered over her. With a cry of fear she slipped down, cowering on the floor, her hands held high for protection. 'I've heard from your papa. He says he don't want you to come home. Don't want you for a daughter no more, and if you return, he'll show you the door. Ever think your darling papa would cast you out as a fallen woman? Dirty? Defiled?'

Only fed scraps, her cheeks were already showing signs of malnourishment and a deficit of fresh air. She pushed back her lank, untidy hair, shaking her head with a weary sigh.

He stood a moment, looking down at her, and gave her a nudge. 'Things would've been much better for both of us, if you'd been a bit more loving to me.'

She shook her head and gave a sob.

'Huh. Have it your way, silly bitch.'

Falling onto his soft bed, he closed his eyes, and within minutes was snoring.

By holding on to whatever furniture was to hand, Merrilla moved across the cabin and, with an effort, closed the dingy lace curtains around his bed without waking him. Returning to the wooden bench, she sat with arms folded, staring into the gloom.

Papa, she cried silently. *Papa, I'm not dirty. I didn't mean things to be like this. He said he loved me, and I believed him.*

Whenever Bill left the cabin, he locked the door, leaving his prisoner to pass the time as best she could. Mostly she would lie on the bench, thinking about her old life in Nottingham, and listen to the water slapping the side of the boat, before falling into a light doze.

One day, she heard raised voices, and thought it sounded like Bill and Jeremy quarrelling, but was too wearisome and demoralised to find out why. She knew that if Bill wanted her to know something he would tell her, or cruelly taunt her.

Later that day, he came into the cabin, and stood looking at her in a speculative manner. She chewed the inside of her cheek with worry.

'Time I got married.'

She gaped at him, open-mouthed.

'I ain't got a family. That's why I need a companion like you, my dear.'

She licked her lips nervously, saying, 'W-Wife?'

'Oh, yes. I mean to wed you. Always have. I made a promise to you, my dear, and as you know, I keep my promises.'

She flinched as he leaned forward to pat her face.

'Ah! Do your bruises hurt, my dear?' He stared at her as she sat with shoulders slumped and head hanging. 'On your bed, dolly,' he said, loosening his trouser belt.

She stretched out on the bench, lifted her skirt, and opened her legs in mute readiness to receive him. No tender kisses or loving caress. It was over quickly, and afterwards, she lay with clenched teeth and closed eyes.

Bill dressed and tightened his belt. 'Yes. I think I've tamed you enough.'

She opened her eyes and looked at him wearily. *Now what's he planning?*

'Jeremy's left us. He wanted to stay in the Midlands, so he's found work as a coachman. We're going up North, so you'll have to help me work the locks and walk the horse. We'll make good money when we reach Ripon. I've heard all the boats up there carry full cargoes every day.' As he unlocked the cabin door, he continued, 'Come up here with me for a while. I'll show you how to steer the boat.'

Holding the door open, he watched with narrowed eyes as she eased herself off the bench and moved towards him. She took a deep breath, shivering as fresh air blew on her face. It was the first time she had left the confines of the cabin. She stumbled up the few steps and stood next to the tiller.

He stared at her white face and sunken eyes. The sunlight showed a half-starved, haggard figure gazing across the water without interest. 'Sit there on that stool, and don't move,' he ordered. 'I'll tell you a bit about the boat while nobody's around.' With one shoulder on the side of the cabin, he picked dirt out of his fingernails. 'Now then, this is the rudder post,' he

68

said, pointing to a sturdy piece of wood, painted with a green and yellow motif of flowers and leaves, 'and that's the towing mast.' The mast was also colourfully decorated.

'What's that for?' Merrilla asked, gesturing to a bunch of long, white hair bound to the post.

'That's the tail of the horse that pulled the boat when my pa worked it. He cut it off when the horse died. It's supposed to bring the boat luck, but it didn't do much for him.'

His lips were tightly compressed. Afraid she'd angered him by reminding him of his father, she attempted to divert his thoughts by nodding towards a brown horse tethered on the bank. 'Is that horse yours?'

'That's Meggie. She's a good worker, and not much bother. I'll perhaps let you take care of her sometime.'

Relaxing, she leaned back on the side of the cabin, her breast showing through a tear in her dress.

'You're not decent. Get you below,' he growled.

Unsurprised by his sudden change of tone, she did as ordered, glancing over her shoulder at the sound of the bolt on the outside of the cabin door shooting home. She lay down on the bench. In spite of the hardness of the wood, she fell asleep in seconds. The fresh air had tired her.

The bang of the door being pushed open awakened her and Bill entered the cabin, carrying a basket. 'Come on, lazy bones. Let's have you doing some work. I've brought you a meat pie for being a good girl. What about this, eh? Do you think this looks tasty?'

Merrilla's mouth watered at the sight of brown flaky pastry. She moved towards him, eyes wide with hope as he held the pie towards her, but unsure whether he was tormenting her or not.

'Don't you want it then? Not hungry enough?' he asked, half joking.

She snatched the pie from his hand and scurried to her bench to eat it. Even though starved she still ate her food in a dainty manner.

'Well, are you going to thank me, then?'

She shivered, wondering what he wanted next, and whispered, 'Thank you, Bill, it was delicious.'

Fixed to a cupboard on the wall was a drop-down table. He undid the lock and, with the table bolted in place, put the basket down.

'That's not all. See these? Eggs, bacon, flour and apples from the farm over there. But you can only have any if you're good,' he warned.

With enormous eyes, she watched him empty the contents of the basket. As he removed each item, he lifted it high, and glanced at her, until everything was on the table. 'Now, what you have to do is to clean up this sty, and wash a pan. I'll make a fire, then you can cook for us.'

Tears welled up and trickled down her cheeks. She had never cooked anything in her life, and as for cleaning—that was why people employed servants. The only washing she had ever done was her hands and face.

'I...I don't know how to,' she sobbed. 'Will...will you show me?' Her expression pleaded for his understanding.

He stared at her in genuine astonishment. Every woman could cook and clean. It was what women did, what they were born for. His fists clenched as his temper exploded. 'Why not?' he yelled.

'We...we always had servants to do all that, Bill. Mamma told them what to do each morning.' Her voice was barely audible. 'She...she had it written in a book.'

'Servants,' he sneered. 'Well, lady, now you are my servant, and you'll do as I tell you.' He paused, chewing on his lip, staring at her. 'Yes, all right. I'll show you what to do. Only once, though.' He lifted a tall, decorated can from the table and held it out to her. 'Here, dry your eyes and drink this. Cow's milk, fresh from the farm. It'll give you strength.'

Milk had never been one of her favourite drinks, but she obediently drank straight from the can.

Bill chuckled. 'You have a moustache,' he said, suddenly good-humoured.

Merrilla gave a weak smile in return. Exhausted, all she wanted to do was sleep.

'We've a pail outside. I'll go and fetch some water, and you put that food away into the cupboard.'

As the days passed, she was allowed to sit beside him on the deck when she prepared vegetables for their meals. She found that she enjoyed working, for it filled the empty hours. Bill continued supplying food, and she learnt how to do simple cookery on the small stove. She felt a sense of achievement when she succeeded in making the pans, which hung over the stove, gleam with her polishing. She made mistakes at first, and was hurt by his sharp comments, but these lessened as the weeks passed, and she relaxed. The day when Bill complimented her on her cooking she felt a glow of pride.

Despite herself, she found herself looking forward to the evenings, when the barge was moored, Meggie was safely tethered, and they could discuss the day's events. Sometimes Bill would bring out a pack of cards, or a set of dominoes, and they would play games.

One afternoon he appeared at the door of the cabin carrying a grey dress, a shawl and kid boots. She had been bare-footed since arriving on the boat.

'Come up here, I want you,' he called.

When she emerged into the sunlight, he pointed at the water swirling around the boat. 'I've some clothes here for you, but first you need to bathe. Have a swim. Time you were cleaned up. There's soft soap here to use.'

She stared, first at him, then down at the river, before shaking her head and backing to the cabin steps with her hand to her mouth. 'I can't swim, Bill. I can't.'

'Oh, struth! What can you do? All boat women swim. Here, we'll get closer to the bank. 'Twill be more shallow.'

Nodding in gratitude, she stood to one side as he leapt onto the riverbank and hauled on the thick ropes, manoeuvring the boat until it nudged the reeds. First making the ropes secure, he then tethered Meggie to an iron peg he'd knocked into a patch of long grass. On his return to the boat, he helped her jump onto the towpath.

It was the first time Merrilla had stood on firm ground since leaving home, and she felt strange and unsteady. For a brief moment, she clung to his arm to keep her balance, smiling, happy at the fact he trusted her enough to let her leave the boat. But her smile faded when he roughly pushed her hand off his arm.

'Let's get you clean, my lady. Into the water. Here's the soap. I'll keep watch. No one should see you. Woods and trees for miles, and not many boats work Sundays. I'll keep your new dress here, so scrub yourself with that rag you're wearing.'

He dropped down, making himself comfortable on the grass as he watched her dip her foot in the river. With a squeal, she turned to look at him over her shoulder.

'Go on in, it ain't cold,' he called.

She took a deep breath and waded into the river. She didn't notice Bill quietly creep to the water's edge and bend down until he splashed her, the water landing on her bare back, making her squeal again.

His face soon became drenched when she retaliated by splashing him back. Seeing him removing his clothes, she tried to run further along the edge of the river.

'I'll show you how to splash, my lady,' he growled. With arms open wide, he waded towards her.

Frightened by his declaration, she attempted to move into deeper water, and all of a sudden found her feet no longer touched the bottom. She was spluttering and gasping for air as he caught hold of her, first by her hair, and then under her arms, lifting her face clear of the water.

'Silly bitch, you could have drowned.'

In panic, she clung to his naked body and, wrapping her arms around him, pulled closer. Unexpectedly, his mouth clamped onto hers. Then his lips brushed over each eye, kissing droplets of water from her long lashes. For a moment, they gazed at each other with astonishment. Then he kissed her again. It was the first time he had kissed her without bruising or drawing blood. She tightened her grip, feeling her breasts contacting with his chest, and his legs moving against hers, forcing them to part.

'Do you know I love you?' His voice sounded gruff. She drew his head down, and with a sweet sadness, kissed him. The kiss, light as the stroke of a feather, lit a flame. Lifting her clear of the water, he carried her to the bank, and lay with her on the grass. There, for the first time, he made love to her, caressing her satin skin and stroking her hair, making her smile and close her eyes. His kisses were tender at first, and then his body throbbed against hers. He cupped her swollen breasts with his hands, and tantalised her nipples with his tongue. Her voice was husky, as she said, 'Oh, Bill!' Oh, Bill!'

Amazed at her response, he drew away, but she clung to him, and kissed him with such a frenzied passion he could not hold back, and he entered her with a suddenness which made her moan with ecstasy. His face buried in her hair, she wrapped her arms around him, both smiling as they slept.

Merrilla woke first, pulled his moustache and ran her fingers lightly over his bare back. He squirmed and joined in her laughter as she found ticklish spots.

She stiffened. 'I can hear something. Bill, someone's coming,' she whispered.

They both lay still for a moment, listening, and then, lifting his head, he peered along the towpath. 'Can't see anyone,' he said, sitting up. Then she saw the movement of a swinging tail. 'It's the bloody horse,' he shouted, leaping to his feet. 'Meggie's got loose.'

Merrilla watched his strong white buttocks flash as he ran after the culprit. Still smiling, she returned to the river. Her tangled hair was difficult to wash, but at last she finished, and found a tattered towel near her clothes.

She returned to the cabin and sat in front of the stove, running her fingers through the strands and towelling her hair until it was dry. When Bill came in, she glanced at him shyly, and asked if he still had her hair ribbons. He opened a drawer and took out one of her old ones.

As he handed it to her he said, 'Meggie had gone a good way before I caught her. Lucky I didn't meet anyone.'

A new understanding between them made life more pleasant and bearable. No luxuries but, instead, hard work and long hours. Bill allowed her to stay on the deck by herself when other barges passed. He taught her how to use the wide sails, how to open and close the different types of locks, and how to steer a straight line through the long, dark tunnels. She found this one of the more difficult tasks. He stayed with her for hours as she stood at the tiller, guiding the boat around the bends and curves of the waterways. Her happy face showed her satisfaction when she mastered the skill of controlling the boat. He responded by placing an arm round her waist, and grinning proudly as other boat people waved and shouted greetings and news.

As they moved northwards, the days became bitterly cold when winter winds blew across the water. Merrilla was often chilled through to her bones as she plodded beside the horse in the rain. Late one winter's night, wearing one of Bill's old caps and a piece of old sacking over her clothes, she noticed a glow coming from an inn stable. Thankfully, she led Meggie inside, and shook the snow from her cap and sacking. Then, after bedding the horse down, she left her deep in straw, munching her feed.

'Snow's getting thick. Be deep by morning. Good thing we've a load of coal for cooking,' Bill said, sniffing appreciatively at a meat and barley stew bubbling on the stove.

Merrilla pulled down the hinged table ready for their meal. 'Meggie's warm enough in the stable.'

During the night, the temperature plummeted. Opening the cabin door the following morning, she caught her breath in wonder at the beauty of the ice-covered water, the now white boat, and the grasses and bushes clad in a mass of jewelled cobwebs.

'You'll not be so happy if you slip. The planks will be treacherous to walk on,' Bill warned. 'We can't move on in this weather. Best if we stay here for a while. Ripon's only a mile or so away. There's a farm across those fields where we might buy food.' He put on extra layers of clothing, and wrapped a knitted muffler around his neck. 'I'll have time now to repair that bit of broken wood on the side of the cabin. You can help.'

Black frost and another fall of snow during the day added to their discomfort, and work which would only have taken an hour or two in the summer seemed to take forever. She was most careful, though, not to let Bill know of her discontentment. He would be very likely to push her overboard in his rage. That night they lay together in bed, listening to the ice cracking against the wooden timbers only inches from their bodies. She snuggled closer to him, and pulled the bed covers higher, pleased that she no longer spent her nights on the wooden bench. As she tried to sleep, she wondered if it was snowing at home, in Nottingham, and if her family were safe and warm. *People will not be on the canal banks, listening to the hurdy-gurdy man if it's snowing.* As she drifted into sleep her last thoughts were of her beloved family.

'I could get used to this weather.' He turned over, and putting his arm around her, drew her even closer.

Although the window of the barge was clean, very little daylight filtered into the cabin. However, the warmth thrown from the stove was comforting. Merrilla sat on the wooden bench with a dish of soft sand beside her feet, polishing the cooking pans with a damp cloth dipped in the sand, and sighing over the fact that she had no food to cook. Bill had been away at Ripon for more than two weeks, and the boat was still gripped by the ice-covered water.

She dropped the cloth and rose to her feet at the sound of footsteps on the deck. An icy blast blew into the cabin as Bill opened the door and half slid down the steps.

With a leap forward she closed the door and rushed to help him take off his sodden clothes. 'Here, let me.' She pushed his hands away, undoing the buttons and unwinding his knitted scarf. 'You're frozen through. I've nothing to feed you with, and you should have a hot meal to warm you. Oh, Bill, come nearer to the stove; at least we have a good fire burning.'

He stood shivering as Merrilla rubbed his back with a warm towel and bustled around, helping him to dress in dry clothes. 'Why's there nothing to eat, woman?' he said, glancing at the cooking pan, and then at the stove.

Upon hearing his gruff tone, all her fear returned. 'You forgot to leave me any money to buy food from the farm,' she murmured. Any glad feelings prompted by his safe return evaporated, and she shrank away from him.

He picked up his jacket, fumbled in a pocket. found a coin and tossed it on the table. 'Get over to the farm, and be quick about it. I'm starving.'

'Yes, Bill, I'll go right away, Bill.' She threw her old woollen shawl over her shoulders, and tied it round her then, snatching hold of a basket, she hurried up the steps, and pulled on one of his old caps.

The lane leading to the farm was thigh-deep in snow, and her long skirts were sodden within minutes and very heavy. Because she was so hungry she soon became exhausted and more than once slipped on ice hidden under the snow, but struggled on, fearful of Bill's anger.

At last she came to a long, low dwelling. Smoke blew from the chimney, and the sound of animals and chickens came from a building across a yard. With what strength she had left, she pounded on the farmhouse door. She clung onto the doorframe as the door opened. Two worried faces peered at her, and then out across the yard at the weather.

'Have…have you any food for sale?' she asked. Her head was now throbbing, and everything seemed to be hazy.

'Oh, you poor thing. Come inside, girl, come and warm yourself.'

Exchanging incredulous looks with each other, the farmer and his wife supported her and helped her to a seat near the fire. A dog moved from his place on the hearthrug, leaving her room to stretch her legs out towards the leaping flames. For a moment or so she closed her eyes. A cup of hot water, laced with brandy and sugar, was handed to her, and she sipped the warm brew with gratitude. Gradually, a glow travelled through her body, and she stopped shivering. Steam rose from her shawl hanging near the fire, and she raised her feet and placed them on a brass fender, as heat rose from her drying boots.

The farmer's wife bustled around and filled her basket with food while Merrilla, although reluctant to leave the cosy warmth of the farmhouse, prepared to make the hazardous journey back to the boat. Before she opened the door, the woman threw a thick woollen cloak around her shoulders, and pulled the hood over her head, saying, 'It's an old one, my dear. You can bring it back the next time you call, or if you don't, it won't matter.'

The farmer handed her a long staff. 'You'd better take this with you. It might prevent you from taking another tumble.'

Merrilla's eyes filled with tears at the couple's kindness. She gave a wistful glance at the fire. How she wished she could stay longer, but she knew Bill would be waiting.

Her return to the boat was almost completed when the snow started once more. Whirling flakes made it difficult to see, and it was only because Bill opened the door to look for her, allowing the lamplight to make a glistening path in the darkness, that she was able to find her way home.

'Ripon's as far as we go in this boat. We'll journey there when the ice breaks up, and then I'll sell the boat,' Bill said, in-between shovelling the hastily-prepared meal into his mouth.

Merrilla's eyes opened with astonishment. The boat meant everything to him. Without it he would be lost. Bargee Bill would become a nobody.

'We can get to Ripon in a day or two. I've met a man in the town who owns a business up North. He has boats in Glasgow. He's going to give us stagecoach tickets to take us to Scotland. Said he'd give me a good price for this old tub. Not as much as he should, but he's offered me permanent work on one of his boats.' Finishing his meal, Bill sat back and, fishing an old matchstick out of his pocket, began picking at his teeth. 'His barges carry coal from the Paxton mine up to Glasgow. They say men working his boats are making a mint of money. We'll be rich in no time, girl.'

'But, Bill, this boat is yours. You're a barge master. It belonged to your father before you.'

'Oh, forget all that. That's all in the past. We must look to the future, and live our own lives now.' Bill's arms wrapped around her as she moved to the stove. 'Do you know why I was given this job, eh?' he said into her still damp hair. She shook her head. 'It's because I told them at my interview in the company office that I was married to a strong boat woman. "She works with me," I said. "She knows how to use the locks, and can help leg through a tunnel". They're always interested when they can hire a married couple—more so if they don't have little 'uns. We'll earn good wages,' he continued. 'I've been hearing how other men have done the same, and after a few years they've bought a pair of barges, and made themselves a fortune. So let's get rid of this old hulk, and travel in style to Glasgow, eh?' Still holding her hands, he took a step back. 'We'd best get you some new things. We can't have you looking shabby when we go to meet your new boss, can we?' He drew her close and kissed her on her forehead.

A week later, the weather changed. The snow and ice had almost gone. The canal water level had risen, and, with Bill steering the barge along the swollen river and negotiating the locks, they arrived in Ripon. The following day they sold both the boat and Meggie.

Upon enquiring as to the departure times of the coach, they were told the road to Penrith was impassable. This gave Bill time to keep his word, and he took Merrilla to a second-hand clothes shop. She stood compliant in the musty-smelling shop, as he selected for her a long-sleeved woollen dress, a cloak, and a pair of shabby but serviceable boots. Afterwards, they went sightseeing. She admired the stately cathedral, and at nine o'clock they stood under a gas lamp in the market place, gazing at the watch blowing his horn. The following day, almost speechless with delight, she clung to his arm as they explored the ruins of Fountains Abbey. They admired the long nave, with its massive columns, but the wind blew chill as they wandered through the cloisters, and Bill muttered that he had seen enough of churches, and it was time to leave. However, they were impressed with the formal water garden and the lake.

'Oh, thank you for taking me. I had read of Fountains Abbey when I was in the schoolroom, but I never dreamed I'd see it.' Her green eyes sparkled, and for a moment, she felt almost as lovely as she knew she used to.

'Thought you'd like it,' he said, pleased that, for once, she seemed really happy.

The green coach and six brown horses stood harnessed for the journey to Penrith that was now possible. Thankfully, Bill had been prudent in buying warm clothes, for the coach felt bitterly cold. Wind blew around their feet, and Merrilla felt grateful to have his surprise gift of a dilapidated fur muff, which she held against her face. She had found it wrapped in the bundle with her new clothes, and had felt a little ashamed of her earlier lack of appreciation at his generosity.

At Penrith, the red and gold coach for Carlisle stood waiting. They had the most expensive tickets and sat inside, but this coach was even colder. Merrilla seated herself next to Bill, by the window, covering her ears when the coachman blew on his long horn to announce their departure.

The road was treacherous, covered with snow, ice, and deep ruts. From time to time everyone climbed out and helped the driver and his companions to push the vehicle, and also encourage the horses to pull the coach away from disaster. They were exhausted when, at last, they alighted at Carlisle.

'Stay here with the baggage. I'll go to the depot, and find out when the next coach leaves for Glasgow.' Bill set off in the direction of a small building.

He seemed to have been gone a long while, and Merrilla grew nervous about a burly man glancing her way. She sighed with relief when she saw Bill walking towards her.

'The next coach is going to Moffat. I could hardly make out what the man said, they all speak so oddly. I managed to understand that the coach wouldn't leave for a couple of days, on account of the weather, so we'd best find lodgings. One of the men in there gave me this address.' He handed her a scrap of paper, then picked up the luggage, and walked along a narrow street. With a weary slump of her shoulders, she looked for street names, and followed a step or so behind him.

They hadn't far to go. The woman owning the lodging house welcomed them and served a hot meal in the privacy of their bedchamber. Almost too tired to eat, Merrilla fell asleep in a bed that took up most of the room.

The following morning, after they had dressed, and whilst they were eating breakfast, a boy banged on the door of the lodging house and announced to everyone in the breakfast-room that there had been a change of plan.

'We've half an hour before the coach leaves. The roads are open. Come girl, hurry. We mustn't be left behind,' Bill called, struggling with his cloak. 'Where's me hat gone?'

After a frenzied rush to pack, they hurried to the depot, and found it swarming with people, all clamouring to reach destinations that Merrilla and Bill had never heard of. With some difficulty, they found their coach. The coachman threw their baggage into the coach boot before they climbed inside, and claimed the last two places. A large woman, carrying a coop containing squawking hens, pressed against Merrilla, who had a corner seat. Bill sat opposite, next to a man who, most of the time, leaned on Bill's shoulder and kept his eyes closed and his mouth open. A young couple sat by the other window, holding hands, whispering, and gazing into each other's eyes. As they travelled, Merrilla almost forgot her discomfort, and watched the spectacular view from the coach window.

'We stop here for half an hour.' The driver's breath puffed out a white mist as he shouted the welcome news. With difficulty, the woman alighted with her hens, followed by the sleepy man. Bill climbed down and helped Merrilla to alight.

'Gretna Green! The blacksmith's over there. Anyone wanting refreshments, follow me,' called the driver, before turning towards the welcoming sight of a low, grey stone building with a chimney belching smoke.

'I'll be pleased to sit by a fire, Bill. My feet are frozen solid,' Merrilla said, following the driver and the sleepy man. She stopped in confusion when Bill, smiling broadly, remained standing near the coach.

'I thought you'd like the blacksmith's fire better,' he chuckled.

She felt her cheeks grow warm as she walked towards him, not knowing for sure if he was teasing. On tiptoe, she gave him a quick kiss on the cheek before taking his arm.

They followed the young couple that had been their travelling companions, and saw a tall pile of rusting horseshoes partly hidden by snow. A pair of old wooden doors were propped open, and the heat from the furnace swept across their faces as they entered the forge. All four travellers threw cloaks back, and undid buttons in the sudden heat.

'Who's first, then? Or shall I marry you all at the same time?' The man, in his work-worn leather apron, beamed at the blushing girls, and winked at Bill and the other young man. 'Over here, then. Girls that side of the anvil, men on this.'

The ceremony was brief, and Bill slipped a ring on Merrilla's finger before bending to kiss her cheek. While they waited for the driver and the other passengers to rejoin the coach, Bill handed her a roll of parchment tied with ribbon. 'Keep that safe. It's the certificate of our marriage. Cost me dear. He's a rob-o'davy with his prices.'

Merrilla smiled, knowing he was only teasing about the cost.

As they travelled the next few miles she turned the ring round and round. She had been in such a daze that when it had been slipped onto her finger she hadn't had the chance to examine it. Somehow, it felt familiar. Slowly, so as not to attract Bill's attention, she drew her left hand out of the muff. Her wedding ring was the ring she had worn when she had left home, the one her sister had given her on her last birthday, the one with the small blue stones. Bill hadn't bothered to buy her a new ring but she beamed in delight, knowing she had a small token to remind her of her family.

The remainder of the coach journey seemed longer and even colder than the others. She sat next to Bill, clinging to his arm in fright each time the coach skidded or lurched. They both gave sighs of relief as they rolled into the sedate little town of Moffat. At the depot, they were told that the coach to Glasgow would arrive in a week's time. That would be the last stage of their journey.

In a narrow street nearby, they found cheap and clean lodgings, and the booking clerk promised to send for them when the Glasgow coach arrived at the depot.

Each evening, Bill left the house without telling Merrilla what time he would be back. On his return, he didn't explain where he had been, or whom he had met. She dared not ask questions, but he always smelt unpleasantly of drink and smoke.

As usual, she was alone on the last evening of their stay when she heard a heavy knocking on the outside door. Curious, she went to the top of the stairs, and tried to peer into the hallway to see what the commotion could be. When the owner of the house opened the door, she could see Bill lying on the doorstep with blood seeping from his scalp. With a cry of, 'Bill! It's my Bill,' she ran down the stairs, and helped the owner to carry him to their room where she poured water into a bowl and, finding a clean cloth, began bathing his wound.

'Robbed! They've taken all my money,' he moaned. 'All the money I had from the sale of Meggie and the boat.'

She made no reply, but put her arms around him and rocked him until his colour returned.

'We still have the tickets for the stage, and a bit of money in the bag over there.' He gestured towards a bundle pushed under a chair. During the journey, he had always taken charge of that bundle. Merrilla had not opened it, for the contents hadn't been needed.

'I'll go and fetch some fresh water. You lie down and rest.' She picked up the ewer and left the room. Halfway down the stairs, she realised she'd forgotten to take the bloodstained bowl to rinse under the pump, and turned back. Through a crack of the door she saw him scurry across the room and pick up a bundle from under the chair. He took out her jewellery box and opened it. As he held up the gold and ruby necklet, the light from the lamp made it sparkle. With her hand over her mouth, and holding back tears, she tiptoed downstairs. Bill had never mentioned her mother's jewellery, and she thought he had sold it. *Somehow, I don't know how or when, but I vow I'll return it to my mother, if it's the last thing I do.*

It took a while to bring her chaotic thoughts under control, but after rinsing her face under the pump, she felt ready to return to their room. Making her footsteps sound loud on the stairs, she gave a throaty cough before entering with the ewer full of fresh water. She didn't refer to what she had seen, or even glance at the bundle, which was now in its old place under the chair. Bill sat on the bed holding his head in his hands, moaning.

Chapter 6

Merrilla liked Glasgow. The wind had turned warmer, and people smiled when they asked the way to Maryhill and the canal wharf.

The Faskin was the name of the boat that would be their new home. It was already moored beside the towing path. Despite its smaller cabin, it was well-fitted with comfortable furnishings, and was a sleeker craft than Bill's old barge.

A young lad led towards them a strong-looking brown horse with a white nose and a white belly. He grinned when Merrilla gave the horse a piece of carrot, and patted its neck.

'His name's Tramp,' he said, putting the rope into her hands. 'He's done the walk before, so he knows the way. I've put his nose tin on the boat, and there's plenty of blacksmiths and stabling along the way.'

The horse shook its head, and pushed its nose against her, as though searching for another titbit.

The company manager joined the group and, as he raised his hat to her, Merrilla bobbed a curtsy.

He turned to Bill. 'You'll have to keep to a strict timetable, Waspill. Those boxes of provisions over there need to be delivered to a Mr Parkinson at his shop. You'll find it easily enough. It's in the village, near the coalmine. Mr Watson, the company superintendent, will be waiting at Paxton Wharf. He'll give you further instructions on where to go when you arrive.'

Merrilla asked the company manager if she could look inside the cabin. When he nodded, Bill hauled on the mooring rope so the boat was close enough for her to step aboard. When she emerged from the cabin she was beaming. 'The cabin's lovely. So large and comfortable,' she called in delight to the two men waiting on the towpath.

Bill and the company manager exchanged amused glances before shaking hands.

'Good luck,' the manager called, as the *Faskin* moved slowly away from the wharf.

Glancing at Bill from time to time, and keeping taut the long towing line that was attached to both the barge and Tramp's harness, Merrilla steered the *Faskin* around the last bend in the canal, grateful it was not a tight one. The weather had changed, and a gentle wind blew ripples on the water. At Bill's enquiry, a man waved and called from a passing boat that the Paxton Coal Wharf was only a few miles further along.

'Thank goodness for that,' Merrilla muttered, only too pleased to hear that the last of the innumerable locks was behind them.

The route from Glasgow had taken the *Faskin* through tunnels, over an aqueduct, and through miles of wild moorland before ending between tree-clad hills. They hadn't hurried, and today Bill walked at a steady pace beside the horse. Upon noticing the noise and the sight of tumbling waters of a weir ahead, he caught hold of the towing rope, and heaved, slowing the boat before undoing the rope from Tramp's harness. Beyond ran the broad river.

'We're here,' he called. 'We keep left and into the river. Hold the boat into me. I'll take it up to the moorings.'

With an ease borne of practice, Merrilla manoeuvred the boat close enough to the bank for him to leap aboard, and then he held the boat steady for her to jump onto the towpath.

'Meet me at the wharf,' he called, and she watched as he lifted the sail. As he did so, the boat caught the breeze, gathering speed.

Walking beside the horse, she watched Bill taking the boat through the water near the weir, then he sailed into the centre of the river, neatly turning the *Faskin* in order to dock at the end of the line of barges waiting to be loaded with coal. She had to admit he was very skilled at his work.

On reaching a field, she led Tramp inside, fastened him to a post while she unbuckled the leather harness and removed the heavy collar from his neck. The horse gave a jump, and galloped across the field, obviously happy to be turned loose to graze with the other barge horses.

Approaching the *Faskin*, Merrilla saw the sails were down, and that Bill had moored the boat close to the one in front. He was standing on the wharf, listening and nodding to a man wearing a black tricorne hat with a braided edging.

Bill turned to her. 'This is Mr Wilkins, the company superintendent, my dear.'

She bobbed a curtsy. The man ignored her, and continued instructing Bill on when to have the *Faskin* moved for loading, and where to find Mr Parkinson's shop.

After Mr Wilkins had left, Merrilla followed Bill into the cabin. As he dressed in his best clothes he kept glancing at her. She was busy washing her hands and face as she made herself ready to accompany him to the village.

'I'd think Mr Parkinson'll want his provisions straight away. Perhaps there's a boy working in the shop who'll help me carry the boxes. Won't be long.' He stepped onto the towpath, adding, 'See you later.'

Merrilla stood beside the tiller, open-mouthed. She had been looking forward to seeing the village shop and, outraged and disappointed, she folded her arms, only just stopping herself from stamping her foot as she used to do as a child. Blinking angry tears away, she watched him stride past the moored boats, stopping more than once to speak to people. Then he walked around the bend and out of sight.

Noticing a group of women further along the towpath near the boats, she gave a resigned sigh, and decided to join them. They had made a coal fire beside the towpath, and were boiling clothes in a large iron cauldron. Most of them wore the traditional style of tight-waisted cotton dress, each bodice elaborately ornamented with lace and smocking, and ankle-length pleated skirts. Two of the older women wore black bonnets with rows of tucks, and from the gathered crown a frilled wimple fell wide and low over their shoulders.

They examined Merrilla with speculation as she introduced herself, and they exchanged wary glances. For a moment, no one spoke. She felt uncomfortable until a woman of about her age, pointing to the steaming cauldron said, 'This is the only time we've got for catching up with washing.'

'I do like clothes well-boiled and white,' said an older woman, looking at Merrilla and then at the *Faskin*.

'Have you come far, my dear?' another woman asked. 'Only I thought Bill Waspill had his own boat, and worked in the Midlands around Nottingham way?'

Merrilla moved closer to the river, and looked along the path, suddenly panicky at the questions. She had thought no-one there would know Bill. Then she espied a familiar figure coming towards her. 'I see Mr Waspill returning. I must go,' she said, edging away from the women, pleased to have an excuse not to answer the probing questions.

Being true boat people, the women were cautious with strangers. With narrowing eyes, they watched Merrilla as she hurried to meet Bill. Boat people usually married their own kind, and the women looked suspiciously at her who, although dressed in a shabby gown, spoke in a cultured voice. Out of earshot, the younger women mimicked her movements.

'Stuck up bitch. Who does she think she is? He owes money everywhere. Never pays his debts. Well known for it.'

'That boat could do with a good clean an' all. It's right squalid,' someone else said with a curl of her lips.

'He'll soon find trouble, if he can't pay my man what he owes. He don't mess. He'll give Bill Waspill a good cudgelling,' another woman said, poking the bubbling contents of the cauldron with a long stick.

When Merrilla joined Bill and entered their cabin, the women turned back to their laundry.

Bill followed Merrilla onto the boat and, with a sheepish grin, handed her a few violets.

'Oh, they're lovely, Bill,' she whispered. 'Thank you.' Blinking back tears, she remembered the day when a bunch of sweet-smelling blooms had landed on her prayer book. She sighed as she glanced at her rough and chapped hands. *Young, and foolish miss'* she thought. *How different I am now.* She found Bill watching her, and smiled. *I'm lucky to have him to care for me so much.* She drew his head down and kissed his cheek.

Very soon boys from the village arrived, ready to help carry the boxes of provisions to the shop and this time Merrilla intended to accompany Bill. He made no comment when, covering her head with her shawl, she fell into step beside him without saying a word.

'Well, that's that job done with,' Bill said once the boxes had been stacked in Mr Parkinson's yard. After giving each boy a coin, they watched them scamper away. Bill allowed her to take his arm, and they walked along the village street together.

They passed a small tavern, with a wooden bench set close against the whitewashed wall. When they reached the forge they stopped and watched the blacksmith expertly fashion a horseshoe. The heat from the fire was fierce, and sparks flew as the blacksmith hammered the red hot metal into shape. Taking hold of the shoe with a pair of long pincers, he dunked it into a nearby pail of water and, supporting an upturned hoof between his legs, he nailed the hot shoe into place. Merrilla and Bill glanced at each other, each recalling their marriage ceremony at Gretna Green. She took a hasty step back and grimaced as acrid fumes from the horse's burning hoof reached her.

'Good lassie. That's my lass,' the smithy said, giving the horse an affectionate pat, allowing it to put its foot to the ground. He noticed them watching and gave them a friendly nod. 'Warm day for this time of year,' he called. 'I've ale here, cool and foaming.' He downed his tools and stretched his back then, lifting a brown stone jug from a shelf near the wide doors, he held it out. 'The wife made this for me.'

Bill approached the man, and Merrilla remembered that warm Sunday morning so long ago, when she'd stood on the bridge, looking down to where people on the canal bank drank from bottles. *I wonder if the young woman married the man who was making love to her.* She gave a sniff, as she thought, *I know what whore means now.*

With a quiet, 'Thank you, sir,' she accepted a cup of ale from the blacksmith, wondering, as she sipped from the cup, if the hurdy-gurdy man in Nottingham would be playing his organ that day.

At an opportune moment, and unnoticed by the blacksmith, although Merrilla saw him, Bill removed his hat, and placed it behind some boxes. The man continued chattering in a friendly manner as he picked up a hammer and returned to his anvil to resume work. Bill seemed reluctant to leave his new friend and, taking Merrilla's arm, they moved on. As soon as they were out of earshot, he said, 'He'll be wanting our custom. Bet he knew we 'ad a horse needing attention.'

Shooting a look at him, she knew it was useless to make a comment about the sour remark. They sauntered along the road, enjoying the sunshine until they reached an open, sagging wooden gate leading into the yard of the Paxton Coalmine. Bill pointed to a group of men and women, all covered with dark dust. 'They're miners. They have to climb down a ladder in that hole over there, and dig out the coal.' He pointed to a large woman standing near a long, low building. 'The woman with the iron band round her waist and chains hanging down is a "drawer". Have to be strong, they do. When she's down the pit, she fastens the chains onto a tub of coal, and pulls it to the bottom of the ladder.' He nodded towards a group of men, pulling and pushing full wooden coal tubs with wooden wheels over the rough ground. 'Those tubs of coal over there are taken to the wharf and the coal's tipped into the boats.'

Merrilla stared in horror at a dozen ragged women waiting in a queue with coal-filled wicker baskets at their feet, and she shuddered. 'It must be dreadful work. Do they live in the village?' she asked, realising how lucky she was to live on the boat and work in the fresh air.

'Suppose most of them live in those houses in the village. They say the coal's coming out easy, and they've not had trouble down the pit for a while now. As soon as they've dropped a full load of coal on the *Faskin,* we'll go back to Glasgow, and get paid for it.'

They moved on again, and had almost reached the boat, when Bill stopped. 'My hat! I've lost my best hat. I bet I left it in the shop. Look, you take these papers Mr Parkinson signed, and keep them safe. I'll go back to the village, and see if I can find it. I won't take so long if I'm by myself. You go back to the boat. Don't go gossiping now. I saw you talking with those women earlier,' he warned, brandishing his finger at her.

Merrilla stood a moment, tight-lipped, watching him hurry away, and then walked towards the *Faskin* with her head bent. *Why on earth couldn't he just say he wanted to see his friends for a drink at the tavern?* she thought. *Why does he always have to be so devious?*

After reaching the boat, she placed the papers inside a cupboard, lit a fire, and then sat near the tiller, waiting for his return. She watched with interest as gangs of workmen manoeuvred tubs of coal along the stony path of the wharf, and tipped the contents into the waiting boats.

Women stood in small groups on the towpath, or sat on their boats, gossiping, others were preparing food for their evening meal. Children played, shouting in shrill voices, and dogs barked at cats, or chased each other across boats and gangplanks. An ordinary scene, but one that made her very lonely.

As darkness fell, she began to worry. The workmen had finished loading the boats and had returned home. Lamps on the other boats were lit, glowing golden through cabin windows, and the aroma of hot meals, drifting on the breeze, made her hungry. She went inside, lit her own lamp, grateful for the warmth coming from the stove. She already had some rabbit stew ready for Bill's dinner. Daylight faded, and a light misty rain began falling.

From time to time she heard footsteps, and men calling goodnight to each other. Hurrying to the window, she peered into the gloom. After cabin doors slammed, the dogs ceased barking, and silence settled. *It's taking a long time to find a hat that you hid*, she thought. After placing a few more coals on the stove, and washing her hands, she lay on the bed, eyes open, tense, listening to the sounds of the night. Bill never stayed out as late as that.

As dawn broke, Merrilla was still lying on the bed, fully dressed, awake, and straining for any sound that could indicate Bill's return. Distant shouts brought her swiftly to her feet. Snatching her shawl from the end of the bed, she swung it round her shoulders before hurrying to open the cabin door. Damp, cold morning air hit her cheeks like a slap, but she noticed nothing but the slow progress of a group of miners coming towards the boats.

'Who does this bugger belong to? We found him drowned, head-first, in a ditch.'

'Come on. All you lot of slug-a-beds in the boats, wake up! Wake up, and tell us who this drowned rat is. Anyone know who we've got here? Drunken sod got himself drowned in a ditch. Hurry up there, and open your eyes, you lot. We've work ter go to. Ain't got all day to hang about here.'

Screaming, Merrilla ran towards the pitmen. They were carrying Bill—head lolling, sodden clothes dripping, and leaving a trail of water on the path.

'Bill,' she sobbed, dropping her shawl, and curling her trembling hands around his pallid face. 'What happened? How did he die like this?' Clutching at the arms of the now silent men, she sobbed out her questions.

'He was reeling drunk when he left the tavern last night, or so someone told us, missus.' The man speaking looked at Merrilla with compassion. The boat people, most of them only half dressed, left their boats and gathered around, watching and listening.

'We saw his boots sticking up. Head first in the ditch, he was. The water's very deep there, missus. He'd have no chance of getting himself out without someone helping him.'

The speaker, who seemed to be the leader, glanced around at the boat people for help, perhaps hoping to be relieved of their burden, but no one stepped forward. Some shuffled their feet and muttered under their breath when Merrilla, sinking to her knees, gave a high wail.

The woman who had spoken to her the previous day took pity on her. Her arm around her, she lifted her up, drew her along the path, and placed her onto the deck of the *Faskin*.

Mr Watson, the company superintendent, came from his small house at the end of the wharf. Sizing up the situation, he ordered the men to lay Bill inside a wooden shack used for storing boat spares, and then ordered them to get back to their work.

Numb with shock, Merrilla sat on her bed, and looked at each of the women who had followed her inside the boat. 'What...?' She swallowed. 'What do I have to do?' Some of the women looked at her with sympathy, but the rest glanced around the cabin, seemingly assessing her belongings.

'These sad arrangements are always made by the men. You'll not have to do anything.' The woman held Merrilla's hand.

Another woman leaned forward, her loosely-braided hair sweeping across Merrilla's arm, as she said, 'You don't have to see him buried, you know. You can leave now if you want.' Her expression was sly, and someone behind her sniggered. Merrilla stared at the woman in disbelief, horrified at her tone. Women didn't usually attend funerals, but in her case? She was the only family Bill had. Not go to the funeral? How callous. *What kind of people are these?* she wondered.

'Your husband worked for the company, Mrs Waspill. Because he hasn't carried a cargo back to Glasgow, he'll not be due to any wages. I would suppose this barge will be given to another couple.'

With frightened eyes, Merrilla looked at each woman in turn. Was it true? The *Faskin* needed two to work her, but she could do most of the work herself. Maybe Mr Watson would find her another man or boy to help until she reached Glasgow, and then she could get permanent help.

A woman, unknown to her, stepped forward, hands on hips and chin thrust forward. 'Your Bill owed money to nearly everyone on the waterways. Whatever he's got will be sold to pay his debts. There'll be nothing left. You can't have anything. Best you leave now, and get back to where you came from.'

With a whimper of fear, she wrapped her arms round her trembling body. Then, taking a deep breath, she rose to her feet and opened the cabin door. 'I need to be alone for a while now, please,' she said, as firmly as her shaking voice would allow. At first they seemed reluctant to leave the cabin, then they pulled their skirts to one side and passed her.

'Upstart! Who does she think she is? Mrs high-and-mighty ain't got nothing to be proud about.' Their spiteful words reached her as the women returned to their own boats, and her lips tightened with fear and anger.

Alone, with no one she could trust. She had nothing but her intelligence and the lessons of her past experience to help her out of her situation. The thought terrified her, and she moaned out loud. How on earth would she manage? Who could she turn to for advice?

She locked the cabin door, pulled the curtains over the windows, and began searching. In the centre of the small cabin she let her eyes rove over each cupboard and drawer, ignoring all the places with which she was familiar, examining those used only by Bill. The contents of one cupboard revealed nothing of interest but the roll of parchment they had received at Gretna Green. It was still tied with a ribbon, and of no monetary value. That tossed on the bed, she continued searching for anything that could be turned into cash. Her eyes lit on the deck cupboard, partly hidden by a rug. Because of the heavy door, she had never used it as storage, and had forgotten its existence. Straining and panting with exertion, she pulled it open. With a loud thud, it dropped back on the floor. A vile stench rose from the darkness, and she knew she had found the origin of the elusive smell she'd been hunting for. A decaying rat.

By the light of a candle, she found spare sails, ropes and other items to do with the boat, which were partly hiding an eighteen-inch square wooden box with metal bands. It took her a moment or two to lift the box out. Bill had not locked it. Inside was a handkerchief—she recognised it as the one she had dropped for him in the bookshop—a small leather pouch that chinked, and the jewellery box she had brought from home. Her hands trembled as she lifted the velvet lid. All that was left of her trinkets were her mother's ruby necklet, the matching earrings, and a single long string of pearls—the pearls given to her by her parents when she was sixteen. *My seventeenth birthday has passed, and I didn't even remember,* she thought. With a sob she lifted the necklet from the jewellery box, and pressed it to her lips.

The boat rocked. Someone had stepped aboard. Catching her breath, and wiping her cheeks with her hand, she replaced the necklet. She snatched up the leather pouch, sprung to her feet, and threw the jewellery box and pouch on the bed. As quietly as she could, she replaced the wooden box inside the deck cupboard and, with some difficulty, closed the door. Frantic, she looked around for a hiding place for her treasure, giving a sob of terror when someone outside called her name and rapped on the cabin door. She moved the rug back into place with her foot to conceal the deck cupboard door before jumping into bed. With shaking hands, she thrust the leather pouch and jewellery box under her pillow.

'Mrs Waspill, Mrs Waspill, let us in. You mustn't be alone at a time like this.' Heavy knocking followed the words.

The cabin darkened as someone peered through the window. A sharp tap on the glass startled her, and she gasped, slid out of bed and let two women enter. She recognised one of them as the one who had used a stick to poke the washing in the cauldron. As they stepped inside, they glanced at the rug covering the deck cupboard. *I was not a moment too soon,* she thought.

'I'm Mrs Staycy, and this is Flo, me daughter,' the older woman said. 'We've come to tell you the arrangements have been made for Friday.'

Merrilla pressed her hand over her mouth, and the woman moved closer, as though to put an arm around her. She sat on the bed. 'That's tomorrow,' she whispered.

'You've to pay for his funeral,' Flo said, looking sideways at her.

'I can't pay for his funeral. What do I pay with? I have no money. The company who owns this boat will have to pay. Bill brought the *Faskin* here safely; they owe him something for doing that.' Her voice was firm as she stared at the women, daring them to contradict her.

'Oh, well, put like that,' the older woman shrugged. 'You'd know, I suppose, if Bill had money, in his trousers, say, or maybe in one of his coats? Most men tuck a little money away in a pocket, and think it's safe from their wives.'

Merrilla shook her head. 'He always carried what money he had with him. He would not have very much. We were expecting to be paid for the cargo of coal when we reached Glasgow.' Her face burned and she hoped she sounded convincing; she'd never been a good liar.

Throughout the rest of the day, and during the night, the boat women took it in turns to stay with her, making sure she didn't pack anything of value with her belongings. Knowing they wanted only a whiff of an excuse to turn her off the boat, she made no attempt to touch any of Bill's things, leaving his clothes still folded inside drawers, and his personal things on shelves. They watched her every move as she collected her own few possessions. No comment was made as she placed the roll of parchment with her things. She had a spare dress that she usually wore on Sundays, her fur muff, and a second pair of boots. She tied an old shawl around her belongings, recalling the time that

Jeremy had tied her clothes into a similar, but much larger, bundle.

During the night, the women dozed, and they were unaware of her surreptitious movements behind the bed curtains as she retrieved the leather pouch and jewellery box from under her pillow, and secreted them inside her clothing.

At daybreak on Friday morning, she swung the cloak the farmer's wife had given to her around her shoulders, drew the hood over her head, picked up her bundle, and, without a backwards glance, left the *Faskin*. With a purposeful stride, she made her way along the wharf to where a group of sombre men waited. Giving a brief nod to Mr Watson, she walked stony-faced in front of the men as they followed a flat wagon pulled by a black-plumed horse. The bone-chilling mist left tiny drops of moisture on the rough planks of the coffin. It bounced as the wagon dipped in and out of the ruts in the road.

You'll have far more bruises on your body than you ever put on mine if we don't get to our destination very soon, Merrilla was thinking, when the wagon came to an abrupt halt and she realised they were under the lych-gate of a small, grey, stone church. Six men moved forward, lifted the coffin onto their shoulders, and walked behind a minister. He led the way between rows of headstones—his words torn away by the wind as he read from his Bible—along the mossy path, past the church, and down a slope to a grave, made ready in the far corner of the churchyard.

The hood of her cloak pulled further over her hair, Merrilla followed the men and stood beside the gaping hole, her bundle in her arms, listening to the minister. As the coffin was lowered, turning her ring round and round on her finger, she stared at the earth crumbling onto the rough planks. *You couldn't even love me enough to buy me a new wedding ring. Still, you made me into a decent woman by marrying me, I'll say that, and I have proof of the ceremony, thank goodness.*

The short service over, Mr Watson came to speak to her, his hair glistening with the mist, and hat in hand. 'You'll be all right, Mrs Waspill? I can't have you taken back to Glasgow. It wouldn't be fair on the new couple to have you sharing a cabin with them.' He could not meet her eyes. 'The money you both earned by bringing the *Faskin* here has been used for all this,' he said, gesturing towards the grave with his hat. 'You're young and strong; you'll soon find work.'

His duty done, he bowed to her, replaced his hat, and hurried away to join the other men shuffling along the path with downcast eyes.

Merrilla turned to the minister, held out her hand, and thanked him for his funeral service. 'Have you a place to go, lassie?' the minister asked as he accompanied her to the lych-gate.

'No, sir, I have no home now, and I need to find accommodation. Do you know if there's a room in the village? I do have a few coins, but I'll need to find work very soon if I'm to make my home here.' She looked at the minister hopefully.

'This is only a small village, and the only place that comes to mind is Mrs O'Keaf's house. It's rough, but I've been told she keeps it clean. Most who live there work at the Paxton Coalmine.' He gave her directions on how to find the way, and hurried off.

As she knocked on the door of Mrs O'Keaf's lodging house, situated in the main village street, she noted flaking brown paint on the door, and a still damp step, which must had been scrubbed and stone-whitened that morning. A child of about five-years old peered out from behind the partly-opened door.

'Mrs O'Keaf. Is this her house?' Merrilla spoke in a soft voice, trying not to frighten the child, who, with her fingers in her mouth, nodded without speaking. 'Can I have a word with her, please?'

The door slammed. She heard the sound of raised voices and footsteps before it reopened. A woman wearing a patched but clean dress leaned against the doorpost, looking at her with suspicious, narrowed eyes. 'Yus?' she snapped.

'I was told by the minister that you might have a room to rent.'

Without speaking, the woman looked at Merrilla clutching her bundle, fingers white with tension, before she opened the door wider, and moved to one side. Merrilla strode over the step to avoid soiling the effect of someone's hard work with a donkey-stone, unimpressed by the sight of a dingy hallway and a bare wooden staircase littered with children of various ages up to about five. She wondered if they all belonged to Mrs O'Keaf and, taking a deep breath, she followed the woman to the first floor, along a passage to the front of the house.

'You in work?' The woman's face brightened when she saw the coin Merrilla held out. 'This is one of my best rooms. On your own, are you, miss?' The woman glanced at Merrilla's left hand. 'Er... Mrs?'

'Waspill. I...' Merrilla swallowed. 'I'm a widow.'

She looked around the shabby room. Brown curtains at a window matched those hanging around the high four-poster bed. A small, bare table with two wooden chairs stood in one corner. She noticed a tall cupboard, with a door hanging half-open, built into the recess beside a fireplace. The fire would supply her with hot water and the means of cooking simple meals. Damp had made a dark stain on the wall beside the window, partly hidden by a washstand that had a rose-patterned ewer and bowl standing on its marble top. A chamber pot sat on a shelf underneath.

'This room will suit me, Mrs O'Keaf.'

Turning at the door, the landlady regarded Merrilla, who flushed with embarrassment. She knew she looked dowdy and unattractive in her old clothes. Her hair straggled over her shoulders, and her complexion was dark and weather-beaten.

When she had worked on the boat, it didn't seem to matter that she looked more than her age, but now?

'I don't allow men in here. This is a respectable house.' The woman seemed satisfied with Merrilla's silent nod and closed the door behind her, making the latch jump noisily in its socket.

After placing her bundle on the table, she went to the bed and pulled back the covers, where clean white sheets covered a soft bolster and a pillow. A great weariness overtook her, and she sank down on the bed, her cheek pressed into the pillow. She had never felt so alone. Tears, held back too long, flowed. 'God, what is to become of me? I'm here without friends or family,' she sobbed. 'I cannot get in touch with my parents. I'm considered a disgrace, and I can never go back home for Bill said my father has disowned me.'

Someone knocked on the door. She lifted her head and rubbed her hand across her eyes, calling, 'Who...who's there?'

A boy of about seven or eight-years old pushed open the door. Clearly noticing that Merrilla had been weeping, he stared at her with sympathetic eyes. 'I've got ter be at work in a little while, but Mam sent me to see if I can 'elp. You want summut fetching from the shop, missus? I can fetch you a pail of water—pump's in the back yard. Make a fire, maybe?' The boy glanced at the empty fireplace, then back at her.

The unexpected offer almost made her tears flow again, but she dared not give in to such an indulgence in front of the child; it would be folly. She rose to her feet with a sniff, then a watery smile, and brushed a strand of tawny hair from her face. 'Thank you, boy. Tell me, what's your name?'

He took a step back. 'It's Freddie Gylby, missus. We live in the room below. You'll need coals for your fire. You'll be able to cook. I can send me mates to the pit to fetch coal. Not cost yer.'

It became clear in the next few hours that Freddie had taken a liking to Merrilla, and had made her his special responsibility.

With his, and also his friends' help, they moved the furniture around, found pots and pans in the cupboard, and, after placing a chair beside the crackling fire, made her small room homely.

'Me mam's made a stew for supper. She wants you ter come down to our room later on, and eat with us. Me mam says you're on your own, and a stranger here, and we 'ave to make yer welcome.'

Merrilla wanted so much to give the boy a hug, but knowing boys could be offended by what they call silly behaviour, she only gave a nod to the earnest child. 'That's very kind of your mother, Freddie.'

'I'll fetch yer down later,' floated back to her, as he shot out of the door and clattered down the stairs.

Chapter 7

Bill's death devastated Merilla, and it took a couple of weeks before she felt strong enough to leave the haven of her lodgings. Freddie Gylby called each day before leaving for work to see if she needed anything, and on his return he brought the food she had ordered from Mr Parkinson's shop.

When she examined the leather pouch she had discovered in the deck cupboard on the boat, she found a number of coins, and a gold sovereign—probably one of those she had taken from her father's study. Remembering the day when she had stolen the money, her eyes brimmed. 'Journeying through life together on our love boat? Some love boat! How on earth could I have been so stupid to believe anything that Bill said, to let someone like him influence me to that extent?' she muttered, dashing away the tears.

Although she was careful, her modest cache of money dwindled until only half a guinea remained. She would need either to earn a wage or remarry.

After the experience of living with Bill she knew she would never remarry, never put herself into the power of a man, to be his skivvy again, besides which there would be little or no opportunity. The best thing would be to find some kind of work.

Her knock on the back door of the rectory brought the housekeeper with a haughty stare. Merrilla enquired as to the availability of work in the house and, in response, had the door shut in her face. She thought of applying to work at the tavern, but swiftly rejected that possibility. She had heard plenty in the past from Bill about the kind of women who worked in those places.

Outside the smithy she remembered the kindness of the man working there. The blacksmith noticed her hovering at the gateway and gave a wave. Taking a deep breath to steady her nerves, she moved towards him. 'Please, sir, do you know of anyone in the district who's wanting to hire a woman?'

He shook his head. 'Hiring for farm labourers is done in the springtime. I know of no other work hereabouts. Maybe the mine's taking on female workers,' he suggested, pointing down the hill with a thumb.

Merrilla's quiet, 'Thank you, sir,' caused the man to sigh as he turned back to his work. As she made her way down the hill, she was close to tears. Anything would be better than going into that black hole in the ground. It had occurred to her that she could ask Mr Watson for work on a barge, but then she remembered the hostility shown to her by the boat people so dismissed the idea. She would not risk being pushed over the side one night and drowned. There was no other way, no means of reaching a town without using a boat. She had to work to live, and the only work available in the small community was at the Paxton Coalmine.

As she trudged to the coalmine, her mind wandered back to the sunny day when, with Bill, she had first seen the dust-covered people in the pit yard. How she had pitied them, and how thankful she had felt to be working in the fresh air.

She wasn't conscious she had come to a decision until she entered the pit yard.

'Worked down a pit before?' the surly manager barked. She stood just inside the office door, her head bowed and hands clasped.

'No. I worked on the boats, but my husband died. I'm strong, and I've been used to working long hours.' Her eyes spoke for her.

Appraising her skinny figure for a long moment, the manager sighed. 'I'll try you as a carrier. You're small for the work, but I'll give you a week to get up to your quota. If you're not carrying a full basket of coal by then, you'll be out.'

'Oh, thank you, sir.'

The manager jerked his head in dismissal. 'Bloody charity, I am!' he muttered.

As she left the office, he shouted, 'Find Mr Lang. Tell him you'll be starting on Monday. He's the overman in charge below.'

After the interview, she found Mary, Freddie's sister, waiting at home to hear her news. Mary told her she had spoken up for Merrilla on the previous day, when she had heard a vacancy for a carrier had opened at the mine. She was a well-built girl, a little older then Merrilla. Her friendly grin exposed the absence of two upper front teeth. Merilla decided to say nothing about her reluctance to work in a coalmine, or about her unsuccessful attempts to find other employment.

They celebrated her success by buying food from Mr Parkinson's shop, and returned to her room to prepare and enjoy a pig's fry dinner. After they had eaten, she told Mary about her elopement, and about the hardships she had experienced on the barge. When she had finished, both girls wept.

'With you working on the barges, I guessed something very bad must have happened to you. You must put it all behind you now and start your life anew,' Mary said. 'You have friends here to turn to now if things get you down.'

Merrilla stood on one of the wooden platforms, halfway up the bell-shaped shaft of the Paxton Coalmine. The ladders up to that section were comparatively easy, but she faced the steepest climb. Her neck craned back as far as she dared, she tried to catch a glimpse of daylight. All she could make out in the hazy glow of a nearby lamp was a pair of blackened feet and the bottom of a wicker basket carried by the woman climbing above her. There was just enough room on the platform for her and two other people, each carrying a load of coal on their back.

'No use you looking up there yet. Long ways to go afore you reach the top.' A flash of white teeth showed in the dim light. 'Come on, girl, stop yer dreaming, do.' The woman gave her an impatient push. 'There's others behind, you know.' She nudged Merrilla's basket.

She turned. They were four ladders high, and she was afraid of causing an accident by dropping some of her load. 'You carry a full basket.' She sounded wistful, knowing her own was only half-full. She knew in her heart that she wasn't built for the work, and would never manage to lift a full basket, let alone carry it up ladders.

'Remember, girl, I've been working as a carrier for years, and you only started this week. It'll take weeks to strengthen your neck muscles. I wager you still get head pains from your strap.'

Merrilla put her hand to the leather band on her forehead, the ends of which were attached to the basket on her back. Truly, she felt the pain. In fact she had many pains, her neck, back, arms, and legs all ached. Taking a deep breath as she hitched up the basket, she put out her hands to grasp the next ladder and climbed. As she moved upward, she thought about the days when she had been a girl, without a care in the world. She also recalled unhappy days. *It was a poor life on the boat. I prayed for death before Bill came to care for me. Now I have an interminable, sordid existence. I've reached the nadir of life, with no future, and no one to love me.* As she pulled herself up, rung by rung, tears streaked the grime on her face.

Women queuing on the ladders and platforms below grumbled, their voices rising up the shaft.

'Weigh-man will've gone home by the time we get on top.'

'Time to finish.'

'When you're slow, your strap digs into your head.'

'It's that new 'un, she's slow.'

Merrilla did her best to hurry, but her calves felt as though they were on fire. She wore the soft kid boots she had brought from home. They were worn through, with a hole in each of the soles, so the rungs of the ladder hurt her feet. With her back bent, she tried to balance the basket, and almost lost her footing. It would be fatal if a person slipped off the ladder.

Her eyes closed, she counted the rungs of the penultimate flight. Twenty-three, twenty-four, twenty-five. As she stepped onto the last platform, she wailed to the woman next to her, 'I have a stitch,' and pressed a fist into her side to ease the pain.

'Only one more ladder. Come now, you must keep moving,' the woman said and placed a hand under Merrilla's basket as they moved slowly towards the light above.

She had to do better, or the manager would dismiss her. Only having done five runs that shift, she would start earlier the following day and raise the number of basket loads.

She staggered across the yard and joined the queue of women waiting for the weighing-in.

'You managed it then, hinny?' the woman in front of her remarked with approval. Comforted by the woman's understanding, Merrilla's face broke into a smile but it faded when it was her turn to have her basket weighed.

'Huh, 'tis not worth you having your basket weighed. Would've been best if you'd stayed below,' the man sneered. With rippling muscles, he lifted her basket of coal with one hand and dropped it on the huge scales.

Merrilla didn't bother replying. She stared, stony-faced, as the man wrote the weight of her load in his ledger. He scribbled the same figures onto a piece of paper, and thrust it in her direction. 'Put your mark on here!'

With a sense of satisfaction, she signed her name with a flourish, probably the only woman there who could read and write.

'Next,' yelled the man, snatching the paper from her hand. It fluttered onto a pile of others.

As she walked she unknotted the string around her waist and released her skirt, partially covering her bare legs. She no longer dropped her eyes in embarrassment at the sight of women scantily clothed.

It was her fourth day. She had begun work at five o'clock that morning, and felt extremely weary. She walked slowly, examining her hands, pressing on blisters, and wincing at the pain of the broken ones. *Who ever would think I once did fine needlework and embroidery?* Her thoughts were interrupted by a piercing, 'Coo-ee!' Recognising the call, she turned and smiled warmly at the girl running towards her.

'Wait for me, hinny,' panted her friend. 'I've been waiting for you to come up pit. Coming to bathe with me in the river, Merr? I have a towel and soap.' Mary Gylby giggled as she linked arms with Merrilla, matching her steps. 'It's warm tonight. Come on in, hinny,' she coaxed, when Merrilla hesitated on the riverbank. The girls had peeled off their dirty shawls and boots and left them with Mary's towels, well away from the water, but they still wore ragged dresses.

As she stepped into the river, Merrilla gasped. 'Oh, Mary, it's very deep just here.' Arms wide to keep her balance, she glanced across the water at her friend's laughing face. Somehow she found courage and followed as Mary waded around the reeds into deeper water. Standing on submerged roots, she tried hard not to let her imagination dwell on what slimy creatures might be slithering over her feet or considering biting her toes.

Further along the river, women stood waist-deep, washing coal dust from their bodies and dipping their heads under the water to rinse the dirt out of their hair. As they splashed, a greasy, sooty film floated on the water, breaking up into small islands. It was less trouble to endure the cold river than to fill heavy wooden hipbaths at home, where every drop of hot water had to be boiled in pans over the fire. The menfolk always bathed first. The women would use the same water by then, dirty and cool, but fortunately Merrilla did not have to suffer that indignity. Although she didn't have a bathtub, she did have a large bowl, and found it adequate for her needs.

The two girls had almost finished when she noticed a barge moving around the bend in the river, travelling in their direction. 'Quick, Mary, a boat. I don't want anyone to see me in this state,' she said, wading through the water. She tried to hurry, knowing her wet clothing revealed every line of her figure. Both girls scrambled out and ran to pick up their belongings before taking cover behind a thick bush.

Mary twisted her ragged skirt into a rope and squeezed out as much water as she could. Merrilla copied her, and braided her long, tawny hair into a style similar to her friend's.

'Did you recognise the boat?'

'No. At first, I thought it might be the *Faskin*, but when it drew nearer, I saw it wasn't.'

The girls started on the long walk home, hoping the stale smell of sweat and coal dust would not still cling to them. Only hot water and soap could really dispel the odour. From time to time, they stopped to pull at the wet skirts that wound around their legs, hindering their movements.

'Wearing wet clothing is most uncomfortable.' Merrilla gave an exaggerated shiver as she attempted to dry her skirt by holding it away from her legs.

'You're just unaccustomed,' Mary laughed over her shoulder, waiting until Merrilla caught up with her. 'I must call at Mr Parkinson's shop. Mammy told me to bring home oats and flour. Our Freddie won't be back from work yet, and Mammy'll want them for dinner.'

'Mr Parkinson won't let me have any further credit, but I have enough food to make a meal tonight.' Merrilla knew she had to go to bed straight after her meal, to arise before daybreak and walk to the coalmine.

'If that man can make a groat out of a person he'll give anyone credit. He must be a proper miser.' The expression on Mary's face caused Merrilla to lift an eyebrow in surprise. She had never heard her friend sound so bitter.

'With any dealing I've had with Mr Parkinson he's been most courteous,' she said, remembering his kindness to Bill on the day they had made the delivery to his shop.

'He'll give you nothing, that one,' Mary went on. 'That's his way. I blame his mother, stuck in that room up there. I dare bet you she's in her room right this minute, looking down on us. Evil old witch.' Spitting on the ground, she pulled her tattered shawl closer around her shoulders, and shuddered.

'Have you seen Mrs Parkinson?' asked Merrilla, curious about the woman who spent all her days in seclusion.

'Me mammy's seen her, though no one else has caught sight of her for years. Me mammy remembers the time when she came to live here. William Parkinson was only a wee bairn then. They say Mrs Parkinson was a nob. She talked posh, a bit like you do.' Mary laughed, and dodged, as Merrilla pretended to smack her friend.

'When I was a young lass talk in the village said how Mrs Parkinson was a proper lady with a title, but her husband had done something really wicked, and was sent to prison. Her family didn't want anything to do with her after that, so she came here and bought the shop. No one liked her, and if there'd been another shop in the village she wouldn't have had any customers.'

The two girls were almost level with the shop doorway when a horrendous-sounding hooter, together with a bell clanging a sombre alarm, drowned Mary's next words. She turned fear-filled eyes towards Merrilla, and yelled, 'Trouble! It's the pit. Come on.' Lifting their skirts, they pelted back down the way they had come.

With unexpected energy, Merrilla tried to keep pace with her friend. Men ran past, their nail-studded boots sparking from the flint stones on the road. Everyone, it seemed, was heading for the Paxton Coalmine.

Just as the girls reached the church, a woman staggered up the hill towards them with staring eyes, and holding both hands over her mouth.

'It's Betty. She lives next door and works down the pit, alongside our Freddie.' Mary bit her lip because Betty was still wearing a thick leather belt around her waist. The belt would usually be removed and left at the bottom of the shaft, ready for use the following day. As the woman moved forward, the chains attached to the belt bounced and clanked over the stony road.

'What is it? What's happened?' Mary shouted questions as she shook Betty's shoulders.

'My tub was empty, so I was down on my hands and feet, pulling it along. You know, that part in the tunnel where it's steep? I had just reached the top of the roadway, ready to make for the coalface, when I heard this bang in the distance and a whoosh of wind and dust, all aflame, blew over the top of the tub, and along the tunnel.' The woman covered her face with her hands, whispering, 'It missed me.'

Merrilla and Mary glanced at each other in horror. There was no need for words. They raced down the road, and joined a group of grim-faced people in the pit yard. Everyone stood, some in silence, most praying, as they waited to hear news of their loved ones trapped in the darkness below.

In the great hall of the Change Building in Nottingham Town the applause died away as members of the large audience rose to their feet, among them John Larcombe, his son, Philip, and their friends, Nathan Denstone and his son, Hugo. The four men stood looking around them. They had arrived together in Nottingham the previous day, and had looked forward to hearing the speakers.

'It's a year ago, but it seems like only yesterday that we were here giving our own lecture on factory reforms.' John Larcombe stretched his back, looking around for other businessmen he might know. He always seemed to be stiff whenever he sat awhile.

The hall was packed with men of commerce, most of whom owned manufacturing outlets in or near the town. One and all were keen to hear of any available new methods that might be profitable in their respective businesses. Everyone in the hall seemed to be relaxed, and as people joined friends and colleagues, a babble of noise broke out, for each man wanted to state his opinion about the lecture they had just heard.

'We may see something of Mr Cooper whilst we're in Nottingham. I'd like to know if he did as he promised me last year, and carried out all the changes I recommended for his factory,' Nathan Denstone said, acknowledging a wave from an acquaintance on the far side of the hall.

'Is Mr Cooper a successful man, Papa? A man who would welcome new business ventures?' Hugo asked.

John and Nathan exchanged quizzical glances. They had heard disquieting whispers about Mr Cooper's family affairs: specifically, the disgrace of a runaway daughter.

John stood swinging a gold and diamond fob on a long chain. 'We met the gentleman last year when we were in Grantham. He seemed most interested in our ideas, and later he met us for dinner. Among other things, we discussed reforms for his factory, most importantly his worker's safety and well-being.'

'That was just before we heard from a friend that when Mr Cooper returned to his home in Nottingham he found his youngest daughter, Merrilla, had disappeared. Packed her clothes, and ran away,' said Nathan. 'She was never found, and it's broken her parents' hearts.'

'Something like that would certainly have changed the man, and soured his nature,' said Philip. 'I've heard since then, from more than one source, that he's one of the most unfeeling employers in Nottingham. His people work very long hours in the factory.'

His father's lips pursed with disapproval, and frowning brought his fine eyebrows together. 'Dreadful. Dreadful for the Cooper family. Imagine raising a daughter who could do such a wanton thing. I heard talk about an elopement, but whether it's true... Well, who knows?'

Philip glanced at him. Most people knew about John Larcombe's rigid moral principles, and how he detested ill-judged and rash behaviour.

Hugo and Philip moved away, and joined some younger friends. John and Nathan watched them as they disappeared among the crowd.

'You haven't said much about your stay in London, John.' Nathan matched his steps with his friend's as they moved towards the open doorway.

'Did I tell you? I was invited to a grand event one evening. A ball. Very nice it was. I met Mr William Pitt—an eloquent speaker, and a first class Prime Minister. He was extremely worried about the King's madness, but reports now say that His Majesty is improving daily.'

'You'll have to tell us about it over dinner. I shall be most interested,' said Nathan.

113

'Drat…where are the boys?' John lifted his quizzing glass and scanned the room.

The "boys", both in their early thirties, and dressed in the latest fashion, were very different in appearance. Philip, tall and slim, had a long, thin face and was ready to break into a smile at every opportunity. Disliking wigs, he kept his straight, brown hair in a que, tied with a black ribbon.

Hugo had brown, soulful eyes underneath his bushy eyebrows, which were exactly the same colour as his dark, curly beard. He was serious, seldom smiled, and spent most of his time on working, among other things, the many financial accounts for the Larcombe and Denstone partnership. Philip had spoken to him of various ideas about expanding the business, and had said paperwork bored him, and that he hoped Hugo would always deal with monetary matters concerning the partnership.

Hugo and Philip were speaking to a group of their peers. Philip gestured with his hands as he made his meaning clear to those around him. A lock of hair fell over his left eye, and he shook it back into place. 'I tell you this, gentlemen: coal is the thing to invest in. Coalmines will become invaluable as more steam machines are used. Steam trains use it, and I saw, with my own eyes, coal turned into coke, producing heat hot enough to smelt iron ore. Most certainly it will replace charcoal.' He shook back his hair once more and, seeing Hugo's expression, grinned ruefully. 'Have I been talking too much? I beg pardon for getting on my hobbyhorse, gentlemen.'

Waving a well-manicured hand heavy with rings, Hugo drawled, 'Not at all, Philip. I'm pleased to hear your visit to the coalmine in Yorkshire was of value. Please continue.'

'Flooding is a problem below ground, as is poisonous air and collapsing tunnels. A good strong steam engine built by the engineer, Mr Watts, is able to pump air in and water out, with great efficiency. Most coalmines can produce extremely healthy profits if up to date methods are used.'

Those listening murmured to each other and nodded in approval. It wasn't the first time Philip Larcombe had spoken about a profitable business enterprise, and those who had taken his advice in the past had made a handsome profit.

Their fathers were waiting beside the door so Hugo spoke to Philip, who nodded, made his excuses, and shook hands with the gentlemen nearby, before following his childhood friend.

Nathan broke the silence in the carriage. 'Remember when we returned to Nottingham from abroad all those years ago, John? There were so many new houses we became lost, and still they construct more buildings.' He pointed with a gloved hand towards piles of bricks and a night watchman huddled over a charcoal brazier on an open site.

'That was before I married my Esther. Do you know? She still has that same dark hair and laughing eyes. Not changed a bit.' John Larcombe's expression was tender as he thought of his wife and daughter, Elysabeth, waiting at home for his return.

The Black Boy Inn in the centre of Nottingham Town never seemed to change. Lights shone from windows behind low, black, wooden balconies, and the numerous tall chimneys belched smoke. The driver of the carriage, Samuel Harris, had to wait a while in the busy street before there was room to enter the inn yard. At last, a smart phaeton was driven away, and as the head groom directed the coaches to manoeuvre around the yard into their appointed positions, he found a safe place for his passengers to alight.

The landlord, in his smart blue coat and white wig, hurried across the yard, risking injury as horses whinnied and reared, causing sedan chair carriers to curse and at least one coach to roll back. As Nathan Denstone and John Larcombe stepped stiffly from the carriage, he smiled warmly to his patrons and bowed low, pleased that these important gentlemen used his hostelry whenever they visited Nottingham Town. He nodded approval as ostlers, wearing yellow and black vertical-striped waistcoats, ran forward to lead the horses into the stables.

The two comfortable rooms allotted to the gentlemen were on the first floor with fires blazing in each hearth. The Larcombes' room had a view overlooking the street.

'We will require our meal in this room, landlord. We're all dining together,' John declared. There was adequate room at the table near the window for four people, and it was not too far from the fire. The evening had turned chilly.

As the landlord bowed his way out he held the door open for Nathan and Hugo to enter.

'There you are. We've ordered dinner to be served in here,' John Larcombe said, kicking a fallen log back onto the fire to burn with the others. 'Didn't fancy going down to the parlour or the coffee room; it's bound to be busy, and it's difficult to talk about business there.'

Nathan gave a wide yawn. 'I'm suited, John. I don't fancy changing my coat and wig to go downstairs. Too tired.' He stretched his arms. 'It always feels strange sleeping in a—'

A sharp rap on the door interrupted him. Men-servants, shirtsleeves rolled up, carried in dishes of mouth-watering food. Maidservants, wearing crisp aprons, threw a white cloth over the table and proceeded to set out silver cutlery.

'I see the landlord has not forgotten your taste in wine, Papa.' Philip grinned, holding up a slender bottle of red claret, from a selection on the side-table.

When the servants had left the room, the gentlemen eyed the table and the large joint of crisp roast beef in a silver dish next to a plate of game birds surrounded by buttered carrots. Other vegetables lay in warm dishes.

'The man has not forgotten your partiality for well-cooked meat either, John.' Nathan pulled up his chair to the table and, taking up a starched linen napkin, tucked it under his chin, and smoothed it over his chest.

It was not until the men were passing the port and enjoying snuff from one of the jars on the table, that John Larcombe referred again to his recent visit to London. 'At that same ball I spoke of earlier, I met a Mr Robert Owen. We shared similar views on children working in factories. Mr Owen has the cotton spinning mills at New Lanark, near Edinburgh. His information was fascinating. He's built a settlement for his older workers, and has provided them with low-rent cottages.' He looked at the attentive faces around him as he refilled his glass. 'I told him t we had similar ambitions, and I mentioned sick pay for men unable to work, owing to an injury.'

Philip leaned forward. 'What did Mr Pitt have to say when he heard about Mr Owen's ideas, sir?'

'He made no comment, but he appeared to be pleased. I told them about our factories, and other proposed schemes. I also mentioned that we never employ children under ten years old. They were both extremely interested in the Sunday School that you started, Nathan.'

Nathan went to the fire and relit his pipe using a taper. He waited until it was drawing properly before sitting down again. 'I promised Mrs Denstone faithfully that while I was here, I'd inspect the school, and make sure the children were happy and well fed,' he said.

Hugo grinned across the table at his father. 'Mother charged me with a similar errand, Papa,' he said with a chuckle.

'Will you two dashing blades be going out tonight?' John asked, hiding a yawn with the back of his hand.

Philip and Hugo glanced at each other. Hugo shrugged and Philip said, 'Not unless we have a few minutes downstairs in the coffee room before turning in.'

As the young men left the room, Nathan called, 'I'm going to my bedchamber very soon, so don't disturb me with your drunken singing on your return, Hugo.'

The men raised their eyebrows. Hugo had never been drunk in his life. The bottle of port was still half full and Nathan said, 'We may as well finish this before retiring, John.' As he refilled the two glasses, raucous laughter reached them and they said simultaneously, 'I recognise that laugh.'

Chapter 8

Their agent, Mr Harwood, had known John Larcombe and Nathan Denstone for many years, and was godfather to all three of their children. He enjoyed visiting their homes, either Clemmants, the home of the Larcombe family, or Ghyll House, both of which were near to each other, in the county of Yorkshire.

Standing in his library, with its floor-to-ceiling bookcases, he waited for his clients, who were also good friends. With his back to the fire, and with his coattails lifted, he ran a critical eye over the table and twelve matching chairs in the centre of the room. Two silver candelabra, each containing four expensive wax candles, stood at each end of the table. Neat piles of papers, ledgers, and law books lay ready for inspection.

He stepped forward, letting his coattails drop, as the door opened, and his secretary ushered in the Larcombe and Denstone gentlemen. As the door closed, he bowed and welcomed them, gesturing towards the chairs nearest to the books and papers. 'Good day to you, sirs. Please sit down. Everything is ready.'

Cloaks, gloves and hats had been left in the outer office. It only took a moment for John and Nathan to sit facing each other, their sons beside them. Philip and Hugo were wearing new coats, with the latest bone-buttoned turned-back sleeves, and braided edging, Philip in olive green, while Hugo wore a midnight blue coat with velvet trim. Both sported a white cravat, embellished with a band of narrow lace and tied with a bow high under the chin. They showed no signs of their late night, and were instantly attentive as Mr Harwood, clearing his throat and placing a pair of pince-nez on his prominent nose, began to speak.

The first few hours were spent discussing the satisfactory state of their business interests. The main issues of the meeting were addressed when Mr Harwood passed papers to each man at the table. 'Gentlemen, I have made widespread enquiries about the acquisition of several businesses during recent months. I thought at one time the factory belonging to Mr Cooper would be placed on the market, but it was withdrawn, so we have turned our attention to two other very different businesses. A coalmine and a cotton mill. If you will refer to the papers in front of you, these show maps of the area around the Paxton Coalmine, in Scotland. As you see, it is the only habitation for miles, apart from a few farms. The village was built to house the miners and their families.' He walked to a large board on an easel and, with the feather end of his quill pen, pointed to a map pinned to the board. 'This is Glasgow, and this line is the canal waterway, running from Glasgow to the Paxton Coalmine. A fleet of narrow boats and barges carry all of the coal production, and they are owned by a Glaswegian company that is willing to negotiate profitable working arrangements.'

The gentlemen examined the papers in front of them, and referred to the map.

'The coalmine is a stair pit. Men, women and children work below. The amount of coal brought out varies from day to day because of poor conditions below ground. According to the information given by the owner, there is still a great deal of coal down there. The wages are very low, but I have estimated that future profits would easily enable you to raise them, if you so wish.'

Hugo, writing some figures on the paper in front of him, held his quill poised as he asked, 'In your opinion, sir, how much capital do you estimate it will take to bring this coalmine to a safe and profitable level?'

'If you refer to page 4c, Mr Hugo, you will see the estimates. I listed the sale of the mine first, followed by a summary of all relevant information.' Mr Harwood referred to a long line of figures running neatly down the page.

'Tell me, Mr Harwood, why is Mr Paxton selling this coalmine if it can be made so profitable?' A silence followed John Larcombe's quietly spoken question, and for a moment everyone looked at the honest face of the agent.

'Mr Paxton is in extremely poor health. His only family is one son. Although the son is old enough, he has no wish to continue working the mine. He has no interest in business matters, and wants to leave Scotland. So Paxton Hall will become empty when Mr Paxton, Senior, leaves. This building will be included in the sale, but it is in a very poor state of repair—'

Clerks interrupted, entering the library carrying trays of wine and crystal goblets.

Nathan leaned back, stretching in his chair and yawning, and Mr Harwood made for the wine. 'Mrs Larcombe and Mrs Denstone are well, I trust, gentlemen?' he asked, as each man accepted a glass of ruby wine. He smiled as they assured him that Esther and Joan were in the best of health, and had sent their felicitations to Mrs Harwood.

Philip and Hugo, taking their wine across to the fireplace, stood speaking in low voices. 'It will be best if you stay here, Hugo. I will travel to the coalmine. Your grasp of profit and loss matters is far better than mine.'

Hugo nodded. He had to agree. Philip was a man of action and inclined to impulsive behaviour, whereas he liked a quiet, orderly, considered life. 'Let's consult our fathers. Maybe one of them will wish to accompany you, Philip.'

Looking serious, they joined the other men. Philip cleared his throat as he replaced his glass on the tray. 'We think someone ought to travel to Scotland and inspect this coalmine. I have a working knowledge of the coalmines in Yorkshire, and I'm willing to meet with Mr Paxton.'

As everyone seated themselves once more at the table, Nathan and John exchanged glances. Nathan said, 'I'll travel with you, Philip. Your father and Hugo can look over this cotton mill in Nottingham. They will soon get it up and running should we be interested in purchasing it.' John and Hugo nodded agreement.

Mr Harwood busied himself with paperwork, before saying, 'Because the owner of the cotton mill is intending to live overseas, he has decided to sell his business. It's situated in the Hollowstone area of the town, near the Church of St. Mary the Virgin. An overseer, who seems to be very capable, runs the mill. It is profitable at the moment, but new machinery and changes to the working conditions would vastly improve matters. I'm very sorry to say the owner still uses child labour. Men, women and young children work in the mill, and they live in neighbouring streets. The building's large, and there's room for expansion on land behind it. This also belongs to the owner, and will be included in the sale.' He pinned a ground plan of the mill on the board.

'The spun cotton is of a fine quality, and is quickly sold to lace makers. Gentlemen, you have before you all the relevant information. The mill has possibilities for future development, but needs an owner who is far-sighted, and able to invest in new machinery.'

'And someone who does not use children,' John Larcombe said firmly.

'Yes, sir. Just so, just so.' Shuffling the papers, Mr Harwood glanced at him over the top of his pince-nez, before continuing. 'I have briefly examined the accounts. If you buy the firm you could expect a very high yield on the investment in a year or two, but it needs someone like yourselves, gentlemen, with foresight, to get the place to meet its full potential.'

There was silence for a moment before Nathan said, leaning back in his chair, 'Right then. The next thing is for our solicitors to get on with matters once we have inspected the place.'

'If, after the viewing, we feel the business is viable, then arrange for meetings as soon as possible, Mr Harwood,' John said, following Nathan's example. He shook hands with the agent.

Philip gave Hugo a rueful glance. They had arranged to watch aquatic races on the river Leen, and had been hopeful the meeting with Mr Harwood would have ended earlier.

'I know of a boxing match being held this evening, and if that sport doesn't find favour, I know where a cock-fight is to be held,' Hugo murmured, as they left the offices.

'Lead me to it,' Philip laughed over his shoulder, as he climbed inside the waiting carriage to join their parents.

After accompanying their fathers to business meetings with Mr Harwood in the mornings, Philip and Hugo spent their evenings enjoying the various entertainments Nottingham had to offer. At midday they would go to an eating-house not far from Mr Harwood's office. Although small, it had clean, white, plaster walls, a scrubbed red brick floor, and serving maids dressed in a uniform of a black dress and a spotlessly clean apron and cap. A portrait of King George the Third hung over the fireplace, dominating the small, private room where they dined.

The four men once again deliberated on their financial situation and Mr Harwood's recommendations, and were in full agreement as to their proposed venture. Relaxed, they finished their excellent meal and spoke about acquiring new horses sound enough for a strenuous journey to Scotland. Nathan pushed his heavy cadogan wig back from his forehead and frowned towards the logs on the fire, as though blaming them for making his chubby face hot.

'Yesterday Philip and I rode out of town, and we saw a horse dealer's animals in a field,' Hugo said, carrying a taper from the fire and giving it to his father to light his pipe. 'From a distance they looked sound, so I told the man to bring his best horses to the inn this afternoon for our inspection.'

'Let us hope he's trustworthy.' John wafted his slender hand in an effort to dispel the smoke rising from Nathan's pipe.

Nathan sat with one foot resting on a footstool and, puffing his pipe, used his thumb as a pointer. 'I'm pleased I ordered these boots the last time I was in Nottingham. The boot maker has done a splendid job. Look how snugly they fit.' Lifting his other foot, he rested them both on the footstool and admired the hand-stitched brown leather.

'A good, strong pair of boots will be necessary for your journey in the saddle, Nathan.' John grinned at his friend, who scowled back. They both knew Nathan preferred to ride in comfort in a carriage since he had become portly.

'Have you come to a decision about the cotton mill, sirs?' Philip spoke, glancing at the others in turn.

'We cannot come to a firm conclusion before we have seen each business, Philip,' Hugo replied.

'If we had a lace-making factory we could have expanded in that direction, but as we haven't...' With a shrug, Nathan pressed his thumb in the bowl of his pipe.

His friend interrupted his thoughts. 'We could explore the possibility of Mr Cooper being able to use some of our yarn in his factory.'

'I know what you're hoping for, John. You think you might be able to persuade him to treat his workers better. You may well do so because, at heart, he seemed to be a good man. I quite liked him,' Nathan Denstone said, with an incline of his head.

John grinned, and flicked a crumb from his sleeve. 'If these horses are suitable, will you both be leaving tomorrow?' He rose to his feet.

'Yes. Friday is a good day to travel, and everything will be ready by the morning. We can make a steady journey and choose where we want to stop for lodgings. Pity the Paxton Coalmine is so remote, the route to get there will not allow us time to call at home,' Nathan said, following the others into the street.

The men had not ordered the carriage to collect them for the day was fine and they preferred to walk back to the inn. Philip and Hugo sauntered along behind their respective fathers.

'Have you any idea how long you'll be in Scotland, Philip?' Hugo asked, just before dodging a cascade of dirty water thrown from an upstairs window. Philip's handsome face broke into a grin as Hugo swore and gave an angry glare up at the woman with the bowl, who moved out of sight.

'Don't know. Don't care. I intend to enjoy my trip though,' he said, watching Hugo using a handkerchief to dry his sleeve. He gave Hugo's arm a nudge. 'I'll see if I can bring you back a pretty highland lassie, one with plaid ribbons,' he teased, fully aware that Hugo was engaged to be married to his sister Elysabeth. The families had arranged the union nineteen years earlier, when Elysabeth was born.

'You bring a girl for yourself. I already have my own love, with big hazel eyes, at home, longing for my return' Hugo retorted in mock anger. Philip grinned with delight. Nothing would please him more than to have Hugo as his brother-in-law.

Stars were still visible when the four men gathered in the inn yard. Ostlers attached luggage to the packhorse, saddled up the horses and led them to where they waited.

'I still think you should have made a later start. You would have had time for a cooked breakfast, and it's deuced cold this time of the morning,' John Larcombe grumbled. Giving an exaggerated shiver, he drew his cloak close around his lean figure. 'Do your best to keep in touch. I know the place is far from a town, but send letters if you can, Nathan.' He squeezed his friend's arm.

'At least we believe the snow in Scotland will be all gone by now,' Nathan grunted. He stared at his new polished boots, looking annoyed that one was already muddy.

'The Quicksilver coach driver told me all the roads are passable now, but he couldn't say anything about the hills over the border,' Philip called, as he gave a last minute check to the bellyband of his mount. He smothered a curse as the chestnut baulked from his attentions and almost stood on his toe.

The packhorse was ready and roped to Philip's horse. One of the ostlers held the bridle of the grey as Nathan attempted to mount. By the time he had swung into the saddle his plump face was ruddy with concentration and exertion. It took a moment or two to bring his horse around to stand beside Hugo, and then he leaned over to shake his son's hand.

'I'll write to mother regularly, sir,' Hugo said, grinning at him.

Placing an arm across Philip's shoulders, John said in a low voice, 'Take care of Mr Denstone, Philip. Recently I've noticed he's looking his age, and it's a long time since he rode a horse for any distance.'

'I will, sir. Take care of yourself also, and when you write home, please send my love to Mamma and Elysabeth.'

'Ready, Philip?' Nathan Denstone called, moving his horse forward. With a cheery wave, he made steady progress out of the yard. Philip mounted, shook his father's hand, saluted Hugo, and, holding the rope of the packhorse, followed Nathan at a smart trot.

John and Hugo stood listening to the sound of the horses moving along the street until they faded away. 'Shall we go back inside, Mr Larcombe?' Hugo smiled at the sombre man. 'We have a busy day ahead.'

Meanwhile, things at the Paxton Coalmine were chaotic. People huddled together in the pit yard with haunted faces, fearful and silent. Those waiting near as possible to the mineshaft had already voiced their awful anxiety about their loved ones, and stood numbly waiting for news. They knew some people in the mine, far below their feet, would be deeply shocked, injured, or even dead, but those above desperately needed to know who was in which state. No news seemed worse than any news, good or bad.

The onlookers pressed forward as a man emerged from the mineshaft and stumbled towards them. 'Any of you here carriers?' he called. His gaunt face was covered with grime, anguish clear by the way he twisted his cap in his hands as he waited for volunteers.

Merrilla stepped forward after Mary and other women followed their example.

'We both work as carriers,' Mary said with a tremor.

'Yer needed below. Some trappers, and others, killed. Someone must have had a flame—a child, maybe.' The man's words were brusque.

A fire meant folk would have perished from burns, or scarred for life. Mary's face blanched as she grabbed the man's sleeve and stared into his eyes. 'Who? Me brother's below, is he...is he safe?' He could not hold her gaze, and turned away, calling to some other women to hurry below.

Supporting each other, the girls hurried to the top of the first ladder. They had difficulty tying their ragged skirts, which were still wet, around their waists.

When ready, Merrilla turned to Mary. 'Whatever we find down there, my dear, I'll be by your side.' Clearly full of dread, Mary shrugged and they began their long descent, each busy with their own thoughts. A mixture of smoke and dust drifted up the shaft, causing them to cough and wipe their streaming eyes. They heard the sound of weeping and smelt the acrid stench of burned flesh long before they reached the horrific sight at the bottom of the mineshaft.

Lamps, glowing yellow like a pale sun through fog but barely penetrating the atmosphere, were enough to show men, women, and children lying in a pitiful row. For a moment or so, the girls became separated in the chaos. It was not the sight or stench that made Merrilla put her hands to her cheeks, but the sound of Mary's strident scream. She had found her brother's body laid out among the corpses. Merrilla pushed her way through groups of people to reach both the still figure and Mary, who was hysterical.

'Freddie! Oh, my Freddie!' She dropped to her knees and, with abnormal strength, pulled her brother's body into her arms, rocking him, and sobbing. 'Oh...why? Why do they bring candles down when they know...? Oh...'

Tears flowed down her own cheeks. She felt such deep sadness for the loss of this boy, who had been the first person to befriend her since leaving her parents' home.

A workman, noticing the distressed girls, left one of the groups and knelt beside Mary. 'Miss Gylby. It were quick. He didn't feel nothing.' The man placed a calloused hand on Mary's shoulder in comfort.

'Is...is this...? Are these all?' Merrilla, her eyes swimming with tears, looked at the devastation all around her. So many dead, surely everyone in the village would be grieving that day. Her throat felt tight and she had difficulty speaking.

'Them lying over there, they had burns. We think some folk are still missing. Sarah Goodligh hasn't come forward yet, and three of the men and a woman ain't been counted in.'

Merrilla swallowed hard. 'How... What age is Sarah?'

The eyes of the man flickered in the direction of Mary before he replied. 'She's only a wee bairn, just seven.'

Though the words were spoken quietly, Mary clearly heard. 'A year younger than our Freddie,' she moaned, still rocking her brother, and kissing his still face.

As Merrilla crouched by her friend, she noticed a man with a basket, and knew without being told what it would be used for. 'Mary, come now, my dear. Let's go back to the surface. I'll carry Freddie.' She drew Mary close, and kissed the grief-stricken girl.

'I don't know how I'm going to tell Mammy. Freddie's the second of my brothers to die down here.' Two men lifted Mary to her feet, and took Freddie from her. Wrapping her arms around her shaking body, she watched as they placed the boy's skinny body reverently into one of the deep wicker baskets. Merrilla noticed other baskets being brought forward, and being filled. Making sure that her skirt was tied out of the way, she stood to allow the men to strap the basket over her shoulders. Then, with the head-strap in place, she held it ready. The girls looked at each other through tears and the murky atmosphere. 'You go first, Mary. I'll be close behind you,' she whispered, knowing Mary was too upset to do any carrying.

The man who had spoken to the girls climbed with them, and at each platform, with gentle hands, he steadied the basket. She had to make use of a newfound strength, for the dead boy was much heavier than the coal she usually carried.

When she reached the surface, a group closed around her.

'I'll help you, Mrs Waspill,' someone said, and they supported the basket as she unfastened the straps. Others hurried forward to help lay Freddie on a rough stretcher and to cover him with a blanket. The crowd moved aside as a distraught woman pushed her way through to stand beside the stretcher.

'Mammy, Mammy!' Watching from a distance, Merrilla saw Mary throw herself into her mother's arms, weeping bitterly. Then the Gylby family closed around the pair. Other bodies, brought out of the mine in the same way, were laid on stretchers. Their families, too, were waiting. The slow cortege moved up the hill in the direction of the village. Men removed their caps, and women brought their shawls forward to cover their heads and dropped their gaze as the sorrowful people passed by. Merrilla walked forlornly behind the Gylby family, shivering in her damp clothes. She could hear murmurs and cries of distress coming from homes on both sides of the street but, overwhelmingly weary, she continued walking with her head bent. She knew everyone in the village would know the dreadful details by then.

'Mrs Waspill, a moment of your time, please.'

Merrilla looked up. It took a moment to focus her gaze. William Parkinson, wearing a white shirt and a sacking apron tied around his middle, stepped down from the top step outside his shop, his muscular arms folded. 'If the Gylby family need any provisions, will you tell them they only have to ask?'

She looked into his concerned hazel eyes with surprise, remembering Mary's earlier condemnation of the man, and pleased he wasn't as tight-fisted as Mary had said.

'I do know they need some oats and flour, Mr Parkinson,' she said.

'Come into the shop, Mrs Waspill, and I'll weigh some out for you. If you could take them to the family, with my condolences, I would be very much obliged to you.' The Scot's voice was soft and musical, but it was his kind tone that made Merrilla feel a

130

pricking behind her eyes. Did she have the strength to climb the two steps leading into the shop?

The aroma in the shop came from an assortment of food: smoked hams and herbs hanging from the high ceiling; wooden boxes filled with tea and spices; bacon, ready to be cut into juicy slices; and fruit piled into boxes. Sweets and jams in glass jars sat on the mahogany counter next to a thick tub of butter, ready to be cut with a wire and patted into handy blocks, and numerous cheaper goods were piled around, for few folk in the village could afford luxuries.

Although the shop was warm, Merrilla shivered and pulled her shawl closer as she watched the big man lift a large sack of oats, shake off the clinging sawdust, and carry the sack to a set of scales on the long counter. All of a sudden reaction set in, and she began shaking. Unable to keep them back any longer, tears flowed. She tried wiping them away with a corner of her shawl in the hope that Mr Parkinson wouldn't notice. Strong arms wrapped around her and, incapable of preventing it, she was drawn against the shopkeeper's broad chest, weeping too hard to protest at the spontaneous consolation.

'Hist. Hist, now. Weep. Weep away.'

It had been many years since she had had such a feeling of security and oh, how she wanted to stay locked in his strong arms.

A caring hand smoothed and patted her head. She flushed, aware that her hair was clogged with damp coal dust. At last, her tears abated and she saw a well-trimmed beard, a sensitive mouth, a mop of curly brown hair, and hazel eyes smiling into hers.

'Have you finished now, lassie?' William still held her close. 'You should feel better for that, I'd imagine.'

Merrilla pushed against his waistcoat in embarrassment but William seemed reluctant to let her go. 'Oh, sir, I'm so sorry.

Please, I don't know what came over me.' Mortified that a strange man should have touched her so intimately, her cheeks were fiery as she stammered out her apology. 'It...It was horrendous down there. Never in my life have I been subjected to such a sight,' she murmured, with another shiver.

He looked at her with concern. 'Yes, Mrs Waspill. I heard it was a bad one. I'm told they had fire this time. You've been very brave, Mrs Waspill. After all, you're new here, and unused to these kinds of disasters. I heard it was you who carried Freddie up the ladders.'

Nodding, she shivered again. *What's the matter with me? Why can't I control myself?* Glancing at her trembling hands, she thought, *I'll perhaps feel better when I've had a hot drink.*

'You're cold. Will you allow me to take you upstairs? My mother has a good fire in her room, and she'll help you dry your things and refresh yourself.'

Startled when they heard a banging on the floor above, they glanced up at the high ceiling and she looked at William with alarm as a querulous voice echoed through the room. 'William! William! What are you doing down there? William, have you a customer?'

Leaving Merrilla standing by the counter, William strode to a flight of wooden stairs in the corner and, leaning on the stair rail, shouted, 'I have a young lady here, Mamma. May I bring her to meet you?' A voice floated down, telling her to join a lonely old lady starved of company. Smiling, he beckoned her forward.

She followed him up the staircase and found herself in a space covering the whole shop area, part of which was divided into cubicles, through a combination of boxes of stock and oak furniture, coupled with velvet curtains hanging on poles and tied in place with tasselled ropes. Her eyes were drawn to an old lady dressed in black, her silver hair curled in a style she recognised as one her grandmother favoured.

Before moving forward, she sank into a deep curtsy, her back poker straight and her chin held high, in the manner of a lady of fashion. Sadly, she spoilt the effect by collapsing in a heap on the floor.

'What on earth? William! Whatever are you thinking of, bringing this bunch of rags here. Get rid of her!' Mrs Parkinson cried, rising swiftly for such an elderly lady, and flapping her hands at her son. 'Oh, the stench of her!' With a hand over her nose, the old lady backed away.

'This young woman has seen sights today, Mother, that you could never imagine. Go and fetch a blanket to cover her.' William's tone permitted no argument.

He lifted her and carried her nearer to the fire. Then, laying her on the rug, he pulled a cushion from his mother's chair and placed it under her head. His hands were on her bodice, ready to unbutton it, when his mother pushed him away.

'Go and lock the shop door, and fetch me some water. I'll do this.' All the time she worked on Merrilla, Mrs Parkinson grumbled. 'Look here, wet through. Filthy rags. Holes as large as sovereigns in the soles of her boots. Better find something to make her decent. I have an old dress somewhere.' She continued muttering under her breath when she found numerous cuts and grazes. After washing her with perfumed soap, none too gently, she wrapped her in an old blanket.

Her son spoke from behind the curtain in a firm voice that invited no comment. 'A nightgown will be best, Mother.'

Mrs Parkinson pulled back the curtain and looked at him in astonishment. Her lips pursed, she obeyed and found her oldest nightgown, placed the garment, with its innumerable neatly-sewn darns, over Merrilla's head and pulled it into place. 'Boil a kettle, William. She needs a hot drink.' Pointing with distaste at the discarded clothes, she added, 'And get rid of that filth.'

A long moan from Merrilla made them both turn to her in dismay. Her eyelids fluttered. She saw a blurred figure bending over her. 'Grandmamma,' she whispered.

'I say she's not staying here. I cannot have this creature in my home. You don't know who she is or where she's from. I'll probably wake tomorrow and find we've been robbed, or worse.'

'Mother, we cannot just turn her out. She's ill.'

'Oh, yes, we can. Send her back to her friends; let them take care of her. I will not nurse her, and you cannot. You have a shop to run.'

Merrilla struggled to sit up. With surprise she found herself in a comfortable chair, covered with blankets. 'I am... I'm so sorry,' she whispered.

'I should think so too. A fine thing to do, swooning on a person's hearthrug. Stay the night, but you go home in the morning. You need someone to look after you, and I'll not turn myself into a nurse at my time of life.' The clipped tone left Merrilla in no doubt that she was unwelcome.

'Please, Mrs Waspill, drink this.' William shot a warning glance at his mother, before holding out a steaming tankard towards Merrilla.

She took it nervously. 'Thank you. What is this?' she whispered.

'It's a hot flannel. Beer, gin, sugar, and a dash of nutmeg. It will dispel your chill. When you've drunk it all, you can sleep.' He tucked the blanket over Merrilla's shoulder and smiled. 'Tomorrow I'll take you home.'

As the warmth from the drink flowed through her, she closed her eyes. *Tomorrow I can go home to Mamma and Papa*, she thought, as she drifted into a deep slumber. She barely felt her legs being lifted onto a footstool, or another blanket being gently draped over her. Even in the early hours of the morning, when

William put more coals on the fire and removed the wooden shutters from the shop windows, she hardly stirred.

'Do you wish breakfast, Mrs Waspill?' It was a man's voice.

Merrilla's eyes flew open. She looked in astonishment at the face near to her own.

'Oh. How? Where? Oh...' Memories of the previous evening came back, and she struggled to sit upright in the chair. She relaxed when she saw Mrs Parkinson, wearing a nightgown and cap, walk across the room towards her.

'After breakfast, you go home. Wash your face over there, in that corner.' Mrs Parkinson pointed to a curtain which had been partly pushed to one side.

Still a little dizzy when she rose to her feet, and with a great deal of concentration, Merrilla rose to her feet and walked towards the curtain without falling. A jug of warm water and a bowl stood on a washstand, and a soft towel lay beside it. After washing her hands and face with a bar of lavender-scented soap she felt better.

'I have salt with my porridge. If you don't enjoy it made this way, you'll have to go without,' Mrs. Parkinson said when Merrilla returned to her chair.

'I prefer porridge with salt, Mrs Parkinson,' she replied. She smiled at William when he placed a tray on her knees containing a bowl of porridge and a cup of tea.

'I sent a boy to Mrs O'Keaf's house for fresh clothes, and to let them know you were safe,' he said.

Merrilla murmured, 'Thank you,' and began to eat. It was the first meal she had eaten since the previous morning, and she felt ravenous. William toasted bread with the heat of the fire; it smelt wonderful. He buttered it and passed some to each of them. Merrilla enjoyed every mouthful.

Mrs Parkinson watched her. 'You can change over there behind the curtain. Perhaps then I can sit in my own chair,' the old lady said, nodding towards a pile of clothes on a stool.

It didn't take many minutes to dress. She felt thankful to see someone had had the wits to send her best dress, her Sunday shawl, and her other pair of boots. When she appeared from behind the curtain, she found William's mother alone. 'I thank you for your hospitality, Mrs Parkinson,' she said, holding out her hand.

The old lady coughed as she picked up the breakfast tray, ignoring the proffered hand. 'Best thing for you is to get home to your family. Your husband will be sober by now, no doubt, and your children will be crying for their mother.'

'I'm a widow, Mrs Parkinson, and I have no children or...or family,' she said, fighting back tears. She had no intention of letting this old harridan know how cutting her words were. 'Good day, madam.'

When she went down into the shop, she had to wait for a moment while William served a customer she recognised as a woman living a few doors away from her lodgings on the same street. She was dressed in black.

'You look much better this morning, lassie. Can I offer an apology for my mother?' William said, pushing his fingers through his hair in embarrassment. Bobbing a curtsy and thanking him in her soft voice, Merrilla left the shop with some oatmeal and flour, and returned home, determined to do her best to help the Gylby family in their grief.

Chapter 9

Nancy Turpin's transformation into a beautiful and confident young woman rapidly brought her to the attention of Mr Pugh, the cotton mill's supervisor. At first, her natural cunning and artful scheming concealed her lack of education. When Polly Goodly took her in hand, and began teaching her how sentences and paragraphs were put together, her writing improved, and once she had mastered her times-tables, she found the adding and subtracting of numbers came easily.

At first Mr Pugh had laughed at her efforts to understand the complexities of the running of the factory and how to use the workforce to its full capacity. But when he realised that the girl seriously wanted to learn, he kept her by his side and explained patiently, so she understood why things were done. Gradually, Nancy became indispensable, and ended up as his second in command. He increased her wage, which led her, one day, to wave her wage-packet joyfully at Polly, and insist they had a splendid meal at a nearby inn and that she would pay the bill. She kept her wits about her, watched and listened to Mr Pugh's orders, and began to understand how each job in the mill was analysed in terms of cost-benefit.

One day he allowed her to write columns of figures in the firm's ledgers, and he patted and squeezed her shoulder in approval at her neat writing.

Everything turned sour when he grew too attentive. He clearly saw her as more than just a mill girl but as his creation. Having taught her everything, she owed him for raising her from the workforce on the factory floor, or so he obviously thought. A moment in the dark corner of the stockroom gave him the opportunity to push Nancy against a bale of cotton and lift her skirts. Instinctively she raised her knee. Luckily for him, his hand was fumbling with his trouser buttons, and he was saved from a more painful injury.

'You bitch, I didn't mean any harm!'

'I'm a good girl,' she panted, as she dodged around a bail of cotton. She managed to reach the lamp beside the door and held it high, ready to dash it on the ground. 'I'll torch the place if you come any closer.'

He slithered to a halt, a hand stretched towards her. Her eyes were blazing, and her bosom heaving. 'Now, Nancy, Nancy, my dear one. Don't get so upset. You can't blame me for trying to steal a little kiss. Being so close to you made me forget myself.'

'I bet it did. Well, in future, keep you hands to yourself. I'll let you know when a liberty can be taken.'

Her eyes narrowed as he stepped closer. After a slight movement of her arm, he moved back. 'We have work to do, girl. Can't play about here all day. Get to the office and make a start on those books. I'll see to things in here,' he said, as he fastened his buttons. With a flick of her long skirt, she left.

After that encounter, she endeavoured not to be alone in the stockroom with him, although she allowed him a touch or two when they were in the office. He could dismiss her. And where would she be without her wage, which had now been increased to almost double its original amount? Apart from that, she enjoyed the thrill of watching the workers below, busy with their tedious work, unaware that Mr Pugh was enjoying furtive fumbling under her skirts.

As the coach driver drove through Nottingham Town, he cursed most prolifically, and at the same time whipped his horse, and beggar any crossing-sweeper in his way. Thankful to alight from the rocking vehicle, John Larcombe and Hugo Denstone gazed in dismay at the factory walls towering on either side of the street. Rows of rusty iron bars, set in crumbling brickwork, were only inches from filthy windows, some rising four and five stories high. The air of gloom and neglect caused them to glance up and down the street and then at each other. A slatternly woman standing in a doorway, holding a snivelling child to her uncovered breast, glanced at them before turning her back on them. An ill-clad man, further along, tried to tempt a group of gossiping women to buy pots and pans or have their knives sharpened. Urchins appeared as though from nowhere, artfully walking with outstretched hands, sensing that the two toffs would be a pushover for a sad tale. Discreetly, Hugo dropped some small coins into their eager hands and shook his head at the remaining pleading children.

John Larcombe turned to climb back into the carriage, but the driver had cracked his whip, and the vehicle was already in motion, pursued along the street by small boys and barking dogs.

'Look, sir, there's Mr Harwood.' Hugo sounded as relieved as John felt when they saw the familiar figure of their agent hurrying towards them.

'This location is dreadful. I feel most unsafe,' John said, shaking the agent's hand.

'It wouldn't do to linger here after dark. Taverns abound in these parts, and drunken people often lurk in doors and alleyways.' The agent glanced over his shoulder at a bearded man who leaned against a wall, watching them. 'The people who work at the mill live locally. Families are employed together wherever possible, so the parents can keep the young ones in order. If they don't control their children at work, the whole family are sacked. There are plenty of others to take their places.' With annoyance, a handkerchief to his nose, he glared at half a dozen ragged children, close enough for their odour to upset him. He waved his cane at them and the children scattered. They followed at a distance and stared at the men until the party passed through a pair of open ornamental gates into a yard stinking of horse mess. It was obviously a busy place.

'This is where deliveries to the mill are made,' said Mr Harwood, pointing with his cane to a wide, open wooden door. As a horse and cart entered the yard, the men moved to one side and backed into place in front of the doors. The driver called two workmen out of the building, and they helped him to unload a number of heavy, square bales, wrapped in sacking.

As the agent moved towards the yard gates, John saw a small child in the doorway, near to the bales of cotton. He touched Hugo's arm and pointed to the child.

'The main doors leading into the factory are in the street around the corner,' Mr Harwood called. 'Please follow me, gentlemen.'

He climbed three wide, stone steps, freshly whitened with a donkey stone, and pushed open a pair of brown-painted doors. John Larcombe, needing the aid of his gold-topped cane, followed him.

Hugo wrinkled his nose as a warm damp stench enveloped them. The place was very different to their mill, although a similar rough-wooden floor vibrated with the throbbing of working machinery. They cast their eyes over the nearest machines with interest. Haggard, weary, grim-faced workers, ignoring the three men who were appraising the situation, continued working on the threads with automatic concentration.

Hugo's heart gave a lurch and he caught his breath. He removed his hat, fighting off the impulse to catch hold of the slender hand of a girl whose eyes shone like amethysts. Instead, he gave her a slight bow and a smile. The girl, lowering her eyelashes, gave a perfect curtsy and charmed him with her dimpled cheeks and flashing smile.

Her hands clasped in front of her, she shouted above the clamour of the machinery, 'Is there someone you wish to see, gentlemen?'

Mr Harwood stepped forward and, cupping his hand round his mouth, said loudly, 'We wish to speak to the overseer.'

'Mr Pugh, he's the overseer. He's up there, in his office.' She pointed to a high window where a man looked down at them. The office door slammed open, and the portly man with a high complexion hurried down a wooden staircase, pulling on his coat and straightening his wig.

'I'm Pugh, gentlemen. I've been expecting you. Will you please come this way up to my office?' He shot an annoyed glance at the girl, hovering nearby, probably trying to catch the conversation.

As he reached the office, Hugo watched her walk to where one of the machines was being re-threaded. Her movements were graceful, and he could see the rise of her milky breasts above the neckline of her dress. *However did that beauty get employment in this dreadful place?* he thought. She lifted both arms, and tucked a stray curl inside her cap. Upon hearing a small cough, he realised Mr Harwood was waiting for him on the staircase. With a sheepish grin and another glance at the girl, he hurried to join the others.

Mr Pugh pulled out chairs and placed a high stool next to the ink-stained table that filled the centre of the office. Above their heads, sunshine struggled through a dirt-covered skylight. Further illumination came from a common oil lamp, its untrimmed wick giving off an acrid smell.

Mr Harwood seated himself on the stool, and rested his hands on the table as Mr Pugh unlocked a glass-fronted bookcase. 'I had a message from the owner saying to expect a visit from you gentlemen, and to have all the ledgers ready for your inspection, sirs.' The obese man lifted half a dozen heavy books from the bookcase and laid them out side-by-side on the table. No one spoke as he proceeded to make a great show of taking a key from his waistcoat pocket and opening a small safe. He placed the contents on the table in front of the agent and, his chest puffed out, and both hands behind his back, he stood near the door and watched Mr Harwood open the largest ledger.

Hugo and John turned to look out of the window overlooking the factory floor. Men and women, deftly using their fingers on the threads, worked along the walkway in front of long machines. Hugo leaned forward and pointed with a shaking finger. 'See there? Look, a small child. She's just come out from under that working machine. There's another one, see?' Girls as young as five or six were emptying small baskets filled with wads of cotton into a round tub almost as high as themselves. Set at the end of each machine, waiting to be used, were other tubs full of greasy cotton.

John pointed with his cane to a boy, a little older, but still a child, working close to some spinning bobbins, using a broom taller than himself. 'See there? The boy?' he said, with tight lips. He beckoned the overseer to stand beside them. 'That will have to change.' He pointed down at the factory floor. 'I'll not have children near moving machinery.' Frowning, and tapping the gold knob of his cane on his chin, he glanced at Hugo, adding, 'None of the machines have safety rails. We would have to alter them and do something similar to what we did in our Stoney Street factory.'

'I see the girls all have their hair hanging loose,' said Hugo. 'That habit must change immediately. Get them all to wear caps, for we don't want long hair caught in the moving machinery. That must be one of the first changes.'

At Mr Pugh's sly glance, John motioned him to move closer. The mixture of body odour and his cheap pomade was powerful and Hugo, nearest to him, moved a step away.

'How many hours do these children work, Mr Pugh?' John asked. The tightness of his gloved hands squeezing his cane showed the extent of his displeasure.

'Erm...they start work at six each morning, sir. They finish between seven or eight o'clock at night. I lets them have a half-hour break at midday if they've worked their quota, so they can play awhile.' The overseer swallowed nervously, and mopped his sweating face with a grubby handkerchief. He glanced uneasily at Mr Harwood, who was still turning pages in the first ledger, and tried to see which page he was looking at.

'Sunday School?' John Larcombe snapped, staring through the window at the workers below.

The piggy eyes of the overseer bulged in amazement. 'Sunday School?' he echoed, glancing at Hugo, and back again at John Larcombe. 'I...I don't quite understand you, sir.'

'Do these children attend a school each Sunday? Are they taught to read? Do they have religious instruction, Mr Pugh?' John spoke slowly so the overseer could not fail to understand.

'No, sir. No, Mr Larcombe. We can't stop the machines, and we need brats to keep the under parts of the machines oiled.' Again Mr Pugh used his handkerchief, sweat running freely.

'Come, come, man. Low rents, Mr Pugh? Do these people receive a wage if they are sick?' John's eyes were a flinty blue as he stared into those of the overseer. Mr Pugh, giving a shiver, dropped his gaze and shook his head. 'Do those workers down there get any benefits?' John continued.

With a backward step, Mr Pugh lifted his chin. 'Sir, I'm the overseer. I do only what the owner tells me. As long as the machines are working and we produce our full quota of thread, everyone's satisfied.' His shoulders lifted in an indifferent shrug, he continued, 'They're paid a wage for the work they do, Mr Larcombe. They don't ask for more than that.'

The sharp snap of a book closing made the overseer jump and spin around to face Mr Harwood.

'I find difficulties with your records, Mr Pugh. I'll need to look at them in much more detail.' The agent looked at John. 'Maybe it would be best if both Mr Hugo and my accounts clerks examined these books? The owner has given me carte-blanche in my enquiries.'

Mr Pugh mopped his face again.

'We will examine the premises, and take a closer look at the machinery now, Mr Pugh.' Hugo opened the office door. The noise of chugging machines filled their ears, like a pulse beating its way out of their heads. John and Hugo walked together. Mr Harwood followed, and Mr Pugh moved from one man to the other, trying to explain the working of the mill and answer questions.

Hugo asked why the tall and narrow windows couldn't be opened to let in fresh air. Mr Pugh informed him that the windows remained sealed because the temperature needed to be kept constant. John's concern was evident in his expression, as he watched pale children flitting around the machines like spectres. He glared when a man yelled insults at a woman who'd allowed a thread to break, but made no comment.

The tour of the mill completed, Mr Pugh beckoned Nancy forward. She'd been watching every movement they had made, following behind the men.

'Go fetch a hackney cab. Tell the driver to wait outside the front door for the gentlemen,' he ordered.

She curtsied, fluttering her eyelashes in Hugo's direction before hurrying away.

Bowing and scraping, Mr Pugh escorted the three men outside. As they passed her, she bobbed another curtsy. While he waited to enter the cab Hugo glanced towards her standing in the factory doorway and acknowledged her by slightly lifting his hand. Nancy stepped further inside, hugged herself, and half-smiled at the cow-like looks he gave her. *You'll do for me, my dear. You can be my first real lover. It seems likely, by the looks of you, it'll be your first time, so I'll not be catching the pox. I'll let you go all the way. With luck I might get in the family way, and then I'd be set up for life,* she thought.

As the cab moved along the street, urchins clung to the back of the vehicle, whooping with fright and delight as they hitched a ride. The overseer had bowed low so many times he looked giddy. He rubbed his bulbous nose with his finger and, a sneer twisting his lips, he stomped across the cobblestones to where she stood. He pushed her so roughly to one side she overbalanced. She let out a cry of, 'What you do that for?'

'What was you looking at, you no good slattern? Giving the young 'un the glad-eye won't do you any good.' Pushing his face near to hers, he growled, 'Tell this lot here to double their quota, else their pay packets will be light. And fetch me a jug of ale!'

Still muttering under his breath, he strode towards the office. Unfortunately, he stumbled over a child. His hand shot out, clouting the child's ear. 'Get from under my feet, you bloody nuisance!' he yelled.

With a hand over her stinging ear, the little girl slunk away to hide in a corner to snivel out of sight. The child knew better than to weep or complain to her elders. The workers nearby bent their heads, and pretended not to have seen the incident.

Nancy hurried to the tavern across the street. The taproom was busy, but as soon as the landlord saw the identity of his customer, she was served a full measure. With a white napkin covering the jug of ale, she hurried back to the mill. She gasped when she saw the state of the office. Books and papers were strewn across the table and the floor. Standing in the doorway open-mouthed, she stared at the overseer.

145

He gave a snort of disgust, swore, and threw down a paper he was reading. 'All these bloody years I've been left in charge. I've always made a nice little profit for the owner, and a bit extra to put away for my old age. Now these so-called gentlemen come here. "There will be changes if we buy the business,"' he sneered, 'Bah!' A sheaf of papers fluttered to the floor as a thick arm swept them off the table. 'It's a good thing I have you to depend on, Nancy. At least you'll help me to run this place as it should be run, won't you, my pet?'

She made no reply. Keeping the table between them, she placed the jug alongside a tankard, closed the office door, and hurried down the stairs with her thoughts whirling. *Maybe this is my chance for a rich lover. Or even a husband. Lots of new men working here, and if I can't catch that gentleman I've seen today I might snare one of the others. I'll make my fortune, one way or the other. I'll get out of this place and be like that young lady Bill Waspill knows and have beautiful clothes and my own carriage, just like her.*

Nathan Denstone turned in his saddle to look towards his companion, and called, 'Strange we have not seen any people in the village, Philip.'

'It's this storm, damn it. Everyone's staying inside next to a fireplace, and I for one don't blame them.' Philip bent his head and allowed water to run off the brim of his sodden hat, but the water splashed onto his breeches and ran down his leg into his leather boot, causing him even more discomfort. He swore under his breath. His heavy box coat had, until then, kept his breeches almost dry.

It was late afternoon. Hooves splashed and slipped. The horses were as weary as the men who rode them. A sudden shaft of sunlight struggling through the clouds threw up rainbow colours

146

from the cobblestones, but the men were in no mood to appreciate the rare beauty. They eyed the mud and filth running along the gutter with trepidation for they had no wish to tumble into it. With no direct road from Glasgow to Paxton Village the men had followed numerous unmarked sheep tracks through miles of moorland.

Along a street with rows of low grey-tiled houses, the glow of a lantern shone in a window. 'It seems there's some kind of shop over there, Mr Denstone,' said Philip. 'Shall I go and enquire if there's any chance of racking up somewhere for the night? There may be an inn nearby. If not, they'll say if we have much further to go before reaching Paxton Village.' As he handed the reins of his horse to Nathan, a spectacular sight of sheet lightning flashed over the hills in the far distance.

When he came out of the shop he said, 'We have arrived. The shopkeeper said the only place to lodge with comfort in Paxton is with a Mrs O'Keaf. Her house is a step or two along the street, and she may not be at home. Most folk are at the kirk, attending a funeral. Some days ago, an accident at the mine killed a dozen or more people. Seems it's a frequent calamity.' He took the reins of his horse, and made his way along the street, trying to avoid the puddles.

Philip's knock brought Mrs O'Keaf to the door, wearing a bonnet with black ribbons. Obviously surprised to see strangers, she opened the door wide. He removed his hat, and giving a slight bow, inquired about accommodation. Small faces, pressing against the banister rails, tried to catch a view of the posh-sounding visitor. Philip grinned.

Mrs O'Keaf went all of a twitter. Still holding the door, she called, 'Come down, you boys. Look sharp, and hold the gentlemen's horses.' As the children scampered towards them, she stepped back to prevent her toes being trampled. She turned back to Philip. 'I've a room at the top of the house, sir, large enough for two.'

When Nathan moved forward to stand next to Philip, her eyes widened at the fine cut of his clothes, and she bobbed a curtsy to the elder gentleman. 'Oh, sirs, please come in.'

'Seems we're in luck, Mr Denstone.'

'Champion.'

Nathan bowed to Mrs O'Keaf and gave her such a winning smile that the poor woman became all the more flustered, and stumbled over herself in her haste to escort them to the room. The smell of cooked food and cheap candles wafted from behind the closed doors on each landing, reminding them they had not eaten since that morning.

On the top landing she flung open a door. They followed her inside to find the furnishings rather shabby, but the room contained a large four-poster bed, with clean sheets and a thick feather quilt. A bare wooden cupboard stood beside the fireplace, and a table and chairs occupied the space next to two large windows overlooking the street.

'You can stable the horses in the shed behind the house. They'll have to share with my hens, but I don't suppose they'll mind.' After lighting a candle on the table, she pulled the drapes closed at the windows, stood with her hands clasped in front of her, and looked at each man in turn. 'I usually ask for two weeks rent up front.' Her face brightened, and she bobbed a curtsy when Nathan handed her without question not only what she had asked for, but also a further month's rent.

With a thankful sigh, Philip closed the door behind her, and leaned against it.

Nathan tried to hide a yawn, glancing longingly at the bed.

'Will it suit, Mr Denstone?'

'Aye.'

'You rest awhile now, and I'll go and fetch the luggage and rub down the horses.'

Giving a weary nod of agreement, Nathan shrugged off his sodden coat.

Philip hung it on one of the nails placed in the door for that purpose, before making his way to the shed at the back of the house, pleasantly surprised to find the building warm with a good supply of straw stacked in the corner.

Most of the children from the lodging house were gathered there. They were too young to appreciate the quality of the hand-stitched leather baggage and saddlebags, but they watched his every movement as he unsaddled the horses, brushed mud from their coats, and inspected and cleaned each hoof. It wasn't until he beckoned the tallest boy forward to ask where the water pump was that the children relaxed.

'Where you from, mister? You talk funny. Have you come a long way?'

Philip carried a leather bucket to the pump and they followed him. With one glance at their upturned faces, he motioned the eldest boy to step forward, took a coin from his pocket, and slipped it into the boy's hand, whispering, 'Go to the shop and buy some bread, butter and cheese, and treat yourself and the other children with the money left over.'

The boy gave a whoop of delight, and shot out the door, calling to the other children to follow him to Parkinson's shop for sweet bonbons and comfits.

At three-thirty the following morning, Philip and Nathan were awakened by noise. They lay listening to the sounds of movement in the house. Doors banged, and the murmuring of voices was like disjointed music. At the clatter of boots marching on the cobblestones under their windows, Philip sat up and threw back the bedclothes. Curiosity drew him to the window to find out what it was all about. People walking to work. Stars were still visible. He scratched his chest, and yawned as he moved towards the bed. The bed curtains were still drawn together, but he heard Nathan grunt and turn over. It would be quite some time before he arose. Heat still radiated from the fire and, using a metal poker to stir the embers, he dropped a few coals on top in the hope of heating a kettle for water to shave.

The sun shone and the streets were dry when they emerged from Mrs O'Keaf's lodging house. It seemed that every housewife in the village needed to donkey-stone her front step, or to polish a window. At each curtsy from the women, Nathan lifted his hat, and Philip nodded an acknowledgement.

'Word has flown around that strangers are in the district, Mr Denstone,' Philip said, as they left the last house behind, and walked past the gate of the smithy.

Nathan chuckled. 'Happen you're reet!' he said jovially, in a broad Yorkshire accent.

Philip strode forward with a grin. That was how most of the lower servants spoke at home, and his thoughts turned to his family.

They had reached as far as the churchyard when Nathan's expression became serious. 'Last night, while you were seeing to the horses, I wrote a letter to Mr Paxton, asking him to meet us at the coalmine. I want to see for myself what he has to offer before we talk business. We mustn't waste our brass.' He stopped, removed his hat, and dabbed at his face with a handkerchief, before adding, 'I'm wishing now that I had put on my other wig instead of this heavy periwig.'

They did not hasten, enjoying their stroll in the sunshine after riding for so long in all kinds of weather. At a gap in a blackthorn hedge, Philip used his cane to bend back a prickly branch, to see how much further they had to walk. 'Have you noticed how quiet it is, Mr Denstone? The mines I visited in Yorkshire were noisy with clanking winding gear, and the iron straked wheels on the coal-tubs rumbled like thunder. The only sounds here are birdsong and our footsteps. You would never think there were folk working nearby,' he added as he let the branches spring back into place.

Further along the road, they had a clear view down the hill to the river and the wharf. Four barges were moored in line, and a dozen or so distant figures were going about their business. He pointed with his cane. 'Those barges are ready to take on coal, so the mine must be nearby.'

'Mr Paxton claims the coal is of an excellent quality, and is brought to the surface in great quantities. I must say the signs so far do not bear out his opinion.'

'Why are not more people loading the boats, if the coal is coming out in such great quantities? And I would have expected many more boats waiting to take coal on board,' Philip said, with a frown. 'Whereas actually there are a fair number of tubs standing on the wharf.'

They continued walking in silence until Nathan stopped. 'You're right, my boy. I'd have thought we'd have heard something more from this distance. This silence is unnatural.'

'Maybe they've closed the mine because of the funeral. After all...'

The sound of a bell and a hooter made them glance at each other in alarm.

'Struth! What on earth's that?' Nathan said, turning pale.

'It's trouble! Another disaster!' yelled Philip. Sprinting away down the road, he prayed, 'Oh God, not more lives lost.'

His hat gripped with one hand, and his wig with the other, Nathan followed as quickly as his legs would allow, but Philip was well out of sight by the time the portly man reached the bend in the road.

Untidy tufts of grass and clumps of stunted weeds, covered in a coating of dust, grew alongside the walls of the low brick buildings in the colliery yard. A dozen or so tearful women stood looking around and talking together, each with a wicker basket on the ground by her feet. Their eyes brightened with hope when Philip ran towards them, but their shoulders slumped again when they saw that it was a gentleman wearing fine clothes.

In his haste Philip skidded and almost fell as he hurried across the stony ground. Grim-faced men glanced at him as they shuffled around the yard, some gathered in small groups, muttering and gesturing to their companions. He could almost taste the tension and the hatred of the miners, and he saw how they glowered at a man standing beside a pair of matching bays harnessed to a smart green and black curricle.

He stared in amazement at the extraordinary appearance of a man, about his own age, standing with one hand on his hip and the other holding a tall gold and ivory staff trimmed with blue tassels. The man was in a coat of palest blue silk and a waistcoat of silver grey, yellow breeches, and grey silk stockings without a hint of a wrinkle. His beaver hat sat at a jaunty angle on top of his shoulder-length ginger curls, and was embellished with small blue bows. He would not have looked out of place walking in Hyde Park... but there? The contrast of such a person against the surrounding greyness seemed unreal.

Dishevelled and feeling at a disadvantage after his run, Philip approached the vision in blue, who elaborately and pompously shook back the ruffles from his wrist, raised a quizzing glass to his eye, and directed his gaze at him. It was an effort to keep a straight face as he approached the curricle.

An old man wrapped in a large plaid shawl peered at him from the open doorway. His eyes darted from one young man to the other, obviously amused by the comparison.

'Mr Paxton? Philip Larcombe at your service, sir.' Bowing low, he hastily raised a hand to his mouth to hide his grin, as the dandy lifted his nose higher and waved a lace handkerchief at him. As Nathan Denstone's portly figure puffed across the yard towards them, the dandy once more raised his eyeglass, and turned his full attention to the stranger.

The alarm continued to echo.

'I am Denstone, sir. Streuth! What a dreadful noise.' Leaning on his cane, Nathan tried to catch his breath, while his eyes roved over the man in blue with awed wonder. He swallowed hard, before saying, 'Thought you would be somewhat older, lad.' His blunt statement made the young man pale under his make-up, and the black velvet patch showed more clearly on his rouged cheek.

'This, sir, is Mr Paxton, the owner of the colliery. I am his son, Anthony.' He gave another wave of the scent-drenched handkerchief, this time directed towards the open door of the curricle.

'Good day to you, sirs.' A weak, quavering voice emerged from the depths of the shawl.

'What is all the noise about, Mr Paxton? What is all the to-do?' Philip directed his question to the man in the curricle but he glanced at Anthony.

From where he stood, Philip could see people streaming down the road from the direction of the village, entering the yard at a run. Some, finding a husband, wife, son or daughter, hugged them and wept with relief to find them safe. The dark looks aimed at him by a group of scowling miners hovering nearby made him uncomfortable.

'Oh, it's nothing of import. These fellows will say that there's been a kind of accident or some such thing. Gives them an excuse to stop working. Rabble will say anything to justify their lazy ways. Sure to be a pack of lies.'

Anthony Paxton's careless words were followed by a chuckle from his father. 'Years ago, I employed an army of masons to cut stone for building houses in the village, just so this rabble had a roof over their mucky heads. I treat them well enough. Most of the people living here were paupers brought from Glasgow. A few families are Irish peasants who complained they were starving in their own country. This place is so remote they can't find other work or move away, so you'll always have coalminers. Pay little and work them hard. You'll soon reap your reward if you purchase the pit.' Both father and son sniggered, old Mr Paxton coughing and wheezing.

Philip's hands tightened into fists, and he drew back his arm as though to hit the dandy in his sneering mouth. Anthony stepped back with his arm lifted in alarm.

Nathan Denstone caught hold of Philip, saying, 'Now, lad, that won't help the workers.'

With a glare of disapproval at the dandy, Philip relaxed.

A furious yell rang out from the crowd of miners as a cloud of black dust belched out of the mineshaft. Nathan gasped with horror and nudged Philip, pulling out his handkerchief, and holding it over his nose and mouth. When the dust settled over them everyone coughed.

Philip turned to the Paxton men and asked, 'Where is the winding machinery to bring up the people from below? And how do you pump out the water?'

There was no answer from the father. The son, holding his perfumed scrap of lace against his lips, shrugged his padded shoulders.

The hubbub around them worsened. Workmen ran, yelling at each other, pointing towards the entrance of the mine. Weeping women had hands over their faces, or wiped away tears with the corner of their shawls.

The dandy gave a limp wave with his handkerchief in the general direction of the coal-blackened people. 'Oh, they manage well enough,' he drawled. 'They climb a ladder, and bring water up in buckets when it becomes a problem.'

'Buckets?' Philip's jaw dropped.

A dozen or so workmen moved closer, gesturing in their direction while speaking earnestly to one of their companions. He was pushed forward by his workmates. The man dropped to his knees a spit away from Philip's feet. 'Sirs, I beg you, hear me.' The man twisted his cap with grimed hands and pushed it under his unshaven chin.

Nathan stepped nearer.

Philip crouched and said, 'Speak, man. What is it? What do you wish to tell me?'

'Disaster, sir. Calamity. Another roof fall. Some trapped, some dead, sir.' The coal dust covering the miner's pit pallor emphasised his pinched face and fear-filled eyes.

Philip paled. He directed a sharp glance at the man in delicate blue. 'Are you coming to see what we can do to help, Mr Paxton?' His expression showed his contempt when he saw the horrified look on the young man's rouged face, and saw him dab at his forehead with his lace-edged handkerchief. Throwing his cane inside the carriage, the elegant figure clambered into the curricle, ignoring his father's curses as he fell over the old man's knees. As he yelled to the driver to whip the horses, Philip ran towards the mineshaft, ignoring Nathan calling, 'Wait, Philip. See what we have to do from up here first.'

He pulled off his coat and threw it to a group of women standing by the entrance before lowering himself onto the rungs of the ladder. On the first platform he waited, leaning to one side, to make way for a woman carrying a heavy basket on her back. She continued climbing to the surface. The dusty air making him cough, he pulled out his handkerchief, and tied it around his mouth.

Voices shouted, 'Roofs gone.'

'Fire's burned some folk.'

'Childer killed.'

'Mr Lang's missing at t'other end of pit.'

The words echoed, and bounced off the walls.

Before the explosion, Merrilla had been instructed to take a message to Mr Lang. She was standing beside him when the explosion threw them both on the floor. She was scared witless, and the inevitable hysterics led him to smack her face. Then he held her trembling body until she finished weeping and became calm.

'It's all right, lass. Don't worry. We'll get out,' he said, glancing at the roof. A shower of stones rained down, and he pulled her to one side. More cracks appeared and a wooden support nearby groaned under the added weight. If it gave way they would be buried. Four other people who were also uninjured joined them.

He picked up the miner's lamp he'd dropped, fortunately still alight. With it held high, he moved the few yards to a pile of solid earth and rubble. Everyone stared at the debris blocking the tunnel.

'We don't know how far we'll have to dig, but if we start from this side the people who'll be coming to fetch us out will have less work to do.' Hooking the handle of the lamp on a projection of rock, he bent to lift a large stone near his feet.

'They know we're here. I told my husband I'd be in these workings,' a woman said, as she rolled her sleeves almost up to her shoulders.

Without another word, everyone began the dangerous work of reopening the tunnel.

When he stepped off the ladder at the bottom of the mineshaft, Philip stared in disbelief. A crowd of people milled around in the dim light, some in deep shock, weeping or gazing into nothingness. Grim-faced women tried to comfort children and each other whilst their menfolk dug and pulled at the debris. Two women placed baskets near to a row of motionless bodies in readiness to carry the dreadful contents to the surface.

A man, arms wide open, staggered towards him. 'We can't do owt 'ere mister. The whole damn roof's come down. Can't tell how far in it's blocked.'

Philip's expression mirrored his mixture of despair and anguish.

Jumping back from a rumble of falling stones and thick dust, another man yelled, 'Never get the poor buggers out now. The whole tunnel's closed up.'

Wiping his mouth with the back of his hand, Philip shouldered his way through the throng to where other men were digging, using anything they could find for a shovel, and helping each other lift larger boulders.

'Is this where the tunnel begins?' he asked a man who had paused to take a mouthful of water from his tin flask.

The man spat a stream of liquid onto the pile of dirt and answered, 'Used to. Went down steep then straightened out. Tunnels lead off on both sides, and then smaller workings lead off from them. Be lucky to move this lot before the air...'

They both spun around and ran towards the sweat-lathered men when someone shouted, 'Haa! Look you here—part of a tub.'

The find spurred on the men who increased their efforts. Steady work allowed them to move forward, stone by stone.

157

They shored up the roof with timber as they progressed. It was difficult, backbreaking work.

One man straightened, cursing. 'Always bin dangerous, but never bin as bad as lately. Constantly shoring it up with wood cut too short, or not strong enough to take the weight. Bloody roof, timber's mostly rotten afore it gets to pit!'

'That's why roof comes down so often,' another voice chipped in.

'Bet they buy the cheapest.'

Angry and bitter, the men made their feelings clear in the way they tugged at the stones and threw them onto a growing pile.

As Philip tried to help the man next to him to lift a heavy stone he yelled and snatched his hand away. 'I felt something cold. I think it may be a...' He looked around, embarrassed by his lack of nerve.

They continued working in silence, uncovering first feet, then legs, now cold and still. Fallen rocks had crushed the woman's chest. After passing the body to people waiting with baskets, the men returned to their dismal work.

Eventually Philip found he was working at the front of the team. Old wooden props, slimy with damp, and any odd pieces of timber were used to shore up the roof, making a low tunnel. Face down, his back cut and bruised, he inched his way forward, disregarding his torn nails and bleeding fingers. With red-rimmed eyes he peered between the stones and thought he saw a light. When he tugged at a stone a puff of air blow into his face.

'Are you there, mister?' a young voice called.

'Alive. Someone's alive!' he yelled to the man behind him. Before they could make another move a bewildering array of sounds attacked them, clattering, and thudding as the earth around them moved and a whoosh as the roof above him dropped. He felt a sharp pain in his right leg, then blackness.

Chapter 10

'You all right, mister?'

Philip felt small fingers touch his face and jerked his head back, blinking dust out of his eyes.

'Who...who are you?' he croaked, squinting at the hand. For a moment, he couldn't think where he was. Then his memory returned, and with it, teeth-clenching pain.

'You'll have to dig the rest yourself. We've pulled you a bit, but we ain't strong enough to pull you any further.' The boy's speech was very matter of fact, almost as though he was used to talking to a half-buried man.

'Shoulders too big to get through the gap.' A girl who sounded very young was close enough to feel her breath on his face, and he could see her silhouette in the dim light.

One of his arms lay above his head, almost touching the children, the other arm beneath him. He tried to move it, and froze as stones rained down on his back. When he tried inching forward again he gasped at the pain in his leg. In a bid to widen the hole, the children constantly called encouragement as he struggled to free himself. At last, by manoeuvring his back and shaking off some of the debris, he pulled himself forward, and found himself lying full-length in a part of the original tunnel that, fortunately, was still shored up with timber props.

He took a deep breath and made a determined effort to sit upright and lean against the wall, but closed his eyes when everything spun. When he did open them, he found himself facing three children with tear-streaked faces. A small stub of a candle burned on the floor beside the girl. He tried to give them a reassuring smile, but only managed a grimace as he realised his painful leg lay at an unnatural angle, and both of his shoes were missing.

'You're not uncle!' the girl wailed.

'Mum yer dubber, Bridget. Uncle Joe'll be next one in. Ain't that right, mister?' The boy, with a sprinkling of freckles, spoke as though he'd placed himself in charge.

'Of course he will.' Philip tried his best to sound convincing. 'He knows you're down here. I told him before the roof fell.'

The homemade candle stub flickered in its pool of tallow fat. Philip frowned. 'Should that be lit? It may have been a flame that set off the explosion. Shall I blow it out?' He knew candles were strictly forbidden down mines. At his suggestion, Bridget's face crumpled. 'We could all hold hands,' he said, noticing the fresh flow of tears.

Bridget scrambled to sit with the older boy. 'I want to hold Toby's hand.'

Toby gave an exaggerated sigh as he slipped his arm around her shoulders. 'She don't like the dark, mister. She's a trapper, see, and she 'as to stay in the dark all the time she's down pit. If they found her with a light, she'd be in right trouble. Maybe sacked.'

Philip was puzzled. 'What do you do as a trapper, child?'

'Strike me lucky,' said Toby. 'Don't you know owt? We have to sit all day pulling a leather flap forward and back to draw air along the tunnels, so everyone can breathe. It's very important work.'

The second boy crawled over to sit on his other side. A pair of blue eyes looked at him. 'My name's Robbie Lang. What's yours?'

Toby blew out the candle. The darkness was total. Philip expected it to be silent in the black world, yet he soon became aware of trickling water, a falling stone, and then the clatter of smaller pebbles echoed around the tunnel. Creaks and groans came from the moving mass around them. A sharp crack from the wooden support in the roof filled him with apprehension, and he stared in the direction of the perceived danger. He shifted, and attempted to straighten his leg, but bit back a cry when the movement caused shooting pains from his leg up to his teeth.

A small hand crept into his, and he felt comforted by the squeeze, but blackness almost overtook him once more.

'Hey! The cove's fallen on top of me, Toby. Light the candle, quick!' he vaguely heard Robbie call. He sensed Toby holding the light high to examine his face.

'What's wrong with him?' Bridget asked, with a voice that quivered with fear.

Toby replied. 'He's all right. Just fell asleep. He'll not be put ter bed with a shovel just yet.' The candle moved. 'That leg's broke.' He felt the boy touch it. 'I'll have to pull it straight while he's still asleep. You find summat to bind it with, Bridget. Robbie, you hold his shoulders down.'

'Wait,' said Bridget. 'His torn shirt'll be best to bind it, but you want a stick to keep it straight. Uncle Joe did that once to our old dog.'

Philip could make out the candle stub moving from side to side. With a shout of triumph, Robbie pounced on the shaft of an old wooden shovel. Together the children rolled and pulled him, tearing the once white shirt until they had removed it from his limp body.

'Right, are you ready? Hold him tight, you two.' Toby gritted his teeth, and pulled the leg so it lay straight. Soon the blood began to flow.

'Quick, Bridget, wrap it up while he's still asleep. Maybe it won't hurt when he wakes up.'

The pain was so excruciating he could not tell them how much it hurt already. The children wrapped part of the shirt around his leg and tied strips of cloth over the wood to keep it in place and, with a groan, he opened his eyes, and struggled to sit upright. Wiping beads of sweat from his face he peered at the watching children.

'You've broke your leg. Will it have to be cut off now?' Bridget's eyes were wide with innocence.

He found himself giving a crooked smile in response to her childish curiosity. 'I do hope not, little one.' With a worried frown he looked down at the children's handiwork. It was not unusual to lose a leg once broken. Sometimes it could be saved if a skilful doctor could be summoned at the time of the accident. The leg would invariably be shorter and the person left with a limp, but using a cane was much better than a crutch.

Leaning forward to look into Philip's face, Toby said, 'You ain't going to sleep again, are you, mister?'

With a supreme effort he opened his eyes wide and smiled at each young face in turn. 'No. I am quite chipper now you have awakened me. When we get out of here I'll take you all for a ride in my big balloon.'

The words diverted the children, as Philip knew they would. He tried to ignore the throbbing pains in various parts of his body.

'What's a balloon?'

'How do you ride in it?'

'Will it hold us all inside it?' Questions tumbled from their lips.

'Blow out the candle, and I'll tell you all about it.'

More questions came from the children when the light went out.

'Do you mean in the sky?'

'Up there, with people's souls?'

'Does the minister in the kirk know about it?' they asked in wonder.

The hours passed. Philip gave information about balloons and anything else he could think of. He told them about Yorkshire and his beloved moorland, of how his family lived at Clemmants, and about a lady ghost that had once haunted his Elizabethan home. From time to time a strange weakness overtook him, and he felt as though he were floating.

'Hush!' Toby ordered. 'What was that? Did you hear it? There it is again.' They all strained their ears and heard a crunching, and a scattering of stones. On the far side of the tunnel, a yellowish light appeared through a crack in the wall.

'Who's there?' Philip called. His voice sounded loud in the darkness, and small hands found his.

'Eh. There's someone else,' a man's voice called. 'I told you I could hear talking. Come on here, hurry up. Lift the light up higher, Mrs Waspill.'

'Can you reach us?' Philip called. 'There are four of us in here.'

'Six of us here,' came the reply.

The light glowed stronger as the barrier of stones, rock and coal was removed. The three children helped as best they could from their side.

'Dada. Is that you, Dada?' Robbie called, scrambling towards a big man digging with his hands. 'It's me, Dada. Robbie.'

Mr Lang struggled through the hole and hugged the boy. His voice sounded gruff, as he said, 'We had to dig through a fall. Took us an age, but we managed it without getting hurt.' Taking the lamp with the thick horn window from the young lady, he looked at Philip and his bandaged leg.

'You've not finished yet, Mr Lang,' replied Philip. 'I'm afraid you have another fall of rocks to dig through. I can't say how far the tunnel's blocked. Ahh!' he yelled, startling everyone. Someone had accidentally kicked his broken leg.

'Struth! What's the to-do?' a woman asked in a scared voice.

'Mister broke his leg when trying to rescue us, and now he's trapped, too,' Bridget said, tearfully stroking Philip's arm.

'Didn't think I knowed you. How did you get into this lot, then?' Mr Lang asked, crouching beside him.

163

Holding Bridget's hand, Philip told the man his name, and explained he would probably be one of the new owners of the mine. 'I thought I would see for myself what the conditions were like down here, and intended to help. I didn't expect ending up like this.'

Mr Lang gave a hoot of derision that was echoed by the others. 'I just bet you didn't, mister. Pray you have a very clever partner on pit top. Only God and them up there can help us now.'

'Blast and damn! I hate to be in the dark,' one of the women said when Mr Lang crawled closer to the fall, taking the lamp with him. Silence fell as everyone studied the blockage.

'I've a little piece of candle,' someone offered.

'Don't be daft. Do you want another explosion?' The woman had spoken softly, but Mr Lang had clearly heard. He held up the lamp as he shouted, 'A bit of fire-damp, and we'll all end up dead!'

Philip glanced at Toby, who responded with a pleading shake of the head, so he rested his head against the wall and closed his eyes and drifted into a doze.

'Water. Do you have any water to drink?' he asked an hour or so later, thinking he lay beside the river near his home, listening to the water lapping against the banks. Someone shaking his arm made him open his eyes. He squinted but the face above him was indistinct.

'Sorry, mister. We've no water here,' said Mr Lang. 'We're going to have to move you over to the far side. We're making a start on the tunnel from our side, or else we'll never leave here.'

Philip nodded before closing his eyes. He barely felt the men lift and carry him away from the entrance to the new tunnel, and had no idea on whose soft lap his head was pillowed. He felt a cool hand on his forehead, and licked his dry lips as he opened his eyes. 'You're my angel,' he said.

'Are you comfortable, sir? Please lie still. The men are still trying to open the tunnel, but they're not through yet.'

'The Gypsies are camping on the river bank again,' he murmured.

The cool hand stroked his hair until he closed his eyes. His mind drifted, half listening to the rattling of stones and men cursing. He thought Bridget squealed, and wanted to go to help the child, but couldn't lift himself.

Someone's hair brushed his dirty cheek. 'They say they can hear people on the other side, in the tunnel, sir. We'll be out of here very soon,' the girl whispered.

He sensed himself being placed on a stretcher, and manoeuvred through narrow spaces along the opened tunnel.

Nathan Denstone spared no expense in organising the rescue of those trapped underground. Men were sent to Glasgow and other mines, upon the village's swiftest horses, carrying news of the disaster and a plea for help. Others, carrying axes and ropes, hurried to fell trees in the nearby woods. All the barge horses were put to work dragging the tree trunks to the mine yard, where a sawing pit was soon dug out, and willing men cut the timber into planks and stout pit props. Women helped to carry the wood down the mineshaft's ladders, and stones and debris up to the surface. The men working below ground used the timber to support the roof as they reopened the tunnels.

Nathan showed people how to make an ingenious device, using horses, strong wooden beams, ropes and pulleys. Working day and night, hollow-eyed men installed the new contraption and the old ladders in the mineshaft were dismantled. Once it was complete, it allowed them to be drawn up and down the shaft, clinging to ropes fitted with seats and loops. The new method seemed strange and rather dangerous, not to mention extremely noisy. However, they were more worried about their injured companions below, and bravely set their fears to one side. When small numbers of rescued miners arrived at the bottom of the mineshaft, they were shown the new lifting contraption. They were instructed on how to sit on it, but it was clear they were apprehensive, and thankful to arrive safely into the waiting arms of their families.

At last, Philip, still semi-conscious on the stretcher, was carried through the narrow passageways until he reached the mineshaft. With hands clenched over her mouth, and biting hard on her thumb, Merrilla watched as Philip, still securely fastened to the stretcher, swung as he was hoisted to the surface. When it became her turn to ascend, she shook with fear. Someone helped her to be seated, warning her not to loosen her grip. Eyes closed, clinging to the taut rope, and with both feet resting in a rope loop, she felt the wind on her face as she was pulled through the darkness. She opened her eyes to see a glorious golden sunset. A strong breeze lifted her lank hair. Willing hands supported her, and helped her onto firm ground. Her face raised to the sky, she breathed in the pine-scented air.

Mary, pushing through the crowd of waiting families, ran forward and hugged her close, and whispered that she had prayed for her friend to be returned unharmed. 'I thought... Well, you know what we were thinking,' she said, trying to pull Merrilla towards the waiting Gylby family, and laughing through her tears. 'I've sent off our little Billy to tell Mam you're safe. She'll make a fire, and see there's a meal waiting on the table for you.'

Nathan watched as Philip regained his senses in the fresh air. Men rested his stretcher on the ground and they covered him with a blanket, his dirty face twisting with pain. He recognised Nathan bending over him. 'Papa—please inform him...' he croaked.

'I sent, poste-haste. He'll soon be with us, lad.' Nathan fought to keep back tears. He had stayed by the mine entrance since Philip had disappeared down the ladder, and almost collapsed on hearing he had become trapped below.

Women had cleaned the manager's office, and a couch, with pillows and blankets, had been placed ready for his comfort, but he had not made use of them, even though he knew he should get some sleep, and looked as though he had aged ten years.

The next person to be lifted to safety was a young woman. She hugged another woman, hurried to Philip, and bent over his stretcher. Nathan watched with concern as Philip clasped the young woman's hand and held it against his face, before closing his eyes.

'Seems he wants you to come with us, ma'am,' he told her. The girl's eyes widened in surprise, as if she recognised him, but he fussed around Philip's stretcher, twitching the blanket into place, and smoothing a wayward lock of the young man's dirty hair. Four men hurried forward at his signal, lifted the stretcher and carried Philip up the hill to the village. Nathan walked on one side, and the girl, still holding Philip's hand, kept pace on the other. Members of the Gylby family, along with others from the village, walked with them, each person ready to provide comfort and assistance.

The room used by Philip and Nathan in Mrs O'Keaf's house had been made ready for their arrival. Any unnecessary furniture had been removed or pushed to the side. A wide, wooden board lay on top of the bed, covered by a clean linen sheet. The fire burned under a kettle of boiling water that spluttered and sizzled on the hot coals.

Mary's mother, hearing of the successful rescue, had already lit a fire in Merrilla's room. Warm water and a tin bath stood near the fire, ready for her. Her filthy dress tore as she pulled it off, and she tossed it onto the floor with an expression of disgust. She sank into the comfort of warm water, gave a sigh of pleasure and closed her eyes, but scenes of the dangerous time below ground intruded. Unable to relax, she poured jugs of warm water over her hair, and washed it with soft soap until it squeaked when she ran her fingers through it. After towelling it as dry as possible, she braided it into a neat coil, and pinned it into place, shook the creases from her Sunday gown, and dressed. It had been two days since she had eaten. A basin of steaming hot broth sat on the table, alongside fresh crusty bread and a glass of milk. Drawing up a chair, she gave her full attention to enjoying the food.

The bed had the top cover turned down, the pillow covered with a white linen case, smooth and inviting. *I'll just lie down for a moment or two, and then I'll go and see how Mr Larcombe's faring,* she thought.

She awakened with a start, and saw it was well past sunrise.

At eight o clock she stood by Nathan at Philip's bedside whilst two doctors argued. The older man held a long knife in a way that frightened her.

'I say take it off. It will ne'er be any good to him. It will wither away,' the paunchy old doctor said, gesturing with the knife.

Merrilla gasped and pressed the back of her hand to her mouth.

'And I say no, doctor. Let me try and save it. I've done this kind of operation many times at the Glasgow Hospital and, I may say without boasting, I've been extremely successful. Only recently, I saved the limb of a thirteen-year-old boy. He's now walking well with the aid of crutches, and will very soon be throwing them away.' The younger, red-haired doctor stood defiantly with arms outstretched, attempting to prevent the older doctor from moving closer to the bed.

The older man gave an exasperated snort, before shouting, 'This is not one of your grand hospitals, Doctor Grant. You could

168

never achieve anything like the same results here. Look around you, man. The leg will be putrefied and gangrenous in no time. I can smell it from here, even now.'

Nathan Denstone looked gaunt and pale. The lack of sleep, Philip's predicament, and now this medical debate were clearly too much for the elderly man. Merilla had gasped when she had first seen him. He had reminded her so much of her grandfather, although a little younger and stouter, but his eyebrows were as bushy, and his hair as white and cut short so he could wear a wig.

With a steadying hand under his arm, she led him to a chair near the fireplace. 'Sit down here, sir,' she said. She had no intention of interrupting the two doctors. She squeezed his hand, whispering, 'They will do what is best for Mr Larcombe.'

His eyes swimming with tears, the manager looked up at her. 'I wish he had never gone down there. I know not how I'm going to face his parents when they arrive. His father will never forgive me if...if...' He put his head into his hands, and his shoulders shook.

Merrilla bent over and rubbed his back with sympathy. Everyone in the room fell silent and turned to look at the bed when Philip gave a long, shuddering sigh.

'He's regaining consciousness, doctor,' Dr Grant said, taking hold of the other doctor's arm. 'Quickly now, tell me, sir, are you going to allow me to save the leg?' A groan escaped Philip as his eyelids fluttered open. He stared in horror at the knife hovering near his leg. For a moment, he watched its movement, and groaned again. 'Damn fool idea. I warn you now, Dr Grant. If you lose him, you'll ne'er practice medicine again, laddie. I'll see to that.' The elderly doctor still brandished the knife. For a moment, they glared at each other. The older man was the first to turn from the bed. 'I'm away, for it's evident I'm not needed here. Just don't come to my door for help when things go wrong, Dr Grant, for they will. I'll stake my life on it,' he warned, throwing the knife into his bag. He closed it with a sharp snap, snatched his cloak from a chair and stomped across the room. 'I'll bid you all good day,' he called, before slamming the door behind him.

Merrilla moved to the bedside. At her touch Philip gave her a puzzled look and, as her hand closed round his with a reassuring grip, he relaxed. 'I remember you. You were down the mine.' He lifted her hand, whispering, 'The children? Where are...?'

She bent closer and said, 'They are safe. Everyone in our group was able to leave unharmed.' It was not the moment to tell him that five other children, two women, and seven men had perished in the latest explosion.

Doctor Grant regarded her with a doubtful expression. 'I'll need your help, ma'am, if I'm to save the leg. Help from both of you.' The young doctor turned towards Nathan, and held out a small ribbed bottle of carbolic acid. 'This cleanses. The idea is to make everything aseptic. Any dressings that go near the wound must be boiled first. Everything in the room needs to be as clean as possible.'

Merrilla's heart skipped a beat when he turned in her direction. She took a step backwards.

'What's your name, my dear?' he asked.

'Mrs Waspill,' she whispered.

'Please, Mrs Waspill, forgive me. I sometimes forget I'm not speaking to one of my hospital nurses.' He moved across the room to where his bag lay on a small table, and removed the necessary instruments. Then he returned to the bed and inspected Philip's leg. 'Now then, we must first remove the rags. Mr Denstone, will you bring that small table over here, please? The rags must be burnt. Mrs Waspill, bring me a large bowl and the kettle of boiling water, please.'

They all watched as he wrapped himself in a large white apron, poured the boiling water into the bowl and added a few drops of carbolic acid from the brown bottle. He dropped his knives one by one into the cloudy liquid, before turning to face Philip, who lay staring at the bottle with horror. 'Mr Larcombe. Philip.'

It clearly took a great deal of effort for Philip to remove his gaze from the bowl, and to look at him.

'Mr Larcombe, I have done this kind of work before. You have no need to fear, although you will feel discomfort.'

Philip stared at the kindly face without speaking.

'The laudanum will deaden the pain. Do you understand, Mr Larcombe?'

Philip nodded, though he did not look convinced, and his eyes flew back to the bowl of instruments. The doctor continued speaking in a low, steady voice, trying to reduce his patient's fear. He placed a piece of wood between Philip's teeth, and he bit down hard and closed his eyes.

The doctor worked quickly, passing blood-stained rags to Nathan, and asking Merrilla for fresh supplies of boiling water. The leg was a mass of bruises, and proud flesh protruded from the torn area. He brought his head back sharply as a stench rose.

'Not a moment too soon,' Merrilla thought she heard him whisper as he lifted his eyes to glance at his patient's face. His deft hands worked confidently, and he paused only when Philip moaned and tried to move.

'Mrs Waspill, please hold Mr Larcombe's shoulders down. I can't have him moving about. Sit on him if you have to, but keep him still. Mr Denstone, come and stand opposite me and hold his leg still, please. Place your knee on his left leg, and hold onto his right. That's the way, good man.' The doctor nodded approval at Nathan and continued working. The effect of the laudanum was lessening, and Philip was growing restless. As he worked, the doctor glanced constantly at his face.

At last it was time to remove the piece of wood from his mouth. 'Mr Larcombe, we have finished for now. You have done very well, very well indeed. Try to sleep now, laddie.'

Philip attempted to raise his head high enough to look to the bottom of the bed. 'Both legs are there,' assured the doctor. 'But you must keep them still. That is most important.'

With a weak smile he whispered, 'Thank you, sir,' and closed his eyes.

John Larcombe and Hugo Denstone were kept busy in Nottingham Town. Their meetings with Mr Harwood and the representatives of the cotton mill owner were eventually concluded to everyone's satisfaction.

John had other business interests in the town that needed his attention, but Hugo arrived early at the mill on the first day of their ownership. He stood a moment, getting used to the noise and the vibrating floor, and watching the mill hands twisting and knotting broken threads on the machinery. All the workers were very much aware of the new owner's scrutiny and, half believing some of the rumours that were flying around, kept their heads bent over their work. With the slightest of nods and eager to begin his work, Hugo acknowledged a girl who moved closer, fluttering her eyelashes at him, and made his way towards the office, where a nervous Mr Pugh waited for him.

The overseer had clearly attempted to smarten his appearance by wearing a cravat, but the bow hung as limp as the points on his shirt collar, and bore traces of snuff. Bowing and scraping, he drew a chair from the table, and dipped a freshly-sharpened feathered quill into the inkpot. He held the quill out towards Hugo.

'Close down the machines, Mr Pugh.'

The portly man goggled. 'C-close down?'

'Stop the machines, and fetch the girl, your supervisor. I'll speak with you both before I tell the people below about some of the changes that will be made.'

Mr Pugh's hand froze in the act of lifting the door latch when Hugo said, 'I'll have your keys, Mr Pugh.'

The overseer almost threw the bunch of keys onto the table.

It was not the first time Hugo had needed to curb his staff, who often had their own ideas on the subject of how to run a factory. He remembered from his first visit that the overseer kept the safe key in a separate pocket. 'And the safe key?' It landed next to the others.

Light footsteps and a swish of skirts caused him to lift his eyes from an open ledger, and to return the girl's curtsy and enquiring expression with a nod. 'Your name, miss?'

'Turpin, sir.' She looking concerned, and with her hands clasped at waist height, bobbed another curtsy.

'Gather everyone together at the foot of the stairs, Turpin. I have something to say to you all.'

'Yes, sir.'

It took some time to stop the machines, but the workers drifted to the foot of the stairs. They stood muttering, looking rather bemused by this unexpected event.

Standing on the office stairway, Hugo held up a hand for silence. 'It is possible that some of you may have a rise in your wages,' he called.

A surprised murmuring rose at the news, and anxious people who had expected to be laid off from work relaxed.

Again raising his hand, Hugo waited for silence before continuing. 'The doors of the mill will open at seven each morning. You will not be late for work. If you are you will be sent home. A meal of bread and soup will be given to each worker at midday, as soon as we are able to have a kitchen built. You will finish work at half-past seven in the evening, unless you are asked to work later, in which case you will be paid a small extra amount.' He glanced at the papers he held and, as an excited gabbling broke out, he looked up. 'When working... When working...' He waited a moment for silence, 'All girls and women will keep their hair completely covered with a tight-fitting cap, and wear an apron which will be provided by me.' He paused for a moment for the idea to take hold, and then continued, 'In future, children under ten will no longer be employed at this mill.'

Immediately rebellious grumbling broke out, and suspicious glances were directed at him.

'They're upset, Mr Denstone,' Mr Pugh said out of the corner of his mouth.

'We can't live on the wages without the brats' money to put to it!' a man shouted.

'How can we run machines proper without oil brats?' another person yelled.

Hugo couldn't see who had called. Everyone ducked down when shouting, in order to avoid being dismissed as troublemakers.

The movement of Hugo's hand once again silenced the workers.

'Hush! Hush!' The voices died as he continued. 'There will be many other changes made here, and you will be told about those later.'

It seemed that everyone had an opinion and wanted to discuss what had been said. Silence fell, however, when a man, raising his fist, yelled, 'What I want to know... I want to know what I'll take home end of each week.'

Others, finding the courage to speak out, broke the hush.

'Yes, I want to know that too,' was the cry from different people around the room. Hugo, looking at the worried, upturned faces, understood their concern.

'In the past, those of you who fell sick and were unable to work used to lose their wages, but in the future a small amount of money will be paid to you. Get back to your work now. When you hear your name called, come to the office. I will speak to each of you individually.'

For a moment the silence was absolute. Everyone stared as Hugo and the overseer entered the office and closed the door.

Nancy's mind whirled. She desperately wanted to dash upstairs and question Hugo further. What other changes? Would she still be needed as a supervisor? Would other men be employed? She clapped her hands sharply. 'That's it, show's over. Get those machines started again. Come on, move along there.'

Excitement filled the air; it seemed as though everyone had something to say. Nancy was as surprised as everyone else by the mention of sick pay. She knew some factories in Nottingham paid a sick wage, but no one expected it to happen at their mill. Maybe the new partners owned the other workplaces receiving this benefit. A sharp rap on the office window broke into her reveries, and she sent the workers one by one to meet their new employer. When they left the office, most of the adults looked pleased.

John Larcombe and Hugo were at the mill on the day that two machines were to be exchanged for the latest steam-powered models. Several engineers had already examined the floor to ensure it could bear the weight of the new machinery.

'They've measured everything they could lay a rule on. Surely they know by now whether the thing will fit into the space,' John grumbled. He drew Hugo to one side as men manoeuvred parts of machinery past them. 'I hope this new technology is worth the outlay we've invested,' he added.

'Everything will be working in a few days, and they need to be certain it all fits into place just as it should, Mr Larcombe,' said Hugo. 'The heaviest part of the machinery is the steam engine.' He wore a pair of old brown woollen breeches that were slightly too tight, and an open-necked shirt, revealing dark curly hair on his chest. He drew many admiring glances from the women, but was far too engrossed in supervising the installation of the machinery to take any notice.

Nancy, noticing one of the younger girls displaying rather too much interest in her new master, pinched her arm and hissed, 'You'll be working in the streets if I see you ogling the master's backside again.'

Her cheeks reddened by fear and embarrassment, the girl scuttled off to her workplace without a word.

Out of earshot of the workers Hugo said, 'If these machines do what we expect, we may need to employ more people, Mr Larcombe.'

'We should be able to find extra people if we need them,' John said. He winced and glared at some workers who had just dropped a piece of iron casting, shaking the windows in the building.

'According to Nancy...em...Miss Turpin, people who are looking for work make a queue outside the front of the building each morning. Miss Turpin keeps a record of each name.' His ears burning, Hugo hoped John hadn't noticed his slip of the tongue. It was unusual for an owner to refer to a worker by their Christian name. Nancy should have been referred to as plain Turpin.

'This Boulton and Watt engine will be the first of many if it powers the machines as their engineer, Mr Watt, claims,' John said.

To make the working conditions more pleasant, the day being warm, the big mill doors stood ajar. An urchin slipped in and stood pressed against a bale of cotton, open-mouthed, watching the workmen until a set of steel-like fingers took hold of his ear and marched him towards the door. 'Ouch! Let go, yer hurting,' he wailed.

'No brats come in here. Now get out,' Nancy hissed, pushing the child outside.

'Got an important letter for Mr Larcombe. Got ter give it to him right away,' the child blubbered at the top of his voice.

'Give it to me, brat. I'll see he gets it.' Nancy held out her hand.

The chance of a reward for bringing the letter seemed to be rapidly disappearing, for the urchin bellowed as loudly as he could, 'No. I was told I must see Mr Larcombe myself, and give the letter only ter him.'

With an amused eyebrow cocked at Hugo, John went to find out what the commotion was about. He frowned at Nancy. She stood with her hands on her hips, facing the tearful urchin who was rubbing his reddened ear. As soon as she noticed John watching her, she moved away from the child, blushed, and bobbed a curtsy.

He ignored her and smiled at the boy. 'I am Mr Larcombe. What do you want with me?'

'I've run all the way from the hotel, sir. The landlord sent me ter find yer, and give yer this, sir.'

Amused by the situation, John handed him a coin, and the boy gave Nancy a triumphant grin before skipping away.

Waving the letter to Hugo, he gestured for him to come to the office. The letter was addressed, in a familiar hand, to Mr Larcombe at the Black Boy Hotel, Nottingham, and bore the unmistakable Denstone seal in a blob of red wax. 'This letter's from your father, Hugo. It was sent to the hotel, so he must have assumed we would not yet have left Nottingham. Strange. It's unlike Nathan to write so soon from Scotland. I hope nothing has gone amiss with the sale of the coalmine. I would have thought Philip would be more likely to write about their news than your father.' He broke the seal, unfolded the closely-written pages, and tilted the paper towards the light of the oil lamp.

His face turned ashen. Hugo ran to take hold of his arm and drew him to a chair. 'Please, sir. Sit down, Mr Larcombe. Whatever's happened to shock you so?'

John held out the letter with trembling hands. Hugo scanned it.

'Read it. Read it out loud. Perhaps I did not understand the words properly. Your father is not the best of writers. His pen always blots, which doesn't help to make his missives legible.'

'It's from my father, as you say, sir. The coalmine is to be called the Larcombe and Denstone. Oh.' He glanced up. 'An explosion has occurred, injuring and killing a number of workers. Philip went down the coalmine to help with the rescue. He was...emm...'

'Yes, yes, go on, Hugo. Read on.'

'He was in a tunnel when it collapsed and buried him. They were able to rescue him.' Again Hugo paused. 'He's alive, but his leg is badly broken, and he has many cuts and bruises.'

Giving a loud groan, John covered his face with his hands.

Chapter 11

Hugo wiped his forehead with his handkerchief, and fought back tears. Philip was only a few months older than him, and more than just neighbours and partners in business, they were friends. It was rare to be apart for any length of time, and now Philip, so active and full of fun, would possibly be a cripple for the rest of his life. He placed a hand on Mister Larcombe's shoulder, squeezing it in mute sympathy, and swallowed hard before continuing to read the letter. 'My father says they are fortunate to have one of the best doctors in Scotland. He's greatly admired for the work he does in the Glasgow Hospital.' John's shoulders shook. 'Please, sir, try not to distress yourself so. You know more than anyone how well my father can organise things to advantage in an emergency.'

John took out his handkerchief, wiped his eyes and blew his nose. He rose to his feet and stared at the busy scene below. With quiet dignity, he said, 'I shall be quite composed in a moment. It was the shock. I know very well we can trust your father to see Philip is well taken care of, my boy.' Nodding, he continued, 'I shall leave you here in charge, Hugo. You now have the mill running smoothly. Keep it going. If you continue to be unhappy with Pugh, and think you need another overseer, use a man from one of our other factories.'

Hugo felt startled at being given such authority.

'I will leave you now, but, before leaving Nottingham I'll speak to Mr Harwood. He should be at his office.' John looked at his pocket watch and moved towards the door.

Hugo followed him into the street. After watching him climb into a carriage and drive away, he returned to the mill, deep in thought. The success of the mill lay in his hands.

The following weeks found the oldest machines halting with monotonous regularity. The new machine had also stopped a few

179

times, mostly because the men were not yet fully trained to use it. Hugo's plan was to bring in workers from another factory, but at the moment they couldn't be spared from their primary workplace.

'We can't keep standing like this, Mr Denstone. It's the oil. It works itself away ter fast. We need oil brats to err...' Mr Pugh stood bent over in front of the office table, wringing his hands. Hugo could hear the man's heavy wheezing, and smell the overseer's body odour. 'To use thicker oil.'

Hugo waved a hand in dismissal, without looking up from his writing.

Nancy sat in the corner of the office, also writing. She gave a discreet cough, and he half turned towards her. 'Roden and Bails use a thicker lubricant. I can find out what they use and who their suppliers are, if you would like me to, Mr Denstone,' she said in a low, throaty voice. She smiled bewitchingly at him. His heart leapt, and a feeling of warmth crept into his loins. The flowery scent from her body reached him. It took a great deal of willpower not to rush over and kiss a curl that had escaped from her cap.

During the weeks Hugo had worked at the mill, she had made sure he noticed her; the arrival of fresh bread with cheese and wine at midday; the brushing of his hat and coat; plus the waiting carriage when it was time for him to leave. These, and other attentions, brought a quiet, 'Thank you, Miss Turpin.'

On the day he decided to examine the smallest stockroom, Nancy was nearby. He beckoned to her. 'Please fetch a lamp.'

She placed the lamp on a table near the door. The room had only one small, grime-covered window, set high at the far end of the room. 'This room's used for storing cotton for special orders, sir. Bales have to be raised on pallets or else we'd get rats making their nests in it, Mr Denstone, sir.'

'If I had it cleared out, another window put in over here, and with a table and benches, this room would be suitable for use as a Sunday School. Without those bales, it would be large enough for a dozen children or more.'

Nancy followed him to the back of the room. 'Oh, yes, Mr Denstone. You do have wonderful ideas.' She fluttered her eyelashes.

Hugo ran his tongue over lips suddenly dry. He found it almost impossible to keep his mind on the job in hand and his eyes off her, using any excuse to be in her company. If she smiled in his direction, his heart skipped a beat, and he would feel elated for hours.

In the half-light, he took hold of her hand and lifted it. For weeks, he had dreamed of being alone with her. He often spoke her name aloud in the privacy of his bedchamber. 'You darling girl, bewitching me with your beauty.' Close enough for her breasts to touch his waistcoat, she gazed at him, her lips moist and slightly parted. 'You should not be among this grease and dirt. You should be out in flower-filled meadows, where sunshine would...'

'There you are, Mr Denstone. Mr Harwood's waiting for you in the office.' Mr Pugh stood in the open doorway, allowing light to stream into the stockroom. Hugo and Nancy sprang apart at the sound of the mocking voice.

Cursing under his breath, Hugo pushed past the man, leaving Nancy to follow.

The door swung closed. Nancy bit her lip with annoyance as the overseer chuckled. 'Thought you had 'im hooked, didn't you m'lady? You has a long way to go yet.'

Her cheeks flamed and she tossed her head in vexation that her carefully contrived plan had come to nothing. 'You have a low and vulgar mind, Mr Pugh. I am a pure maid, and Mr Denstone is a gentleman.'

He leered at her. 'Bah! You're a fiendish doxy like all the rest. You led me on in that way at first, and I fell for it. But I say this, my little beauty, I still want you, and if he don't have yer, I will.'

Nancy darted out of reach of his soiled, nail-bitten fingers.

'Sir, what have you here?' The scandalised tone of Mr. Harwood's voice caused the overseer to spin on his heel. He had clearly not expected Mr Harwood to follow him to the stockroom.

Nancy pulled down her bodice to show a bare breast and made sure both Mr Harwood and Hugo saw her tearful face and quivering lips.

On her return home that evening, the story lost nothing in the telling. 'I've never seen anything so funny. I saw the door opening, and I pulled down my gown to show a bit more, you know, like this.'

Polly put both hands to her face in horror. 'Oh, my, you're playing a dangerous game, Nancy. A lady would never let herself be so compromised.'

'I tell you, Polly, never have I seen anyone look so dumbstruck. He'll lose his position at the mill for certain. Mr Denstone brought in an overseer from another factory the other day to show the men how to use the new machine.' She smirked. 'He'll take Pugh's place permanently at our mill if Mr Denstone sees him so much as look in my direction again.'

'Oh, Nancy, have a care. He'll try to spoil things between Hugo and you if he can. He's bad through and through, that man.'

Nancy gave a toss of her head, making her golden curls bounce. The glint of laughter still shone in her eyes, as she said, 'I know what I'm about, Polly.'

'You just remember when Mr Pugh sacked Joe. The poor man had just lost his wife in childbirth, and had six other children to feed. He had to go to the poorhouse. Pugh has no pity. He's wicked.'

'Don't be fearful, Polly. I mean to get Mr Denstone for my husband, and if he'll not marry me, well, he can be my lover. You, my dear, will be my personal maid. Together we'll be rich and have a happy life without me working in that mill. Just wait and see if my words don't come true.'

Polly's mouth hung open. 'But where are your dreams of working in a big house?'

'Who wants to be a servant when they've chance of marrying a rich man?'

Polly frowned, and shook her head.

Unable to control her passion, and without Polly's knowledge, Nancy had a string of lovers. All of her suitors were poor working-class men, and so only used for her pleasure. She was careful to take precautions to minimise the risk of pregnancy. Sometimes she used a wad of cotton soaked in a mixture of herbs, lemon and vinegar, or insisted that each man used a knotted animal intestine, but mostly she satisfied them, and herself, by using hands or mouth. She also found that the small amount of money they gave her was useful, though she did not always charge.

Nancy tantalised Hugo with her smile and fluttering eyelashes. Each day she wore a new starched white cap with a protruding lace frill that encircled her face like petals on a flower. She dominated his thoughts, and everything she did charmed him. Without his friend, Philip, to talk him out of his lovesick daze, or John Larcombe to put an end to the affair by dismissing her, he passed many hours indulging in his favourite pastime—watching his adored Nancy. He chose to forget Elizabeth Larcombe, waiting at home for his return so they could be married.

Each evening when the machinery was switched off and the only sounds in the building were calls of goodnight and the shuffling of feet, Hugo watched Nancy swing her shawl into place and put on her bonnet. She tied the shawl in such a way that it emphasised her breasts and small waist, but gave no indication that she knew he was nearby.

On one occasion he caught sight of Mr Pugh giving him a speculative stare. He gave a short laugh, realising he had almost given away his secret by saying, aloud, 'How I wish I could escort you home, my darling.' Pulling on his gloves, he muttered a sharp, 'Good night,' to the overseer, and hurried down the steps into his waiting carriage.

Later, dressed in a nightshirt and tasselled cap, he lay in his bed in the inn, thinking of her. He remembered how she had looked at him that morning, how she had tilted her head, the tip of her tongue resting on her moist lips whilst he explained why he wanted a certain thread to be made thicker.

Coming to a decision, he sat bolt upright. He slid down from the high four-poster bed, ignoring his slippers, and carried his oil lamp to the oak bureau. He opened the lid and took out a sharpened quill and paper, and began writing.

The Black Boy Hotel
Nottingham.
Monday April 18th. 1797.

Dear Miss Turpin,
My dearest love. There. At last the words are written for your glorious eyes to read. Those are the words I say a million times within my heart. You may laugh at me, you may scoff, I fear, when I say that it is you I adore.

On the day we were together in the stockroom, I held your hand. Only the two of us were on this earth. The walls crumbled away, and in my imagination we danced together, as in a resplendent ballroom. We stood in the light of your beautiful soul, my angel.

You have no idea how I wait for each dawn, knowing that in a few hours I will behold your beauty. My only concern is that you may not smile when you greet me at those great doors of the mill each morning.

Do you know that a frown from you makes my day a misery? There is nothing I want in life but your kind regard, my dearest love. Ought I to be ashamed at my boldness? Do you feel any less for me because I declare my undying love? No. You would never harbour any but the most virtuous, prudent and honourable of thoughts, and have the most beauteous of feelings, my dearest.

I send to you a golden locket, within which is a snip of my hair. If I see my gift resting where I wish my cheek to lie, my joy will be complete.

Adieu,

Hugo D.

The following day, it took a long time before Hugo found the opportunity, not to mention the courage, to hand his letter to Nancy. It seemed that whenever he stood close to her someone would want to speak to him, or he became aware of Mr Pugh watching him. Late in the afternoon, unable to wait any longer, he summoned her to the office.

She curtsied.

'Mmm…Miss Turpin. Please take this, and r…read it this evening, when you are alone.'

Her eyes widened. As he sat behind his new desk, blushing and stammering, an overpowering sense of triumph surged through her. She recognised Mr Pugh's heavy tread on the wooden staircase. With a quick smile at Hugo, she pushed the letter into the pocket of her skirt, and pulled her apron into place before hurrying out of the office.

During the remainder of the day, she fingered the letter through the fabric of her clothes with a feeling of satisfaction and curiosity. She had noticed the paper had a blob of hard sealing wax, and she traced the pattern of the Denstone seal with her finger. But there was something else, something hard inside the folded paper. She could hardly wait to get home to show Polly her first love-letter.

Her meal was ready and waiting on the table when she returned, but as soon as Polly saw her excited expression, the meal was forgotten. Nancy placed the letter on the table. For a moment, both women stood looking at it. 'You open it, Polly.'

Polly opened it with a knife, trying to avoid spoiling the seal. The locket, on a long gold chain, slithered onto the table. Nancy snatched the missive and gave a gasp of delight as she read the sincerely-penned words.

Polly took hold of her arm and tried to read it, but Nancy pulled away. 'What does it say? Are you dismissed? Has he said anything? Oh, stop dancing around the room in that silly way, girl, and come and sit down here. Now, tell me what he's written.'

Nancy, twirling round the table, bounced across, and kissed her on the cheek before sitting down. 'This, my dearest Polly, is what I've been working for. It's from Mr Denstone, as you guessed from the seal. It says he loves me, and he's sent me this bauble with a lock of his hair. Look.'

Polly's incredulous expression as she read the letter made Nancy laugh merrily.

'You have caught his fancy, you clever little girl. He can't back out now he's declared himself in writing. You have the proof here. Keep this letter in a very safe place indeed.'

'Don't you worry. You just make sure my gown is clean and pressed, ready for tomorrow morning. This locket will be perfect to wear with its low neckline, and I'll make sure he can see where it's lying,' she said as she fastened the chain around her neck.

The Back Boy Hotel
Nottingham.

My dearest Miss Turpin,
I saw the locket, my secret love. Dare I hope? I tremble with joy. Do you care for me just a little?
You smiled at me today. It made my heart soar.
Mr Pugh stayed beside me the whole day, vexing me.
My darling, here I sit in my lonely chamber dreaming of you, and waiting with impatience for tomorrow's dawn.
Adieu,
Hugo D.

Some weeks later, Nancy closed the street door with a slam. Polly was so startled that she dropped a plate onto the table with a clatter. Noticing Nancy's peevish expression, her heart sank; these sour moods had become a regular thing.

Nancy threw her bonnet on her bed with such a force that the brim bent. She flopped on a chair, and gracelessly stretched out both legs. 'Oh, Polly, Hugo watches every move I make and follows me round the mill all day like a puppy. Pugh knows what's going on and walks behind him, smirking. Oh, I could smack his fat, ugly face. And I'm annoyed at the way Hugo writes every day. Where on earth does the man find the time?

187

That's what I'd like to know.' She kicked off her shoes, continuing, 'Pugh's trying to cause trouble. I think he knows about my old love, Fred Pullings, and I'm worried the troublemaker will say something to Mr Denstone.'

With a wag of her finger, Polly bent over the sulky girl. 'Don't you come here with your groans and ill temper, miss. You know as well as I that Mr Denstone would never listen to what Pugh has to say. He'd consider it low gossip, unworthy of his attention.' Polly tut-tutted, and tried to straighten the twisted brim of the bonnet.

In the market that morning, a friend had grinned as she had told her Nancy had been seen more than once in the company of a well-known philanderer, and he had walked beside her with his arm around her waist. 'Cooing and all lovey-dovey. Closer than two love birds they were,' she'd said.

Polly waited to see if she would tell her about the man, but her friend was not in the mood for idle chitchat.

'I had another letter today. He placed it between some papers, but I'm sure Pugh knows about it.' With a frown, she held out a crumpled piece of paper. 'I know I'm being silly, but if Pugh gets to know Mr Denstone loves me, he'll try to spoil things, I know he will. You once told me he's a wicked man, and I'm sure you're right, Polly.'

Taking the letter closer to an oil lamp, Polly smiled as she read it. 'Don't you worry, my dear. Whatever is said by Pugh, or any one else, no one will put out this fire. Not now. The man is too smitten.' She placed the letter on the table. 'You'd best put this one with the others. How many have you received now?'

'Oh, I don't know. Lots.' With a shrug, Nancy picked it up and tossed it onto the bed, before pouring some water into a bowl and washing the factory grime from her hands and face.

The Black Boy Hotel,
Nottingham.
My Dearest Nancy,

    Beloved. You have heard, I am sure, that Mr Larcombe has left Nottingham to travel to Scotland. What you may not know is that he was informed that his son, Philip, has suffered a terrible injury. Philip Larcombe is my friend, my greatest friend, and I pray constantly for his speedy recovery.

    Clemmants is the name of the Larcombe estate. It is in the county of Yorkshire, and they are our nearest neighbours. Although I have sent a letter to Philip's mother, I now feel it necessary to leave Nottingham to console Mrs Larcombe and her daughter, Elysabeth.

    May I ask - dare I ask, after such a short acquaintance - whether you would consider accompanying me to my home? It would mean leaving Nottingham, and your friends behind. You would meet my mother, who is sure to love you.

    I want you always by my side, my darling one. Wear this scarf when you are at the mill tomorrow, or in church on Sunday, and I will know you will be prepared to come away with me. I breathlessly await the future days with anticipation.

    Adieu,

      Hugo D.

On Thursday afternoon, when the deliverymen returned to their wagon for more tubs of greased cotton, Nancy was left alone for a moment. Hugo moved forward and handed over the letter before hurrying away.

She thrust it into her pocket without looking at it and forgot about it until she was ready to leave the mill. It seemed to be thicker than usual. She broke the seal.

A shadow darkened the cream-coloured paper. Mr Pugh towered over her with an outstretched hand. 'What you got there, girl?' Scorn screwed up his face, and his eyes seemed almost to disappear.

She backed away, shoving the letter into her pocket. 'Nothing that concerns you, Mr Pugh. It's of a private nature.' Her shawl drawn around her shoulders, she lifted her skirts ready to leave. Mr Pugh grabbed her arm, and squeezed it until she cried out with pain.

In desperation she looked around for Hugh, trying to twist away from the overseer's grasp. 'Leave me alone, Mr Pugh! You've no right to stop me leaving. My work's done for the day,' she panted.

'No good looking for him, he's gone off early. You think he wants to wed you? A mill girl? Ten-a-penny, mill sluts are. Use them, and then get another when you've done. Bah! Get off, yer little fool. Get off 'ome to yer hovel.' With a savage push, he sent her stumbling into the street.

Nancy, trembling with temper and fear, hurried home. She almost fell down the steps leading to Polly's door. It took soothing words and a drink laced with brandy to calm her enough to look at Hugo's letter. With a rapt expression, she drew out a pale blue gauze scarf from the folded pages. 'Oh! This is lovely, Polly.' She dropped the scarf onto the table, and tilted the notepaper to catch the light from the lamp.

'What does it say, my dear?' Polly asked, trying to make out the words over Nancy's shoulder.

A cry made her draw back. 'He wants me to leave Nottingham and go home with him. He wants me to meet his mother, but says nothing about marriage. Polly, tell me quick, what shall I do?'

Polly stared in disbelief. 'Do? Do, you silly girl? What have we been working for all this time? You are a lady. The man wants you. He's in love with you.'

'But, Polly, he hasn't been on his knees to propose, and now I don't want to be just his mistress,' she wailed.

'Don't be more stupid than you need to be, girl. He's a gentleman. He'll not be allowed to marry unless the girl is either rich or he's able to persuade his doting mamma to take kindly to her. You have a great deal of work to do yet, Nancy. Let's hope Mrs Denstone's the kind of mother who lets her darling boy have anything he asks for. If she doesn't, you'll either lose him or you'll have to settle for being his mistress.'

Nancy sat a moment, fingering the scarf and re-reading the letter. 'You'll be able to come with me, Polly? I don't know enough etiquette yet, and I'd be lost in a posh house without your help.'

'Bless you, dear. Yes, of course I will.' She smiled into Nancy's eyes. 'You'll have to take someone with you, for his mother most certainly wouldn't accept you into her home without a chaperone.'

Returning from work the following Friday evening, Nancy hesitated on the bottom step as the door flew open. Polly, with a broad grin, held a large parcel in her arms.

'What's this? What have you there?' Nancy's eyes sparkled in anticipation as she took hold of the package.

'It's another gift from your laddie. Hurry and unwrap it. Let's see what he's sent you this time.'

'Oh!' Both women gave a gasp of delight as blue velvet shimmered in the lamplight. It was an opulent blue-green full-length velvet cloak, with a large hood trimmed with white swan down. Nancy swung the cloak around her shoulders. The folds brushed the tops of her shoes. She draped the hood over her head and looked in the mirror. The aquamarine velvet made her eyes look darkly mysterious. Throughout the evening, the women continually admired it, and Polly tried it on so Nancy could see what it looked like from behind. At bedtime, she draped it over a chair beside her bed so during the night she could reach out and touch the exquisite material.

The Black Boy Hotel,
Nottingham.

My Angel. My Nancy,
My love. My life. I sent you the cloak, searching all Nottingham to find a blue to match the perfection of your eyes.
I saw you wearing the scarf, and now I am counting the days until we can travel to Yorkshire. Beloved, please send all your dressmaker's bills to my address.
I hang my head. I know now how foolish it was to try to win a kiss from you when alone in the office. You were right, I know, to be vexed with me.
I have pressed this lovely flower. I am sure that its fragrance will delight you, my dearest. Pray accept it with my devoted love.
Adieu,
Hugo D.

'Polly, I'm home,' Nancy called, sniffing appreciatively at the smell of baking as she noticed her favourite ham pie on the table. She kissed Polly's cheek. 'He sent another letter today, Polly, with a dead flower inside.' She giggled. 'Poor thing is all shrivelled up, look.' She held out the flower. With a snort of disgust, she threw it onto the fire, and watched it burn.

'Why on earth did you do that, girl?' Polly shivered, and moved away. 'Burning flowers or any greenery on an indoor fire will bring bad luck into the house.'

'Pah, dead things won't pay for anything. The pretty gold pin he sent me last week, now that's different. I can always sell that.' She tossed her head. 'I've no time to eat, though I must say it smells lovely. I have to change my gown for Mr Denstone is taking his sweetheart out tonight. He stuttered out his invitation when I was in the office this morning. So delighted when I said yes.' Laughing violet eyes twinkled. 'Now, are you prepared to be my tire-woman on our journey to Yorkshire, Polly? We're meeting tonight to make plans for leaving Nottingham. I suppose you must also make arrangements if you're to come with us,' she called as she hurried across the room.

Making a sweeping curtsy, Polly returned Nancy's jubilant smile. 'Yes, ma-am,' she said.

The Black Boy Hotel.
Nottingham.

My darling angel, Nancy.
Tomorrow we fly away together behind swift horses. I feel pleased to know your friend Polly will chaperone you, my Nancy. Although I write to my mother with regularity, I have not told her of our abiding love. I want to tell Mamma in person, and let her see for herself what a paragon of virtue I have found in you.

I have carried out your wishes, and employed two postillions and a coachman. All three consider themselves mighty fine, and wear linen as white as any gentleman, and I have heard reports that they are masters of driving, and we will be perfectly safe in their coach.

The mill is now running smoothly, and I can leave Mr Pugh in charge with an easy mind.

I have glimpses of paradise as I plan our glorious future together, secure in our love. When we leave this place, we will have all our lives to discover each other, and revel in our abiding love.

My dearest darling. My goddess without a flaw.

Until tomorrow,

Adieu,

Your Hugo.

Chapter 12

Everyone who lived in the street came out to gape when a shiny green and black travelling coach came to a halt outside Polly's door. Never in living memory had such a smart vehicle been seen in the impoverished area.

They all moved closer as a groom and a coachman in long green coats with three shoulder-capes and matching tricorn hats sat on the driving seat, eying the circling urchins. They were ready to use a whip or cudgel on anyone who soiled the coach paintwork with grubby fingers.

Hugo ignored the footmen, opened the coach door himself, calling, 'Ready?' as he leapt down the steps two at a time.

Nancy, on a chair with a pile of luggage near her feet, smiled as he removed his hat with an elaborate flourish and bowed over her gloved fingers.

'I have never seen you look as lovely as you do at this moment, Miss Turpin,' he said, placing his lips on the back of her gloved fingers. Indeed, she did look charming in her new honey-gold travelling dress and a tall straw bonnet trimmed with ruched violet ribbon.

Hugo wore a knee-length brown coat trimmed with bands of wide braid, and a pair of pale yellow breeches. A diamond sparkled between the folds of his necktie, and six diamonds were set in the buckle of each of his shoes.

As the couple emerged into the sunshine, a cheer went up from the waiting crowd.

Hugo flushed with embarrassment when an old woman said, 'Ah, they do look lovely together.'

The groom gave Nancy a half-smile, and touched his hat with his whip. She stared in astonishment when she realised he was Fred Pullings, one of her regular lovers. Excitement surged through her, and her buttocks clenched. She had not been with a man for weeks, and the urge to have someone fondle her in an intimate way was overpowering. Without anyone else noticing, he gave her a saucy wink. She turned her back, and gave her attention to Hugo. Two footmen in white wigs and green coats stood stiffly on either side of the coach door as Hugo assisted Nancy and Polly to their seats. The groom placed the luggage in the coach boot and the journey to Yorkshire began. Nancy waved her handkerchief at the neighbours while Hugo, leaning back in his seat, watched her with an indulgent smile.

The roads from Nottingham were busy, and it was over an hour before they left the last dwelling behind, but the travellers were in no hurry. Knowing this was the first time Nancy had left the town, Hugo spent the time watching her reaction to the meadows, woodlands and rivers.

During refreshment breaks and overnight stops at inns en route, he escorted the women to private parlours, and always engaged the best rooms available for their comfort. Nothing was too good for his Nancy. At his command, each landlord, bowing and scraping, sent servants running to perform any necessary service.

Eventually, they stopped at an inn for what would be the last night of their journey to Ghyll House.

While Hugo spoke to the landlord and Polly gave instructions to one of the footmen, Fred Pullings sidled up close to Nancy and said in a low voice, 'Meet me in the coach house tonight at ten. I'll wait for you beside the carriage.'

She turned startled eyes on him. 'I can't do that,' she whispered.

'Oh, Nancy, please. It's dreadful watching you with him and remembering it was once me you were thinking of marrying. And now I'm not even able to talk to yer.'

She noticed Hugo coming towards her. With a hand covering her trembling lips to hide her panic, she lifted her skirts and walked across the yard to join him. *If I don't meet Fred tonight he might tell Hugo about us being more than friends. He's spiteful enough and that would ruin all my plans,* she thought.

Hugo offered Nancy his arm and escorted her into a private parlour. 'I have everything ordered for our comfort, Miss Turpin. A room for you and Mistress Goodley on the quiet side of the building.' She tried to hide her agitation, but it took a huge effort to behave as though nothing were amiss.

The clock on the coach house struck ten as Nancy, her hooded cloak concealing her identity, hurried across the yard.

'You managed it, then. I've missed holding you in my arms, Nancy,' Fred Pullings said, moving out of the shadows, and beckoning to her.

'Fred, this is madness. I've so much to lose. If Hugo finds out I've been with you he will... Oh...' Her protests were cut short as he covered her mouth with kisses. Her passion was swiftly aroused and two pairs of hands fumbled with restraining fastenings. Pushed against the wheel at the back of the carriage, she let his fingers part the golden hairs—already damp with lust—and fill her, whilst she stroked and played with his hard erection. At last she moaned, satisfied, and they drew apart. She had been lost at that first kiss, her response, as always, wild and abandoned.

'I must go,' she panted. 'Hugo thinks I'm in bed, and Polly thinks I'm with Hugo. If they should meet and find me missing, all hell will break loose.' She pulled her clothing into place and lifted the hood of her cloak over her curls so her face was in shadow.

As they stepped away from the carriage, they noticed a figure against the wall, watching them from under an oil lamp. 'Evening!' he said.

Nancy gave a gasp as she recognised Jeremy.

'I didn't think you recognised me earlier dressed in my smart green footman's uniform.'

Fred pushed Nancy behind him. 'How long have you been there?'

'Long enough to know what's going on between you two.'

'Nothing's going on,' Nancy hissed.

'Didn't look that way to me. If I was to tell what I know, somebody would be in trouble up to her pretty neck,' Jeremy said, with a grin.

'You say one word, and...' Fred lunged forward, fist raised.

Jeremy was too quick. He darted out of the coach house door and, keeping to the shadows, disappeared into the darkness.

Nancy, weeping with fear and anger, said, 'This is your fault, Fred Pullings. I know that little rat, and what he can do. He's a friend of Bill Waspill. They kidnap girls for the brothels. They took a young lady called Merrilla Cooper from her family and she was never heard of again. He's sure to tell Hugo what he saw and that'll be me finished.'

'Don't talk daft. No need for you to worry. I'll sort something out to stop him gossiping,' Fred said with not much conviction.

Somehow Nancy gained entry into the inn without being seen. She let the hood of her cloak fall and put her hand to the door latch of her bedchamber. She froze.

Hugo, wearing a loose robe and carrying a book, stood a few steps behind her. 'Have you been out, Miss Turpin?'

She held out her wrist to show him a gold chain with a medallion hanging from it. 'I dropped my bracelet in the carriage and I didn't want to lose it. It's the one you bought for me, Mr Denstone.' Batting her eyelashes, she peeped up at him.

'A servant could have performed the task. I hope you do not take a chill from the night air, Miss Turpin.'

She stepped forward, lifted her face so her lips were temptingly close, and shook her head, gesturing towards the book. 'Were you bringing that for me to read, Mr Denstone?' she asked in a throaty voice.

He seemed about to kiss her but drew back. 'I thought you would enjoy reading this book of poems.'

With another flutter of her eyelashes, she thanked him and went to her room.

Polly sat in a chair beside a lamp, reading her Bible. 'Where on earth have you been? I've waited here for a good hour to undress you and ready you for bed.'

'I've been with Mr Denstone. He's given me this book of poems, see?' She thrust the book into Polly's hands.

Polly sniffed. 'By the state of you, you've been doing more than just reading.'

Breakfast, consisting of a dozen delectable dishes, was served to Hugo and Nancy in a private parlour. They had finished their meal, and were about to leave, when the landlord entered and asked for a private word with Hugo. At the man's grim expression, Nancy caught her breath with fear. Something must have been seriously amiss for the man to speak to Hugo in such a manner, and her guilty secret made her cheeks glow. With a bow to her, and a murmured apology, the men left the room.

The door had hardly closed behind them when Polly rushed in, all of a twitter, saying, 'There's been a murder in one of the stables. They say one of our footmen was found with a hayfork through his neck.'

Nancy blanched as she remembered Fred Pullings's words. Lifting her coffee cup, she tried to hide her trembling and appear unconcerned. 'What has that to do with us?'

'What has it to do with us?' Polly's eyebrows raised in astonishment. 'We'll be delayed. That's what it'll mean. They've caught the man who did it, and taken him off to a gaol in York, thank goodness, so he won't be murdering anyone else.'

'Really? Who do they think's done it?'

'The groom, or was he the coachman? Anyway. Fred Pullings. Someone overheard them quarrelling. I dare say Mr Denstone will be extremely vexed, especially when he finds he'll have to hire another coachman for the remainder of the journey.' Polly peered out of the window. 'Maybe he'll just hire some man who works at the inn.' Her eyes rounded with suspicion. 'I hope you haven't had anything to do with this bother, Nancy.'

'Course not. It has nothing to do with me. Why should it?'

By midday another coach driver had been hired and stood waiting in the yard. Polly went outside to instruct the new man on how to stack her lady's luggage.

Hugo escorted Nancy to the coach and, knowing how chilly the wind could be, blowing over the moorland, tucked a rug around her knees.

Nancy was quieter than usual, thinking about the previous evening, and worrying about whether Fred Pullings would talk and involve her in the incident to save himself from hanging. She hoped Hugo surmised she was nervous at the prospect of meeting his mother, for he left her to gaze out of the coach window in peace.

However, Nancy forgot about Fred Pullings when they entered the grounds of Ghyll House. As they travelled along the long gravel drive leading to the front of the house, Nancy and Polly stared with amazement at a herd of deer grazing in the parkland. Nancy had never seen anything like it in her life and, forgetting herself for a moment, squealed and pointed her finger in a most unladylike way.

Hugo held out his arm and she rested her hand on it as she stepped down from the coach. She hid her nervousness by holding her chin high and looking haughty as he escorted her past a row of servants who curtsied and bowed a welcome.

In the entrance hall, a maid stepped forward and took her cloak and bonnet. Polly seated herself on a wooden chair by the wall, waiting, as any good servant should, for her next instructions.

Joan Denstone sat writing at her escritoire in her sitting room when Nancy and Hugo were announced. 'Hugo?' she exclaimed in delight, rising from her chair and taking a step towards her son. She held out a slim hand in his direction, staring at Nancy with an enquiring expression.

'Mamma.' Hugo seemed unable to meet his mother's eyes. He bowed low over her hand before moving to one side and drawing Nancy forward. 'May I present Miss Nancy Turpin, Mamma.'

She dropped her long lashes, blushed, and sank in a curtsy as though being presented to royalty. She also made the mistake of looking up at her hostess and giving a brilliant smile before being welcomed.

His mother stared in astonishment. Nancy held her breath, realising she had forgotten the first rule of etiquette but was greeted as courtesy demanded. 'Welcome to our home, my dear. I do hope you enjoy your stay with us.'

'You are most kind, Mrs Denstone.'

'I came home sooner than expected, not only to see you and Mrs Larcombe, Mamma, but also because, if the need arises, I will be travelling to the Paxton coalmine.'

'Most commendable, Hugo. Will Miss Turpin be making a long visit with us?' She gave Nancy a cool look.

Hugo took Nancy's hand and, holding it tightly, said, 'Mamma. I have asked Miss Turpin to be my wife, and she has agreed.'

The sound of ticking clocks filled the room and Nancy held her breath once more. Joan Denstone stared at her son for a long moment, before saying, 'I feel your father will very much want a say in the matter, Hugo. I do hope you will wait until he arrives home before formally announcing your engagement.'

'Yes. Of course, Mamma.'

His mother did not try to hide her stricken expression. 'I will expect to see you here, alone, in one hour, Hugo.'

In Scotland, Mrs O'Keaf's house became the centre of activity. People came and went at all times, visiting Nathan Denstone on business, and the doctor continued his twice-daily attendance on Philip Larcombe. Mrs O'Keaf had given permission for Merrilla's room to be used as a bedchamber for the person resting from nursing Philip.

On the fourth evening after the operation, Merrilla noticed a change in Philip. He felt hot to the touch and restless. Only the restraining straps prevented him from moving his leg. She ran to the bedchamber and hammered with both fists on the door and rattled the door latch. It was Nathan's turn to enjoy the comfortable bed that night. 'Mr Denstone, sir,' she called. 'Mr Denstone, wake up!' A faint light appeared under the door.

When the door flew open, a worried looking Nathan, nightcap askew, stood in the draughty passageway, his trembling hand shielding a flickering candle.

'Mr Denstone, sir, I've sent one of the children for Doctor Grant. I'm sure something is dreadfully amiss with Mr Larcombe,' Merrilla said, a catch in her voice.

The candle shook and he leaped back with a shout as a drip of hot wax fell onto his bare toe.

She didn't wait but hurried back to be with Philip. Hugo joined her at the bedside, having pulled on a pair of breeches over his nightshirt. Philip lay with eyes closed, groaning, moving his head from side to side. Near to tears, Merrilla tried to hold his hand, but he pulled it away. She gave a gasp of relief when Doctor

Grant walked into the room. She explained what she had been doing to make Philip comfortable.

'You've done just as you ought, Mrs Waspill. Cool cloths on his brow is the best way to bring down his temperature. Now, let me see if we can find the cause of the trouble.' The doctor's calm manner steadied her nerves. On his instructions, she held the oil lamp high, watching closely as he stripped away the dressings. Although the wound still looked angry, the only smell was that of carbolic. He redressed the leg. 'Something's disturbing him. The trouble must be coming from his back, Mrs Waspill. Most of the cuts are deep, and will be painful when he lies on them. When they do heal, he'll have permanent blue scars, since the coal is to blame for most of the cuts.'

She gasped with horror when he lifted Philip. The sheet was sodden with puss and perspiration.

'I hadn't noticed. I tried to make him lie still,' she whispered. In a bid to hide her anxiety and tearfulness, she went to fetch clean linen and hot water, wondering if she would be dismissed for not noticing his condition sooner. She felt drained and took some deep breaths to regain her usual air of composure.

After the doctor had cleaned and dressed his patient's wounds and Philip had fallen into a doze, Nathan yawned and said goodnight, closing the door behind him. Merrilla and the doctor drew chairs up to the fireside and sat waiting for Philip's fever to abate. They spoke together quietly, constantly glancing to check on his condition.

'Mrs Waspill, have you given any thought as what you will do when Mr Larcombe has recovered?'

Shaking her head, she gave a deep sigh. 'All I know is that I could never go back to that dreadful coalmine.' She picked up the poker and prodded the coals, causing a bevy of sparks to fly up the chimney.

'Would you ever consider joining my staff at the Glasgow Hospital? We desperately need young helpers with abilities such as yours.' She opened her mouth to reply, but the doctor lifted his hand and rose to his feet. 'Please don't answer me now. Give careful thought to my suggestion. I'll ask what you've decided nearer the day I leave Paxton.'

He carried the lamp over to the bed and stood looking down at Philip, shading the light with his hand so the glare would not disturb his patient. 'He appears to have settled down again now, and is much cooler.' A weary sigh escaped him as he added, 'I'll be away to my own bed now, Mrs Waspill.' As the only doctor in the village, he had spent many hours tending others hurt in the mining disaster and, Merilla had heard, knowing how poor most of the families were, hadn't charged for his services.

Once he had left, Merrilla returned to her chair by the fire. Before she could sit down, she heard Philip croak, 'Water,' but by the time she had filled a cup, he was sound asleep.

In the three weeks following the night visit Doctor Grant continued to call twice a day. Once he was satisfied all was progressing well he taught Merrilla how to change the dressings and cut his visits to once a day.

'You'll soon be sitting on the side of the bed if you continue to improve like this, Mr Larcombe. Now, let me see you move your toes. Ah. Yes. Good.' The doctor nodded in approval. Philip, clearly proud of his accomplishment, grinned in triumph.

Merrilla watched with mixed feelings. Another few weeks and her patient would no longer need her. She had no money, and was seriously worried about her future. Doctor Grant hadn't mentioned anything more about her working in the Glasgow Hospital. On top of that, she realised she had fallen hopelessly in love with Philip.

She was tidying the sick room when a loud knock on the door startled her. She hurried to open it. Three well-washed faces

204

gazed up at her. It took a moment or two to recognise Toby, Robbie and Bridget.

'We's come to see Mister.' Toby, as usual, was the spokesman.

'Is he getting better, Mrs Waspill?' Robbie almost sang the words in his soft highland voice.

'Will he be leaving in his balloon?' Bridget asked. She was wearing her best dress and a starched white pinafore for the visit. Thick plaits hung to her waist from under a neat linen bonnet.

'You had best come inside and see for yourselves,' Merrilla said, holding the door open. She smiled at the way the children tried to tiptoe across the uncarpeted floorboards in their nail-studded boots.

At first, conversation was awkward, for the man on the bed must have seemed a different person to the one they had rescued from the coalmine. When he had told them about flying balloons, and a far away house in Yorkshire called Clemmants, he had been dirty, more like one of them. They were clearly not sure how to speak to this gentleman now he was clean.

'My dada's in charge of the pit. He's the manager now. He had a letter from Glasgow the other day, and he says I've to go away to a school there.' Robbie sounded proud of his father, but when he spoke about going to school his mouth turned down.

Not to be outdone, Toby pronounced, 'I been talking to Mr Denstone. He's a good friend of mine and says I'm to be trained as a groom. He's going to take me to Yorkshire when he goes home to his big house. It's bigger than yours, mister. A big stable with lots and lots of horses.'

'Perhaps we can travel to Yorkshire together, Toby.' Philip said. 'I live very near to Mr Denstone. We're neighbours, so we should see each other often.'

Bridget tugged the sleeve of Philip's nightshirt to claim his attention. Two front teeth missing, she gave him a gappy smile as he turned to look at her.

'I can't work down the pit no more. My mammy wants me to go into service, so I'm going to live in a big house and learn to be a skivvy. Can I go up in your balloon one day, mister?' The girl's eyes were wide with hopeful anticipation. She had not forgotten Philip's stories about floating through the clouds.

'Not until my leg's better, but you'll have to grow a little taller first, my dear,' Philip said, taking the child's hand and patting it. Merrilla noticed that the children's chatter had begun to tire him so, placing an arm around Bridget's shoulder, she ushered them out of the room with a promise that they could call and see him again. She smiled at their anxious expressions. 'Yes. Very soon,' she added as she closed the door.

Philip had closed his eyes so she crept across the room to place more coal on the fire. 'My back's sore, Mrs Was pill.'

'I thought you were ready for a sleep, Mr Larcombe.' She hurried to the bed and straightened the bedcovers. 'I'll bathe your back and then you can have a bowl of the meat and barley broth Mary's mother made for you.' Reaching behind him, she fluffed up the pillows. Not alarmed at first when his arms stayed around her waist, she was astonished when he drew her head down and kissed her lips. She responded with a sharp cry, struggling to free herself from his grasp. 'How dare you? You...you... Oh, how could you do such a thing?' Tears pricked the back of her eyes and, blinking them away, she backed out of his reach.

He held out his arms. 'Mrs Waspill. Merrilla. Please, my dear... Oh, I've frightened you. I do beg your pardon. I wanted you to know how much... That is...I've grown so fond of you.'

She stared at him. Was it true? Did he mean it? She placed a hand on her heart, thudding so loudly she was sure he could hear it.

'You...you care for me?' she whispered, through pale lips.

'My dear, I don't know what I would have done without you. Down in the pit, you cradled me in your arms. We were together in the foul blackness of the mine. I called you my angel then, and now I know you better I...I...don't know what to say. Can you forgive me?'

'Oh, Mr Larcombe, you know nothing about me. I am...I've been married. I was...'

'My dearest, sit beside me and let us talk. I want to know everything about you.'

She couldn't tell him about Bill. How could she bear to? He'd spurn her; he'd surely be disgusted to learn she'd eloped to live with a stranger on a barge. Tears flowed, and, lifting her apron, she covered her face.

'Whatever you say about your past history it will make scant difference to my feelings for you, Merrilla.'

She gave an incredulous look. Could they have a future together? It was too soon, and she would need to know more about his feelings before telling him her secrets. She edged forward. Their fingers intertwined. Exchanging a smile, she leaned towards him. He blinked, bringing her face into focus. 'How beautiful you are,' he breathed.

She accepted the tribute with a rosy blush and bent closer.

The following day, Nathan Denstone had to go to the coalmine, leaving the couple alone.

'Merrilla, my dear,' Philip whispered.

She put down the shirt she was sewing and hurried to the bed.

'We must speak of our future, Merrilla. My father will soon arrive, and I must tell him, for he will want to know why we are such...er...close friends. Do you care for me, Merrilla?'

She nodded as she pulled a chair closer to the bed and sat down.

'Begin by telling me about your childhood. Have you a mamma and papa?'

Again she nodded and then took a deep breath. 'I was born in Grantham.'

'That's not far from Nottingham.' He didn't take his eyes from her face, listening without interrupting as she told him about her family, about Bill, and how she'd secretly left home expecting to marry him and have a romantic life. How she had became a prisoner, and worked on the barge. She didn't criticise her late husband but trembled, twisting her fingers, and cringing at times.

'Put all those unhappy days behind you and look towards the future,' he said, covering her hand with his own. They sat in silence as he stared towards the door, deep in thought, and she gazed down at her hands.

His grave expression made her heart sink. *I daren't mention anything else,* she thought. *I don't suppose for a moment that his parents will accept me as a daughter, once they know my history. However hard I try to change myself, I'll never become a fashionable young lady again. As soon as people hear I was a coalminer, and that now I'm a penniless widow, I'll be ostracised. Philip's business may suffer. Perhaps if we stayed in the village, married at the kirk, and then made our home at Paxton Hall, things would work out.* She knew very well that, like all parents, Philip's would want him to marry well and, if possible, marry someone in his own social circle. If the woman came with a dowry or business assets it would please his father.

'There...there's something else Mr Larcombe...Philip.'

He tensed and waited until she had composed herself. 'The night I arrived here I...I was very ill.' Unable to restrain herself any longer, she wept so loudly that Philip glanced towards the door in case someone would hear. Fortunately no one came to the room.

'Hush, hush, my dear, it's no wonder you fell ill. But it's finished. That part of your life is over.' He ran his fingers through his hair.

She wiped her eyes. 'You now know everything about me,' she said, rising to her feet. 'I'm going to fetch my shawl and bonnet, and then I shall walk to the shop. When I return we will not say anything more about...about...' With a rush she closed the door.

More than an hour passed before she returned, carrying a steaming dish. 'Mrs Gylby has sent you more broth, Mr Larcombe,' she said, placing it on the table.

Philip lay on his pillows, staring at her. 'Will you please come here, Mrs Waspill.' Unable to hide her apprehension, she walked to the bed and stood looking at the floor, hands clasped.

'Mrs Waspill, will you do me the great honour of becoming my wife?' His eyes radiated love.

She blushed and then paled as she shook her head. How could he love her? Had he heard her disclosures? Did he realise she would never be received into society if ever her history became known?

'Mrs Was pill, I have thought long and hard about our future. If my father dislikes the concept of our marriage, we'll stay here in the village, although I expect him to become accustomed to the idea in time.'

'Do...do you think so?' she whispered.

'I do, Merrilla. So what do you say?'

'I will marry you, Mr Larcombe, but not if your father objects.'

'Come now. What kind of answer is that? It's me you'll be marrying, not my father.'

'I will not be the cause of any estrangement between you and your family. To lose the love of your parents is a most terrible thing. I know.'

He had to be satisfied, but before the matter was settled, they agreed that John Larcombe must know of their love before they mentioned it to anyone else. The issue of marriage could keep for another day.

Allowing the reins to slacken, Nathan Denstone let the horse move at its own pace along the meandering lanes leading to Paxton Hall. He had allowed plenty of time for his appointment with Mr Paxton, and found the sounds of the countryside and the warmth of the morning sunshine relaxing. As he entered the grounds he noticed the neglected flowerbeds and the meadowland with weeds growing through the gravel around the house, and pursed his mouth with disapproval.

'Damn and blast!' he cursed when the overhanging branch of a tree knocked his hat off, sending his wig askew. He cursed again when he tied the reins of his horse to an iron ring set into the crumbling stonework of the house and, to his dismay, the ring fell off. Hoping no one had seen the incident, he tethered the horse to a nearby bush and approached the front door. His pull on the bell chain made a clanging echo.

A shrunken old man in a kilt opened the huge, wooden, iron-studded door and ushered Nathan into an entrance hall, made gloomy by the heavy curtains covering the windows. After stating his business, he watched the old man hurry away along a corridor, and then spent his time peering at a number of dilapidated Paxton family portraits. A thick layer of dust over everything provided evidence of lack of care.

After the accident, Mr Paxton had offered the use of Paxton Hall for Philip's operation and convalescence, but it had been the thought of the long journey carrying the stretcher to and along the long drive of the hall that made Nathan decide to use Mrs O'Keaf's house instead.

'Streuth! I thank my stars we didn't take up Paxton's offer to bring Philip to this mausoleum. The lad would have been dead by now,' he muttered to a dead spider inside a stained, cracked bowl on a side-table.

At the sound of a cough, he turned towards the black oak staircase. A younger Mr Paxton walked down the bare wooden stairs, and Nathan marvelled at the sight of his russet silk smoking jacket and matching hat with its long swinging tassel. As the young man drew closer, he became aware of his powdered face, rouged and embellished with a variety of face patches, and heavy perfume. He would be at home in London among the dandy set. Nathan hid a grin by bending his head in response to Anthony Paxton's elaborate bow.

'My father is in the library, Mr Denstone. This way, sir.'

The servant returned, but was dismissed by a wave of the young man's handkerchief. Nathan followed the man's mincing steps. The library felt as cold as the entrance hall, and the small ineffectual peat fire in the wide grate did little to banish the musty smell of old books.

'Mr Denstone is here, father.' Anthony said, in a loud, high voice.

Mr Paxton Senior sat enthroned in a deep-buttoned chair, a number of plaid shawls wrapped around his small body, and a nightcap covering his ears. A dewdrop on the end of his nose caught Nathan's attention. He waited for it to fall, but it hung, glistening, as if defying gravity. The old man gestured towards some papers on a large oval table in the centre of the room. Nathan proceeded to spread out his own documents on the same table before drawing out a chair and seating himself.

Anthony lit a single candle and set it on the table near Nathan's elbow before moving closer to his father.

'My lawyer has prepared all the necessary papers, Mr Denstone. They are on the table, ready for your seal.' Giving a rasping cough, Mr Paxton continued, 'My son, Anthony, and I feel that the price is a fair one, for though we are not a wealthy family, we have never cheated anyone.' The words ended with a wheeze, and another cough.

Some weeks earlier, in Nottingham, both Mr Harwood and the lawyers acting for the Paxton family had negotiated reasonable terms. All that remained to complete the deal was Nathan's signature and the Larcombe and Denstone partners' seal on the documents.

Nathan signed his name on each paper with a flourish and, dribbling a blob of red sealing wax onto each of the papers, pressed the seal into the soft wax. He then pushed all of the documents across the table in the direction of the young Mr Paxton.

'I shall leave first thing tomorrow for Glasgow, Mr Denstone, so the lawyers will have these without delay,' Anthony said, before blowing on each wax seal to dry it. 'These documents belong to you, sir,' he added, moving another pile of papers and ledgers across the table towards Nathan with effeminate grace.

'I have lived here man and boy. I brought my bride to this house, and I thought I would be buried at yonder kirk, but it seems as though it's not to be.' The old man, sighing deeply, pushed his chin into the folds of his shawl.

'I see no reason for you to leave the hall yet awhile, Mr Paxton. We can give you three months, or longer at our discretion, as in the agreement,' he said, extending his hand to the old man.

The old man's face brightened, and he shook his hand warmly.

'Thank ye. I thank ye, sir,' he said, waving from his chair as Nathan bowed himself from the room. The manservant had been waiting outside the library and, after deftly pocketing the coin he gave him, showed him out.

He rode his horse at a smart pace back to Mrs O'Keaf's house. Ned, one of Mary Gylby's brothers, was pleased to stable the horse, and received a penny in return.

Near to his room a burst of merry laughter caused him to hesitate before he placed his hand on the door latch. It had not escaped his notice during the last few weeks that Merrilla and

Philip had been exchanging loving glances, and touched fingers at every opportunity. He had said nothing, knowing Philip would wish to speak to his father before the couple shared their secret. But what would be John Larcombe's reaction when he heard his son had formed a liaison with a coal carrier? His friend would certainly be appalled, and all the more so by the knowledge that she had also worked on a barge. He rattled the door latch before entering the room and greeting the happy pair.

'We've done it, Philip. We are now the owners of the Larcombe and Denstone coalmine. It has been signed over to us this very day, my boy.' He drew a chair nearer to the bed and sat down. 'We will be informed officially by Mr Harwood when he is in receipt of the documents. Because of your accident, the price is very much less than the one we first agreed. It's a good thing they hired a clever lawyer, for neither of the Paxton men have a head for business, and that young man's a complete fool with paperwork.' He stretched out his legs and allowed Merrilla to pull off his boots. Without speaking, she carried his slippers from the hearth, where they had been warming, placed them on his feet and returned to her seat beside the fire.

'Does that include Paxton Hall and its surrounding grounds, sir?' Philip asked, drawing himself up into a more comfortable position on his pillows.

'Yes. There are acres of land on both sides of the river and the canal. It also includes the village. Not the shop, though. That was sold to a Mrs Parkinson many years ago.'

'Do you think we should have the shop, Nathan?'

Merrilla turned at Philip's question.

'If you think it would be of benefit to us, I can make an offer,' Nathan replied.

With an expression of alarm, Merrilla rose. 'Sirs, excuse me, I know something about the shop. May I tell you?'

'If you think it's of consequence,' said Nathan.

213

She moved a step closer. 'Mr Denstone, Philip, I've met the old lady, and the shop is all she has. Years ago, after her husband was gaoled, she came to live here. Her family had turned her out with her baby. Since then she's had no contact with them, and has no close friends. She'll have nowhere to go.' She stood, biting her lip and wringing her hands. 'I met Mrs Parkinson a while ago. She was born a lady,' she added. 'I thought it best to say something. I'm sorry if you think I've spoken out of turn.'

'You were right to say something, my dear. We can make them an offer one day if she wants to sell and move from the district.' Nathan yawned.

Merrilla continued, 'Doctor Grant knows Mrs Parkinson and her son quite well. Once, when we were discussing the village, I told him how they had helped me. Dr Grant mentioned that William once wanted to be a doctor, but his mother wouldn't have any of that nonsense (as she called it) and he had to give up his dream. She has a very strong will and a most deplorable manner, but her son can bring her around most kindly.' She smiled and added, 'I can understand her not wanting her son to leave home, as she entirely depends on him.'

Nathan gave her a sharp look. 'Things have a way of happening in this life of ours. If it's in his blood, he will be what he wants to be. Time will tell.' He changed the subject, and said no more about the Parkinsons. He had met and spoken to William Parkinson a few times, and had decided to discuss his suspicion about the Parkinson family with John Larcombe when he went to see Philip.

Chapter 13

En route to the Paxton Village in Scotland, John Larcombe watched the ever-changing views as the barge moved along the canal, the white ruffles of his shirt fluttering in the breeze. Irritated at the barge's leisurely pace, he glanced over his shoulder towards the man sitting at the tiller. The *Eastwood* was capable of carrying about twenty tons, but the only cargo she carried that day was his travelling coach.

'Can you not get your horse to go any faster, Mr Clayton?' he called. He nibbled at his thumbnail, a habit that came on when worried. 'Your employer said this was the quickest route to the Paxton Coalmine.'

Mr Clayton removed the clay pipe from his mouth and pressed a stained finger inside its bowl before answering, 'So it is, sir.' The wind seemed to be stronger, and the man glanced up at the clouds. 'My employer's very familiar with the route, and knows it's quite the quickest.' The bargee pointed the stem of his pipe towards the coach that had been secured with stout ropes for the journey. 'Seems slow to you, maybe, but we've made excellent time. We run steady like. A mile an hour is a good speed for a boat like ours.'

John squinted in the sunlight across the tranquil water as the boat slid between the canal banks. The boat horse plodded along, led by the Clayton's youngest boy. It knew the towpath well, and recognised where to snatch at a nibble of grass, which was just as well, since the boy had forgotten to put the tin on the horse to feed it. How different were the beautiful four greys, following one behind the other. They tossed their heads, pulling taut their chestnut coloured tack, but the grooms, Dick and Samuel Harris, had them well in hand. John watched the men gripping the harnesses of their charges.

215

When news of Philip's accident had reached him, he had considered using the public stage, but Hugo and Mr Harwood had persuaded him to take his own carriage. Although a trifle old-fashioned and heavy, it would be far more comfortable than a public stagecoach, and he would have the added security of Dick and Samuel to assist him on the journey.

His thoughts were interrupted when Mrs Clayton emerged from the cabin. Leaving his wife to hoist the sail and navigate the bend ahead, Mr Clayton moved to John's side. 'Not long to go now, Mr Larcombe. One more bend and we'll see the wharf where you'll disembark.'

They stood listening to the sound of buzzing insects as a flotilla of plump mallards paddled along. Staring at the birds and puffing on his pipe, Mr Clayton said, 'You're not the first passenger we've carried on the *Eastwood* just lately. Bin all manner of experts up at the Paxton Mine. The pit stopped working for a while, but they've got it started again now, we understand. They're making all kinds of changes. Ponies instead of people pull the tubs of coal to the wharf. You'll see the empty boats lined up, waiting to be filled, when we get to the river.' He sent puffs of smoke into the air before saying, 'There. You see?' Again, he used his pipe as a pointer.

Shielding his eyes from the sun, John watched workmen guiding ponies between newly-laid wooden rails on the wharf, and coal being tipped into a barge, causing the dust-laden water to undulate.

'I've heard tell the workers at Paxton's are to be laid off. New owners want to bring in their own men. Bin a lot of hot talk in the village.' Mr Clayton glanced at John out of the corner of his eye, to see what effect his words had made.

John, as always, kept his own counsel. They were travelling smoothly towards the wharf using the wide sail. He noticed some grey-slated houses high on the hill, between the foliage of bushes and trees.

'That there is the village, Mr Larcombe. The coalmine I spoke of is over there, see?'

John gave a relieved nod as he realised his journey had almost ended. The *Eastwood* was moored at the wharf, and he followed the bargee ashore.

'Hey, lads, there's good money to be earned if you can unload the coach for this gentleman.'

The workmen stopped what they were doing and stared at the unusual load on the *Eastwood*, before a couple of them moved forward.

'You'll wait your turn, Clayton, like the rest of us. You know how easy it is to have accidents to your boat.' Standing on his cabin roof, the master of the adjacent barge scowled menacingly at the men, and they hastily returned to their work.

Mr Clayton turned to John with an apologetic shrug and said, 'Seems we have to wait awhile, Mr Larcombe. Bob ain't a man to be crossed.' He lowered his voice as he half-turned to face him. 'He could cause me to lose my living, making me late on my runs, among other things. They do say he knows everything about a certain bargee's death, but no one's telling.'

His cane for support on the rough ground, John walked along the wharf.

Dick and Samuel Harris came towards him, leading the four horses. 'These boys are in good shape, Mr Larcombe. They can't wait to be put back in harness,' Samuel said, keeping a firm hold on his charges.

'The coach will be unloaded soon. When it's ready, meet me at the coalmine.'

Mr Clayton had already given John the directions. Pleased to stretch his legs after being restricted for so long on the boat, he walked at a steady pace, and soon reached the clearing leading to the pit shaft. A timber hut encased the new shaft mechanism, and people were walking around the yard in a purposeful way.

He caught sight of his friend leaving one of the new buildings. 'Nathan! Nathan!' he called.

With arms held wide in welcome and eyes moist, they hugged each other.

'It's so good to see you here, John. We didn't expect to see you for at least another month.'

John clutched hold of Nathan's arm and stared into his friend's eyes. 'Philip? How is he?'

His answer was a reassuring grin, and, for the first time in weeks, he relaxed.

As they walked across the clearing, his arm around John's shoulders Nathan said, 'It was extremely worrying at first. He had a dreadful time when he was trapped down the mine. The conditions were terrible. We were remarkably fortunate to find an excellent doctor, name of Grant, from Glasgow. He happened to be visiting his friend in the village. He's experienced in dealing with cases of this nature. Anyway, now you're here you can see how things are for yourself. Oh, I see you've brought Dick and Samuel with you.' He gave a cheerful wave to the two brothers, whom he had known since their childhood.

'I left them on the wharf. I couldn't wait for the coach to be disembarked.'

They walked towards the vehicle. John glanced at his friend, and gave a puzzled frown. Nathan wore his bagwig, with bushy sideburns low on each cheek. *Surely his hair was not as snowy as that when I last saw him,* he thought, but made no comment as he followed him into the coach.

The greys' hooves pounded rhythmically on the hard ground as they pulled the coach through the village. People dodged the strong gust of air and the debris thrown up by the large, ironclad wheels. Intending to call out directions to Samuel, who was driving, John put his head out of the coach window as a woman dressed in black turned to face the coach. She gave a high, piercing scream, lifted her mittened hands, and her long, flapping shawl slipped from her shoulders. Samuel swore as he tried to control the plunging horses, and yanked hard on the reins to dissuade them from bolting. Dick tried to help by grasping his brother's hands. When the coach gave a violent lurch, John fell to the floor, and Nathan, his wig askew, grabbed hold of the leather safety strap and hung on.

The offside coach wheel struck the woman with such force it threw her high against the shop wall.

As the horses were hauled to a halt they jumped from the coach and ran back to the scene of the accident. Her son knelt at the woman's side. He lifted her in his arms.

As John bent over them, she opened her eyes. 'John. John Larcombe... So many years.' Her words were only just audible.

John glanced at Nathan, disconcerted and said, 'Yes. Yes, that's my name.'

'Sally Grashod. Charles.' The whisper was feeble, and the men leaned closer to catch what she said.

'Strewth! But how? Did you know about this, Nathan?'

Nathan made no answer.

'I came here to live. The disgrace was too much for my family...' She tried to raise her head, but it dropped when she coughed. A thin trickle of blood ran from the corner of her mouth.

John was stupefied. It must have been more than thirty years since he had seen or heard from his sister-in-law. She had written to him and his wife only once, and nothing had been mentioned about a child.

'Lay still, Mamma. Someone has gone to fetch the doctor.' The son fought hard to keep his voice steady. He looked at the men as he said, bitterly, 'It's the first time in years my mother has left the shop, and this has to happen. She'd heard about a young man with a broken leg, and thought she may have known his family.'

'John.' The whisper brought him closer. 'My William here is Charles's son. Take care. No one else.' The words ended with a sigh.

'No!' wailed William.

'Sir, I'm so sorry. Let us help you carry her inside.' John placed his hand on the man's shoulder in solace.

With a sharp cry, William shrugged off the hand, and pulled his mother's body closer. Tears ran down his face. 'No! Don't touch her. I'll be the one to move her. She's my mother.'

With dignity, he lifted the diminutive body, carried her inside the shop and kicked the door closed behind him.

A babble of voices broke out around them. It seemed as though the whole village had gathered.

Nathan breathed a sigh of relief when Merrilla ran towards him. 'Oh, Mrs Waspill. It's a most dreadful accident. Mrs Parkinson has died. Could you bring yourself to go inside and give Mr Parkinson some support? Please tell him we'll communicate with him later.'

'Yes, indeed I will. Oh, the poor man, he'll be overwhelmed with grief.'

Merrilla hurried into the shop. She pulled down the blinds, for business had finished for the day.

'Come, John, let's see Philip,' said Nathan. 'Mrs Waspill is well able to look after things here. I should have introduced you, but it wasn't the right moment. She was the young lady who nursed Philip back to health. I must say that without her constant care, you would have lost him.' His hand on his friend's arm, he led the dazed man to the waiting coach and helped him inside.

'That young man is Charles' son, Nathan.'

'He must be about the same age as Philip.'

'I don't know what Esther will say when she hears the news.' John's face was ashen with shock. 'She and Sally Grashod used to be best friends when they were girls. Struth, she will... she'll... Oh, what a waste of years.' John turned with sad eyes.

'If I know Esther, and I know her well, she'll be extremely pleased to meet William. She'll have one more chick to cluck over and pet.'

Philip sat on the edge of his bed. He held out his arms. The three men grinned inanely as John hugged his son. It seemed they all had news that could not wait another moment. When Philip heard that William, who owned the village shop, was his cousin, his mouth fell open. He laughed. His laughter was so infectious that Nathan and John joined in.

'We've travelled all these miles, only to find we have relatives living here,' Philip said, looking at his father. 'I don't remember you speaking of an Uncle Charles, Papa.'

For a moment or two, John twisted the rings on his fingers, before saying, 'I'll tell you all about it at another time, my boy.'

'I have no doubt you would rather be alone for a while to talk over family matters.' Nathan rose to his feet and, swinging his cloak round his shoulders, added, 'I'll see if Dick and Samuel have found the tavern. I made arrangements weeks ago to use their stable, and to put your coach in their barn. There's a room over the tavern large enough for them. They'll be comfortable together, and be able to keep watch over the horses.'

When the door had closed behind him, John gestured towards Philip's leg. 'You've been extremely lucky, my son.'

Philip looked like a child caught out in a wrongdoing. His face flushed crimson. He took a deep breath before he spoke. 'Papa?' He turned so pale that John stepped forward. 'Err...Papa, I need to bring certain matters to your attention. Err...when I... we...were entombed inside the coalmine, I was tended by a young woman. During these past weeks I have...we have fallen

221

in love. She's everything I wish to find in a lady. I...I wish to marry her, Papa.'

John stared at him, open-mouthed. *The boy has lost his wits. The accident has been more serious than anyone thought. Philip to marry a common woman? My only beloved son wants to marry a coalminer?* These and other thoughts shot through his mind. He tried not to show his dismay as he carried a chair nearer to the bed. It took a moment to find his voice. 'Marry? You met this young woman down in the coalmine, and you now wish to marry her? She must be very remarkable.' He sat bolt upright on his seat, gripping the top of his cane with both hands. His eyes were steel blue as he stared at his son and his eyebrows rose in silent enquiry.

'She is, Papa. Mrs Waspill is the most remarkable and wonderful woman.'

'What of her family background? That has to count. How can she possibly be suitable?' he asked, wondering how Esther would take the news.

'She's told me everything about herself: how a man enticed her to leave home, her dreadful life as a boat woman; and how she came to be in this village.'

John lifted an elegant hand, causing a prism of light to flash from his jewelled rings. 'Did...you...say...boat woman?' He had no need to raise his voice.

'Her husband treated Merrilla, Mrs Waspill, appallingly. She has nightmares.'

Was it love or pity his son felt for this woman? Did she assume she would become rich and live a life of luxury if she had a Larcombe as a husband? He moved to the window and stared out.

'Nathan likes her, Papa. She really is wonderful. I...I would like you to approve of her.'

'How old is she?'

'Eighteen, Papa.'

'Are there children?'

'No.'

'Where is she from?' John still faced the window as he asked his questions.

'Nottingham, Papa.'

He turned round slowly. 'Her maiden name?'

'Cooper. Merrilla Cooper.'

'Since buying the mill in Nottingham, we have had business dealings with Mr Cooper. I recall hearing something about his runaway daughter.' With a nod, John returned to his chair. 'She seems rather unstable. Can you say why she hasn't contacted her family since becoming widowed?'

'She told me that, years ago, her husband received a letter from Mr Cooper, informing him that her father had disowned her. It also said Mr Cooper wanted no further word as to her well-being or whereabouts.'

'Hmm...does Nathan know the girl's name?'

Philip slowly shook his head.

'No, Papa. I don't think so. I've never discussed Merrilla with Mr Denstone. Err...will...will you speak with her, Papa?' Philip's eyes pleaded for his father's understanding. He sighed deeply when John nodded.

There was no time to say more, for a knock on the door announced the arrival of Dick and Samuel with the luggage and the three younger men had a swift exchange of banter.

Nathan returned. After closing the door behind the servants, he sat on the bed and turned to John. 'I've just seen Mrs Waspill. She's spoken with Mrs O'Keaf, and obtained her permission to move rooms. She is to stay with the Gylby family, downstairs. I'll use her room, and you'll be able to stay in here with Philip.' He beamed, receiving a slight nod in return.

'Mrs Waspill seems to be able to organise things very well. Do I take it she's also arranged Mr Parkinson's affairs?' John's eyes were flinty blue as he looked at his friend.

'You have no need to be concerned about anything but resting after your long journey, John. May I suggest you use my room for an hour or so? Then we can have dinner together.'

Without speaking, he allowed himself to be ushered downstairs into a room that was spotlessly clean and smelled faintly of lavender. Nathan lifted the latch, ready to leave, when John's hand on his arm stopped him. 'Tell me, friend...Merrilla. What kind of young woman is she?' He relaxed a little as the younger man smiled warmly.

'She's kind and generous. Still a lady, for all her sad experiences.'

'You know of her history?'

'But of course. When I saw how fond Philip was becoming of her, I asked questions. A bargee said he had changed an earlier opinion since becoming more acquainted with her. Everyone speaks very respectfully of her.'

'She must be a very exceptional young woman, Nathan.'

'She is. She is,' was the quiet reply.

Mrs Gylby and Merrilla had prepared a meal and it was ready to be served as they entered Philip's room. Merrilla, with eyes cast down, sank into a curtsy. Philip plucked at his bed covers.

Nathan indicated towards Merilla. 'John, may I present Mrs Waspill? This is the young lady who has looked after Philip so marvellously.'

Everyone held their breath and watched as he stepped forward and, with a gallant gesture, took Merrilla's hand and bowed over it.

'I have heard reports of your tender care of my son and Mr Denstone. I am much indebted to you, my dear.'

A pulse beat rapidly in her throat and her colour heightened. She inclined her head and murmured, 'It was a pleasure to be of service, sir.'

Hmm, he thought, *at least her voice is cultured.*

Philip visibly relaxed at the benign expression settling on his father's face, and the smile he directed at Merrilla.

Nathan pulled a chair near to his own and patted it, inviting John to sit beside him. 'Come and enjoy this rabbit pie, John. I wager my gold studs that you'll say you have never tasted better pastry.'

At midnight, the three men were still talking. Merrilla had cleared the table hours before and gone to bed.

John said, 'The coalmine can be left in the capable hands of Mr Lang. Hugo had everything under control at the Nottingham mill when I left, so when you are able to travel, Philip, we'll return home.' The men agreed, each, for his own reasons, eager to leave Paxton and return to home comforts in Yorkshire.

As the coachman cleaned the mud-spattered coach in the stable yard at Ghyll House in Yorkshire, he repeated everything he had heard about Jeremy's murder to the Denstones' head stable lad. His account was overheard and, as the maid helped Joan dress for dinner, she brought the gossip to the ears of her mistress. Joan rebuked the maid for repeating tales from the stable, but did not dismiss the story as mere tittle-tattle. Concerned to hear that Nancy might have played a part in it, she decided to send for the man and find out for herself what he knew. His account of the events horrified her.

Hugo's subsequent interview with his mother was stormy. He was unable to reply to many of her searching questions about Nancy's background, and stuttered and stammered as he had as a small boy.

'And what are you going to do about Miss Elysabeth Larcombe? Are you going to tell her about this latest turn of events, or were you intending to let her know on the day of your wedding to this... this person?' She could hardly spit out the words. 'And another thing—a tale of a murder has been brought to my attention. Would this person you've brought here have anything to do with it? I understand from the newsmonger that the accused man has stated he knows her. They used to be close friends in Nottingham Town, and "close" could mean anything.'

Hugo sprang to Nancy's defence, saying she had spent the evening with him. He had escorted her to her bedchamber and given her into the care of her maid.

That evening Nancy's behaviour at dinner was beyond reproach. As they withdrew to the sitting room, however, Joan caught her smiling and fluttering her eyelashes seductively at a young footman. Her lips tightened with fury, but she said nothing to Nancy although she gave a quelling glance at the footman, who coloured up with embarrassment.

Hugo spent a sleepless night thinking about his future with Nancy. He had left his mother and returned to his room but, changing his mind, had dismissed the manservant, saying he was going for a walk around the garden before dressing for dinner.

Remembering Nancy's breathlessness and her tousled appearance that night, he couldn't help but wonder. He called to mind her account of the lost bracelet, and the way she looked and smiled at other men when she thought she was unobserved. He remembered the sly look Mr Pugh had given him when he had told the man he was now in sole charge of the workforce, and that Miss Turpin would no longer be working at the mill. Could he do anything to extricate himself from his difficult predicament? For he realised he had been foolishly infatuated with her. It might be possible for Nancy to return to Nottingham, but she would be bound to talk, and would the Denstone family live down the resulting scandal?

Blurry-eyed the following morning, he made ready to ride to Clemmants with a letter written by John for Esther Larcombe. He was told, on his arrival at the house, that Mrs Larcombe had already set off for Stagill Village to arrange the church flowers. It was usual at that time of day for Miss Elysabeth Larcombe to be preparing for an early morning ride so he made a wide detour of the stables.

On his way to the church, he hardly noticed the picturesque thatched cottages behind their flower-filled gardens, nor the village pond, where ducks waddled away to safety, and flopped into the water, quacking in alarm. He dismounted at the church gates and tethered his horse to a hitching-rail before making his way along one of the paths. As he approached the south door, he saw Esther Larcombe leaving the church, the grey, stone doorway making a fitting background to her yellow gown and flower-decked bonnet. Although in her fifties, her brown hair shone without a trace of grey, and only the laughter lines about her eyes indicated maturity. With an empty wicker basket over her slender arm, she started to set off to where her groom and carriage waited.

'Mrs Larcombe! Mrs Larcombe, ma'am.'

She turned, but her warm smile of welcome faded as he turned his tricorn hat round and round in his hands, an embarrassed expression on his face. She took a step forward to place her usual kiss on her godson's cheek, but drew back.

'I...err...Mrs Larcombe. I have a letter from Mr Larcombe, and I h-have to tell you...' He stuttered to a halt. How on earth could he tell this woman, who was like a second mother to him, that he was no longer eligible to marry her beautiful daughter, Elysabeth?

'What is it, Hugo? What are you trying to say?' Her fingers pressed to her forehead, she stared at his pale face with fear-filled eyes. 'Is...is it Philip? Have you had bad news from Scotland? My husband?' She swayed, and Hugo placed his hand under her arm to steady her.

'No, no, Mrs Larcombe. Please do not distress yourself. Mr Larcombe and my father will bring Philip home safely, you'll see.'

With a tremulous smile, she said, 'We have been so worried. You see, we had only the one brief letter from my husband.'

'Paxton Village is very isolated, and it might be some time before they can get word to us. Mr Larcombe did stress that you were not to join them. He left some weeks ago, and is sure to be with Philip and my father by now, ma'am.' He handed her the letter from John and, with her hand resting lightly on his arm, he escorted her to the waiting carriage.

They were both silent, deep in thought, until, leaning forward to speak through the carriage window, she said, 'Thank-you for the letter, my dear, and do not worry. Come to dinner tonight with your mamma. I'm sure Elysabeth will be delighted to see you.'

Hugo watched the carriage until it was out of sight. Dinner? How could he possibly face Elysabeth at her home, and introduce her to Nancy before they all walked into dinner? It would be impossible. With a curse, he mounted his horse, kicking it into movement, and galloped through the village, onward to the moors, as though pursued by demons. Never before had he ridden with such recklessness. His horse leapt over swiftly flowing becks, onto peat hags where the going was wet and treacherous, and along shelving scree beds, where an incautious movement could create a rush and flurry of falling rock. He rode for miles until at last his horse halted, trembling, covered in white lather.

On his return from his wild ride on the moors, knowing that his mother would be making her usual midday visit to Clemmants, he went to the study to write a letter for Elysabeth. It took several attempts before he succeeded in placing a seal on it. Hearing his mother giving instructions to the servants as she made her departure, he hurried outside and was just in time to hand her his letter through the carriage window. 'Please, Mamma. Give this to Elysabeth for me.' His eyes spoke for him, but Joan only gave her son a cool nod as she took the letter, and curtly instructed the coachman to drive on.

At Clemmants, shafts of afternoon sunlight slanted through the long windows and the open doors, lighting the black and white chequered floor in the entrance hall. A crackling log fire in a vast, elaborate fireplace was never allowed to go out, and it warmed the hall throughout both summer and winter.

Elysabeth Larcombe was a tall slim girl with a ready smile. Her wavy brown hair, similar in colour to that of her brother, reached her waist. That day she wore it confined by a wide satin ribbon matching the colour of her pink gown.

She had seen Joan Denstone's carriage approach the house and, wearing a welcoming smile, ran to greet her. She had almost reached the bottom of the main staircase when Joan stepped into the entrance hall looking annoyed. 'Your mamma, Elysabeth?'

Chilled by the tone of voice, and noticing the unusual way she clutched the folds of her skirt as she strode forward, Elysabeth's smile faded. She pointed wordlessly at the drawing room door and watched Joan enter. No greeting, no curtsy, not even a smile.

'What ever can be amiss?' she wondered aloud. Joan Denstone had not looked at her in such a manner since the occasion, years before, when she had indulged in childish mischief with Hugo and he had broken a tooth. She decided to wait a moment in the hallway before joining the two women.

When the door of the drawing room opened, Esther gave a cry of pleasure at the sight of her friend, Joan. She dropped the tapestry she was working on, scattering the assortment of coloured threads over the carpet as she rose to her feet. 'Hugo met me this morning at the church, and gave me a letter from John. I am expecting you both for dinner this evening, Joan,' she said as she took hold of her friend's hand and drew her forward, kissing her cheek. Her smile faded when she noticed the frown creasing Joan's brow, and the puckered tightness of her lips. 'Please, Joan, cease worrying. I am positive the men will bring Philip home safely. Come and sit here by me.'

Joan sank onto the sofa next to her and burst into tears. Esther turned pale as goose bumps rose on her arms. Something must be very wrong for her friend to behave in such a manner. She usually acted so sensibly, with a level head. Her immediate thought was concern for her loved ones. Had bad news arrived from Scotland? Did Hugo know more than he had told her?

'Joan. Joan, tell me what's wrong! For goodness sake, tell me,' she pleaded, grasping her friend's arm in alarm.

Mopping her eyes, Joan sniffed a few times, and then composed herself. 'It's Hugo.'

Esther looked blankly at her. 'Hugo? But I saw him only this morning. He seemed to be quite well.'

'He has brought home a…a person. He says they are to marry.' The words ended on a high wail.

Esther blinked to bring Joan's face back into focus. Her beautiful daughter, Elysabeth, jilted? That was the last thing she had expected her friend to say. 'A…a person?'

Joan pressed her lips together and nodded. 'She…they arrived yesterday, late afternoon. They met when he went to work at the new cotton mill in Nottingham. She worked there. A mill girl…'

She stopped and looked over her shoulder as Esther put her finger to her mouth, staring past her at the door.

Elysabeth stood in the open doorway, her hands over her cheeks, her eyes round and disbelieving. Alarmed at the sight of her daughter's grief-stricken face, Esther hurried to put an arm around her shoulders.

Joan fumbled inside her reticule and took out a letter bearing the Denstone seal. 'Hugo asked me to give you this, Elysabeth.' She offered the letter to the dumbfounded girl.

Elysabeth moved to stand in front of Joan. 'It cannot be true, Mrs Denstone. Hugo loves me. We are betrothed. He always said...' She put her hand over her mouth, unable to continue.

'Hugo gave me the letter as I was leaving.' Joan's tone was flat.

Taking the letter, Elysabeth faced her mother. 'Will...will you please excuse me, Mamma, Mrs Denstone?' She sank into a curtsy before leaving the room but forgot to close the door behind her.

They listened as she ran up the stairs to the sanctuary of her bedchamber. Esther spoke first. 'I saw Hugo this morning, but he only spoke of Philip. Nothing else. He never said a word about a young lady.'

Giving a loud sniff, Joan muttered, 'No lady, that one! She does try her best to act the part, but she is without the right breeding.' She sat staring at the rug at her feet, and moved a skein of thread with her foot.

Her head jerked up as Esther spoke. 'I never thought Hugo capable of hurting Elysabeth in this way. I know they used to have quarrels as children, but this! I don't know what to say. This will break Elysabeth's heart.'

They both sniffed and wiped their eyes, until Joan burst out, 'He didn't even have the decency to send a note to warn me. Must be besotted. Just turned up with this woman, this Miss

Turpin, hanging on his arm, without so much as a by your leave. I've no idea who her people are, nor if they own property or have money, although there can't be much chance of that if she worked in a cotton mill. Miss Turpin says they love each other. Well, we will see. I think she leaves much to be desired. The wedding ring is not yet on her finger, and I hope it never will be. Whatever his father will have to say, I dread to think.'

It was clear Joan was hurt and bitter. From the time of Elysabeth's birth both women had looked forward to the day when the girl would become Hugo's bride.

Once her friend had left, Esther went straight to her daughter's bedchamber. She found Elysabeth lying across her bed, swollen faced, her eyes red from weeping.

'Oh, my dear, don't. It's not worthy of him to treat you like this.' She held her close, trying to console her, rocking the broken-hearted girl as though she was still a baby, murmuring soft words of comfort and stroking her dark curls.

'It is me Hugo loves, Mamma. I know it is. Somehow, he must have been tricked. We have always said...' Her slender body shook with more sobs.

'Hush, my dear. You'll make yourself ill if you weep like this.'

Her tears mingled with those of her daughter as they clung to each other.

Sometime later, Elysabeth said, 'Mamma dear, I'll stay here in my room awhile. Please excuse me. I cannot face dinner.'

'Of course... The letter, dear? What excuse does Hugo give for bringing this young woman home?'

'Very little that makes any sense. Oh, how I wish Papa and Philip were here. They could perhaps talk to him, and make him see reason.'

After searching for the letter among the rumpled bed covers, Elysabeth handed it to her mother. Small fragments of sealing wax were still attached to the damp and crumpled paper. It wasn't easy to smooth out the letter.

GHYLL HOUSE

Thursday

26th May 1797

My dear Miss Larcombe,

I fear that I have some news which may upset you. I know that our families have always thought we should marry, but I have met a young lady whom I have asked to be my wife.

When in Nottingham with your papa, we purchased a cotton mill. Nancy Turpin, the young lady who has come home with me, worked there, and she was a great help to your papa and myself. When your papa left for Scotland, Miss Turpin and I grew to know each other much better, and I have brought her home to meet my mamma. I do hope you, my closest ally, will befriend her, for she knows no one in Yorkshire, and I am sure she will welcome a female companion.

We are now both adults, and have the opportunity to go into the world and meet other people. I am sure that in time you will put aside our childish infatuation, and will fall in love with a man worthy of you. I do value your friendship, Elysabeth, and hope to keep it.

Adieu,

Hugo Denstone.

Esther folded the letter before giving it back to Elysabeth. 'Seems a mite strange he makes no mention of loving her, or anything about her family. This is not the kind of letter I expected to read, and when I saw Hugo this morning, he certainly didn't strike me as a man in a joyous fever of love.'

233

Elysabeth lay still. Esther sat on the bed, holding her hand in silence.

Chapter 14

No one at Clemmants discussed Elysabeth, but it was evident to everyone that she had changed from a vivacious girl who rushed through life with a careless laughter, into an introvert who crept quietly around the house. Her complexion had turned blotchy from constant weeping, and she only replied briefly when addressed. She had also forsaken her beloved horse.

When the Larcombe coach, followed by a carriage and a flat wagon, swept along Clemmants drive and halted in front of the house, Elysabeth stood unsmiling beside her mother. It was Esther who ran down the steps with a glad cry to greet John and Philip. Waiting until the kisses were finished, Elysabeth moved sedately forward to greet the travellers.

'My love, thank God you have all arrived home safely,' Esther said. After exchanging hugs with her husband, she turned to her son, still seated in the coach. 'My dear.' As she grasped Philip's hands, she froze on seeing a young woman sitting in the coach beside him, and her eyes widened in surprise.

Merrilla saw a glimpse of dismay, and knew at once that sooner, rather than later, there'd have to be a private interview with Philip's mother.

Before the journey, John had slipped a purse to Philip, along with instructions to encourage Merrilla to buy new clothes, as well as anything of which she may be in need. Once they had reached Glasgow, and with only a slight protest, she had made a visit to a dressmaker.

The dressmaker had made a number of garments for customers who had not collected them, and was delighted to receive a client who would take some off her hands. She brought Merrilla a selection of gowns, holding each one out to show off the style and fabric, before laying it over a chair. Merrilla chose a dove-grey silk with simple trimmings as a travelling dress and a light brown morning dress with a modest neckline, trimmed with ruffles of narrow ecru lace. The dressmaker also supplied her with matching petticoats and other essentials, including a reticule and three pairs of kid gloves. The gloves delighted her. Since the accident in the coalmine, she had constantly rubbed goose-grease on her hands, and gradually they had become less sore and rough. She wore her new finery for her journey to Clemmants.

Alighting from the coach with downcast eyes, she curtsied to Philip's mother.

'My dear, we have so many things to tell you,' John said, keeping his arm tightly around his wife's trim waist. 'But first, may I present Mrs Waspill, a widow who nursed Philip back to health.'

William, hat in hand, and smart in a new green coat, came to stand beside Merrilla. 'This is Mr William Parkinson, my dear,' John continued. His wife stiffened, and she turned questioning eyes on him. 'He is very like Philip, is he not, my dear?' he added.

William bowed low, and when introduced to the aloof girl, nodded his head in Elysabeth's direction.

Elysabeth gave her father a hug and a kiss, but made no attempt to welcome the strangers. She only gave her brother a half-smile and stood back to watch the menservants help him from the coach and carry him inside.

Philip and Elysabeth each had a bedchamber on the same corridor. The vacant room next to Elysabeth's was made ready for Merrilla.

'I hope that you will be comfortable in here, Mrs Waspill,' Elysabeth said, giving a cursory look around the sunny room. 'Do you have a maid?'

'Yes, Miss Larcombe. Bridget. She's only a child. I'm training her.' Merrilla gave a hesitant smile, and held out her hand.

'Would you...? Could you bring yourself to call me Merrilla, Miss Larcombe? I would like so much for us to be friends.'

Elysabeth had turned to leave the room, but at the words she paused with a hand on the door handle. With dark, sad eyes, she looked intently at her. 'It will be very nice to have a female companion near my own age, Merrilla.'

William Parkinson sat in the spacious drawing room as John and Esther recounted the attributes of his father, and told him of the work he'd carried out at the Nottingham Medical School years before.

'My brother was a virtuous man, and a very clever physician,' Esther said, with a catch in her voice. 'Much of his knowledge came from your grandpapa. I loved Charles very much.'

'I didn't know anything about you and all this,' said William. 'Mother only spoke bitterly about him, and very little about her life in Nottingham. She never encouraged me to ask questions about the family,'

The only sounds in the room were those of a clock ticking, and a sudden movement of a burning log. William broke the silence. 'My mother felt deeply wounded by the treatment she received from everyone in Nottingham. She said she'd chosen to cut herself off from her family by travelling to Scotland, and that's all I know, except that she'd promised to tell me about the past "one day".'

Tears filled his aunt's eyes. 'She was once my dearest friend, but not a clever lady. And always kept under her mother's influence. Had we known all the facts... Anyway, we will never know now.' She dabbed her eyes with a handkerchief. John hovered over her, patting her hand in sympathy.

A knock on the door heralded the entrance of Philip, helped into the room by two footmen, followed by Merrilla carrying a light blanket. While attention was on him Elysabeth drifted into

237

the room. After curtsying to her parents, and murmuring a vague greeting to everyone else, she settled herself in a chair near the window and bent her head over her needlework.

'We left Mr Denstone at Ghyll House.' Philip smiled across the hearthrug at his parents. 'He half-promised to come with Mrs Denstone and Hugo for dinner, Mamma.' 'Time we saw Hugo. I've so much to discuss with him.'

An expression of horror covered his mother's face and, with a sharp cry of distress his sister made a hurried exit.

'Goodness, Mamma, what have I said? Why did Elysabeth run away in that manner?'

'Hugo has returned home, but he is engaged to be married to a Miss Turpin,' Esther said, in a low voice. 'Elysabeth has made herself quite ill by the news, and now refuses to leave the house, in case she meets the woman.'

John's eyes bulged with temper. 'That…that damn young puppy. I've met this Turpin wench. She has nothing but a pretty face. Did she beguile him by lifting her skirts, and then get him to propose marriage? Bah! Needs bringing to his senses with a whipping. Nathan will give him one, and if not, I will.'

'John, my dear. Please.' Esther fanned her face to cool her blushes as she gestured in Merrilla's direction.

Merrilla cheeks had also reddened, and she kept her eyes lowered.

Esther gave her husband a speaking glance, rose to her feet, and moved to join William at the window in the late afternoon sunlight. She placed her hand on his sleeve. 'William, you are so much like your papa. He had a small moustache. Did you know that? I see you favour a full beard. You have similar coloured hair. His used to curl across his forehead just like yours.' Chattering on about past history, she drew him to the door, and out of the room.

After she left him at the door of his bedchamber, he looked around the spacious room with appreciation. Dark oak panelling on the walls was partly hidden by an assortment of etchings and paintings. Comfortable chairs were set on a patterned carpet, some near to the high windows, with sweeping views across the moorland. Next to the four-poster bed stood a bookcase full of miscellaneous reading matter. A number of medical journals brought a contented smile to his face.

He remembered John's words. "Although disgraced, you can be proud in the knowledge that your father was a very intelligent and gifted man." He put a hand to his face, and wiped away a tear. He now understood why his mother had been ostracised by her family. So many things that had puzzled him in the past were becoming clear.

After his mother's funeral, he had gratefully accepted John's suggestion that he accompany the party to Yorkshire, and meet his father's side of the family. They arranged for Mary Gylby and her brothers to manage the shop, with the option to rent it sometime in the future. He had no idea when he would return to Scotland—or, indeed, whether or not he would wish to do so, now he had found his family.

John moved to sit on the arm of his son's chair.

'Papa. What can we do to help Elysabeth?' Philip asked, watching his father rub his thumb on his lips. He exchanged a glance with Merrilla. 'This means our plan for a double wedding with Hugo and Elysabeth will have to be changed, but we will still have our lovely day.' Prompted by this thought, a sunny smile lit his face.

John stood up and, with both hands behind his back, faced them. 'We do nothing. We pretend that nothing is amiss. Merrilla, you, my dear, will need to work very hard to keep Elysabeth's spirits up. I will ride over to Ghyll House and see

Hugo's parents, to find out the facts. Who knows? Perhaps they will allow Hugo to marry this Miss Turpin. She may even have tried to charm Nathan with her flashing eyes, and he might have fallen for it. I remember seeing her at the mill. She would try and charm anything in breeches, if I remember her aright. But Nathan will soon see through her deception, I'm sure.'

At Ghyll House, the atmosphere was strained. Nathan Denstone arrived home to a wife who, after giving him a warm greeting in front of the servants, hurried him into her sitting room, and burst into tears.

'This is a fine welcome home, wife. Is the gossip I heard true?'

Lifting her head out of her handkerchief, Joan stared at her husband. 'G...gossip?'

'The girl who travelled here with Hugo. I heard she might be involved in the murder at the inn. If that's so, pack her off back to Nottingham.'

'No, it was nothing to do with her. Hugo told me she was with him that evening.'

'Thank goodness. I thought...' He tugged at his cravat. 'What made him bring her here?'

'They...they are to marry.' Joan held out her hands imploringly, tears streaming down her cheeks. 'Oh, please, Nathan, can you do something to stop them?'

'Marry? What do you mean, marry? Is he the head of this house? Has he gone mad? And what about asking my permission?' His eyes bulged. He snatched off his wig and threw it on a nearby chair. It slid to the floor as he yanked open the door and shouted to the butler to bring him a bottle of claret, and to be quick about it.

'Where is the young fool?' he growled, after slamming the door closed.

'He's out riding. I seldom see him during the day. He usually returns home in time to join us for dinner.'

He went to stand by the fireplace, looking into the fire. 'Does he love her?'

'I haven't seen any sign of loving behaviour between them. She tends to stay in the garden, or in the drawing room on her own. It seems as though she enjoys her own company.'

A knock on the door announced the butler with a bottle of claret and two glasses on a silver tray. Nathan waited until the man had withdrawn, before saying, 'I remember seeing the minx. She had a pretty face, but obviously working class. She'll never be capable of being the mistress of this house, or of giving Hugo the support he needs from a wife.'

'I've been giving the matter a great deal of thought, and I have an idea how we might get rid of her, Nathan. Your study is next to the drawing room, where she likes to sit, and there is a connecting door that can be left ajar. We'll be as devious and scheming as she is. Bring your wine to your bedchamber. We can discuss my idea without fear of interruption, or of being overheard by anyone.' Joan rose to her feet.

They sat late into the night, discussing ways of disrupting the affair between their son and Nancy. Nathan proposed paying her money, but Joan had heard a whisper about the girl's behaviour towards the male staff, and persuaded her husband to wait awhile.

'We'll drop her some corn, and see if she chokes on it,' she said, before coaching Nathan on what to say when they were behind his open study door.

Nancy sat by the open window in the opulent drawing room, allowing the floral fragrance to drift in. Polly had worked hard to improve her neglected complexion, and she always had her chair positioned to prevent the sun from darkening her skin. Shining glass droplets from the chandelier sparkled rainbow colours onto furniture as the sunlight crept across the room. She sat enjoying the luxury of doing absolutely nothing. With her back straight, she made a charming picture in her lilac gown. She had a cream fichu around her shoulders, arranged, as usual, to enhance the sight of her breasts.

Of the two doors in the drawing room, one led to the extensive entrance hall and the other to Nathan's study. She hadn't noticed the study door was slightly open until she heard voices.

'How do you know for certain that William is the son of Charles Parkinson?'

Recognising Joan Denstone's voice, she cocked her head in order to hear more clearly.

'Sally's accident was terrible. What a dreadful end. William found her marriage certificate and other papers among her possessions and showed them to us. John Larcombe knew that both Lord Grashod and his wife had died, and he sent word to Mr Harwood immediately, to find out if William had inherited anything from the Grashod estate. When the will was examined William discovered he would be a very wealthy person indeed.' Nancy strained to hear better, as Nathan Denstone continued. 'As the only daughter of Lord Grashod, Sally would have certainly inherited something, and if they had known her address...'

Joan must have moved closer to the door, since her voice became louder as she asked in a clear voice, 'Does that mean William Parkinson will inherit the title? Oh, Nathan, he will be Lord Grashod, and may go to the King's Court in London. Every hostess in London will want him at her social evenings, especially if she has an unmarried daughter.'

'That is most likely, my dear. William will probably inherit the title, and be rich by any standard. And I know John Larcombe will be generous to his nephew. He has always been open-handed with his family.'

'William Parkinson will be an admirable suitor for any girl who can capture his heart. I suppose Elysabeth Larcombe is eligible for such a prize now Hugo is no longer available.'

Nancy heard a low chuckle, and the sound of a chair creaking as someone moved.

'I must ride over to Clemmants, my dear. John and I have business to discuss.'

'Let's walk to the stables together. Will you have time to...?' The sound of a door closing shut off the rest of the conversation.

Nancy sat motionless. How could she turn this new knowledge to her own advantage? The words "rich" and "title" and "social evenings" rang in her ears. She'd be Lady Grashod if she were to marry William, a real lady, with a crown and a castle. A surge of excitement swept through her. Thank goodness she'd overheard that titbit of information. Funny how a person's direction could change with just a few overheard words. That poxy Larcombe girl wouldn't have chance to get the prize. It would be she who accompanied William Parkinson to London. She'd have jewels on her thumbs, and six gowns to wear every day in the week, and twice that many on Sundays. And shoes. A wardrobe full of lovely shoes.

A movement of the window drapes drew her attention to the entrance hall door being opened. A young girl in a maid's uniform, and carrying a brass coalscuttle, hesitated in the doorway.

'Well, girl? Don't stand there making a draught.'

The maid bobbed a curtsy. 'Sorry, Miss Turpin. The fire needs laying, ready for lighting this evening. I thought there was no one in here.'

The girl jumped when Nancy snapped her fan closed, pointed to the study door with it, and ordered, 'Close that door over there.'

With a frightened glance the girl hurried to do as she was told, and hastened to finish her task. Nancy could be spiteful to those she considered below her station, and there were many. After a soft click of the door, she was once more alone. Her contemplation of marriage to William Parkinson spun around in her mind. *How can I win Mr Parkinson without announcing my intention to the Denstone family? I must keep my muckworm, in case William doesn't come up to scratch.*

Later, as she made her way to her bedchamber, her mind still grappled with her problem. A new gown had been laid out, ready to wear at dinner that evening. Polly had stayed up most of the previous night to finish making it. She turned to look at Nancy, who was humming a tune.

'Polly, we have been invited to dine at Clemmants this evening. I had intended to say I felt unwell, or some such excuse, but after what I overheard today, I've changed my mind. I'll go and meet this high-stomached Larcombe family. Put out my pink gown, and we'll place fresh roses on my bosom. When the petals fall, (or when I pluck them), they'll be more of me to see.' She stood admiring herself in the long mirror, her hands raising her breasts whilst she practised a pouting smile. 'My hair needs to be dressed higher, and use plenty of powder. A curl must come over my shoulder, like this.' Tugging her hair from the restraining pins, she allowed it to cascade almost to her waist. Still examining herself, she continued, 'Make sure you pick the best blooms. And I don't want any thorns on the rose stems. Your fingers are so clumsy nowadays, Polly. Just lately, I've been thinking I'd be happier with a maid more suitable, someone nearer my own age, maybe. You could return to your friends in Nottingham. There's plenty of carriers' carts journeying south that could take you.'

An opportunity arose for Merrilla to speak with Esther the following evening after dinner when Elysabeth excused herself from accompanying them to Esther's sitting room. It was evident Esther wanted her to feel at ease. She patted the couch invitingly. 'Come and sit by me, my dear.'

She obeyed, and, tongue-tied, sat staring at the pastoral scene painted on the chicken-skin of her fan.

With a light hand on Merrilla's arm, Esther said, 'Perhaps you'd care to tell me a little about yourself, Merrilla?'

'My life has been nothing but folly, ma-am. Stupid and wicked folly.'

'My husband told me a little of your history. Did you elope for the romance of it?'

Her head lowered, she nodded, and haltingly recounted her story. Esther sat still and silent, her face showing outrage and distress in turn. At the end of her narrative, Merrilla wept with the relief of being able to unburden herself, and Esther allowed her to cry for a while, before saying, 'My dear.'

Those two words, said with such feeling, touched her and, from time to time, she wiped her eyes as they talked.

At last, Esther said, 'Thank you for confiding in me, Merrilla. I understand how difficult it must have been for you to recount that unhappy time. Now you are here, we must leave all that behind you. Think of the present, and look forward to the future.'

Polly's lips were tightly compressed as she worked on Nancy's hair, automatically brushing and curling it into a high coiffure. She didn't ask why Nancy wanted to engage a new maid, knowing the reason would probably be something of which she didn't approve. She hadn't yet mentioned her own news. Her plans were already in place.

Each Sunday, she attended the church in Stagill Village. She had met one of the tenant farmers from the Clemmants estate and

245

welcomed his attention. Although she hadn't yet told the farmer, she still had a little money. Older than her, he hadn't been married before. When he'd asked her to be his wife, it hadn't taken long to make up her mind, and she'd accepted.

He'd mentioned that her mistress was news for the gossips. She'd been mortified. As her fingers worked, her thoughts ran on. *That girl wants too much too quickly and she's heading for a fall. The jump from a mill worker to society life was far too ambitious for a girl brought up as she was. Never thought she'd have turned out like this, or I wouldn't have come with her. I don't want her reputation staining my character. Thank goodness I've found a kind and honest man to marry. Otherwise, my situation here would be intolerable. I'll tell my love we'll marry as soon as he can arrange it, and then I'll leave that baggage to get on with her own life.*

A sharp rap on the door interrupted her thoughts, and she sprang across the room to answer it. She moved to one side and bobbed a curtsy as Joan walked in, carrying a small, chased silver casket.

Nancy rose to her feet, bobbed a curtsy, and, noticing the casket, gave an eager smile.

'As we will all be dining at Clemmants this evening, and I have no doubt you will wish to look your best, I have brought you this necklace to wear. I shall want it back on your return.'

Nancy's eyes glittered when Joan lifted the lid of the casket. Even Polly gave a gasp of wonder. The velvet-lined box revealed a diamond and amethyst necklace, a pair of matching earrings and a ring.

'Mr Denstone suggested you ought to wear these this evening.'

The jewels rivalled Nancy's eyes in brilliance, and her smile of genuine pleasure broadened as she took the earrings and held them against her ears.

'They'll look well on you. When you marry Hugo, they'll be yours.' Joan studied the girl as she postured in front of her looking glass. 'Wear no flowers tonight, Miss Turpin. Young girls must not gild the lily. Their natural beauty is enough.' She lifted Nancy's new gown, allowing the satin to slither into slinky folds over her arms. 'The neckline is very deep on this gown, my dear. Do you have a wrap to drape over it?'

Polly hurried to fetch a selection of shawls from the wooden chest. Joan selected a multi-coloured silk with a long fringe, and held it out. Nancy took it, draped it high over her shoulders, and curtsied.

Joan nodded her approval. 'Very nice. I always had an eye for matching colours,' she said, with a smile for Polly, who smiled in return.

After she had left, Nancy gave way to temper. Dashing the silk shawl onto the floor, she threw brushes and trinkets from her dressing table, as well as anything else that came to hand. 'That odious, hateful woman! I wanted to wear flowers. Just you wait. If I marry that muckworm, Hugo, I'll be the mistress here, and that stuck-up bitch will be moved out. Let her go and live at precious Clemmants, out of my sight. Neckline too low, indeed! At least I fill it, which is more than that scrawny bitch is able to do.' She threw a vase, and it landed on the polished door.

When she left her bedchamber for the evening revels, all signs of her temper tantrum had vanished. Waiting until she was sure she'd be the last person down, she drifted down the wide staircase to join the family, and waited for the usual murmurs of admiration at her stunning appearance. She managed to keep her smile fixed in place, even though the only expected accolade came from Nathan.

'You look very pretty this evening, Miss Turpin.'

Nancy did look lovely in her pink gown, but she had defied Joan by attaching clusters of rosebuds to the lifted hem around the skirt that opened to show a cream and pink striped underskirt. Pink rosebuds were also threaded through her curls, which fell over one shoulder. Polly had excelled herself.

As Nathan bowed to her, Hugo stepped forward to take her hand. Flashing him a brilliant smile, she gazed into his eyes and lifted her half-open fan to her cheek. She stroked it in a seductive manner, and ran her tongue over her lips.

'We have all been waiting this half-hour past, Miss Turpin. Now you are finally here, we can leave,' said Joan, clearly unable to hide her displeasure at being kept waiting by the twitching of her shawl. With a grim expression, she placed a hand on her husband's arm, and moved towards the door.

Nancy kept silent throughout the drive to Clemmants. She gave a most charming smile to Hugo as he helped her down from the carriage, but he gave no sign of loving emotion as their hands touched. His expression seemed chilled.

'Come along. Why do you dally?' called Joan, who had been the first to be helped from the carriage, and stood waiting on the wide sweeping steps.

Once in the entrance hall, Nancy allowed a maid to remove her cloak, while her eyes appraised the gracious furnishings. Liveried servants seemed to be everywhere. As she moved to stand in front of a high court cupboard, she lifted her hand to touch the rich carvings. She shivered when she felt what seemed to be a cold breath on her bare neck, and looked around, but no other person stood near.

With a shrug at her foolish fancy, she joined the others and placed her gloved hand on Hugo's arm, allowing him to lead her along the corridor behind his parents. Without the Denstone family noticing, she smiled and fluttered her eyelashes at a footman, who looked back wooden-faced. She guessed he would mention it later to his cronies in the servants' hall.

John and Esther Larcombe greeted Hugo warmly, as usual. Elysabeth, however, conveyed her unhappy feelings in her very brief greeting, and seated herself well away from him and Nancy. Throughout the whole evening, she stayed either beside a member of her family or Merrilla.

Nancy recognised Merrilla immediately. She gave her a condescending nod, and fingered the jewels around her throat. *As good as you, Miss Lady*, she thought. *You won't look down on me now. I wonder what happened to Bill Waspill. Has she told them she was once living as a common boat woman? Lower than a scullery skivvy, they are.* The knowledge that she was now of a higher social position than Merrilla made her eyes sparkle, and she became so vivacious that the older women exchanged speaking glances.

The huge, polished dining room table reflected the silver and the crystal glassware. High towers of mixed flowers and fruits, many unknown to her, were placed at intervals along the centre of the table, and wide floral arrangements were positioned on either side of her. Hugo sat on her right, Philip to her left, and, with delight, she found William directly opposite. By a sly tug to her bodice and leaning forward, she managed to attract his interest to such an extent that he didn't hear a question put to him by Esther, who had to repeat herself.

Her etiquette was faultless. She ate a little of each dish presented to her, drank very little, was attentive when spoken to, and most charming to Esther and John.

The meal finished, the ladies formally returned to the withdrawing room. Merrilla seated herself next to Nancy, but was ignored when she tried to speak to her. Some time later, the menfolk joined them, and the atmosphere lightened. Nancy chattered and glanced at each of the men to catch any admiring looks thrown her way.

Although the numerous windows and the glass doors leading to the terrace were open, everyone felt warm, most of the ladies using a fan. Nancy had twice moved to a different seat, and she welcomed what little breeze came from the windows. She gave a surreptitious glance around, and found William was missing. Everyone else appeared to be deep in conversation, and she assumed no one would notice if she rose to her feet and wandered outside.

As she made her way to the end of the terrace, her embroidered slippers soundless on the flagstones, she tapped her closed fan on her left hand, and looked across the lawn towards a fountain. The splashing was loud in the evening hush, and she breathed in, enjoying the scents wafting from nearby flowering bushes.

'Is that you, Miss Larcombe?' Cigar smoke and the light tread of footsteps accompanied the voice. William appeared from the shadows. 'Miss Turpin.' He gave a low chuckle. 'However could I have mistaken you?' He bowed low, his eyes looking into hers with an almost hypnotic stare.

Nancy gave a glittering smile, interpreting his look. She had seen that expression many times on a man's face.

'Do you wish to take a stroll, Miss Turpin? Perhaps I can show you the fish fountain that everyone admires?'

She fluttered her eyelashes as she gazed into his eyes, and flicked open her fan with a well-practised flourish.

'As far as the fish fountain, Mr Parkinson?' She glanced over her shoulder. They were still alone.

'Yes. We'll hear should anyone call.'

Her fan snapped closed, she placed her hand on his proffered arm and lifted her skirts clear of the grass. He led her across the lawn and, covering her hand with his, looked into her eyes. Behind the fountain, in shadow, he slipped his arm around her waist.

'Sir!' Pretended scandalised shock shook her voice as she moved out of his embrace. 'I...I would not like you to think...' She paused. How tight his breeches had become. With a guess at his thoughts, she took deep breaths so her bosom heaved, white in the dim light. At that moment, she caught sight of a figure on the terrace and stepped away. 'Hugo's watching,' she whispered.

'Nancy, where are you, my dear?' Silhouetted against the light from the drawing room, Hugo stood staring in their direction.

With a satisfied smile, she moved towards the light. *I must contrive to meet rich William in private as soon as possible,* she thought.

'Here we are, my love,' she called. 'Mr Parkinson had taken me to see the fish, but it was too dark to see them properly.' Using her eyelashes, and with a winning smile, she tried to charm Hugo, but he was poker-faced and tight-lipped as he bowed over her proffered hand. He gave William a speculative glance and took her by the arm, his fingers digging into her flesh as he led her back into the drawing room, followed by William, wearing a sheepish grin.

Everyone fell silent and turned to look at Nancy, who flushed with annoyance. *Another mistake. Don't leave the room when in company. Like a bloody maze, learning all the rules of the gentry,* she thought. Chin high, ignoring the bruising on her arm, she walked to where Joan and Esther were sitting together, and swept a curtsy.

'Pray forgive my manners, ma'am, I felt a little giddy and needed fresh air.'

The older women smiled, and Esther murmured, 'It is a warm night, my dear.'

Nancy gave a sigh of relief when, a short time later, Joan and Nathan thanked Esther and John for a pleasant evening.

'Good night, Miss Turpin. Maybe you will allow me to call?' suggested William.

The question hung between them, and as William bowed over her hand she shot an anxious glance towards Hugo and his parents, who were speaking to Merrilla.

'I'm not sure. Would it be correct?' Biting her lip, and looking confused, she portrayed herself as a demure young lady.

'Don't you fret yourself. I'll be seeing you very soon,' he whispered, as he picked up the glove she had dropped.

Philip and Merrilla had only been at home a month, but already everyone could see a change for the better in Elysabeth, especially since she had been approached to become a bridal attendant. Both Merrilla and William Parkinson found life at Clemmants most pleasant. They had been introduced to most of the families in the district, encouraged to join in social events, and had enjoyed many sunny days exploring the countryside.

In the garden room Esther was busying herself arranging flowers, but peals of laughter drew her into the long, vine-shaded terrace overlooking the lawns. She heard Elysabeth's voice raised in a cheerful discussion with Philip, as they played lottery chances with Merrilla and William. Philip lay on a chaise-longue, and the other three sat close by, bantering. Philip was the target of gentle ribbing, as he had drawn the winning ticket in the last three games.

Catching sight of his mother, he beckoned her to come closer. 'Mamma, come and join us. Would you believe it? They maintain I couldn't possibly win three games in a row, but how could I cheat? I cannot leave my seat.' He assumed a hurt expression until Elysabeth and Merrilla pounced on a bunch of tickets half-hidden underneath a cushion. Unable to keep up the pretence any longer, he burst out laughing.

'Forfeit! Forfeit! You must pay for your misdemeanour,' they cried, standing over him, each wagging a finger at the unrepentant miscreant. Esther wondered if Philip and William were in cahoots, if it had been William's idea to hide the tickets. 'You're like a bunch of small children,' she said, with a laugh in her voice, pleased to see them enjoying themselves. 'Merrilla, Elysabeth, leave them to their clowning, and come with me, I have something to show you.' As the girls walked towards her, she noticed with pleasure what close friends they had become. She had been extremely concerned when she had first seen Merrilla, worrying she would be another Nancy Turpin, but now she knew her fears were groundless. The girl's evident devotion to Philip, her sweet nature, and her ladylike manners had endeared her to everyone. The indoor and outside staff all liked and respected her. They were already planning what bridal gift to give her.

'I sent to York for silks and furbelows to make your wedding gown. They have arrived, and I thought we ladies would enjoy the afternoon examining them.'

Merrilla's eyes opened wide in surprise, her face glowing with happiness and, holding Elysabeth's hand, she followed Esther into the sitting room. They were captivated by the sight of silks, satins, cambric and matching ribbons, trimmings and threads, in a profusion of colours. Esther smiled, and watched as the excited pair gave a gasp of pleasure when each roll of fabric was unfurled. They lost no time in holding up lengths of material and displaying them against their slender bodies. Only once did she notice an expression of sadness cross her daughter's face.

The last piece of fabric inspected, Elysabeth left the room to find the fashion plates, and other books.

Esther sat alone with Merrilla. 'Have you had a reply from your family, my dear?' she said.

Merrilla ceased folding a fragment of torn wrapping paper and rose to her feet without looking at her.

'No, not yet, Mrs Larcombe, but I will write to them once more. Maybe my papa will come to the church when I marry

Philip. If not, Mr Larcombe has promised to escort me to the altar.' The wistfulness in her voice was unmistakable, and Esther's skirts rustled as she hurried across the room and gathered her into her arms. She felt her give a shuddering breath, and held the distressed girl until she had composed herself.

'Would you like me to ask Mr Larcombe to visit your family home and speak to your papa, my dear? I know he will be pleased to do so, but only if you wish it.'

Her long ringlets bounced as she shook her head. 'No. Thank you. It's kind of you to make the offer, Mrs Larcombe, and believe me when I say I'm very grateful, indeed I am, but no. If my papa forgives me and wishes to be reconciled, I'm sure he'll write to me.'

Realising the painful subject was upsetting the girl, she said no more, though she intended to have a talk with her husband about the matter.

The atmosphere of the room brightened when Elysabeth returned, carrying an assortment of books. She dropped them on the table. 'I've found them all, Mamma.'

The three women spent the following hours looking at fashion plates, choosing and rejecting styles and fabrics for the most important gown in a woman's life.

Gradually, as the weeks passed, Philip grew stronger, and was able to put his foot to the ground. His nightmarish dreams of being buried alive in blackness became less frequent.

'I can see you walking down the aisle without support if you continue to improve like this, Philip,' Elysabeth said one day, as she accompanied her brother's slow progress along a path leading to the stables.

Each day he did the exercises taught to him by Doctor Grant, and could soon walk with the aid of only one stick. Merrilla and Elysabeth gave him every encouragement, and either one or both girls were in constant attendance. It had been a long and painful business, but his confidence grew daily.

'I'm walking further each day,' he said, proudly. 'I do own that I'm slow, but if I keep practising, I'll run to the church on my wedding day.' He half turned to give Elysabeth a boyish grin, but it changed into a grimace when he stepped on a loose stone, toppled over, and twisted his leg. In dismay, Elysabeth rushed forward to support him. She gave a cry of distress at his expression of agony.

'Damn! Damn! Damn!' he swore through gritted teeth. Beads of perspiration broke out on his forehead. One arm over Elysabeth's shoulders and, using his stick, he gained his feet. They stood for a moment while he took deep breaths.

'Stay where you are, Philip. I'll go and fetch someone to help.'

'No. I must make an effort to reach the house. I'll do it, if you help me.'

'We'll only manage if you take it very slowly. We don't want to push you to church in a bath chair. Merrilla's liable to scold us if your leg worsens.'

They stopped every few steps so he could catch his breath. At a stop longer than usual, Elysabeth asked, 'Have you spoken to William yet? Will he be your best man, do you think?' She hoped that by asking questions, it would take his mind off his injury. His arm around her shoulders weighed her down, making her breathless, and she kept looking towards the house, praying someone had noticed their predicament.

'I'd have asked Hugo, if he'd not been so stupid and brought that ladybird home on his arm. Always has been impulsive. He's nothing but a damn fool. Fancy throwing you away for a trollop like her. Anyone with half an eye can see what she is. Consider yourself lucky to have found how impetuous he is, sister.'

If he hadn't been in such pain, he would never have spoken to Elysabeth so candidly. He had discussed her situation with his parents and Merrilla, and they all agreed the least said about Nancy and Hugo in Elysabeth's presence, the better it would be for everyone concerned.

His sister kept her head lowered as she supported him, clearly distressed. She gave a huge sigh of relief when Merrilla, skirts held high, raced across the lawn towards them. Trembling with concern, she put both arms around him and helped to support him.

'Whatever is amiss?' she panted. 'I saw you struggling from the window. I didn't have time to summon help.' She moved to one side and placed Philip's arm across her shoulders.

'He walked too far, and stumbled on a stone,' Elysabeth said. 'We need a man to help him into the house. I'll go and fetch someone.'

With her skirts clear of the grass, she ran towards the house as Merrilla beseeched Philip to remain still, for he had turned ashen with pain, and leaned heavily on his stick.

Chapter 15

'No, no, no!' Merrilla sat bolt upright in bed with her bed linen clutched to her chest, staring wide-eyed into the darkness. The drapes were still closed around her bed, just as Bridget had left them. A nightmare. A horrible dream. So real. She had seen herself in her wedding gown inside Stagill Church, but instead of Philip, Bill Waspill stood waiting, dripping water onto the altar steps.

With a shuddering sigh, she slipped back under the covers, and tears oozed from her closed eyes.

Oh, Mamma, I've been so foolish. I'm sorry. I'm so very sorry. It's no wonder my family have not replied to my correspondence. Why bother with such a vexatious person as me?

Rings rattled as the drapes around the bed were drawn open. Sunlight flooded the room as she opened her eyes.

'It's morning, mistress. I've brought your chocolate, and hot water ready for you to wash.' Bridget held a cup of hot chocolate, her childish face beaming with a gappy smile. 'The sun's shining for your big day. Miss Elysabeth says she's bringing your breakfast herself.' She said the words almost in one breath.

Merrilla relaxed, and forgot her nightmare. A commotion in the corridor had them looking towards the door. Bridget bobbed a curtsy when Elysabeth walked into the room, carrying a large, silver tray.

'Here's your breakfast, bride-girl. When you've eaten every scrap, we can begin to beautify you, so Philip... ' she paused, as she settled the tray in front of her, 'so Philip will love you twice as much.'

As the morning progressed, the household found itself in a flurry of excitement. Happy servants waited on arriving guests

257

and friends who had been invited to the wedding, as well as those who called to leave gifts.

As Elysabeth helped Merrilla to dress, Esther, who sat near the window, gave orders to the maids to fetch, carry and tidy. The bride had chosen a rich, cream, satin gown, with minute tucks and bows on the bodice. A loose, floating overdress of damask, painted with a dainty floral pattern and fastened in place under the bust with tiny seed pearls, flowed open from the waist. The low neckline enhanced her shoulders, and the elbow-length sleeves, with rows of falling lace ruffles, flattered her smooth arms. The only jewellery comprised of her own pearl necklace, and a pair of pearl earrings which Esther had lent to her. She had looked at the ruby necklet and earrings the previous day but, after pressing them to her lips, she had wrapped them in velvet and put them back in a drawer. Matching satin slippers and long, ivory-coloured gloves completed the ensemble, and earned Esther's approval.

'I think those cream rosebuds among your curls are exactly right, Merrilla,' Elysabeth said, gently shaking Merrilla's skirts into place before standing beside her mother. They watched her walk around the room. With short steps, her natural grace allowed her skirts to swing becomingly.

'You look lovely. Every inch a bride. Papa may let us have more gowns made in this style when he sees how fine we look today.' Elysabeth, in her new gown of palest primrose over a golden underskirt, looked beautiful. Her dark hair had been twisted into a knot of curls, and arranged on the top of her head.

'Well, I think the styles of today are indecent for an older lady. I for one will never leave off my whalebones. You might well smile, you two, but when you reach my age...' Esther broke off as the girls exchanged amused glances. 'Stop your giggles, you naughty pair. Don't you dare mark your gown, Elysabeth. Drape the gauze shawl over your arms, Merrilla, and I'll place your bonnet. There, that's perfect.' She sighed, looking wishful. 'I remember my own wedding day, with my brother, Charles, wishing me happiness.' She walked towards the door. 'Mr Larcombe will be waiting for you in the hall when you go downstairs, my dear. Myself and Elysabeth will travel to the old village church together.'

Philip fidgeted as he waited for his bride. He had decided to wear his hair naturally, without powder. 'Time for a wig when I lose my hair,' he had told his father, who had given him a wry smile.

The rich claret colour of his coat gleamed in the mellow light of the church and the glow of the altar candles. His beige, satin breeches were a perfect fit. His cane left at home, he stood straight and proud, William standing nervously beside him.

The sound of the organ reverberated in the church, and he turned to see his bride drifting down the aisle, her hand resting on his father's arm. With a most gallant gesture, he gave her a low, courtly bow, and then stood beside her. Elysabeth stepped forward to take Merrilla's bouquet from her as the short service started. He spoke in a clear, firm voice, and she sounded no less firm as she pledged her vows. They gazed into each other's eyes, smiling, and he placed a ring on her finger. When the parson pronounced the happy pair man and wife, their lips met in a tender kiss.

As they left the altar, they paused in front of John and Esther. Merrilla swept a low curtsy, whilst Philip, with a broad grin, bowed. Choristers sang like angels as the newly-married couple progressed down the aisle, followed by Esther, who clutched John's hand, and dabbed her eyes.

Once outside, family and friends, all jostling, surrounded them. Merrilla's green eyes sparkled with joy as people hugged and kissed the happy pair, wishing them well.

A tall, thin man stood unsmiling in front of her. She looked into eyes as green as her own, set in a careworn face encircled with white hair and whiskers. The sound of merry laughter and the joyful pealing bells faded. She felt herself sway as she gazed into her father's sad face. 'Papa. Oh, Papa,' she whispered. 'You've come.'

Gradually, Mr Cooper's stern mouth relaxed, and he half smiled, as though unsure of his welcome. As his smile deepened, he lifted his hands. With a glad cry, she flung herself forward and hugged him, her tears wetting his waistcoat, his gold watch chain and fob pressed into her cheek.

She became aware of Philip's scrutiny. The two men stared for a moment over her head, then a relieved expression crossed Philip's face, and he moved forward to shake the hand of his father-in-law, to bid him welcome.

'Your Mamma's here, Merrilla. She insisted on seeing you married, my dear.' Visibly emotional, he stepped to one side, to let his wife hug her daughter. Her tears mingled with those of the happy bride.

Philip brought his parents forward, and introductions were made. Men shook hands and women curtsied, while Philip drew Merrilla to one side, and whispered in her ear, 'We have to run, Mrs Larcombe. Your carriage is waiting to transport you home, my darling.'

At the sound of her new name, she glanced across to where her parents were in conversation with Esther and John.

'Do not worry, my dearest. They are to follow us to Clemmants. My papa made all the arrangements. It is a bridal gift to you.'

Eyes sparkling like bright emeralds, she blushed as he bent and kissed his bride full on the lips.

'Come with me, my precious,' he murmured. He took hold of her hand, and they hurried along a path lined with people intent on showering them with rice and flower petals.

The carriage horses had ribbon plaited through their manes and tails. More bows decorated the coachman's whip, and banks of flowers and ribbons adorned the carriage.

Merrilla sat next to Philip, clutching his hand. Taking a deep breath and closing her eyes tightly, she threw her bouquet as far as she could towards a group of young women with upturned faces. As the carriage moved away, she witnessed Elysabeth holding the bunch of sweet-smelling blossoms and wearing a bemused expression. Nearby, watching Elysabeth with a look of adoration, stood Hugo.

'It's said whoever catches the bride's bouquet will be the next happy bride.' Hugo's voice, very low, addressed Elysabeth, and no one else heard him speak. He saw the hurt in her eyes, and cursed himself for his clumsy remark. 'Oh, Miss Larcombe. Elysabeth, my dear, I did not think.'

'That, Hugo is your most mammoth fault. You do and say things without first thinking. Until you change, Mr Denstone, you will never be wise.' With a withering glance, she turned away as Nancy, escorted by William, walked in their direction. 'Here, give these to your, your....' Thrusting the bouquet at Hugo, she hurried away, back into the cool church.

William was enchanted as Nancy hugged his arm, chattering about trivial things, gazing into his face and smiling. Hugo joined them and William nodded a greeting to him.

'Oh, Mr Denstone. You have the bride's bouquet for me,' gushed Nancy. 'How kind of Merrilla to let me have it. Thank you, my dear.' Taking the flowers, she abandoned William, and clung to Hugo as they made their way across the churchyard to where the Denstone carriage stood waiting.

William's face was inscrutable as he watched the couple move away. During the past few weeks he had grown to know Nancy. At first, it had been flattering to have her making excuses to be alone with him. But now he only had scorn for her flirtatious behaviour. He had lain awake many nights, trying to work out some way of bringing Elysabeth and Hugo together, and trying to devise some kind of plan to remove Nancy from the scene. One way would be to persuade her to elope with him. Judging by her recent actions, she would be happy to accept, but he would have to pay the price of marriage to her. He certainly had no wish to dishonour the Larcombe name by causing a scandal, too aware of how much he owed to them to hurt Esther and John in such a way. He admired Elysabeth, and had become extremely fond of the gentle girl.

He turned with the intention of returning to the church, knowing Elysabeth had been upset by the way she had thrust the flowers at Hugo, before marching away from him.

As he stood in the open doorway of the church, he heard the desolate weeping of the young lady, and decided the best thing to do would be to wait outside for her. He found a shady spot under a yew tree, spread out a handkerchief and sat thinking.

When Elysabeth left the church he made up his mind. He kept pace behind her as she began her long walk home to Clammants.

'You do not care for company, Miss Larcombe?'

She spun around, her hand to her mouth. 'Oh, Cousin William. I didn't hear you. I thought everyone had left for the wedding celebrations.'

He fell in step beside her, and continued walking in companionable silence. From time to time, he plucked a leaf from the hedgerow, and threw it down, watching her out of the corner of his eye. They were crossing the packhorse bridge over the river when he spoke again. 'Cousin Elysabeth, would you marry me? I'm well aware we've only known each other for a short time, but I hold you in the highest esteem. We could make our home at Paxton Hall, and it would surely be better than being a neighbour to Hugo and Nancy.'

She halted, her mouth open, staring at him.

He placed a finger under her chin, and closed her mouth. 'Your papa and Mr Denstone have given the Paxton Coalmine and the surrounding lands to me, and that includes the hall. At the moment it's very shabby, but together we could make a comfortable home. It's not as large as Clemmants, or as grand as Ghyll House, but you could have a free hand to furnish it to your liking.'

It was probably the longest speech she had ever heard him make. 'William. You cannot marry me just because I've been jilted,' she gasped.

He kicked a stone off the side of the bridge, and they watched it plop into the river. 'I can assure you, I would be most happy to marry you. I've grown very fond of you, Elysabeth, and I know we could deal famously together as man and wife.'

'No. I am very much obliged to you, cousin William, but I cannot marry you. I cannot marry anyone. You see, William, I love Hugo.' Head bent, she gazed into the water, playing with her bonnet ribbons. After a moment or two, she looked up and her eyes glistened with tears. Her voice quivered, as she said, 'I must point out that we're first cousins. Papa would never agree, and the church maintains that first cousins are unable to marry. But, dearest cousin William, I thank you from the bottom of my heart, and I'll never forget your kindness to me.'

She touched his sleeve and he leaned towards her. 'Are you sure? These reasons are not insurmountable, Elysabeth.'

'Yes, William, quite sure. I'll be leaving Clemmants myself very soon.' She linked her arm in his.

'We'll miss all the festivities if we don't hurry,' he said as they continued their long walk in the sunshine to Clemmants.

Merrilla and Philip's wedding celebrations were well under way at Clemmants, and everyone was enjoying the warm summer's day.

The tenants were holding their own party in the gardens. Polly's fiancé climbed onto an empty beer barrel to gain attention, and informed his friends there would be another wedding, for he intended to marry Polly. A roar of approval went up, for she was well liked by both the Clemmants and Ghyll House staff alike.

Music and a loud burst of laughter from the celebration party in the garden made everyone on the terrace glance in the direction of the revellers.

John Larcombe had moved outside with his wife and daughter and they were sitting with Mr and Mrs Cooper on the shady terrace when the bride and groom rejoined them. Merrilla was still wearing her wedding gown, but had removed her bonnet. She gave Philip an adoring look as he pulled a chair out for her.

'My, what a crush! So many people here. Everyone has been very kind to us,' Philip said, seating himself between his wife and mother.

Leaning forward, Esther placed a hand on her son's arm. 'Before you go on your honeymoon may we ask if some of your plans could be altered, my dears?'

The bridal pair looked at each other and grinned.

Mr Cooper cleared his throat. 'We have a house near St James, in London. Elysabeth has already agreed to be our guest for as long as she desires. It would give us great pleasure if you would both join us after your honeymoon.' His wife clasped her hands, clearly longing to have her daughter back home again.

'Nathan and I can attend to all the business concerns while you're absent,' said John.

Leaning closer to Merrilla, Philip asked, 'Would you wish to do that, my dear? We can have some time on our own, and then go and stay with your parents.'

Merrilla's sparkling eyes shone with joy. 'Oh, yes, please,' she breathed.

Mrs Cooper sat back in her chair and beamed with pleasure. 'That would be wonderful. I'll find out who's in town, and make certain you all receive vouchers for Almack's, and are invited to any other social occasions this season.' Turning to Elysabeth, who sat quietly beside her father, she added, 'Merrilla's sister lives nearby, and knows many suitable young men who will escort you, Elysabeth.' She tapped Elysabeth's arm with her fan. 'To be sure, I'm looking forward to showing London to you lovely young creatures,' she laughed.

After making arrangements with her parents, the bride went to her rooms to change into her travelling outfit. The suite once occupied by Esther's parents had been completely refurbished by Merrilla and Philip, for it would be their future home. Most of the windows overlooked gardens, and beyond them, one could see the moorland and hills rising in the distance. Merrilla had spotted Esther smiling to herself when she had run a finger over a new table, her mother-in-law probably remembering her own delight at redecorating Clemmants years before.

Philip had agreed to change in his father's dressing room, leaving the new suite for Merrilla. He turned at a knock on the door.

'Ah, Papa, I'd hoped to have a private word with you before we left,' he said, as John entered the room. 'It's crossed my mind that it may be best if you spoke to Elysabeth. Would you tell her to do as I bid while we are away? You know how deuced awkward she can be.'

John placed a chair nearer to the window and sat down. 'That's why I'm here. She's quite liable to choose a husband on the rebound, if you're not there to guide her. If a whiff of her fortune is known to anyone in the London set, she will be the target of every fleecer in town. Yours and Merrilla's steadying influence will give me less cause to worry.'

'Have you had time to speak with Mr Cooper about business affairs?' Philip asked a moment or two later, as he shrugged himself into his new coat that had been made by a London tailor, and showed off his broad shoulders to perfection.

'I'm certain things will change for the better at his Nottingham factory, especially when Nathan and I have had a discussion with him, my boy. But don't you think about things like that. Just look after your wife, and enjoy yourselves.' John followed Philip from the room.

The Larcombe travelling coach stood ready at the door, with a wagon standing close behind. Whilst Philip and Merrilla had been changing, some wag had fastened old shoes and horseshoes to the back of the coach. All the guests stood outside, waiting for the bridal pair to appear.

The family stood in a group at the bottom of the staircase, waiting to make their private farewells. A rustle of silk occasioned a silence, as everyone turned to see the bride descend the stairs in her green taffeta gown. A full silken cloak, in a deep lustrous gold, fanned out behind her as she and her husband walked towards those who loved them.

Each lady held a handkerchief ready to dab her eyes, and the men watched indulgently as tearful farewells were made.

Turning to his father, Philip held out his hand. 'Thank you for everything, Papa.' His eyes filled when his father drew him close and hugged him.

'Take care, my boy. Bring your bride back safely. We look forward to having you both home again with us.'

Merrilla had arranged for Bridget to accompany them, and the girl sat perched on a box in the wagon, waving excitedly. Philip saw his new wife's sweet expression as she smiled at the child, and felt a longing to rush her away into a private corner and kiss her. He contented himself by giving her hand a squeeze, before stepping forward and helping her into the coach.

'Write and tell of your stay in London whenever you have the time, my dears,' called Esther, as the vehicles moved away. A handkerchief fluttering out of the coach window was her answer.

It had been arranged that the following week, Elysabeth would leave Clemmants with Mr and Mrs Cooper in their light travelling chase. As she stood on the wide steps outside the house, close to her father, she looked up at him with miserable eyes. 'I do wish I felt less nervous, Papa. London seems so far away.'

'Nonsense, my girl. You enjoy yourself, and try to forget everyone here. Both Mr and Mrs Cooper tell me they'll be delighted to have your company, and there's plenty of room at their town house.' John spoke briskly, and glanced at Esther, who was fighting to control her tears.

'You will have Philip to take care of you, dear,' Esther said.

'Of course I will, Mamma. I'm being silly. I must forget Hugo and his broken promises.' With straight shoulders, she smiled at her parents. 'I intend to use the time I have in London to make a good match, and one day give you beautiful grandchildren.' She blushed and played with her bonnet strings.

Mrs Cooper's eyes rounded at Elysabeth's forthright speech. 'Mrs Larcombe, you're very fortunate to have such a sensible daughter. Miss Larcombe, you're a most good-natured young woman. I hope you meet and marry a gentleman of standing, and I'll certainly do all in my power to assist you.' She looked at her husband and Elysabeth's parents and beamed. 'When we reach London, I'll make certain you enjoy yourself. Merrilla's sister knows all the best places to visit.' She patted Elysabeth's arm. 'The people Maude doesn't know in society are not worth the knowing.'

Mr Cooper held out his hand to John. 'Mr Larcombe, may we thank you for your hospitality. The stay at your home has been most pleasant. We thought we had lost our dear Merrilla, but now, thanks to you, sir, we are reunited. I will never be able to repay you for inviting us to the wedding. All I can say is "Thank you," sir.'

Both men cleared their throats, and glanced to where their spouses were hugging each other.

'We are delighted to have Merrilla as a daughter,' Esther said.

It was time for them to leave, and Mr Cooper bowed low over Esther's proffered hand, before taking his wife's arm and moving her towards the coach.

John lifted Elysabeth's hand to his lips, before drawing her close and giving her a hug.

'I gave Philip some money—my present to you. Buy yourself some pretty bonnets and gowns,' he whispered in her ear, before allowing her to turn to her mother. His words brought a tremulous smile to her face and, holding her mother's hand, she walked towards the coach and waved to William, who stood in the doorway watching the departure. He had said goodbye to her earlier. Mother and daughter clung together for a moment, before Elysabeth climbed into the coach and sat facing Mr and Mrs Cooper.

'Write and tell us of your activities, my dear,' Esther called, before the footman closed the door. The sounds of moving horses and wheels on the gravel drowned out Elysabeth's answer. Esther's comfort was John's strong arm around her shoulders.

William observed the departure of Elysabeth and the Coopers with mixed feelings. He would miss the young Larcombe couple, and Elysabeth. Over the past weeks he had come to know them all very well, and had enjoyed long rides over the moors with Philip and Merrilla. Although upset to see Elysabeth leave, she was, in his opinion, wise to go to London. He had noticed how she had flitted around the great old house, looking, when she thought herself alone, very sad. He wished he could think of a way to bring her and Hugo back together. Apart from simply wanting to help them, he felt indebted to both families.

Recently, Elysabeth's beloved horse had missed his customary early morning gallop with his mistress, although she still brought him a titbit each day. William thought she had been afraid of meeting Nancy, though it would have been unlikely for the two girls to have met. Nancy had been taking riding lessons, and had a peach and cream-coloured habit with matching accessories, but she so disliked sitting on a horse, the outfit had only been seen a few times.

William cleared his throat and moved to John's side as Esther hurried into the house with a handkerchief to her mouth. 'Mr Larcombe.' He swallowed audibly, still very much in awe of his rich uncle. 'Sir, I will also be leaving in the near future. I have enjoyed visiting Clemmants, and getting to know the family, but Scotland calls. I only wish I could repay you in some way for your kindness.'

John pointed with his cane down the steps. They strolled along the path leading to the stables. Although spry for his age, he needed his long cane for support when tired. William's hands were clasped behind his back, matching his steps.

'The man, Mr Lang, whom we placed in charge at the coalmine, is a stout fellow and knows his work well, but I think I should be at the mine with him.' William glanced at him, hoping for his assent, but when his uncle made no comment, he continued, 'I thought of having a house built for him. His rent could be low. There's a plot of land near the kirk that would be suitable. I haven't forgotten that, if it had not been for him, Philip and Merrilla would have perished with those other poor souls. The house would reward him, but without giving offence. He is very proud, and I have no wish to patronise him.'

John stopped. 'That idea is sound, my boy. If you employ a good man who can be trusted, he is worth his weight in gold. Go ahead with the building of the house. I will be only too pleased to help in any way I can. You are now the sole owner of the coalmine, William. Mr Denstone and the boys have signed all the necessary documents, but remember, if at any time you need help or advice, contact one of us. Before you return to Scotland, you must arrange to call on Mr Harwood in Nottingham. He will be expecting you, and will explain about the assignment of the Paxton Mine.'

'I...You have all been most generous, sir,' William stammered.

'Nonsense. I'm sure I can give my only nephew a rightful gift. I only wish we had known of your existence earlier. Your mother always was a proud woman—not that that's a bad thing,' John added when William's lips tightened, 'and you seem to have inherited Sally's sunny nature.'

They continued in silence towards the stables until John stopped, and asked, 'What will you do about medical school? Will you contact Doctor Grant?'

William exhaled deeply, looking into the distance. 'I'm not sure. Maybe I've left it too late.' He gave a chuckle. 'I'm not yet used to the fact that I'm rich, and can do as I please. But you may rest assured, Mr Larcombe, I would never rush into anything thoughtlessly.'

'I know that, young man. Whatever decision you make, I will always back you absolutely. Now then, I've walked far enough, and must return to your aunt. We'll see you later, after your ride.'

Full of emotion, William entered the stables. He heard the grooms and ostlers talking. 'It's said she comes out of the side door. She doesn't charge owt. Someone told me how she'd six men around her, and when she'd served them all, she ran off laughing.'

'There's a name for women like her, who enjoy having a lot of men. Ninfer, Minfer something.' William guessed it was old Tom speaking.

''Tis whore,' another man said. Someone hawked and spat.

'Ner. Summat very long and fancy. I know'd it once, but it's slipped me mind.

'She had a full pair, by all accounts. Wouldn't mind getting me mouth around them.' The men joined in coarse laughter with the speaker.

'I heard she comes out about once a week, and waits on the path under that big oak near the lake.'

William gradually became aware of other sounds in the stable: a horse munching; a tuneless whistle, stomping hoofs. He was about to step forward when someone else spoke loudly.

'She wears a mask, and smells just like a flower. She ain't no scullery maid, that's for sure.'

'Tell you one thing... Oh, morning, Mr Parkinson. Saddle your horse, sir?'

As soon as William moved inside the long stable block, with its whitewashed stalls and red brick floor, the men busied themselves. He nodded to old Tom, who put a finger to his cap in salutation, before hurrying to fetch the hunter used by him. On his return to the yard, he stared at the distant crags, unappreciative of their beauty, as he pondered instead on the conversation he had overheard. If the woman the men spoke of was whom he thought, maybe his half-formed plan could be carried out after all.

'No, surely not. She would never be so stupid as to throw a life of luxury away, not unless she had something else...' He shook his head. Surely the silly girl wouldn't risk losing Hugo unless she had another richer man in sight. Or maybe the Denstone family were about to send her home. He turned as the ostler brought his horse clip-clopping over the cobblestone yard.

Still deep in thought, he rode along the narrow roads and sheep tracks until he found himself inside the grounds of Ghyll House. After a quick scan of the area, he made his way to the lake, where a large oak tree towered over the bushes and trees near a path. Best to return after dark, and see if the lady of the night were the person he suspected it might be. With Hugo away on business it will be the perfect time to find out. He urged his horse along the path until he was in sight of the house. Partly hidden by bushes, he sat there, studying the building. She would probably leave by that side door without being seen, and it would be unlikely anyone could see over the lawns as far as the path, especially on a moonless night. Turning his horse's head, he returned to Clemmants, thinking out his plan. The outcome would all depend on Nancy believing whatever tale he chose to tell her.

That evening, knowing that grooms slept in the rooms above the stables, and would be certain to wake at the slightest sound from below, William decided to walk to Ghyll House. Wearing his long, dark cloak and a hat pulled well down over his eyes, he stood in the shadow of bushes, not far from the oak tree. He became aware of the night sounds of hunting owls and small creatures scurrying around, intent on their nocturnal activities. A shrill cry nearby from an animal made him shiver and draw his cloak closer. Chilled, and a little foolish, he wondered if he was maligning the lady. However, his heart raced when he heard muted laughter coming from near the oak tree, and saw one of two people scramble to their feet and slink away. He expelled a long breath. *At last, my dear. Now let me see who you are.* As the woman passed, a waft of perfume and the sight of golden curls gave him his answer.

Knowing Nancy disliked rising early, he waited until mid-morning of the following day before riding to Ghyll House. Again, he followed the path past the lake and the oak tree and approached the house from the rear. As he was about to leave the path and cross the lawns, he noticed a man in a footman's uniform emerging from some thick bushes and scurrying towards the house. A few moments later, Nancy appeared from behind the same group of bushes, carrying a small basket containing wild flowers. For a moment, his lips pursed.

He knew that if he told Nathan Denstone about her, she would be sent away, but she would certainly retaliate by spreading gossip, and in so doing it would bring the Denstone name into disrepute. No, the permanent removal of Nancy Turpin had to be tackled in a cunning and devious way.

As he urged his horse forward, he removed his hat and called, 'Nancy. Miss Turpin!'

She stopped, and her anxious expression disappeared as she watched him leap from his horse, and bow over her hand.

'I had hoped to see you, Miss Turpin. I'm overjoyed to have the opportunity to speak with you alone.' He gave her a winning smile.

'It would be best if we were not observed. My maid's not with me, Mr Parkinson.'

With a glance towards the house, the pair moved to stand beneath the trees. Taking hold of her hand, he gazed into her eyes. 'Nancy. My love. I came to ask you to elope with me. I intend to leave for Scotland tomorrow, and I beg you to come with me.'

She hesitated for a moment, gave him a searching look, and sat on a fallen tree. William tethered his horse and joined her.

Her eyes never left his face as he fabricated a country mansion near Glasgow. He embroidered a tale of theatres, balls attended by the smartest of London society, fictitious family jewels, and the time Mary Queen of Scots visited his family home. 'I leave early tomorrow, my darling. I pray you will say yes, and come with me. We could make our home in my castle in the glen. It's a hard decision to make, for I know you love Hugo deeply, and it will mean you'll never be the mistress of Ghyll House. When you do make up your mind, please remember that I love you with all my heart.' He gave her a tender kiss on her cheek.

'It'll be a big disappointment for Hugo. He loves me, and I know he'd do his best to make me happy; but I don't love him like I love you, William. You're so strong. I've listened to stories about the wonders of beautiful Scotland from others, and I'm sure I'd like living there.' She ran a finger along his arm, not quite succeeding in hiding a look of triumph.

'Is that true? Do you mean you'll leave with me, Nancy?'

She nodded. 'I'll be as happy as a lark if you take me with you, Mr Parkinson. How I'll mask my bliss and my love for you, I don't know. This day and night will seem unending.'

'Remember to be here at first light before the servants stir. Not much luggage—just bring what you'll need on the journey. We may need to hurry, and so must travel light. One day I'll buy you your own carriage, my sweet love.'

Nancy turned her gaze away from his face, and rose to her feet. 'Rest assured, I'll be early, and I'll meet you where you said, William.'

He watched her walk towards the house, and couldn't help but give a chuckle. 'This day and night will seem to be unending indeed.'

Chapter 16

A day and night had passed since William's meeting with Nancy, and he hoped she had not changed her mercenary mind about leaving with him. Three horses stood tethered to a bush in the early morning mist. As he peered along the path leading towards Ghyll House, he noticed the sound of creatures moving unseen in the undergrowth.

If she didn't arrive soon he would have to leave without her. He walked across the grassy clearing and checked once again that the ropes on the packhorse were secure. He didn't want to lose his luggage, and had also placed the bulky documents John had given him inside one of the panniers on the horse for safekeeping. In his inside coat pocket he had some money and the address of a decent lodging house in Nottingham. A letter had already been sent to Mr Harwood to secure a room in time for his arrival.

Upon hearing a light step, and a silken rustle of skirts, he turned around with an overwhelming sense of relief at knowing Nancy had kept her word and joined him for their tryst.

'You've brought a horse,' she said, her eyes wide in dismay. 'That's not a ladies' mount. The saddle...' Various items of luggage, including a gaily striped hatbox, dropped from her hands as she gaped at a strong, well-boned horse. It turned its head in her direction, showing its yellow teeth champing its bit.

'My darling, they are to whisk you off to paradise. No one will catch us and bring you back here if we use these beauties.' Slapping the rump of the nearest horse, he caused it to sidestep and toss its head.

She pressed her thumb knuckle to her teeth and backed away. 'But I can't ride that. It's far too high, and there's no mounting block for me to use.'

'When you're in the saddle you'll feel quite secure. This is a good-natured animal, and all you have to do is to sit on its back until we reach York. Come, my darling, let me help you mount.' He held out both hands, smiling in what he hoped was a mollifying manner.

Her face crumpled, and she stepped back from him. 'No. Get away. I'm not going. No!' In her effort to flee, she stumbled over her scattered luggage.

With desperate strength, he caught hold of her, and threw her up into the saddle of the nearest horse—the largest one. Feeling the sudden load on its back, it bolted, and the reins, pulled free from the bush to which they had been tethered, trailed along the ground. Nancy's screams unsettled the other two horses, and they tossed their heads and struck the ground with impatient hoofs.

He snatched one of Nancy's dropped bundles and leapt onto his own horse. Somehow, he held onto the packhorse, and caught the reins of her mount, unable to suppress a chuckle at the sight of her, with tightly closed eyes, desperately clinging to the upturned front of the saddle.

He led the team at a smart pace through the grounds of Ghyll House and out onto the narrow bridle paths of the lonely moorland. He had spent many hours riding, alone, and with Philip and Merrilla, and felt confident he would find his way to York City, and on to Nottingham, without using any main roads. After the first hour or so, Nancy stopped shouting at him. The only sounds she gave were hiccups and sniffles. Eventually, she said, 'William.'

No reply.

She raised her voice. 'Mr Parkinson, I need to stop.'

For an answer, he gave a sharp tug on the reins, making her mount quicken its pace. She squealed and clung on with eyes closed as they passed beautiful lichen-covered rocks and a rippling tarn, her ears blocked to the sound of a curlew calling

277

with haunting sweetness. The town girl paid no heed to the charms of the moorland and fells.

At midday she tried again. 'Please, Mr Parkinson. I beg you, let's stop for a minute.'

William ignored her. He knew that if he allowed her to dismount he would never get her back on the horse, and they were still close enough to Ghyll House for her to attempt walking back.

For many miles, Nancy swore and shrieked, calling him everything she could lay her tongue to. Stiff-backed, he rode with his face expressionless. Her fluent gutter vocabulary amazed him, and his disgust intensified. She was as beautiful as the sea, and as deep and treacherous. It was no wonder Hugo found himself ensnared by her wiles.

When darkness approached, they were too far from Ghyll House for her to return either on foot or horseback, even had she known the way. William was grateful for her silence. He glanced over his shoulder, and saw her swaying with each movement of the horse, so halted in a clearing inside a small wood, dismounted and went to her.

'Come, my dear, let me help you.' He reached up with the intention of assisting her to dismount but jumped back as she kicked out at him.

'Get away. Don't you dare touch me!' she hissed, through clenched teeth as she half slithered, half jumped from her horse. For a while she stood clinging to the saddle, not trusting her trembling legs to support her weight. Her face screwed up in agony when her muscles were forced into movement, she glared at him. 'You... Bastard!' she spat and he looked at the wetness on his coat without surprise.

Tears streamed down her face as she sobbed. 'I told you I couldn't ride well, and that's not even a lady's side-saddle.'

'The only way to learn is to get on a horse and ride, my darling. Anyway, you'll find it far less tiring to use this saddle.' He returned to his own mount, unfastened the straps holding his luggage and put it under a tree.

'Oh, you...you poaching pirate. I'm not your darling, and never will be. I shall write to Hugo the first chance I get. When he knows what you've done, he...he'll break your neck and fetch me back to Ghyll House.' She tottered across the clearing and perched carefully on the branch of a fallen tree, watching in sulky silence as he continued attending to the horses.

Once the animals had been made ready for the night, William collected a small bundle which was lying next to his saddle, and offered Nancy bread and cheese wrapped in a fine linen cloth. She gobbled it down, continually glancing towards the packs that had been removed from the horses and lay on the ground.

She bawled out, 'Where's me 'at box? All me jewellery's in that box. If you've lost it, you'll replace every last piece. Took me long 'ard work ter get them trinkets.' She spat out the words with venom, and scowled, clearly past caring about lapsing into her broad midlands dialect. Her veneer as a lady of fashion had fled, and during the following hours, she continued to curse and berate him.

After checking that the horses were securely tethered, he threw her one of the horse-blankets. 'The night's warm. You'll not take hurt in the open air,' he said, lying down and wrapping himself in his own blanket. Throughout the night, at every small sound, his eyes flew open to observe her, but she lay sleeping with her hair spilling over a branch that acted as her pillow. He felt thankful when the sky lightened and they were able to continue their journey.

He made no attempt to enter the city of York, using the roads on the outer side of the city walls that were far enough away to make it difficult for Nancy to run off and find someone to help her in the great city.

'I'm not wasting good coin on soft beds for your idle bones,' he snarled, in response to her protestations against spending another night under a damp hedgerow.

By the fourth day, his eyes were red-rimmed and sore from lack of sleep, for he was determined she be delivered safely back to Nottingham. He felt unwilling to explain his future plans to the angry girl.

They were a sorry sight entering Nottingham Town. Remembering the instructions given to him by John, William led the way to a residential street lined by trees. Nancy was so exhausted and uncaring that, turning in his saddle, he had to shout to her that they had reached the end of their journey before she lifted her head and looked around.

'You can stop here or leave. I don't mind what you do. I'm quite sure you'll find someone to give you accommodation.' He swung down and tied his horses to a set of railings enclosing a set of steps leading to a basement with a lace-curtained window. The house had a set of freshly-scrubbed steps leading up to a green painted door.

Shooting a venomous look, Nancy clumsily dismounted. An urchin whistled when he caught sight of a bare knee. Her temper showed in her reddened cheeks, but apart from giving the child a rude sign, she made no comment. When she noticed the railing and steps leading to the basement she turned pale and glanced at William.

The street-door above opened and a boy ran down the steps, ready to take hold of the horses. He was followed more slowly by a woman, neatly dressed in black, wearing a white, frilled day cap, set back, revealing grey curls. Keys hung from a chain on her waist belt.

'Are you Mr Parkinson, sir? Mr Harwood told us you were travelling from Yorkshire, and that I was to keep a room ready for you. My boy will take your horses to the stables, and bring in your luggage.' She bobbed a curtsy before leading the way into the house. 'My name is Mrs Wood, sir, the housekeeper. My husband helps me run the place.' She looked at Nancy. 'I wasn't told there'd be a young woman, sir.' Standing in the hallway with hands clasped in front of her, she scrutinised Nancy's dishevelled appearance.

'I decided to leave Yorkshire at the last minute. As you see, I'm not dressed for travel, and my clothes are quite ruined.' Nancy smiled at the housekeeper, using all her charm. It was true. She still wore the same clothes in which she had left. Her outfit looked travel-worn, stained, and crumpled. The bonnet she had chosen most carefully for her "elopement" had fallen off some days before, and, too weary to retrieve it, she had left it where it lay.

'Fortunately, I do have one room free. It can soon be made ready, Miss...Mam...' Mrs Wood was not sure how to address a young lady travelling with a single man and no chaperone. The housekeeper looked from one to the other, obviously puzzled to see her new lodgers regarding each other with apparent hostility.

They were shown into a well-furnished parlour with a sideboard, other pieces of furniture and a dining table in the centre, with numerous attractive ornaments on the mantelshelf. Mrs Wood left them alone, saying she would prepare a bedchamber for her extra guest.

As soon as the door had closed, Nancy took hold of William's arm to spin him around for battle, but he remained unyielding. 'I shall write to Hugo at the first opportunity, and tell him how you abducted me. And I'll say how you promised to take me to your castle in Scotland, and then brought me to Nottingham instead,' she hissed.

'Huh, do you think for one minute he would believe you? He'll only have to question the stablemen at Clemmants about your night-time activities. And, may I ask, how you will get your letter franked? For I will not do it.'

'I could never have stayed long with that muckworm, anyway. I need to have a real man with hot blood.' She smiled roguishly. 'A man such as you, Mr Parkinson.' She stretched a hand towards him. He had no need to answer. His expression said it all, and she drew back with a pout. Before she could retaliate, Mrs Wood entered and invited them to see their bedchambers. Nancy shot a baleful glance at William and entered her room. The latch rattled as she banged the door behind her.

Once in his room, he arranged the contents of his luggage in some semblance of order. As he did so, he noticed the small bundle belonging to Nancy. He walked along the passage, and knocked on her door. 'This is yours. The only thing I caught.' He held out the bundle towards the sullen girl. She snatched it from him, and he stepped back, otherwise the door would have slammed in his face.

Nancy's bundle was made up of a couple of gowns, a large fringed silk shawl, and a pair of kid boots. Both gowns were badly creased, and the muslin one needed a brisk shake before she could wear it. She found a brush and comb on the dressing table, but it was impossible to dress her hair in her usual elaborate style without Polly's help.

Polly would be tetchy when she knew she'd gone off without telling her where. Shame she'd already left to marry her dozy farmer. Joan Denstone would certainly have dismissed her, and she might have had to come back to Nottingham, and they could have lived together again. She shrugged. 'All those months of hard work for nothing but experience,' she muttered, as she peered into the mirror on the dressing table.

Before she had left Nancy's employment, Polly had sat for many hours making the second gown in the bundle, trimming it with ribbons. She unpicked the stitches, using the ribbon to tie up her hair. Then, with a deep breath, she pulled the deep neckline of her gown well down, and left her room.

She found William already seated at the table in the parlour, eating his meal. Drawing up a chair, she scrutinised the many knickknacks and ornaments scattered around the parlour.

When she had been served with her meal and Mrs Wood had left the room, she said, 'I dropped me box. The striped box.'

William looked at her in mute enquiry, before lifting a glass of claret to his lips.

'All me money and my best jewellery was in that box. I only have these two rings and this silver necklace...' She broke off what she was about to say as Mrs Wood entered the room, carrying a jug of ale. She placed it on the table, glancing at the couple, then gave a quick curtsy towards William before leaving the room.

'Really?' said William, when the door closed. He yawned and stretched. 'I'm tired. I'll be pleased to sleep between sheets tonight.'

The parlour table had been covered with a chenille cloth, and the bang made by Nancy's fist hitting it wasn't as loud as she would have liked. She was unused to indifference from a man. William had paid almost no attention to her since he had thrown her onto the back of the horse. She had tried to tempt and seduce him from time to time on their journey to Nottingham, but her stratagem had not worked. In fact, he had seemed even more indifferent.

'You made me drop my hatbox. You'll damn well replace the contents. And when are you going do as you said, and marry me? I could please you in a married state, as you very well know,' she said, in a husky voice, leaning over the table, revealing her breasts and fluttering her eyelashes.

'No!'

Her violet eyes sparkled with tears, and her bottom lip trembled. 'No? But I love you truly, William.' She dabbed a tear with her smallest finger. 'You said you loved me, and that we would be married and be together forever,' she wailed.

'No, I did not. I said, "Will you come away with me and we could be together for ever". I said nothing about marrying you. I wouldn't dream of marrying you. I would never have a moment's peace, knowing your scheming and loose ways.'

He had left his coat hanging on a chair, and she watched with a crafty expression as he picked it up and walked towards the door. 'William. I'm with child.'

The softly spoken words made him spin on his heel to face her. His face flushed and his eyes narrowed with anger. 'If you're pregnant, it would not be with Hugo. Besides which, one evening I happened to be in the Clemmants stables. The men working there didn't see me. I heard bets put on how many men you could serve in one night, madam. They laughed when they said you could never have enough, and they recognised you by your perfume and silk clothing,' he rebuked, in obvious disgust.

'No.' She shook her head violently, and jumped to her feet. 'You must believe me. It was someone else they were speaking about, not me.' She gripped the back of a chair.

'Bah! Get on the street where you belong, and earn your bread. I never want to touch you. The thought of lovemaking with you sickens me. You're loathsome.'

With a piercing cry, she threw herself on the floor and put her face on his boot. He looked down for a moment, removed his boot and left the room, leaving her sobbing. Lifting her head, she listened as he climbed the stairs. Furious, she sprang to her feet and flounced across the room to look in the mirror over the fireplace.

'You're not the only one looking for a wife, my lad. Plenty of men would be only too pleased to place a ring on my finger.' She stroked her face and examined her flawless complexion. 'I shall soon find another fool to love me,' she told her reflection, with a smirk. 'I just have to smile at a young buck, and he'll be only too pleased to marry me.'

Nancy opened the bed drapes and slid out of the high bed upon hearing familiar sounds. Throwing a coverlet around her shoulders, she padded to the window and gazed at the busy scene below.

A jolly-looking fishmonger walked along the street, ringing a hand-bell, his wheelbarrow filled with rows of glistening herrings. Behind him came a milkmaid, balancing her buckets, calling out in a melodious voice, 'Milk! Fresh milk from my cow.' Further along the street, a pie-boy shouted and cursed as he shielded his tray of hot pies from a horse that was straining forward to take a tasty morsel. The boy spun on his heel and held the tray high, out of the reach of a group of light-fingered urchins.

She giggled at the sight, and pressed her face closer to the glass. A skivvy with red hands, scrubbing the front doorsteps, moved to one side as William appeared. Dressed in his best brown coat and fawn breeches, he darted between horse-drawn vehicles, and almost lost his hat as he turned the corner on the opposite side of the street.

She turned away from the window, and began to dress. *Wonder where he's going in such a hurry*, she mused. Tying the strings of her stays to the bedpost, she pulled until her expanding waist seemed as slim as it had always been. The muslin gown still fitted, and she smirked with pleasure at her reflection. Then she brushed her hair high, twisting the ends into a fashionable knot. She knew she looked her best as she lifted her fringe-edged shawl from the back of a chair and draped it over her arm before making her way downstairs to the parlour.

In daylight, the room was bright and elegant. She looked around the parlour with interest, taking particular notice of the furniture and the tasteful bric-a-brac on the mantelpiece. Her eyes rested speculatively on a brass-faced clock, and she caught sight of a pair of pewter candlesticks half hidden behind the window drapes. When the parlour door opened, she turned to Mrs Wood with an angelic face. 'I'll only have coffee this morning.' She seated herself at the table as she continued, 'I'll be going out later, Mrs Wood. A new bonnet must be my first purchase.' She gave a little giggle, but Mrs Wood gave no answering smile. Neither did the housekeeper make an effort to engage her in conversation as she filled a tray with the dirty breakfast crockery left by William. She bobbed the briefest of curtsies before leaving Nancy to drink her coffee alone.

Nancy stuck out her tongue at the closed door.

She strolled along the familiar streets of the town, stopping from time to time to gaze through shop windows. The shop she chose to enter was quite a distance from the lodging house. A bell on the door jangled as she pushed it open. She had forgotten how unpleasant the stench of worn clothing and dusty household items could be, and covered her nose with her hand. A frail, elderly man with wispy hair and a huge nose shuffled towards her, and she stepped closer to the counter.

'How much for these?' she asked, uncovering a pair of pewter candlesticks that had been hidden under her shawl. 'And this.' She removed the silver necklace Hugo had given her, and dropped it onto the counter next to the clock. It took a few minutes of haggling before she accepted a few coins. She was not displeased by the transaction, and stepped lightly as she made her way towards the centre of town. A street market should be in progress, and at that time of the day an old acquaintance might be there, selling good second-hand clothing.

She caught sight of a milliner's shop, and peered inside the window. *The last time I was here, Hugo took me to buy my blue bonnet.* Her thoughts were interrupted when someone called her name.

'Miss Nancy Turpin? ''Pon my soul! Sound as a roach, and twice as pretty. Miss Nancy Turpin as was, or maybe still is?'

She turned and saw Mr Pugh smiling at her. His lips were pursed, hiding his broken brown teeth. Portly as ever, he had an air of assurance and well-being. Nancy hid her surprise at the meeting by smiling sweetly and doing her old trick with her eyelashes.

'Why, Mr Pugh, how nice.' She gave a quick assessment of the value of his ruby velvet coat, and his pink and cream brocade waistcoat. Her eyes gleamed upon noticing the silver buckles on his shoes. They matched his buttons. A gold watch chain stretched across his paunch, and he gave the impression of being a very affluent businessman.

Graceful as always, she sank into a curtsy and offered her hand. His corsets creaked as he bowed low. 'You are even more charming than I remember, Miss Turpin. May I ask why you dally in Peter's Street?'

Allowing him to keep her hand in his, her nimble mind began to scheme. 'Shopping, Mr Pugh. My maid has taken my purchases home. So many boxes, the girl couldn't manage. I always buy more than I ought, but then, what is money for if not to enjoy?' She giggled, and squeezed his fingers. 'I've noticed a delightful bonnet in this shop window, and I was just thinking I might try it on when you called my name. Would you like to come in with me and say whether you like it or not? I know I can trust your good taste and dress sense.' Hooking her hand around his arm, she guided him through the door before he could protest.

Mr Pugh sat on an uncomfortable chair as shop assistants brought out richly-decorated bonnets and hats for Nancy to try on. Mirrors were held at all angles. Afterwards, he seemed bemused when Nancy left the shop with him following behind her, carrying two hat boxes he had paid for.

When they were in the street, her breath moved the forest of hairs in his ears, as she whispered, 'I must return home, you naughty man. But I do thank you for your wonderful advice. I knew I could rely on you.'

Brick red and breathing hard, he raised his cane and hailed a passing hackney coach. Before she climbed inside, she stroked the whiskers on his jowls with a fingertip. 'Will I see you tomorrow, Mr Pugh?' She leaned closer so he could catch the scent of the perfumed soap she had used, and allowed her breasts to press against his arm.

'Dear Miss Turpin. Yes, oh, yes.' He pressed his lips on her hand as she told him the place and time to meet her—well away from the lodging house.

If, during the next few days, William noticed Nancy's new clothes, he made no comment. Each morning he would breakfast before she came downstairs, and it was late evening before he returned. Often she would be in bed.

Returning home one day from an afternoon shopping with Mr Pugh, Nancy was amazed to find most of William's luggage on the floor in the entrance hall. He stood, holding another bag. She turned pale, realising he was wearing his travelling clothes.

'What's this doing here?' Nudging a bundle with her foot, she looked across the hallway at him.

'I leave tomorrow.' His voice was as cold as his eyes, and she trembled. Without William nearby, she had no protector. After the initial excitement of meeting her again, Mr Pugh now seemed a little reluctant to discuss his affairs, and, although generous with gifts, was not in any hurry to propose marriage.

She was wearing a new green gown, with a matching bonnet trimmed with ecru, coloured lace and feathers, both of which had been paid for by Mr Pugh. William stared at her from her neat shoes up to the feathers, and his sneering expression made her take a step back. 'You ought not to wear that pale shade. It makes you look bilious and sallow. Dead fish turn that colour.'

Flushing scarlet, she bit hard on her bottom lip. *You would turn that colour if I could get someone to knife you,* she thought, but managed not to show her outrage.

'What would you know about such things?' she said, with a toss of her head, wondering if he had heard her retching into her chamber pot each morning.

He shrugged and, after dropping the bag next to his other luggage, returned to his bedchamber.

'Anyway, no one asked for your opinion,' she shouted to his retreating back. He shrugged again, so she gave his luggage a vicious kick before following him upstairs. Although weepy, she became aware of Mrs Wood coming along the corridor towards her, and managed a bright beam.

'Mr Parkinson will be leaving us tomorrow, Miss Turpin.'

She nodded without speaking. Twitching her skirts to one side so the housekeeper could pass, she hurried to William's room where, untying her bonnet ribbons, she stood watching as he rolled the remainder of his belongings into a bundle. She coughed. When he ignored her, she moved further into the room. 'You're travelling alone, Mr Parkinson?'

'No.'

Her heart gave a leap and she flushed.

'Shall... Shall I pack my things?' Her voice was low and unsure.

'No need. Everything here is paid for to the end of the month.'

She could feel the rapid beating of her heart and became breathless. The end of the month was sixteen days away. What would she do for money after that? Knowing the housekeeper watched her every move, she dared not sell any more bric-a-brac from the parlour.

'I...I can leave with you tomorrow. We don't n-need to marry if you wish to wait. Later perhaps, in Scotland...?'

Her stuttering words halted as William stopped what he was doing and stared at her for a long moment without speaking. Then he said, 'I ride with friends to Scotland. You can stay here until the end of the month. After that you'll have to leave or pay the bill.'

Her face drained of colour, and she saw mockery in his eyes. 'You have no idea what happiness you're throwing away, William.' The despair in her voice stilled his busy hands for a moment. He kept his head lowered as she gave a cry and ran to her own room, slamming the door behind her. Throwing herself onto her bed, she pounded her pillow with clenched fists, giving way to tears of rage, and cursing at the way she had misdirected her life.

'Am I to take it you'll be staying on a few days longer, Miss Turpin?' Mrs Wood asked the following morning after William's early departure. She stood in the parlour facing Nancy, her hands clasped, and her bunch of keys jangling from her waist as she moved.

Matching the housekeeper's frown, Nancy snapped, 'The rent for my room is paid, so you should be happy.'

She was irritated by the way Mr and Mrs Wood constantly watched her. One of them would appear in a corridor when she was not expecting them, and each time she left the house she knew the kitchen curtains twitched.

'Your room will not be available after the end of the month, Miss Turpin, and when you leave here, the contents of the house will be listed.' The woman's chin lifted as she continued. 'An account is always made for items broken or missing. I'm just letting you know that Mr Harwood comes here, in person, to check the list. He always does.' Mrs Wood deliberately let her gaze settle on the windowsill when she finished speaking. Following her look, Nancy had the grace to blush. A pottery model of a spaniel looked rather lonely without the pair of pewter candlesticks that usually sat there.

'I'm sure I don't care what you may or may not count, Mrs Wood. Mr Parkinson has gone to his home in Scotland. You'll have to write and ask him about anything you think's missing.' Nancy held out a cup towards the housekeeper, and, giving her a frosty glare, added, 'Now, will you fill my cup with breakfast chocolate or not?'

Mrs Wood returned to her kitchen, rattling and banging the pots and pans with ill humour. 'She's a brass-faced hussy, that one. Never said a word about my missing things. That Mr Parkinson had her measure, though.' She turned to her husband and shook a spoon at him. 'Did you know she tried to get into his bedchamber one night? And each morning her chamber pot contains not only pee, but also vomit.'

Mr Wood raised his eyes from his newssheet and looked across the kitchen table at his wife's indignant face. 'How do you know for sure that she tried to get into his bedchamber, wife?'

'Remember the night of the high wind? Well, I heard a shutter banging, so I went to fasten it. At the end of the corridor, I saw that baggage-on-two-legs trying to lift the latch of his door and push it open. Luckily, he had the sense to keep it bolted. You should have seen the look on her face when she had to return to her own room. Like thunder it was. And as for the chamber pots, you know very well I'm the one to empty them.' With a chuckle she set his meal on the table. 'Just like thunder it was, her face.'

First folding his paper, Mr Wood put an arm around his wife's waist, and gave her a squeeze. 'She won't be here much longer, wife. I've reported everything to Mr Harwood, so we've no need to worry about her, or the tricks she gets up to.'

Nancy sat in the parlour, drinking her chocolate, becoming seriously concerned about her situation. Although she had managed to collect a fashionable wardrobe—mostly second-hand clothes suitable for her condition—she had a small amount of coinage, but not enough to pay for the birth of the child. It had become crucial to find a protector. Husband or lover—she didn't mind which. It was unfortunate she had no connections with a family of social standing in Nottingham, for otherwise she might have been invited to dinner parties or dances, and met gentlemen of a higher station in life. The reverend at the church she had attended in the past with Polly had moved district, and she had no wish to visit her own family, for they couldn't aid her ambitions. Her only way to become respectable would be to seduce Mr Pugh, who had informed her some days before that he was now a widower.

'My name is Edmund. Edmund Pugh.'

The couple were strolling arm in arm in one of the great parks of the town, when Nancy realised she had no idea of his first name. Tilting her parasol to shade her complexion from the sunshine, she smiled into his eyes. 'It suits you. Yes, it suits you well, my dear. Edmund. Nancy and Edmund Pugh. Doesn't that sound lovely?'

'Hmm. Me last wife liked it well enough.' Judging by the tone of his voice, he was obviously not yet convinced he liked the name Nancy Pugh.

Noticing his hesitation, she became even more apprehensive, and realised something drastic had to be done. She angled her parasol to hide her face from the others in the park, and, reaching up, pulled his florid face near enough to kiss. His eyes glinted, and he blushed red with embarrassment at such a wanton display in public.

It took many more days of kissing and titillating love-play before the reluctant man finally proposed marriage, whereupon she was delighted to accept.

Nancy dressed in white for her wedding. She wore a plain muslin gown with a lace ruffle round the hem, and a white muslin curricle jacket. Her bonnet, high-crowned, was decorated with pink and white silk flowers that cascaded down to a bunch of white ribbon on one side.

When they emerged from the parish church the bride wore an anxious expression. Mr Pugh placed an arm around his wife's shoulders, and pulled her close to give her a slobbery kiss, but Nancy turned her head so the kiss landed on her pale cheek. It was only just past eleven o'clock, and she felt nauseous until well past noon.

He hurried her to a waiting carriage, helped her into it, and clambered up, panting and sweating, to sit beside her. She looked with distaste at the podgy hand squeezing her knee, and gave a sigh. Somehow she must make him understand she was the master in the marriage.

'Mr Pugh, you are creasing my gown. This white muslin marks quickly, and your hands are none too clean.' She forgot he was her husband, that his word was law, and that she had just made a vow to obey him until death. 'One has to sit in a certain way in this jacket to show off the beautiful folds.' Her voice raised with vexation, she glanced at him, to find him scowling at her, so added, 'My dearest one,' and reached over to pinch a flabby jowl.

She was certainly not prepared for his reaction. He took her roughly in his arms, her bonnet tipped over one eye, and her lace parasol took a dive over the side of the open-topped carriage. With a scream, she tried to push his bulk off her, but he only held her closer. 'Sir, remember we are in public,' she panted, glancing at the driver who was grinning broadly, enjoying glimpses of her bare thighs.

'I don't care about such things now you are my spouse, Nancy, and neither should you.' Mr Pugh's thick lips were turned down with determination. 'No bridegroom likes to be turned away, wife. I see I've to teach you a few things about being a dutiful wife. But I've had plenty of practice at that.' His voice was sulky, and Nancy realised she needed to be very careful. Polly's words floated through her mind. *He's wicked, that one.*

'I just want to look my best for my handsome bridegroom.' Pressing close to him, she took hold of his hand, and began to kiss each finger. His eyes almost disappeared as he scrutinised her.

'I hope you ain't going to turn out like the last Mrs Pugh.' Nancy lifted her head, and looked at her husband with trepidation. He went on, 'Always wanting things. Spending my hard earned money on frippery. She even wanted a doctor to attend when she was lying in her childbed. I took no notice of her whims. Good thing I didn't. Would have been a waste of money. They both died.'

Nancy paled at his words, and she sat close to him with her head lowered, stroking his hand. Taking a deep breath, she said, 'But, darling Edmund, I'm different. I love you and you love me. We'll have a happy life together, you'll see.'

As he lolled back in his seat with one arm resting on her shoulders, he said, 'Of course we will, me dear. And we can use your money to buy us a house in London, or beside the sea.'

Her blood ran cold, and she stiffened when his words sank in. *Oh my goodness, he thinks I'm a rich woman. Surely he has money saved from working at the mill, and he must have an income from the way he dresses, and is bedecked?* In silence, she pressed the back of her hand to her mouth in panic, nervously twiddling a lock of hair. *God. What have I done?*

Bound together, husband and wife journeying to a future full of pitfalls, Nancy cursed the fact she was pregnant.

Chapter 17

This was Elysabeth's first visit to London and as the party passed through the last of the tollgates she stared wide-eyed at the various sights. She disregarded the way the coach jostled for space with other vehicles as it bounced and rattled through the narrow streets, much too excited to take any notice of the stinking gutters and beggars as she admired the fine buildings. Mr and Mrs Cooper were delighted to see her looking around in wonder, and they laughed kindly at her credulity.

They all grabbed the safety straps when the coach lurched to a halt. A footman, wearing a distinctive purple and silver livery, opened the door of the carriage and dropped the steps into place, before standing back and bowing.

'We have arrived,' said Mrs Cooper. 'Come, Elysabeth.' Gathering her skirts, with the help of the footman, she alighted onto the flagway.

Elysabeth followed and stood looking at a crescent-shaped building that stretched along the entire road, its windows reflecting the late afternoon sunlight.

'Here we are. This is our London residence. I do so hope you'll enjoy your stay with us, Elysabeth.'

Elysabeth curtsied. 'I thank you. Oh, a park. It will be pleasant to take a stroll there.' She gestured towards a wide expanse of grass surrounded by trees and bushes opposite the houses.

'Yes. We often walk in the afternoon. Horses can be hired, if you care to ride.'

'How lovely.'

Black iron railings and a gate parted the flagway from the house. The door stood open to show a row of waiting maids and a footman in a smart uniform, all wearing smiles of welcome. A young maid moved forward and, giving a curtsy, escorted

Elysabeth to her bedchamber and proceeded to unpack her luggage.

She turned towards the door in answer to a knock and sank into a curtsy as Mrs Cooper entered the room.

'Are you comfortable in here, Elysabeth?' she asked, running a critical eye around the pretty room, with its two high windows overlooking the park. 'We dine at eight. We'll rest this evening, for we must all be tired after our journey.' She gave an impish look, which reminded Elysabeth of Merrilla. 'I do own, I would love to take you out and point out some of the sights right this very minute. But still, there will be plenty of time to show you the delights London has to offer. I'll have a tray sent up to you, and then you can relax in peace.'

Elysabeth tried to stifle a yawn behind her hand. 'I, for one, will not be sorry to try my bed. It looks most comfortable.' She sat on the bed and nodded in appreciation of the softness of the goose-down quilt.

After a sound night's sleep, she found she was first down to breakfast the following morning. The door of the breakfast parlour had been left ajar, so she had no difficulty finding the room. Her eyes flew to the enormous epergne, and numerous silver dishes on the sideboard. She stared in amazement as a footman, dressed in morning livery, lifted one lid after the other to reveal a mouth-watering selection of food: a wing of chicken poached in milk and wine; slices of York ham, garnished with parsley; kedgeree of white fillet, or smoked fish; stewed eels, with anchovy essence; galantine of beef in a bed of chopped aspic jelly; game pancakes, and grilled kidneys. There was far more choice for breakfast here than she was accustomed to at home.

Far too excited to eat a full breakfast, she chose an egg and thinly-sliced bread and butter. The footman had just replenished her cup of chocolate when she heard a commotion in the hallway. Recognising the voices, she rose to her feet. The door was flung open, and Merrilla hurried into the parlour, followed more slowly by Philip. Merrilla looked radiant. 'My dear. How wonderful to see you. Did you enjoy the journey? Oh, never mind, tell us about it later,' she cried, as she kissed her. 'We have seen such remarkable sights. The king and queen passed us in their carriage yesterday. I'm sure they waved to me alone.'

Philip grinned at his sister before kissing her cheek. 'No problems on the journey here? And you are comfortable?'

'Oh, no problems at all. We only arrived yesterday evening.' Elysabeth turned to Merrilla. 'Your mamma and papa are still upstairs,' she said, watching Merrilla seat herself at the table.

'I've sent a maid up to Mamma to say we have arrived. We'll have chocolate while we wait for her.' Merrilla looked towards the footman, who hurried to serve her. The man then stood at attention next to the sideboard.

'I had forgotten how well Mamma trains her servants,' she said, in a low, sad voice. Her sunny smile returned when Philip put his arm around her shoulders and gave her a hug.

She had just raised her cup when her mother, giving a glad cry, hurried into the breakfast parlour to greet them. So many questions poured out: where they had been, what they had done, whom they had met, that Merrilla caught hold of her hands, gave her a kiss, and told her they had days to catch up with their news.

Mid-afternoon the following day, Maude Godsen entered the salon on the ground floor of number five in a most stately way. Merrilla looked at her sister for a long moment, before holding out both arms and hurrying to hug her. She drew back, flushed and embarrassed at the light kiss that missed her cheek and the unyielding stiffness of Maude's corset-restrained body.

'So pleased you're returned to us, sister. I understand you're married, Mrs Larcombe?' Maude seated herself on a dainty chair as she drawled the words and waved her fan. The chair creaked in protest at having to bear such a heavy weight.

Elysabeth moved her skirts to make room on the couch for Merrilla to sit beside her.

'Mr Larcombe has gone to visit a coffee house with Papa. May I present Miss Elysabeth Larcombe, my sister-in-law?'

Lifting a tortoiseshell lorgnette, Maude stared at Elysabeth. The girl blushed, and murmured a greeting.

'My dear Maude, so pleased you could call at such a short notice,' Mrs Cooper greeted her daughter, as she swept into the room. 'I know you usually visit your manteau maker on a weekday.' She proceeded to kiss Maude's powdered cheek, before settling herself in a comfortable chair. 'Miss Larcombe here knows no one in London. While she's with us, Elysabeth hopes to acquire some town polish. Her mamma will be pleased to see her agreeably established as a lady, married to a gentleman of standing.' Breaking off, Mrs Cooper motioned to the servants for tea and seed cake to be passed around.

Elysabeth coloured, obviously embarrassed at being discussed as though she were absent.

Maude sniffed. 'That should set us a challenge. I own, Miss Elysabeth is quite an attractive creature, but she will need dressing. Brown hair is not in fashion this season, so she will need to powder. The girl is in a class of her own. She may take or she may not.' The fruit, flowers and feathers on her hat leaped and bobbed as she nodded in Elysabeth's direction. 'I suppose I could take her to see my woman, and have her dressed.'

With downcast eyes, Elysabeth looked as if she was biting back a retort that might have damned her in Mrs Cooper's esteem. Not so Merrilla. Her childhood animosity for Maude surfaced. She sprang to the girl's defence. 'Miss Larcombe does not need you to say she needs a different wardrobe, Maude. She had not expected to be in London. We both wish to visit a wigmaker and choose new fans. Mamma is to take us shopping tomorrow.' Her chin was defiant. She had learned how to defend herself in a hard school, and now she perched on the edge of her seat with her back straight, ready to give battle.

Maude gave her a scornful glance. 'Where was it you disappeared to, sister? Why did you leave home so suddenly? Did you not know that Papa made an extensive search for you? He even employed men from London to make enquiries all over the country. The house was in an uproar for months after, and he became a changed and unwell man because of your wanton disappearance.'

Maude had almost finished speaking when the door opened, and their father and Philip walked into the salon. Mr Cooper shook his head at the stormy faces and tight lips of his daughters.

Philip strode forward, dressed magnificently in a silk coat with an embroidered matching waistcoat, and shoes with jewelled buckles. He looked extremely elegant as he bowed over the hand of his mother-in-law saying, 'Ma'am, we have seen a bonnet in a shop window, with ribbons made to tie under your chin. You must allow me to buy it tomorrow when we go shopping.'

Flushing and giggling girlishly, Mrs Cooper tapped his arm with her fan. 'Fie on you for your flattery, Philip. Come, let me introduce you to my other daughter, Mrs Godsen.'

Philip's eyes flashed a warning to Merrilla before turning to her sister. Maude inclined her head graciously as he legged a bow. 'Pleased to make the acquaintance of my wife's sister, Mrs Godsen.'

Maude lifted a limp hand and he raised it to his lips. 'You must all come and dine with us this evening. London is very short of eligible men at the moment, but I will do my best to have a full table,' Maude murmured, glancing across the room at Elysabeth.

They all gave a sigh of relief when Maude made her adieu, then Elysabeth murmured an excuse and left the room.

With a frown, Mrs Cooper moved to sit beside Merrilla. 'We had best put our heads together and find a story we can tell about your absence, Merrilla. People don't like enigmas, and will quickly begin inventing tales that will fly around the town and beyond.' She exchanged a worried glance with her husband. A person's reputation could be ruined beyond repair by a hint of adverse gossip, and they had no wish to see their daughter hurt further.

'Mamma, we do not have to say anything. It's no one's business, and only we know the truth.' Tears filled Merrilla's eyes. She felt comforted, and her confidence returned when Philip placed a protective arm around her shoulders.

'I agree with Merrilla. She is my wife, and that is all anyone needs to know. If people want more information, let them come and ask me or her father.' Philip's tone brooked no argument. Standing by the fireplace, with a foot on the fender and one arm on the mantelshelf, Mr Cooper nodded agreement, clearly thankful that at last Merrilla had found happiness with such a strong and upright man.

Merrilla, Philip and Elysabeth became frequent dinner guests at Godsen House, and it seemed to them that every person of importance in London was invited. Maude and her husband moved in the "Polite World" and since they had sufficient wealth and charm, both were popular, and they thoroughly enjoyed entertaining their numerous friends and acquaintances. They were perfect hosts, and frequent ripples of laughter ran around the table as they introduced topics of conversation of interest to everyone.

During the following weeks, Elysabeth, together with all the family, experienced an exciting round of shopping, receptions, theatres, balls, concerts in drawing rooms, and pleasurable meals. Innumerable fashion fittings were arranged for the girls, until she laughingly protested to her hosts that her father would be surely ruined by her vast expenditure.

'I bought these silk stockings as a surprise gift for Philip. I do hope he likes the colour.' Merrilla seated herself on Elysabeth's bed, and then dropped back with an audible sigh.

'If Papa knew how much I've spent on my new shoes, he'd have a seizure,' Elysabeth giggled, a happy glow on her face.

Both girls enjoyed every moment with Elysabeth hardly having time to think of Hugo.

Breakfast in London became an informal affair, with everyone coming down when they were ready and helping themselves from the warm dishes on the sideboard. Two servants stood nearby, ready to assist.

A month after their arrival in London, Philip and Merrilla were the last to come downstairs for breakfast, and the rest of the family drifted from the room with vague promises of meeting later. As the door closed behind Elysabeth, Merrilla turned to Philip with a puzzled frown and asked, 'Who was your letter from, dearest? I saw you trying to keep it hidden from Elysabeth's eyes.'

'Oh, dear, am I so transparent, my love? The letter's from Hugo. He's here, in London, staying at Limmers Hotel, although I cannot think why he should want to stay in such a place as that. Mostly elderly gentlemen stay there. He's asked to see me, either at the hotel or somewhere of my choice.'

The colour fled from Merrilla's cheeks. 'Philip. Mr Larcombe. Please do be careful. We have such a happy family here. Don't allow Mr Denstone to bring that woman into our company.'

'It's strange, but Hugo hasn't mentioned anything about Miss Turpin's whereabouts in his letter, and Limmers is certainly not the kind of hotel to which I'd have expected him to take her. It's far too gloomy. No doubt, all will be made clear when I meet him. I've sent word I will be at the hotel at eleven. You must make some excuse to everyone for my absence this morning, my love.'

Hearing a swish of silk skirts as Elysabeth re-entered the room, Philip jumped to his feet with an embarrassed expression, and accidentally spilled his coffee over the table. 'Oh, damn. I...I must beg leave. I've remembered an...an appointment.' He had never been able to keep secrets from his sister. He almost fell over a chair rushing from the breakfast room, leaving Elysabeth and Merrilla staring in astonishment at the closed door.

Limmers Hotel was within walking distance. Ignoring the driver of a hackney carriage who kept pace with him in the hopes of picking up a passenger, Philip strode along the streets at a brisk rate. Nodding to the lackey who held open the hotel door, he glanced around the dimly lit foyer in the hope of seeing Hugo. When his friend walked towards him with a hand outstretched he noticed with satisfaction Nancy's absence.

'So pleased you could come, Philip. The coffee room's busy at this hour, however we can use the lounge.' Hugo led the way to a comfortless room—decorated with huge portraits of solemn-looking men—even more dismal than the foyer. He invited Philip to be seated.

Philip looked around at the dark portraits of anonymous gentlemen, and grinned. 'Must say I don't think much to your choice of hotel, my friend.'

'It suits me for the moment. A place to lay my head, away from bloody scheming women,' he said, rubbing a hand across his eyes.

At first, haltingly, then with more confidence, he told his friend what he knew about Nancy's wanton behaviour. 'The day after William Parkinson's departure one of the game-keepers found her belongings in the grounds and brought everything to my parents. They found a hatbox filled with money and jewellery.

Most of the money had been taken from my father's study, and the jewellery all belonged to Mamma.

"My parents thought at first that William and Nancy had eloped. Papa sent a message for me to return home at once from a business meeting in York, and I apologised to him most sincerely for bringing her to our home in the first place, and also for the appalling way she had behaved while staying with us. He said I was well rid of her.' Again, he rubbed his hand across his eyes, in that same weary gesture an old man makes. 'He was right. I'm surprised he has not disowned me for the trouble I brought into the house.'

'William elope with Nancy? No. I don't think for one moment he'd be so foolish. He had her measure from the start. William may have taken her, but not to marry her. He would do it because he knew you loved my sister.'

'You're right, of course, Philip. We were all relieved to hear it wasn't an elopement, and that William had taken Miss Turpin to rejoin her family and friends. When he reached Nottingham he wrote to me at great length, explaining exactly what had happened. I cannot thank him enough.'

A silence followed as each man sat deep in thought. Hugo glanced more than once at Philip.

'Will you tell me why you got yourself into this mess, Hugo? Could you not have paid her to leave?'

Hugo shook his head. 'She wanted more than I could offer. I felt so ashamed to have brought her away from her friends and family, and I thought she wouldn't be able to face everyone at home as a jilted woman. I didn't know her very well, did I?' He gave a short laugh. 'I wanted to act with honour and principle.'

'You nearly drove poor Elysabeth into a nunnery. Still, we may be able to sort out something, for I'm certain she still loves you.'

As though Philip had lit a candle, Hugo straightened his shoulders and beamed with delight. 'Somehow you always come to my aid, Philip. The thing is, how am I going to see your sister and beg her to forgive me?' He gave another deep sigh when Philip shook his head.

'I dare not bring the subject up. Not even to tell her you're in London. You know better than most how sensitive Elysabeth is. I fear she would immediately pack her bags and return home if she found out you wished to speak to her. I'm not even sure what her reaction would be if she knew we had met.'

There was another heavy silence as they pondered the issue until Philip said, 'And another thing—you've shaved off your beard.'

Shamefaced, Hugo put a hand to his bare chin. 'I...I...err...wanted to look different. Fresh start.'

The two men sat in the gloomy surroundings, drinking burgundy and trying to think of a way of informing Elysabeth of Hugo's new situation. At last, knowing Merrilla and his sister would be waiting for him to take him out shopping, or on some other excursion, Philip rose to his feet. Looking thin and haggard, Hugo walked with him into the foyer.

They shook hands, as Philip said, 'I'll ask Merrilla if she can find a solution. She's a woman with plenty of common sense, and may agree to have a talk with Elysabeth.'

'I do hope she will, Philip. I know I've been extremely stupid, but I did, at first, care for Miss Turpin very much. Once I knew her better, I became afraid of the harm she would cause everyone with her lies, never mind the fool she made of me.'

Philip returned to the Cooper residence. Merilla hurried across the entrance hall as the butler took his hat and gloves. Holding tightly to her husband's arm, she drew him into the downstairs salon, and closed the door.

'Why have you been so long, Philip? I felt so worried when you didn't arrive in time to accompany Elysabeth on her drive. She sounded most put out because you broke your promise. I had a dreadful time explaining your absence.' She led him to a sofa and they sat holding hands as he unfolded the tale about Nancy and William.

'Oh! The wicked, wicked woman. William Parkinson, of all people. I saw him flirting with her more than once, but I had no idea it was a ploy.'

With a grin he said, 'Hugo has declared he must see Elysabeth and explain things to her personally. The thing is, my dear, shall we help him? And if so, how?'

Cupping her husband's face in her hands, Merrilla said, 'However can you ask such a thing? We must give them the chance to be as happy as we are.' She dropped her hands into her lap, and giving a heavy sigh, asked, 'But how? Now, that is the problem.'

He put an arm around her shoulders, and moved his cheek against her curls as he sat thinking. 'It's a hellish puzzle. If my sister finds I've been meddling, I'll be in deep trouble, but if I do nothing, she may marry someone else. Then, after a while, she would certainly find out she could have married Hugo as was planned. Egad! What a mess.'

Kissing the top of Merrilla's head, he continued. 'This has all come about because Hugo wanted to act as an honourable gentleman towards Nancy Turpin. If he had not involved himself with her in the first place none of this upset would have happened.' He ran his hand over his hair in despair. 'I don't know what to do for the best. If someone so much as mentions Hugo, it will upset Elysabeth, and she'll start to mope again. We don't want her going around London like a duck without a pond.'

Merrilla chuckled. 'I think I may know of a way out of this difficulty. Listen closely, now. Tomorrow evening is the big masquerade. Send a message to Hugo to be there in a domino costume. Elysabeth will not expect him, and he can dance with her, and maybe take her into supper. At the unmasking, we can be as surprised as Elysabeth when we see the identity of her partner.'

Merrilla watched various emotions cross her husband's face, then laughed as he gave a sudden whoop, and hugged her. 'My clever little wife! Will it be successful?'

'Of course it will be successful. Send a note to his address tomorrow, but let Mr Denstone do something for himself, Philip. After all, it was his imprudence and timidity that created the problem. If Elysabeth rejects him, that is her choice, and she will not be angry at you, my love.' Her happy face, tilted up to her husband, invited more kisses.

'What ever transpires, my darling, we're together.'

She whispered in his ear, 'I know, my dearest. Shall we go to our room?'

The evening of the masquerade found the street filled with a long line of carriages waiting to set down their passengers. The trio in their carriage were entertained by the magnificence of revellers on foot. Jewels of every colour and description winked and flashed in the light of flaming torches held high by linkboys. Philip escorted Merrilla and Elysabeth. The young ladies stared at an enormous fat woman ablaze with rows of diamonds, and being carried in a sedan chair, escorted by a stick of a man dressed all in purple. Catching Merrilla's eye, Elysabeth broke into peals of laughter. This caused more than one gentleman to raise his quizzing glass and stare at their merry faces.

Footmen helped them to alight onto the red carpet and, with eyes bright in happy anticipation, they moved forward to take their place among the guests under rows of chandeliers aglitter with flickering candles.

Everyone wore a mask, some, like Elysabeth's, feather-covered, matching the wearer's headdress or fan. Others were encrusted with jewels, or plain and coloured to enhance an

307

ensemble. Some masks covered all of their owner's features to the upper lip, and some were attached to a wand and held to the face.

The party found Mr and Mrs Cooper, with some friends, assembled in a small alcove, from where they could watch the dancing. Merrilla looked charming, in blue silk, trimmed with coffee-coloured lace. Her father gave her an elaborate bow, using his handkerchief to great advantage. 'May I claim your hand for the first dance of the evening, my dear?'

First glancing at Philip for his permission, Merrilla gave her father a radiant smile, and allowed him to lead her into the dance. Philip turned to Elysabeth, intending to ask her to be his partner, but a tall, thin man, in a black domino and mask, bowed over her hand. Elysabeth snapped her fan closed. A nod from Philip signalled a clear indication of his approval, and soon a strong hand on her waist whirled her around the dance floor, her steps matching those of the stranger.

'Oh, I did enjoy that.' Her cheeks were rosy, and her eyes sparkled with animation.

'Will the damsel carry me to heavenly heights by allowing me to lead her into the next dance? It will be a quadrille.'

Elysabeth stood motionless, her smile frozen as she tried to penetrate the stranger's disguise. That husky whisper sounded familiar. *No. It could never be him, not here, not in London. I'm being silly,* she thought, crossly. *Anyway, Hugo has a beard, and this man is quite thin.* Hoping the stranger hadn't noticed her hesitation, she agreed and, defying convention, danced most of the evening with him. At a quarter to midnight, she found she had been whirled into a secluded corner. Alone with this strange man behind tall plants and flowers, she glanced around for her brother.

'You are adorable. A goddess in water green.'

An arm around her slim waist, her partner drew her close. She felt his warm breath on her cheek. When a tender whisper of a kiss brushed her lips she felt her heart leap and flutter.

'It is with regret that I have to return you to your party's safekeeping before we unmask. I will behold your perfection from afar.'

She was unable to see the colour of his hair, for the man wore a white wig, but brown eyes glittered through the narrow slits of the stranger's mask.

'I...I do not understand. Would you not like to meet my family and friends?' Her words were drowned when a group of laughing people danced into the screened corner, and she found herself being led across the room to rejoin Mrs Cooper.

Merrilla had been delighted to be reunited with some girlhood friends and acquaintances whom she then introduced to her husband and Elysabeth. The merry circle became merrier.

'Philip, dear, I want you to meet... Oh! He has gone.' Disappointment could be heard in Elysabeth's voice when she realised the stranger was no longer standing beside her. 'No matter, Philip. Just someone I danced with.' She gave her brother a brilliant smile. 'Oh, Philip, I have enjoyed this evening.'

Alone with Philip in their bedchamber, Merrilla's annoyance became apparent. Before removing her shoes or jewellery, she faced him with her hands on her hips. 'Why? Tell me, why Hugo did not reveal his identity when we all unmasked?'

He ran his hands through his hair, wishing he hadn't become entangled with his friend's troubles, and shook his head. He tugged off his cravat and threw it on to a chair, facing her. 'He met me when you were collecting your cloaks and said he thought there might be a public scene, and that people might stare. That would have upset Elysabeth even more. There wasn't time to say more, but I told him we would be at the Vauxhall

Gardens tomorrow evening, and he promised to be there, and to speak to Elysabeth then.'

'Let's hope he keeps his word.' Moving closer, Merrilla smiled roguishly, and her green eyes sparkled as she slid both arms around her husband. Drawing his head down she whispered, 'I have another plan.'

The next day, Elysabeth's bedchamber was in disarray. Merrilla sat on the bed as Elysabeth tried to make up her mind what to wear for the evening revels at Vauxhall's. The dusty pink gown with a paler flounce, or the green gown she had worn to the masquerade?

'Did you keep your mask and fan from last night, Elysabeth?'

Blushing, she sighed. 'I shall always keep them. My partner and I danced so well together. He was so...so masterful.'

Merrilla smiled, and, picking up the green gown, twirled around the room until she stood in front of the long looking-glass.

'Your gentleman in the black domino may be at the Vauxhall Gardens this evening,' she said, watching Elysabeth in the glass. 'I suppose he wanted to appear mysterious. He's succeeded. He's the only man you've spoken about out of all those you've met in London.'

'That's probably because he reminds me most strongly of Hugo. Perhaps it's his height, or maybe it's the way he held me as we danced.'

Merrilla gave her sister-in-law a searching glance, wondering if she suspected anything, for she knew how sharp-witted Elysabeth could be. *We must all be very careful. I couldn't bear anything to spoil our friendship,* she thought.

Chapter 18

That evening, the dusky pink gown, freshly pressed, was laid out for Elysabeth. The maid's nimble fingers had skilfully brushed and curled her hair. Two long curls, threaded with narrow pink ribbon, lay over one shoulder, and elflocks, brushed and dampened, curled around her face.

'I don't know how you do it, Jane. You only touch my hair, and it behaves beautifully.' she laughed at her pretty maid in the mirror.

Jane hurried to answer a knock on the door. A servant carrying a large, flat box stood beside Merrilla. 'Look what's arrived, Elysabeth. The dressmaker must have worked all night to finish our gowns ready for this evening,' she said, hurrying into the room. She dismissed the servant and gestured to the maid to take the box and place it on the bed. All the girls gave a gasp of pleasure when, removing the packing, they discovered a beautiful cream and silver gown and a length of silver ribbon.

Merrilla had promised to pay the dressmaker double and also her future patronage, if the gown could be finished on time. 'Wear it tonight, Elysabeth. Promise me you will. It will shimmer with all different colours from the lights hanging down from the trees at Vauxhall's.'

Nodding happily, Elysabeth sat transfixed, facing her mirror as the maid expertly re-dressed her hair with the silver ribbon. Merrilla seated herself in a chair nearby, and watched until Elysabeth was almost ready. 'Mr Godsen has booked our party a box which opens onto one of the colonnade walks. We'll be able to see all that's going on, and hear the concert during supper. I've heard such tales about Vauxhall Gardens. Even my mother says it's a sensational place.'

311

'I have heard people speak about the fireworks displays. I cannot wait to see them.' Catching her sister-in-law's excitement, she grinned mischievously and wiggled her fingers at her before leaving the room to attend to her own toilette.

The evening started in a most agreeable way. Maude had arrived earlier with her husband and she walked beside her mother as they came downstairs. Merrilla and Elysabeth followed closely behind. All three men bowed low as the ladies entered the salon. No apology was given for keeping them waiting. The four women sank into a deep curtsy in acknowledgment of their men-folk's appraisal.

Mr Cooper stepped forward and offered his arm to his wife. 'We must leave at once, my dear. Mr Godsen and I have made arrangements to enter the gardens by the water gate, and we must be on time to catch the boat.' He winked at Philip as Elysabeth and Mrs Cooper murmured excitedly about this unexpected addition to the evening's entertainment. Only Philip noticed how pale Merrilla had become, and he murmured a quiet reassurance to his wife as he escorted her out to the waiting carriage.

The boat was surprisingly steady as the ladies were assisted in alighting at the landing stage. Merrilla had been quiet through the short journey, so Philip took the opportunity, as they transferred to the pathway, to keep his arm around his wife's waist a moment or two longer than was necessary. 'What a crush! So many people have come. Are you sure you will not find your visit here too exhausting, my love?' he teased, giving her a squeeze.

She dimpled at her husband. 'You're so handsome, even in your mask, Mr Larcombe.'

'Did you know you have the most enchanting way of laughing, my dear?' He bent to kiss the rosy lips which hovered so temptingly close to his. Entwined in each other's arms, they followed other couples along paths lit by shimmering candle lamps.

Standing to one side, Elysabeth watched as a juggler threw blazing torches into the air, deftly catching each one as it fell. She was unaware of being left alone beneath a row of multi-coloured candle lanterns until a husky voice made her gasp. 'My goddess is in silver this evening.' She turned as the tall man in the black domino bowed deeply.

'You...you startled me, sir.' With an expert flick of her fan, she cooled her flushed cheeks, her heart racing, at the same time, hoping she appeared cool and indifferent. She glanced around and, realising the other members of her party had vanished into the pageant of promenading people, felt a sudden panic.

'May I be allowed to escort you, my goddess in silver?'

That husky whisper, somehow so familiar, caused her to stare at the masked face above her. She became even more puzzled. *We must have met before, but where? Who is he?*

'Philip, my brother, regretted you were not introduced at the masquerade,' she said, placing a hand lightly on the stranger's arm.

The man bowed his head. 'This evening we will meet, dear damsel.'

The couple were drawn into the crowds where everyone wore masks. They walked slowly, stopping to watch tumbling clowns in colourful costumes with big, black shoes. Everyone looked on with delight and wonder at a boy and girl in matching pantaloons and sleeveless vests dancing with hoops and ropes upon a high wire that slanted from the tip of a tall pole down to a stake in the grass clearing.

They walked for more than an hour, enjoying both the performances and the sideshows that had such interesting exhibits.

313

'There are so many things to see in the gardens, it'll take most of the evening,' the stranger said, giving a broad smile. As they stood under a lamp, brighter than others in the vicinity, Elysabeth noticed that one of his front teeth was slightly chipped. Her face drained of colour as she remembered that, at twelve years old, Hugo had taken an awkward fall from his horse, and that she had bravely staunched the blood from his mouth with her handkerchief.

'Do you wish to partake of supper, goddess? The Pavilion is but a short walk away.'

'Do not call me goddess, Hugo!' Ice could not have been any colder than her voice.

'Oh!' Hugo seemed disconcerted. They walked side by side in silence. She sensed him glancing at her, but stared ahead.

'Err... When...? H-how did you know, Elysabeth?'

She tossed her head without answering.

'Miss Larcombe.' He caught hold of her arm, and turned her to face him. 'Will you sit on that bench with me, and let me explain? Please, Elysabeth.'

'You will escort me to where my brother is, Mr Denstone. Tomorrow at ten o'clock, you may call at my address. If I am at home, I will see you.' Her words dripped with scorn and frosty disdain. Her eyes glinted dangerously through the slits of her mask. He knew that look of old, and remained silent.

Philip rose to his feet as they approached the supper party. He nudged Merrilla. Her eyes widened with apprehension at Elysabeth's tight lips and stiff back.

Hugo bowed to each of the ladies in the box, and inclined his head to the gentlemen in the party.

'You know my escort, Philip. Adieu, Mr Denstone. You may call tomorrow.' When Elysabeth extended her hand, Hugo raised it to his lips, and tried to catch her eye. But it was no use. She was determined not to look at him. He shot a miserable glance at

314

Philip and Merrilla, before moving away into the cheerful crowds.

The evening was spoiled when a mournful silence fell across the group. In a whisper to her mother, Maude asked the reason. This brought a sharp retort. 'Mind your own affairs. What you don't know, you can't gossip about over tea cups.'

After that exchange, everyone decided they were ready to return home.

Noticing how close to tears Miss Elysabeth seemed, the maid hardly dared to speak as she undressed her and helped her to prepare for bed. When the girl had left the room, she pulled a chair nearer to the fire, and sat looking at the glowing coals. 'I do wish Mamma was here to advise me,' she murmured. Then she thought of Mrs Cooper. Maybe Merrilla's mamma would give her guidance. She pulled a robe over her long nightdress, opened the door and peered into the corridor. Silence. A lamp had been turned down low, but it was light enough to see her way to the last door at the other end of the corridor. She heard a faint 'Come', in answer to her timid tap.

She opened the door, and saw a fire blazing in the hearth. A turkey-red carpet made the room seem even more warm and welcoming. 'Oh, my goodness!' She stood in confusion at the sight of a weeping Merrilla seated at her mother's feet.

Mrs Cooper beckoned. 'Come in and join us, Elysabeth. We were unsure whether to call and see you. How are you feeling, my dear?'

She walked to a low chair, and sat near Merrilla. 'I...I don't know, Mrs Cooper. Relieved, I think.'

Sniffing, Merrilla wiped her face with a damp handkerchief. 'It's so awful. Everything has gone wrong. I wanted Hugo to make himself known to you yesterday evening. At the

315

masquerade.' The words ended on a wail as she buried her face in her hands.

With her mouth open, Elysabeth stared at her. Did everyone know and think her a simpleton for not having seen through his disguise?

'Elysabeth, please give the bell a pull. We'll have hot milk and think together what will be best. Mr Denstone has been foolish, but you are a strong girl, with a good deal of sense. That is just what he needs, my dear.' Mrs Cooper's words were crisp, and Elysabeth hurried to do as bidden.

The milk arrived, and before the maid left the room, she heaped more coals on the fire. Mrs Cooper dragged a stool towards her and lifted the lid. The eyes of both girls widened in astonishment when she took out a bottle of spirits.

'Now you see why I ordered milk. Put a spoonful of sugar into each cup, Merrilla, and pass them to me. This will help us to think, and later, we'll get a good night's sleep.'

Merrilla gasped at the generous measure of the spirit poured into each cup. 'Mamma, what is it?'

'Brandy. Best thing I know for shock. It's good for other things, too.' The elder lady chuckled wickedly as she handed a cup to Elysabeth.

Sipping the mixture appreciatively, Elysabeth smiled, remembering the shocked expression on Hugo's face. 'I feel better already,' she said.

'Now then, young lady, is this Mr Denstone worth having, or would you be better off with another man for a husband?' Mrs Cooper asked, when their cups were half empty.

The girls glanced at each other.

'I want Hugo. I love him still, even though he has been so foolish.' Elysabeth spoke with conviction.

Merrilla nodded as she looked into her mother's face. 'He's nice, Mamma. He loves Elysabeth. I met him once, and he told me he had made a dreadful mistake. That wicked woman tricked him.'

'Men can make themselves look such buffoons...' Mrs Cooper broke off when the door opened. Mr Cooper stood in the doorway, staring at them. His thin, white legs were bare from the knee down. A nightshirt hung loose on his tall frame, and a tassel on his nightcap hung over one eye. 'Oh,' he said. 'Oh dear.'

The first giggle came from Merrilla, soon joined by Mrs Cooper and then Elysabeth. Soon all three were letting out whoops of laughter. With a shake of his head in bewilderment, he left them to their merriment. 'Never will understand women,' they heard him mutter, before he left the room.

Promptly at ten o'clock the following morning, the door opened to a pasty-faced Hugo, holding a bunch of red roses. Shown into the ground floor salon, he trod nervously up and down the carpet as he waited for Elysabeth. He sprang to attention, and held the roses at arm's length as the door opened. Alas, Merrilla came into the room, and he lowered the flowers to his side.

'Elysabeth is out. She asked me to tell you to wait.' Merrilla moved to a sofa and arranged her skirts as she sat down.

Wiping his forehead with his hand, Hugo sighed deeply and held out the roses. 'I brought these. Do you think she'll like them?'

'Mr Denstone. It will take much more than mere flowers. You'll need to work very hard if Elysabeth is to pardon you.'

'I don't deserve that she should even look in my direction, much less regard me with affection.'

Intent on speaking, he didn't notice the door open. Without speaking, Elysabeth seated herself next to Merrilla. He hurried to bow formally over Elysabeth's proffered hand. 'I've brought you these,' he said, holding out the flowers.

317

Elysabeth looked at the roses and then at Hugo. 'Be seated, Mr Denstone,' she said, pointing with her closed fan to a chair on the far side of the room. He placed the roses on a side table, walked to the chair and lifting his coattails, sat down, clenching his teeth. He had spent a sleepless night, and his temper was beginning to show.

'Miss Turpin has gone back to Nottingham. Your cousin William took her away with him.'

Elysabeth's face wore a look of boredom, and she yawned behind her open fan.

'I thought you might enjoy an airing in the park?' He looked despondently at the carpet. 'Perhaps not.'

At the sound of rustling skirts, he raised his eyes, as Mrs Cooper swept into the room in a flowing shawl. 'Mr Denstone. Did no one order tea? Merrilla, ring the bell for tea. Young man, tell me, are you to escort Elysabeth to my other daughter's home for dinner this evening? We will only be a family party, so do not expect a drove of people.'

It seemed as though the sun had come out, and Hugo stuttered and smiled his thanks.

Over the teacups, Merrilla and her mother made light conversation. Elysabeth joined in chattering until a servant appeared with a note for Mrs Cooper and Merrilla. They excused themselves, and left her playing with her fan. As soon as the door closed Hugo hurried across the room and, kneeling in front of Elysabeth, took hold of her hands. 'I am so very sorry, Elysabeth. I will spend my whole life making it up to you, my dearest.' A tear trembled on her eyelashes, and he gently wiped it away with a trembling finger. 'I love you, Elysabeth. I will always love you.' His heart gave a leap when she gave a sniff and a watery smile. After gazing at each other for a brief moment, they fell into each other's arms.

A weak sun shone high in the sky, and a fresh wind whistled past the rider as he bent low over his horse's neck. Familiar with the road from York to Clemmants, the horse needed little guidance as it raced along. A young groom ran forward to catch the bridle as the rider rode into Clemmants' stable yard. The man shouted no pleasant greetings, but ran towards the house, pulling a packet of letters from his pocket. They were placed in the hands of John Larcombe.

'There you are, Esther!' The door of Esther's sitting room burst open and John hurried across the carpet, waving the letters at her. 'We have a letter from London. It's in Philip's handwriting, so I brought it to you immediately. It may tell us what they are doing and when they are all returning home.'

Sweeping the needlework from her lap, Esther settled herself to hear the latest news as John stood near a window to read. He broke the seal on the folded paper and read aloud to his attentive wife.

London   Town.

Dearest Mamma and Papa,

Beloved parents. We leave London with reluctance, for Mr and Mrs Cooper have been most kind to us all. They are not travelling with us, and have decided to return to their country house in Grantham.

Everyone expects to return home before the trees are stripped bare of their leaves. We have seen so many sights here in London; it will take us a lifetime to recount the wonders of this amazing town.

We sat down for dinner with more than two hundred people last night. The meal was tastefully served, and the wines excellent.

During our time here, Mr and Mrs Godsen have introduced Hugo and myself to many worthy persons, some of whom I intend

319

to acquaint you with, Papa, for they are sound business men, with forward-looking ideas.

Last week we met Mr Paxton at a soiree. He was outrageously dressed in a bright pink coat, and had his name sewn on the back with silver embroidery. He paints his face more thickly, and still wears black patches of all shapes on his face. It was obvious that he is happy to be included among the London dandy set. Without sorrow, he told us of his father's recent demise.

<u>Now for news most important</u>! I am sure you must have heard from William by now, and know the story of his departure with Nancy - and the reason for it.

Hugo arrived in London safely, and contacted me. He has now persuaded Elysabeth to allow him to accompany her on all of her outings. Elysabeth's demeanour makes us think she has fully forgiven him. She told Merrilla privately that she has put his foolhardiness behind her, and will say yes when he next proposes. Dining with Hugo last week, he informed me that he expected to be affianced before we reach home. He showed me a very fine ring he had bought for my sister.

Maybe you had best give a hint to your friend, the reverend. Do you remember Merrilla's wedding flowers? She thinks that perhaps there is some truth in the old superstition about the bride's bouquet?

Merrilla and Elysabeth have just walked into the study. They say to be sure to write of their love for you both.

We are packed and ready to leave on the morrow. I send this missive by the new express, and will be cross if we reach home before it.

Merrilla and I also have some news that I am sure will delight you both.

Your loving and obedient son,
Philip Larcombe.

Florence Evelyn Hudson/Wharmby was born in Coventry, one of four children. At the age of twenty, Florence met and married her husband Donald, and they had a lovely daughter, Janet, who needed twenty-four-hour care. This meant Florence gave up her work, stayed at home and after a few years began writing her first novel, Gilded Wagons. The Gypsy story was published in 2013. Her second book, Brides for Clemmants, is a love story published in 2014. All profits from the sale of her books are given to the Salvation Army.

49179868R00177

Made in the USA
Charleston, SC
21 November 2015